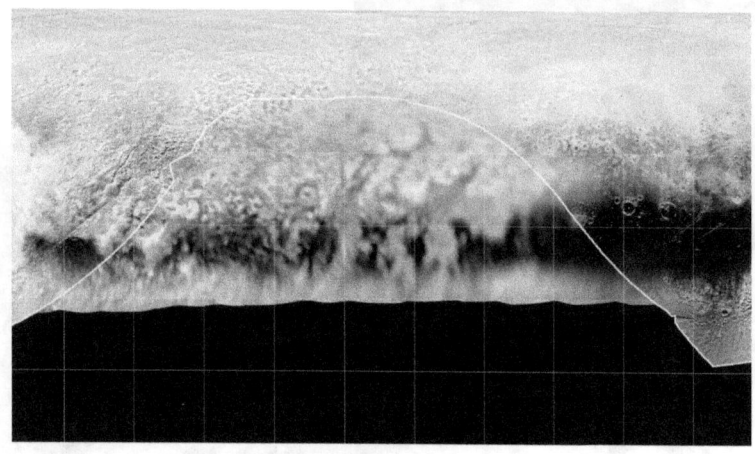

Pluto's far side. Photographed by NASA's New Horizons spacecraft. (Image courtesy NASA/JPL-Caltech)

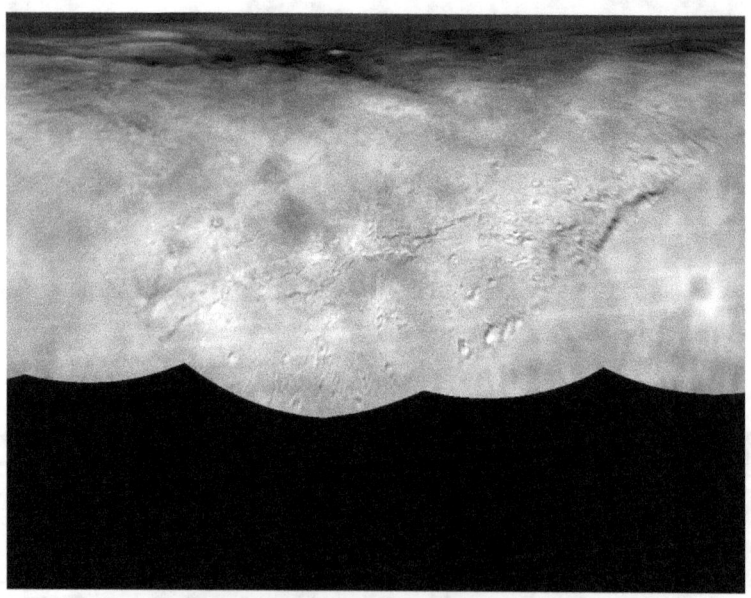

Charon's near side, as would be seen from Pluto. Photographed by NASA's New Horizons spacecraft. (Image courtesy NASA/JPL-Caltech)

CHAR●N

Gordon D'Arcy Christensen

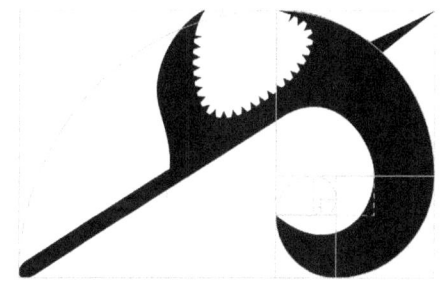

John Dakar's Kpinga Throwing Axe

Book design by Jacky Adelstein

Pluto-Charon System, yr 2111

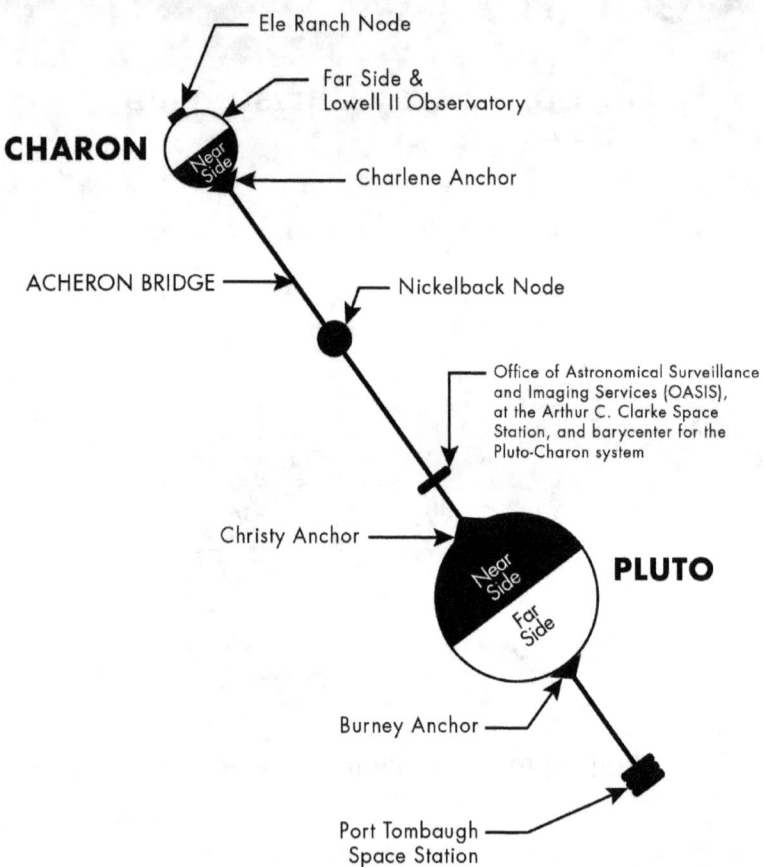

Ele Ranch Node

Far Side &
Lowell II Observatory

CHARON

Near Side

Charlene Anchor

ACHERON BRIDGE

Nickelback Node

Office of Astronomical Surveillance
and Imaging Services (OASIS),
at the Arthur C. Clarke Space
Station, and barycenter for the
Pluto-Charon system

Christy Anchor

Near Side

Far Side

PLUTO

Burney Anchor

Port Tombaugh
Space Station

NOT TO SCALE

DISCLAIMERS

Charon is a work of fiction. The names, characters, businesses, organizations, places, events, and locales are either the products of the author's imagination or are used in a fictitious manner. Any resemblance to actual persons, living or dead, is purely coincidental.

The author has named certain fictitious entities after current and deceased public figures (e.g. political leaders, notable scientists, artists, and writers) who the author believes will become historical figures by the year 2111, when Charon takes place. At no time do any of these public figures or their names appear as characters in the book.

The author has used the following material from the public domain:
- An apparition that looks like the Scarecrow of Oz, as pictured by John R. Neill, appears in Charon. The apparition does not speak and does not act like the Scarecrow in the Oz books by L. Frank Baum.
- Two characters from paintings by Hieronymus Bosch appear in Charon.
- Charon includes a scene where a character recites Gustav Mahler's love poem to his wife Alma while a quartet plays the fourth movement—the Adagietto—of Mahler's Fifth Symphony.

For the center of my universe:

Alice,
Charlotte
and Janara

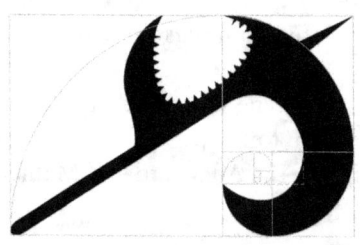

*"Invention, it must be humbly admitted,
does not consist of creating out of void,
but out of chaos ..."*

Mary Wollstonecraft Godwin Shelley

TABLE OF CONTENTS

READER'S GUIDE TO ACRONYMS, NAMES, CHARACTERS, PLACES AND GLOSSARY

Abbreviations and Acronyms
(in order of introduction)

KC: Kansas City

EP: Entangled Photon

CIA: Central Intelligence Agency

US: United States

USDS: United States Department of Space

L2: second Lagrange orbital vantage point

USSS: United States Space Ship

RAIR: Ram-Augmented, Interplanetary Rocket

VR: Virtual Reality movie

OASIS: Office for Astronomical Surveillance and Imaging Services for the Lowell II Observatory (Located at the Arthur C. Clarke Station on the Acheron Bridge)

PT: Port Tombaugh, Space station on Pluto

PC System: the Pluto-Charon System

IAU: International Astronomical Union, amongst many other functions, the IAU assigns names to natural features on Pluto and Charon

NTSB: National Transportation Safety Board

AP: Associated Press

ID: embedded computer IDentity chip

UTC: Coordinated Universal Time (for an explanation, see the Names section)

VC: Violent Crimes

5th FD: Fifth Freedom Directorate of the CIA (for an explanation, see the Names section)

KC Star: *Kansas City Star* (newspaper)

PRB: Peer Review Board

ERC: Emergency Response Computer.

SDD: Star of David District

LUIS: Lunar Union of Islamic States

LLCN: Lunar League of Christian Nations

MIT: Massachusetts Institute of Technology

OTB: Off Track Betting parlor

IT: Information Technology

AA: Administrative Assistant

Cinco-A: All American Academic Athletic Association (AAAAA)

OOD: Officer Of the Deck

LiDAR: Light Detection and Ranging, a remote imaging device that uses pulsed lasers to measure ranging (distance) to an object and create a three-dimensional image of the object

XO: eXecutive Officer

HCO: Hanger Control Officer

LSS: Life Support System

Names

(in order of introduction)

3-Hour War. On July 4, 2041, the Iranians and the North Koreans attacked Israel and the US with nuclear weapons. Israel and the US fought back. The war lasted only three hours, but more than a hundred and thirty million people died. The war destroyed Washington, D.C., New York City, and Los Angeles, all of Israel, nearly all of North Korea, and multiple Iranian cities. History declared the US the victor as it alone survived the war.

Coordinated Universal Time (UTC). Formerly known as Greenwich Mean Time (GMT). In 1972 this became the primary time standard by which the Earth, and then later the solar system, regulated clocks and time. UTC is five hours ahead of Eastern Standard Time (EST) and six hours ahead of Central Standard Time (CST).

Fifth Freedom Directorate (5th FD) of the CIA. This ultra-secret branch of the reorganized CIA has congressional authority to break the law to defend the law. The CIA was reorganized in 2041 after the 3-Hour War and relocated to Kansas City, Missouri.

Interrobang (?!) is a non-standard punctuation mark, introduced in the 1950s. It designates a question expressed as an exclamation. When the CIA reorganized after the 3-Hour War, it coopted the interrobang symbol (written as a question mark followed by an exclamation point) for the title of a 5th FD field agent with the authority to torture and kill in the line of duty.

Caine Toads. A fictional Caribbean criminal organization, noted for cruelty and violence. The Caine Toads used Voodoo imagery to terrify victims. The organization took its name from both the biblical Cain, who murdered his brother, and from the poisonous cane toads. The apex predator for its ecological niche, cane toads are the largest of all toads. Rapid breeders, with voracious appetites and omnivorous tastes, by the 1800s the animals had spread from their origins in the American tropics to invade the Caribbean islands. After that, the animals spread throughout the tropics, becoming a worldwide invasive pest by the end of the 20th century.

Major Characters
(in order of introduction)

CHAPTER 1

Dr. Mary Keator, OASIS astronomer and covert CIA analyst.

Dr. Jim Moxon, Chief of OASIS; directs both the public and secret services.

Kory, wake-word for the Series 2100/Charon ultramax computer manufactured by the ORB Computer Company for the Lowell II Observatory. The most powerful computer ever built.

CHAPTER 2

Inspector Scott Skalay, Homicide Squad Commander for the Port Tombaugh Police Department. Responsible for investigating all homicides in the Pluto-Charon system. Other members of the Homicide Squad:

> **Senior Detective Hildy Kirk,** second in command, assigned to the Port Tombaugh beat.

> **Officer Charlie Baker,** assigned to the Charon beat. Performs physical forensics for the Homicide Squad.

> **Officer Roc Qadeer,** assigned to the Acheron Bridge beat. Performs computer forensics for the Homicide Squad.

Dr. Ronald Best, Director of the Lowell II Observatory.

CHAPTER 3

Dr. Emma Lee (codename **Brick**), Director of the 5th FD. Other members of the Director's office:

> **Colonel Louis Boot,** (codename **Kick**), 5th FD Deputy Director and Colonel John Dakar's handler.

> **Colonel Peter Dawson,** (codename **Rod**), 5th FD Director's Chief of Staff.

Max Thaler, Assistant to Director Lee.

Sergeant Frank Thomas, Director Lee's bodyguard.

Colonel John Dakar, ?! (codename **Steel**), 5th FD agent. He has the authority to torture and kill in the line of duty.

CHAPTER 7

General Ora Barrun. CIA Executive (XO) Director and immediate supervisor to Director Lee, he reports to the CIA Director. As the plot unfolds, he is assigned the codename **Cobra**.

CHAPTER 8

Major Sumate Laoloo (codename **Duke**), 5th FD agent, Sea of Storms CIA Office, Luna.

Dr. Selena Volkova (codename **Kes**), Mossad agent, New Israel, Luna. Mossad has licensed her to torture and kill in the line of duty.

CHAPTER 14

Castor Valerio, assassin and member of the Caine Toads.

CHAPTER 20

Captain Leena Rakis, Captain of the USSS *Odysseus* and later, of the *Lady Annee's Sins*

CHAPTER 27

Ogun, Captain of the Caine Toads' space ship, the *Lady Annee's Sins*.

CHAPTER 30

General Mark Sliffer, Commandant of Fort Resnik.

Important Place Names

(in order of introduction, see map of Pluto Charon System)

Charon: Pluto's largest and closest moon. Tidally locked to Pluto so that the near-side of Charon always s faces the near-side of Pluto.

Valentine: Also known informally as the Heart and formally as Tombaugh Regio, the Valentine is the largest and most prominent feature on Pluto's surface. It is an immense nitrogen glacier, located on the far-side, that resembles a heart.

Kubrick Mons: is the tallest mountain on the near-side of Charon. Named after Stanley Kubrick, who produced and directed the film *2001: A Space Odyssey.*

Edwin Eugene Aldrin Space Station (nicknamed the Buzz). Located near-Earth at L2. The Buzz houses the **New James Webb Space Telescope.** The New Webb public mission is to perform astronomical research. The secret mission is to conduct surveillance of solar system electronic communications and transmit covert messages and data to the Kansas City CIA headquarters.

Lowell II Observatory. Offices are in the Arthur C. Clarke Space Station; the instrument reservation covers the far side of Charon. The observatory's public mission is to perform astronomical research. The secret mission is to conduct surveillance of solar system electronic communications and transmit covert messages and data to the Kansas City CIA headquarters.

Charlene Anchor: The Acheron Bridge space elevator terminus on the near-side of Charon.

Ele Ranch Node: Located in the center of the Charon far-side hemisphere, it is the antipode to the Charlene Anchor. Serves as the node to unite all of the data and transmission lines for the Lowell II instruments.

Port Tombaugh Space Station. Located on the far-side of Pluto, the space station orbits Pluto in a geosynchronous equatorial orbit. Connected to the surface of Pluto at Burney Anchor by a space elevator that spans the gulf between the space station and Pluto's surface.

Arthur C. Clarke Space Station, built on the Acheron Bridge at the Pluto-Charon barycenter. (The **barycenter** is the point in space around which both Pluto and Charon orbit). Houses the offices for Lowell II Observatory, including the OASIS office.

Acheron Bridge: The space elevator that spans the Acheron Gulf between Pluto and Charon.

Christy Anchor: The Acheron Bridge space elevator terminus on the near-side of Pluto.

Burney Anchor: The space elevator terminus on the far-side of Pluto.

Acheron Gulf: The gap between Pluto and Charon.

Nickelback Node: Midpoint of the Acheron Bridge; houses mechanical, electrical, computer, and transportation services for the Acheron Bridge.

Michael Brown District: Adjoining Charlene Anchor, the district includes an industrial park, tourist services, and a space port for the Pluto-Charon system.

Edmond Hamilton District: Located at Ele Ranch Node, the district is similar to the Brown District. It includes an industrial park, residential and food services for transient Lowell staff, and a local space port.

Glossary

(Neologisms, Jargon, Slang, and Unusual Terms,
in order of introduction)

Sumacom: neologism for a super-max computer. Sumacoms are the most powerful computers in the 22nd centuries. The most powerful of all sumacoms, is the **ultramax** computer, Kory.

Nucents: slang for New Centurions, the generation that became adults in the early 22nd century.

'Troid: slang for asteroid, particularly in reference to Psych-16 as a treasure 'troid.

'Scope: slang for telescope.

Goldilocks zone: refers to the orbital zone around a star where water exists in liquid form. Terrestrial planets in the Goldilocks zone have the best chance for the existence of life.

Boffin: British term, dating from the mid-1900s, for scientists and technicians. Popularized in the 21st century.

Klick: slang for kilometer

Ultramax computer: neologism for the largest computer ever built by humans. The word applies to only one computer, commonly known by its wake-word, Kory.

Wake-word: A word spoken by a human that commands a computer to perform a task.

Anchor: jargon for the terminus of a space elevator on the surface of Pluto (Brinkley Anchor and Christy Anchor) or on Charon (Charlene Anchor).

Planemo: refers to an astronomical object with enough gravity to assume a rounded or ellipsoid shape, but not enough gravity to become a star. It includes planets, dwarf planets, and the larger moons of the solar system.

Wristpod: neologism for a computer terminal worn on the wrist, linked to the perscom.

Mag-lev tram: A people mover built with superconducting materials and powered by electricity. Similar to a railroad train, only the tram does not touch the rails, instead it is suspended by electric magnets above the rail. In this story the tram travels on rails suspended over the Plutonian landscape, powered by electricity generated by the Acheron Bridge.

Bot: space slang, used as a single word for a robot or as a prefix for an autonomous (robot) controlled contrivance.

Perscom: neologism for a personal computer that can be either handheld for ease of use or worn in the clothing.

Limbot: neologism for a robot piloted limousine.

loP-loG: neologism for space jargon. Pronounced either "low P-low G" or "lop-log." loP refers to an atmospheric pressure below 0.8 atm (equivalent to the pressure at an altitude of 7,000 feet) and above 0.58 atm (equivalent to the pressure at an altitude of 15,000 feet), where 1.0 atm is the atmospheric pressure at sea level (with a normal partial pressure of oxygen of 21%). loG refers to gravity below 0.8 g and above 0.15 g (Lunar gravity is 0.17), where 1.0 g is equivalent to the gravity on the surface of the Earth.

noP-noG: neologism for space jargon. Pronounced either "no P-no G" or "nop-nog." noP refers to atmospheric pressure that will not sustain human life (exclusive of humans who are adapted to a low atmospheric pressure), meaning an atmospheric pressure below 0.58; in most cases, noP refers to a vacuum. noG refers to gravity less than 0.15 g; 0.01 g or less is essentially weightless or microgravity.

'Stro: neologism space slang for astronaut. In this story, a human who does not live on Earth.

Tailorcom: neologism for a computerized tailor for customizing and creating clothing.

Microdrone: neologism space jargon for a tiny drone equipped with video, audio, recorder, and transmitter capacities.

Battlebot: neologism for an armed robot that can attack humans on command.

Hyperion: Saturnian moon, famous for its holey, sponge-like composition.

Botweb: slang for the internet connection of intelligent devices and service robots, originally known as the internet of things.

Iapetus: Saturnian moon, famous for being two-toned (two-faced). The leading hemisphere is dark and the trailing hemisphere is bright.

HopCrawler: neologism space jargon for a human and cargo transport designed for low gravity, overland travel. It has eight legs for jumping, walking, and crawling. It also has four arms for grasping, loading, and manipulating. It also has rockets for short distance space travel.

Belt: neologism space slang for the colonies in the asteroid belt, the location of many noP-noG mining and support facilities. The Belt police and military are experts in noP-noG hand-to-hand combat.

Avabot: neologism for a robot created to look and act like a particular person. An avabot can resemble a person so closely that the avabot will be mistaken for the living person.

Medbot: neologism for a medical robot.

Quintal: refers to a unit of mass equal to 100 kilograms. Like a cannonball, a **quintal slug** is a projectile that uses the kinetic energy (equal to $\frac{1}{2} mv^2$) of the mass (m) and relative velocity (v) of the slug to destroy the target. It is fired by an electromagnetic rail gun.

CHAR●N

1 MARY BECOMES A LEGEND

Thirty-Seven Minutes Before It Happened

"Jim! When do we get to see the Valentine?" Mary asked. "It's Valentine's Day! Come on! You promised that we would see it." She handed him a bladder of freshly brewed coffee and leaned forward, flashing him a peek at her cleavage, framed in the artificial flower lei he had given her four months earlier.

Caught momentarily speechless by her flirting, Jim stammered, "Hey. Thanks for the coffee. Look, we'll catch the Valentine on the way back, I promise. You know . . . um . . . it's on the far side, the night side. It's . . . um . . . going to be hard to see it in the dark."

"But won't the Valentine's glacial ice shine in the starlight?"

"Yes, it's gorgeous! The frozen methane sparkles like fresh snow on a mountain meadow. But first I thought we'd watch the eclipse from up here, on top of Kubrick Mons. It's a sight that comes along only once every one hundred twenty-four years." He glanced at the ship's chronometer. "It starts in about thirty-five minutes."

"All right," Mary said. "Just wondering. I don't want you to get so caught up in your work that you forget why we're up here."

Jim frowned. "Mary, you know that we've got to make this stop so I can send my message to KC without attracting any attention."

"Yes, I know."

"Well, the thing is, I've never used the EP gun before. I figure it will take me about a half-hour to set the whole thing up and send the message." Then, not wanting to kill the mood, he quickly added with a softer tone. "Look. After you finish landing the transport and I finish sending my message, I promise you we'll have some time to enjoy the fantastic view of the eclipse from up here, four klicks above the Vulcan plain! On our way back to Clarke Station, we'll circle around Pluto to the far side and see the Valentine. I promise."

As she said, "Roger that," he turned away and retreated to the workstation at the stern of the transport. He set the coffee bladder on the steel bench next to his personal tablet and pulled a sheet of numbers and letters out of his pocket. He needed the sheet to encrypt the message he was preparing for laser transmission to Earth: a message asking his superiors to prepare for an emergency entangled photon conference.

After preparing the message, he planned to unpack the EP-Breaker, the device that entangled the photons into couplets and then broke them in half. After preparing the message and the photons, with the help of Kory, the Charon sumacom, he would aim and shoot the EP gun. Resembling an antique Gatling gun, the device sat on the rear external deck of the transport. The gun would send both his laser message and one-half of each photon couplet, down-range to an inner solar system collector for relay to the Central

Intelligence Agency headquarters in Kansas City. In the meantime, the EP breaker would retain the remaining half of each couplet for EP conferencing. Because each photon couplet was entangled, sending and receiving messages between the entangled photons would be instantaneous, no matter the distance separating the two photons—even if they were on opposite sides of the solar system.

While he was working, Mary fired the three transport grappling hooks into the regolith on the mountaintop to anchor the transport in place so that Jim could send his message. After verifying the solid anchorage of the transport, she began working her way through the landing and shutdown protocol, cross-checking environmental systems and winding down the transport engines. Finished with the landing tasks, she then established the communication link with Kory.

Fingering the flowers in her lei and sipping her coffee while she worked, she thought about how her dream had finally become true.

Thirty-One Minutes Before It Happened

For as long as she could remember, Mary had wanted to leave home, explore outer space, and search for alien life. These yearnings had led her to obtain a dual doctorate in computer sciences and comparative exoplanetary studies from the University of Washington. After finishing her post-graduate training at the University of Arizona, she had expected she would have plenty of opportunities to follow her ambitions and obtain a position at any one of the many off-planet observatories. But after having every application rejected, she realized there were just too few positions for all the aspiring astronomers who, like her, wanted to leave Earth. *To escape the Dirt!*

She didn't know why the competition was so great, but she supposed all the other Nucents felt the same as she did, weary of the melancholia that had gripped the US for the past seven decades since the Three Hour War. Like so many in her generation, she wanted a break from the dreariness. A fresh start. Something new and exciting! Something off-planet!

Her parents thought she was crazy to want to leave the Earth. They told her many times Americans never had it as good as they did now. By seizing the treasure 'troid Psyche-16, the US had secured immense wealth that enabled the country to rebuild after the war, eliminated poverty for all Americans, reduced the workweek to twenty-five hours for those who chose to work, and provided a living allowance for those who chose not to work. No more income tax. Lots of jobs in government projects and commercial endeavors for those who wanted one. Psyche-16 wealth financed the reversal of climate change and the extension of life spans by many decades. Psyche-16 wealth promoted the exploration and colonization of the solar system. Psyche-16 wealth funded the expansion of US military and space commands, making the US the most powerful nation that had ever been. Guarantor of world peace! Ruler of space! These were great things! Why would she want to leave?

She told them that was not enough for her. She wanted more. She wanted to see new worlds. She wanted to do something important. She wanted to make a difference.

What she didn't tell them was she was sick of the lingering mourning from the Three Hour War.

My God! she thought.

The war had taken place before her parents were even born. Seventy years had passed. Seventy years during which her parents had grown up and had children, but the country still grieved for the dead and mourned the lost cities.

She regretted the war. But it had happened long before she was born. She had nothing to do with it. New York City, Washington, D.C., Los Angeles—she would've liked to have visited those fabled cities—walked their avenues, visited their museums, seen their monuments. But they were gone. For her, they had no more reality than the Emerald City or Camelot or ancient Rome.

She felt sorry for the people who had died—particularly the Americans, but also, the Israelis, Iranians, and Koreans, whose countries had disappeared in the nuclear cataclysm. But people died throughout history. Sure, some of her parents' relatives had died, but obviously, no one they knew or she knew. It was past time to get over it. Yet it seemed throughout her life, not a month would go by without a memorial or a commemoration by some community group, intent on reminding everyone of the horrors of the Three Hour War. No wonder sorrow, paranoia, and anger still gripped her parents and the country.

She'd had enough. She wanted to leave: *I've got to escape the Dirt*, as people who scorned the Earth would say.

Life is for living, she thought. *Not for grieving the dead.*

When the CIA visited in early 2107 on a recruiting mission to Tucson, where Mary was finishing her postdoctoral studies, they offered her the opportunity to be a data analyst and research astronomer at the New James Webb Space Observatory. She jumped at the chance.

Wow!

Thinking about it even now, nearly four years later, she still felt a thrill from getting the CIA offer.

She didn't understand why the CIA wanted to hire someone with her credentials, but she didn't question her good luck. After completing six months basic training at "the Bush" (the nickname for CIA headquarters in the George H.W. Bush building in North Kansas City) and getting her security clearance, she learned the answer.

The CIA intended to assign her to a dual appointment at the New James Webb Observatory. Her overt assignment would be to the USDS where she would serve as an astronomer conducting research on comparative exoplanetary studies, meaning the search for extrasolar life. Her covert assignment, however, would be to the ultra-classified Central Security Service—a joint CIA and National Security Agency operation—where she would use her computer skills to collect, analyze, and troubleshoot signals intelligence collected by the New James Webb Observatory. In other words, the CIA wanted her to spy on Earth and inner solar system communications, including domestic US communications.

She worried about the task of spying on the US. She knew it was strictly illegal. *Will I regret this? Should I turn down the offer?* But, after much soul searching, she reasoned: *If spying prevents another nuclear war, then I'm willing to do it...*

For her, the thrill of the CIA offer was the chance to live and work in a deep-space observatory. *I can get off the planet! I can escape the Dirt!*

The US Department of Space (USDS), the successor to the old National Aeronautics and Space Administration (NASA), constructed the New James Webb Observatory at the second Lagrange orbital vantage point, the same point in space where NASA had located the original, robotic James Webb Space Telescope. At four times the distance from the Moon to the Earth, L2 had an ideal location, giving it an unimpeded view of the heavens as well as a continuous communications channel with the Earth. When the New Webb saw first light in 2049, it was a hundred times more powerful than any telescope, anywhere else.

Of course, by 2107, when Mary joined the staff of the New Webb, it had slipped in scientific importance, being no longer New and no longer the most powerful. By 2107, the power of more than two dozen 'scopes exceeded that of the Webb. She didn't care.

There's still a lot of science left in the Webb!

And of course, by 2107, the search for extrasolar life had cooled. All of the solar system ocean worlds—Mars, Enceladus, Europa, Calisto, Ganymede, Triton, and even Pluto—proved to be sterile. And, after intensive investigation of the nearest one hundred terrestrial planets in "Goldilocks zones," neither the Webb nor any other 'scope, had found incontrovertible evidence of extrasolar life. A few planets had oxygen or methane-enriched atmospheres, suggesting the possibility of life but not proving its presence. More importantly, after two-hundred

7

years of astronomical research, no observatory anywhere had detected mysterious radio signals, or seen alien city lights, or observed any other signs of intelligent life. She didn't care. Mary was undaunted. *With an estimated four billion terrestrial planets in the Milky Way, the search has just begun!*

What the Feds failed to tell the public when they built the Webb, what she learned when she joined the CIA, was the Feds didn't just intend to build a new toy for space boffins like her to use to look for little green men. No. The Feds had a much larger agenda. They intended to claim L2, to make it into a US space colony, by building the Edwin Eugene Aldrin Jr. Space Station to house the Webb, its support facilities, and much more.

Mary loved its nickname, "the Buzz." It reminded her of her stepfather, who kept bees in the backyard of her parents' home in Columbia, Missouri. When her stepfather wanted to start a new bee colony, he would begin with a small brood chamber in a foundation box, where the queen would lay her eggs and be tended by workers. As the hive increased in numbers, he would add frame after frame to the foundation box for the bees to fill with combs, first combs for the queen to fill with eggs and then combs for the worker bees to fill with pollen and honey. When the foundation box was full, he would place a second, and then a third box, on top of it. Each box would have more and more frames, for more and more bees, to fill with more and more honey. As the hive grew, the colony would buzz louder and louder, with the furious energy of the increasing comings and goings of bees in search of nectar and in defense of the hive.

Like a celestial beekeeper, the Feds used the New Webb Space Telescope for a brood chamber and placed it in the space station foundation box which would become the Buzz. The Feds then added more and more frames and boxes to the station as they crammed more and more functions into it, expanding it to include an interplanetary transportation hub, space docks, warehouses, factories, space farms, hospitality services, healthcare facilities, private residences, shops, banks, and even a space fort for the defense of the Buzz and near-Earth space lanes. And in a secret arrangement which would become Mary's future, the CIA added a slew of radio telescopes for spying on Earth and near-Earth space transmissions and traffic. As the Feds added more and more functions to the Buzz, it filled the cosmic hive with the increasing frenetic energy of the Federal government's search for greater wealth and power.

Over time, the growing Buzz eclipsed the Webb in importance and became, for a while, the largest space station ever built. As humans left Earth and colonized the solar system, they built more outposts. Some, like the Lunar cities Armstrong Base, Marius Hills, and New Jerusalem, the Martian cities Fort Musk, Allen Town, and Bezos City, and the Ceres city Port Gauss, had become many times larger than the Buzz. Nevertheless, because of the proximity to both the terrestrial and Lunar US, and because of its strategic deep space location at L2, the Buzz remained the center for near-Earth commerce, transportation, and science.

For Nucents like Mary, who hated the dreary old twenty-first century and who wanted the bright new world of the twenty-second century, there were few places as exciting as the celestial city known as the Buzz.

What a great job!

Mary had such a wonderful time at the Buzz, she opted to sign on for a second year-long tour. After two years, the CIA said "enough" and sent her back to Missouri to regain her Dirt legs and recover from the cosmic-ray trauma of living a million and a half klicks from Earth.

Mary wasn't happy to return to her parents' home in Columbia. Even though she still worked as an analyst for the CIA, she feared they would never again post her off-planet. Resigned to a life on Earth, she polished her resume and began shopping it around, hoping her tour of duty at the Webb and the publication of her research in *Nature* and *The Astrophysical Journal* would open academic doors for her. But no one invited her in for an interview.

Twelve months later, on September 7, 2110, the CIA saved her again. Same offer as before: public USDS sponsored research on comparative exoplanetary studies and covert spying on space communications. Only this time, the CIA offered her the chance of a lifetime, an assignment to the Lowell II Observatory on Charon!

She remembered her immediate reaction.

Double wow!

On further reflection, though, she started to get cold feet. She considered declining the offer. Pluto was the edge of the human frontier—as far away as you could get from everywhere else. As much as she enjoyed being off of Earth, she feared going that far from it. She feared the dark, the cold, and the isolation.

However, she found courage in the family legends about her great-grandmother, Ruth Beard, whose life as an astronomer inspired Mary's own career.

A little more than a hundred years ago—sometime around the turn of the millennia—after having just obtained her doctorate in astronomy, her great-grandmother left her Iowa home and went to the Parkes Observatory in Australia to study pulsars. At that time, the Parkes must have seemed to Ruth a remote and exotic place, even though it had already been operating for nearly fifty years and was located in a safe, fully developed, modern, English-speaking country. The most exciting things that happened to Ruth while in Australia were taking trips across the Outback and visiting the disappearing Great Barrier Reef. Hardly the stuff of family mythology.

What happened next established her great-grandmother in family legend. Emboldened by her Australian adventure, Ruth went to the Amundsen-Scott South Pole Station to use the South Pole Telescope. At the end of her first summer session, she volunteered to winter over at the station.

For seven months, Mary's great-grandmother lived on the edge of twentieth-century humanity, in unending dark and in the coldest place on Earth. Because there was no transportation in or out of the station during the winter months, she—along with fifty other people—was isolated from everyone else on Earth.

It must have been like living on another planet! A dark, icy planet like Pluto!

Family history included tales of how Ruth scouted ice crevasses which could swallow her whole, how she assisted the station medic in performing emergency surgery on a colleague who had appendicitis, how a colleague had died of a suspected but unsolved murder, and how she endured horrific airplane flights through howling storms over desolate ice plains. An oft-repeated story was how once, while visiting McMurdo Base on the edge of the ice, Ruth saw a colleague die when an orca leaped out of the ocean, snatched her friend, and devoured him on the spot.

Despite all these hardships, Ruth Beard became famous for her astronomical research on pulsars. She also wrote letters and took photos showing the beauty of Antarctica, documents her family cherished and passed on for generations.

Her great-grandmother had many descendants. During the second winter-over, she fell in love with an engineer and married him before returning to the States. Their marriage became a sixty-year fairy tale for all of Ruth's descendants. This was the life Mary wanted!

On that memorable day last August, when Mary had told her parents that the USDS offered her an appointment to the Lowell II Observatory, she had expected her parents would be as pleased as she was by the promotion, but they were not.

Instead, her parents had complained they could not understand why Mary would accept such an assignment. The Buzz was far enough, but Pluto! Why would she want to live so far away? They might never see her again! Why would she agree to such a dangerous assignment? She might get hurt or even killed!

Crushed by her parent's reaction, Mary had reminded them of how few positions there were for research astronomers like her. She had tried for the year after leaving the Buzz to get a new research position, but no one wanted her. Going to the Lowell would open doors for her. She promised them that every year or two she would come home for a visit. Someday, she would even move back to Earth. As far as safety, the Lowell Observatory had an excellent record. She had even gone so far as to remind her mother how great-grandmother Ruth had gone to Antarctica and how wonderful that had been for her.

Her parents countered that if Mary really loved them, she would not leave them.

Mary replied that if her parents really loved her, they would not try to stop her.

But no one heard what the other had said. What had begun as a proud announcement, had slipped into a family discussion, that fell into a heated argument with harsh words, followed by shouting, then slammed doors, and finally tears. It was the only fight she could ever recall having had with her mother and stepfather.

Such fights have no winners. This one ended when Mary simply declared, "I'm going."

After two weeks of orientation to the Lowell II Observatory at the Bush, on a rainy and cheerless 9/11, Mary found herself standing with her parents on the Columbia Station platform, waiting for the hyper-loop to take her to the St. Louis Spaceport. Her mother cried, her step-father withdrew, and Mary felt awful.

During the breaks between transfers from the Spaceport to the International Space Station, and from the Space Station to the Buzz where she would catch her flight to Pluto, when all Mary had to do was sit and ponder, she thought about the fight, trying to understand how she had let things go so wrong between her and her parents, whom she loved very much and whom she knew loved her.

Only after she had discarded her shield of self-delusions, only after she had been honest with herself and soberly explored her feelings—whether she liked them or did not—only then, had she remembered how she had had cold feet when she first got the Lowell assignment. Her argument was not with her parents, it was with herself.

That night, after checking into her hotel room on the Buzz, she had sent a video to her parents, telling them how much she loved them. She told them she wished she had been more understanding and did not want to hurt them. She promised she would return home for a visit as soon as she could.

My parents were right. If I let myself think about it, Pluto is scary. I'll be on the edge of the solar system! I could be killed . . . But damn, if my great-grandmother could dare to go to the South Pole, then I dare to go to Pluto!

Twenty-Nine Minutes Before It Happened

Reaching the end of her task list and breaking from her reverie, she called back to Jim, "I'm all done. How are you doing?"

"I'm just about done encoding my message," Jim replied from the rear of the transport. "After that, I'll need to set up the gun. I'll be another twenty or twenty-five minutes."

"All right. What can I do while you're working?"

"Um . . . well . . . you can stow the spacesuits and unpack our lunch. After I send this message to KC, we'll eat while watching the eclipse."

While Jim worked, Mary wrestled the bulky spacesuits into the storage lockers. Not an easy task, given the high mass of the suits and Charon's negligible gravity (about one-thirtieth of Earth's). By mutual unspoken consent, they had decided to ignore protocol—almost everyone did—and not wear the spacesuits in the transport. It was highly unlikely that they would need the suits, and the suits would interfere with their intimacy. After locking them away, Mary repositioned the cockpit seats into an upright incline and adjusted the seatbelts to hold Jim and her while they watched the eclipse. She then unpacked their lunch.

While performing these simple, even domestic, preparations, her thoughts returned to the Lowell Observatory.

During her two-week Pluto orientation at the Bush, one of the CIA tutors tried to brief her on the dusty history of the Lowell Observatory. At the time she didn't pay much attention to the dull recitation of two-hundred-year-old events, when during the Gay-90's, an American businessman—who seemed to have more money than sense and an overpowering obsession that aliens had dug canals on Mars—built the first Lowell Observatory. Unfortunately for Percival Lowell, the Martian canals proved to be optical illusions and Percival did not live long enough to see the greatest achievement by his Observatory, Clyde Tombaugh's discovery of the ninth planet, Pluto.

Now, while sitting in the transport pilot's seat, parked on the top of a Charon mountain, with Tombaugh's enormous pink Pluto on the horizon—just 18 thousand klicks away, she wasn't so sure. Perhaps she'd been too flippant.

After all, she could call Lowell a prophet. His search for the promised land—the dark skies for the best views of Mars—led him to locate his telescope—at the time, one of the largest in the world—in the most remote, highest, place he could find: the mile-high frontier town of Flagstaff, in what was then the territory of Arizona.

Since then, astronomers have followed Lowell's search for the darkest skies by placing bigger telescopes on higher and more remote locations. The path led astronomers to build the Hale Telescope on Palomar Mountain in California, the Keck Telescope on the Hawaiian volcano Mauna Kea, and the Extremely Large Telescope on the Chilean mountain Cerro Armazones. Having exhausted locations for Earth-bound 'scopes, the quest sprang into space, first with robot telescopes, such as the Hubble Space Telescope orbiting Earth and the robot James Webb Space Telescope orbiting the Sun at L2, followed by the manned James Webb Space Telescope, also at L2.

At the end of the twenty-first century, the USDS trumped all other observatories by taking the next grand step and seizing the highest ground and the darkest sky by building the most powerful and most remote observatory ever imagined, the Lowell II Observatory—her Observatory—on Charon.

The USDS created this immense observatory by covering the entire far side of Charon—an area three times the size of Texas—with a network of more than two-hundred thousand telescopes, including visible light, infrared, ultraviolet, radio, x-ray, gamma-ray, and microwave. The USDS also placed additional 'scopes on Pluto's poles and in orbit around the

Pluto-Charon System. They fused this massive network into a single interferometer observatory, larger than Charon itself, by linking the individual 'scopes to each other at Ele Ranch Node—at the center of the far side of Charon.

To process the massive load of astronomical data, the USDS contracted with ORB Computers to construct the largest computer ever built, the Series 2100/Charon ultramax computer, known to users by its wake-word, Kory.

After building Kory in two components on Luna, ORB shipped the components to Charon, installed the mainframe —for human interface, data analysis, and Charon housekeeping—in the Brown District, next to Charlene Anchor—and installed the subsidiary mainframe—for network data collection and collation and first-pass processing—in the Hamilton District, at Ele Ranch Node.

If the manned James Webb Telescope was a thousand times more powerful than the robotic James Webb Telescope, then the Lowell II Observatory was 100 million times more powerful than the manned James Webb Telescope. Instead of studying light reflected from pinpoint objects, the Lowell II could—if present—image surface features like ice caps, continents, oceans, forests, and even city lights on the nearest exoplanets.

And now, thanks to the USDS and the CIA, this new wonder of the solar system, the biggest, highest, and most remote astronomical observatory ever, is mine to use as I see fit . . . And irony of irony, maybe old man Lowell's alien obsession wasn't so crazy after all.

Twenty-Three Minutes Before It Happened

"Hey, Jim! I'm all done," Mary called out. "What's taking you so long? We're going to miss the eclipse."

From the rear of the transport where he was fiddling with his covert communication devices, Jim replied, "Still working! This is the first time I've set up the gun. It looks like the last person to use it didn't properly shut it down. So, it's taking me a little longer than I expected. Take a break. I'll be ready in about, oh, I don't know, fifteen or twenty minutes."

"All right. But you're in trouble if you miss this!"

Mary sipped from her second bladder of coffee and looked out at the Charon landscape through the forward bow canopy.

It was the middle of the night on Charon. Only the surfaces of planemos—meaning the planets, the dwarf planets, and the larger moons of the solar system—experience night. Night occurs on the dark side of the planemo, the side that faces away from the Sun, and looks into the shadow cast by the planemo. When you ascend above the nocturnal surface and exit the shadow of the planemo, you reenter the glorious sunlit heavens where there is no night, only perpetual sunshine.

Mary had not experienced night since she left Earth more than five months ago. Perhaps for that reason, while sitting alone in the dark, she found the shadowy, desolate, gloomy nightscape alarming, even unnerving. Charon was starting to give her the willies.

Not wanting her increasing uneasiness to ruin their plans, she averted her eyes and picked up the romance novel she'd brought with her. She hoped the trashy book would help her ignore the disturbing view and allow her to recover her composure.

Despite her best efforts, negative thoughts intruded into her consciousness, interrupting her internal dialogue. Like a heckler at a speech, the unwanted thoughts demanded her attention, pushing her to reconsider the wisdom of her big space adventure.

The CIA had warned her that the Lowell Observatory could be dangerous to her health. Feeling the invincibility of youth, she didn't worry about it.

The CIA had also warned her that the Pluto-Charon System had become an international cesspool of intrigue, with all kinds of spies and enemies, people who might harm or even kill her if they discovered her CIA identity. Confident in her new martial art skills, courtesy of CIA training, she dismissed the warnings. Besides, the hush-hush work only made life more interesting.

However, she had not warned the CIA of her fear of the dark. She had always thought her childish phobia would disappear with adulthood, but it hadn't. Ashamed to mention such immature silliness to the recruiter and worried the CIA might reject her if they knew, she could almost pretend it did not exist. Yet, she still avoided dark rooms and walking alone at night. An odd thing for an astronomer, to be afraid of the dark. Perhaps devoting her career to studying the night sky was a coping mechanism. If so, it had failed.

She supposed her fear of the dark came from watching old movies as a child, movies that became nightmares about monsters in her bedroom, ghosts in her basement, and aliens from another planet in her yard.

There's got to be more to it than that! she thought. Everyone grows up watching horror movies, why should I have a problem?

She knew the answer, she just didn't want to admit it.

Her night terrors began when she was only three or four years old. The first one she could recall, the most vivid one —she could still see it in her mind's eye—was the face in the window.

Just thinking about it caused the hair to rise on the back of her neck and a cold sensation to run down her spine. Suddenly, she was no longer a thirty-two-year-old woman, an astronomer and CIA agent, parked on Charon, sitting in the transport pilot's seat, looking at the moonscape through the spaceship canopy. Instead, she was a small child, back in Missouri, in her bed, looking at the white face that appeared in her bedroom window, the white face with the big white eyes and big black pupils that stared back at her and filled her with horror.

It didn't look real.

It didn't look real because the expression didn't change. But the eyes moved.

It felt like a dream.

But, she knew it was real because she couldn't wake-up and escape the eyes.

Instead, slowly, silently, she got out of bed and backed away from the window. The eyes followed her.

Slowly, silently, she slid along the wall to the bedroom door. The eyes followed her.

As soon as she got to the door, she ran out of the room screaming, "MOM! MOM! MOM!"

Her mom grabbed her and held her tight.

Her dad rushed outside and checked the grounds. When he returned, he yelled at her for being a baby, waking him with her nightmare, and making him go outside in his pajamas. He told her there was nothing out there.

She didn't believe him. She knew better. She knew what she had seen.

After her dad went to bed, her mom led Mary back to her bedroom and tucked her into bed. Mary didn't want her mom to leave. She cried and asked her mom to stay.

Her mom sat down on the edge of the bed and asked her, "What did the face look like?"

Mary couldn't tell her.

Then seeing Mary's new bedtime story book on the floor, about the little girl and her little dog who had been swept up by a tornado and taken to a magical world, her mom picked up the book, and flipped through the pages. For Mary's bedtime story that night, her mom had read about how the little girl had met a scarecrow, a real live scarecrow.

Pointing to the picture of the scarecrow, her mom asked. "Is this what it looked like?"

"Yes!" Mary cried. Frightened by seeing it again, she crawled back into her mom's arms. Her mom held her daughter until Mary fell asleep.

The Scarecrow of Oz. Damn! Here I am, an adult, on the very edge of the solar system, and I'm afraid of the dark. And, I'm afraid of the Scarecrow of Oz. Damn!

Still, thinking about the face in the window, trying to figure out what really happened, she was sure that she had seen something . . . perhaps someone wearing a mask . . . maybe a peeping tom. Who knows? Maybe she wasn't so crazy. Only the memory still made her uneasy, even today.

God! What a mess. I should have told the CIA before I got here.

Thinking about her dad caused her buttocks to burn, bringing back the memory of his spankings, which was odd when she thought about it.

After all these years, she thought the memory of her dad's abuse should have faded away with the rest of her forgotten childhood. Particularly since after her dad's death from alcoholism, her mom had married a good man who loved Mary like his own child. Surely her kind stepfather should have doused any lingering paternal trauma.

But, maybe not. She wondered if her painful memories and fear of the dark persisted because most of her encounters with her dad had occurred at night, after he had been drinking, when he would come home and start beating her mom and spanking her.

Or maybe this was all just pop psychology. A rationalization for irrational fears.

Either way, I wish I'd been honest with the CIA, then they might've been honest with me and told me just how frightening I might find the Charon night. Too late now.

Nineteen Minutes Before It Happened

Breaking into a sweat, she could feel her heart beginning to pound and her breath quickening. As a familiar, but nearly forgotten, cold, liquid feeling swept through her bowels, she realized she was having a panic attack. It had been a long time since she had had one, but she had not forgotten what to do to stop it. She closed her eyes, forced herself to slow her breathing, and focused her thoughts on something pleasant, like the first time she met Jim.

It had taken her only a day to travel from the St. Louis Spaceport to the Buzz. She'd had a couple of days there to visit old friends and review her research data, and then it was Sunday, September 14, 2110, time to board the USSS *Hermes*, a Pluto-Class, Ram-Augmented, Interplanetary Rocket (RAIR) that regularly made the loop between the Buzz and Port Tombaugh on the far side of Pluto. Excitement filled her as she stepped aboard the *Hermes* and found her stateroom. She was going to Pluto, to the edge of the solar system!

But after four deadly dull yet nerve-racking weeks, she'd had enough of space travel. She knew too much, like a physician about to go under the knife. As an astronomer and a physicist, she knew the hazards of sub-light-speed travel. She knew that RAIR spaceships swept up interstellar plasma and dust to use for rocket fuel and reaction mass, clearing the path to Pluto. She also knew that at speeds up to two percent the speed of light, just one speck of dust striking the ship in the wrong way could destroy the vehicle in a flash. Knowing it had happened only once before didn't help. Knowing if it did happen, she would never know it, also didn't help. Nature didn't intend for her to travel this fast. Because of her anxiety, she slept poorly, rarely exercised, binged on virtual reality movies, lost money at the casino, fell behind on her research manuscript, and worried all the way to Pluto. When she finally floated out of the debarkation tube at Port Tombaugh and grabbed onto the people mover, she felt tired and grumpy.

And then there it was! The iconic steel arch—reminiscent of the St. Louis Arch—stretched over the entrance to the arrival tube, proclaiming in big, bold, copper letters, WELCOME TO PLUTO—ARCHWAY TO THE STARS!

Wow! I'm really here!

As the people mover pulled her through the arrivals tube toward the gravity zone, she passed poster after poster along the walls, entreating her to see the sites. Across one gigantic picture of a space complex in the foreground and the far side of Pluto with the famous white heart—the Valentine—in the background, splashed the invitation, SEE PORT TOMBAUGH—GATEWAY TO THE KUIPER BELT—THE FIRST DEEP SPACE COLONY!

Another poster showed a picture of the Acheron Bridge and Clarke Station with the caption: DON'T MISS THE ARTHUR C. CLARKE STATION AND THE ACHERON BRIDGE—THE GREATEST MANMADE WONDER OF THE SOLAR SYSTEM! VIEW THE NEAR SIDE OF PLUTO AND THE FAMOUS BRASS KNUCKLES FROM THE BARYCENTER, 1,000 KILOMETERS ABOVE MENG-P'O AND CHRISTY ANCHOR! And, in smaller print at the bottom, HOME OF THE LOWELL II OBSERVATORY, LARGEST IN THE SOLAR SYSTEM!

A gigantic photograph of the near side of Charon proclaimed, RIDE THE ACHERON BRIDGE SPACE ELEVATOR AND TOUR CHARON! SEE KUBRICK MONS, THE CLARKE MONTES, THE RED PLAINS OF

MORDOR, AND THE VULCAN PLANUM! AFTER THE TOUR, DON'T FORGET TO VISIT THE CHARLENE ANCHOR TIMES SQUARE CAFETERIA AND HAYDEN ATRIUM—ENJOY A NEW YORK CITY HOT DOG UNDER THE STARS! Advertisements for Port Tombaugh tourist sites also covered the walls. She knew nothing about Pluto having a Chinese colony until she passed a picture of lamb in a peppercorn sauce labeled VISIT CELESTIAL CHINA! THE ONLY CHINATOWN IN DEEP SPACE! Likewise, she didn't know about the Brazilian colony until she saw a picture of a beautiful bronze woman and a dark, handsome man sitting together in a restaurant and holding wine glasses with the title VISIT SANTA TERESA, PORT TOMBAUGH—THE ONLY ARTS COLONY AND BRAZILIAN BARRIO BEYOND SATURN! There was an advertisement to watch the championship flyball game between the Port Tombaugh Toughs and the Chinatown Dragons. Even the local bank, the First National Bank of Port Tombaugh, had an advertisement touting savings accounts and investments in the Pluto Stock Market. And so it went. Advertisement after advertisement filled the arrivals tube, inviting Mary to patronize restaurants, bars, betting parlors, nightclubs, observation lounges, gift shops, art galleries, athletic events, and financial institutions as well as to visit the parks and museums and see the natural sites. Between the ads were posters displaying the natural beauty of the Pluto and Charon system.

This is hardly a hinterland, she thought. *This is the Buzz, only better!*

As the people mover pulled her through the arrivals tube, she felt the gradual return to gravity, by the time she entered the reception arena she was walking normally with lifted spirits and a big smile on her face.

Stepping out of the tube into the arrivals hall, the public-address system announced her: "Dr. Mary Keator, arriving from St. Louis."

Disoriented by the new surroundings, crowded with people arriving and others meeting the arrivals, she started to look around for the luggage carousel. Just then a tall, slim man swooped down on her, and placed a lei of colorful white, green, and gold artificial flowers over her head. "Dr. Keator, welcome to Pluto!"

Stunned, she could only look up at him in response. He smiled at her look of shock.

"Thanks, what—"

"The lei? Pluto is a treasure house of natural resources —water ice mountain ranges, nitrogen glaciers, methane dunes, star-tar stained and cratered highlands, and unlimited electricity. To celebrate our wealth, we Plutonians adopted the Hawaiian tradition of honoring all our visitors who have traveled so far to visit us, particularly first-time visitors like you, with a lei, using our territorial colors. White orchids symbolize our water ice, gold mums symbolize our star-tar, and green leaves symbolize all of the plants and life we've brought to Pluto. You know we've got a lot of hydrocarbons on Pluto—"

"Yes, I know. But—"

"So, we make a lot of plastic. To add color to our gray world, we use every excuse we can think of to use colored plastic to brighten things up. You now have a genuine souvenir of Pluto, made here with our own star-tar."

"Thank you!" Mary said. "I—I—um. Who are you?"

"Sorry! I'm Dr. Moxon, your new boss. Chief of OASIS, the Office for Astronomical Surveillance and Imaging Services. You can call me Jim."

"Thank you! I wasn't expecting anyone to meet me, particularly not you."

"Port Tombaugh is a maze of tubes and passages, and it can be hard to find your way, even with a wristpod and Talos's help. We usually send someone to meet new staff—it makes it more personal. I, um, had an errand to run at PT. So, I thought I'd greet you myself. Besides, it gives us a chance to talk."

"Thank you for the lei! Tell me about star-tar. I've read about it, but I didn't know you could do anything with it."

"Oh, yes, lots! You saw pictures of star-tar in the arrivals tube. Most of Pluto—and also Charon—is covered by it, coloring the surface in shades of brown and red. The star-tar looks like mud or dead vegetation, but it's actually a crust of hydrocarbons called tholins. Ultraviolet light striking nitrogen glaciers and methane rocks creates the tholins. We call the tholin crust, star-tar because in the laboratory at room temperature, the crust is sticky like tar. But on the surface of Pluto and Charon, at a temperature near absolute zero, the star-tar is as hard as granite. It's a great resource for making plastics, biochemicals, and even food."

With that, he helped her retrieve her baggage from the carousel and make the arrangements for shipping her personal luggage crate to Clarke Station.

Leaving the Interplanetary Travel Pavilion, he ushered her along, explaining, "We could take a transport to Clarke Station, but it takes less than a day to travel overland from PT to Clarke Station. Since your crate won't make it to the station until tomorrow, I thought we'd take the overland route and let you see a little bit of your new home and let you stretch your legs."

"That sounds great!" Mary said.

"We'll get some brunch at our Tavern on the Green, one of my favorite places," Jim said. "Then we'll ride the elevator down to Burney Anchor and transfer to the overland maglev for the trip to Christy Anchor. The maglev follows the equator west, from the far side to the near side, taking us over spectacular mountains and glacial plains. At Christy Anchor, we will transfer to the Acheron Bridge Elevator for the ride up to Clarke Station. It's ten o'clock now. The overland trip takes about eleven hours. We should make it to Clarke by twenty-one. A little late, but the canteen is open twenty-four hours. In the meantime, I'd like to brief you about OASIS and answer any questions you might have about your new job. Sound good?"

"Sure, sounds like fun."

As they marched along the pedway, they passed through the PT Central Park on their way to the Tavern. Planted with tall trees, shrubs, flowers, and grass, and populated with squirrels, rabbits, and many kinds of birds, the park reminded her of Peace Park at home in Columbia. After four weeks of being cooped up in a can, she paused for a moment to enjoy all the life around her.

"Marvelous!" Mary said. "Is that a kestrel?"

"Yes, they help keep the rabbit, mice, and bird populations under control."

"Where do all of the animals come from?"

"These are the same animals that live in the parks on Luna, Mars, and Ceres. We know from experience that they do well in space cities." With that, he urged her on while continuing his monologue.

"Um, back in 2090," he began, "when they started building the Lowell, they needed a staging center for receiving workers, equipment, and supplies. So, they built Port Tombaugh and placed it in geocentric orbit on the far side of Pluto, where human activity would least disturb the new observatory. Because Pluto and Charon always face each other, the engineers planned from the beginning to connect them by bridging the Acheron Gulf with a space elevator. No one had ever built one before, so the engineers decided to develop the technology by first building a space elevator to connect the Port Tombaugh Space Station to the Plutonian surface at Burney Anchor. Burney Anchor sits on Pluto's equator, in the center of the far side hemisphere, on the eastern edge of the Valentine nitrogen glacier. The thing is, no one ever predicted Port Tombaugh would become a boomtown on its own."

"How many people live here?"

Speaking into his wristpod, Jim contacted the Port Tombaugh sumacom by saying, "Talos, How many people live in the Pluto-Charon System?"

With a male voice, Talos replied, "As of seven this morning: 208,245 souls."

"Wow!" she said. *That is more than four times the size of the Buzz and almost half the size of New Jerusalem.*

He continued. "The Station has grown so much that Port Tombaugh now has nineteen habitation rings—we call them Circles—like this one."

The Buzz is just now building its eleventh ring. "Why are you booming? What's out here?"

"Well, we live so far from everybody else—particularly the Earth and the Moon, we had to be self-sufficient. When the USDS started building the Lowell, they made PT the first totally self-sufficient, deep-space colony. We're more self-sufficient than Luna and the Buzz and just as independent as Mars, Ceres, or Ganymede. Because there's a space rush for Kuiper belt and Trans-Uranian planemos, prospectors and colonizers are using PT as their forward staging ground to further explore and settle this side of the outer solar system."

"Wow! I had no idea. All I knew about was the Lowell!"

"We add ten thousand people or more and a new circle every year," Jim continued. "Prospectors are looking for another Psyche-sixteen, or even a piece of one. Smarter prospectors are looking for the raw materials to keep building homes and feeding people out here on the Edge, where life can be sweet. The Chinese are using the PT harbor and manufacturing facilities to build an outpost on Sedna; they want their own Lowell-like observatory and PT-like spaceport. The Brazilians are trying to do the same with Eris. The Russians have teamed with Europa and staked out Titania and Oberon in the Uranus system for colonization. The USDS is pushing forward with plans to colonize Neptune's moon Triton and the twenty to thirty Neptunian Trojans—that's enough territory there to create a whole new country bigger than the US. And that's not counting the more than ten thousand Jupiter Trojans that are up for grabs. People are eager to get what they can! Particularly religious sects, like fundamental Mormons, Orthodox Jews, and Shiites, who want to set up their own religious colonies, free of Dirt ties and secular laws. In addition to the Trojans, their teams have been exploring the Makemake, Quaoar, and the Haumea-Hi'iaka systems, but no claims have been made yet. I forget who else. There're more than ten thousand new planemos bigger than Mimas out here. Some people say more than a million. There's plenty to go around. But," he sighed, "not enough for some."

"What do you mean?"

"Well . . . I can't talk too freely here, but it's no secret we think the Chinese, or maybe the Brazilians, or even the Russians, are trying to undercut the Pluto-Charon system while building their own outposts. Just like every other place, PT has its criminals—con men, human traffickers, pimps, gangs, thieves, and murderers who prey on our citizens and visitors. The Edge also has its pirates who hijack spaceships, attack outposts, and kidnap prospectors. We've got a strong police and military presence here, but not strong enough. We even have to deal with inner solar system politics, like the Lunar Lights controversy. And, we've got our anarchists who don't want any government this far from Earth, our revolutionaries who're pushing the PC system to declare independence, and our patriots who want US statehood for PC. Right now, we're a US territory, but sometimes that doesn't work for us because of the distance."

"I'd no idea so much was going on out here! Does everyone live here at Port Tombaugh? Or do they live elsewhere?"

"Well, not counting outside the Pluto-Charon System, pretty much all of the Plutonians live here, at Port Tombaugh. Oh, I don't know, somewhere between two hundred and two hundred fifty people live at Clarke Station, depending upon how many visiting scientists we have. People have tried to colonize our lesser moons, Styx, Nix, Kerberos, and Hydra, but their motions are so chaotic—randomly tumbling rather than predictably rotating—and their gravity so low, no one has done anything with them except prospect."

"So, no one lives on the surface?"

"Um, not permanently. Rotating crews service Burney Anchor, Christy Anchor, and Charlene Anchor, but as you know, it is hard to live in microgravity for more than a month or so. Also, to avoid disturbing the 'scopes, the only time people go to the far side of Charon is when the observatory requires humans to fix one. Since most repairs can be done by bots, almost no one ever goes to the far side. We have fabrication plants, food production facilities, chemical processing plants, storage facilities, and mining operations on the surfaces of both Pluto and Charon, but these are also staffed by bots. Humans only visit to check on them and troubleshoot. We also have the sumacoms Kory at Charlene Anchor, Robby at Clarke Station, and Talos at Port Tombaugh. Although we usually call her a sumacom, properly speaking Kory is an ultramax computer, because she is unique and by several magnitudes the most powerful computer ever built. You'll get to meet her sometime. You just heard me speak to Talos."

"Where do those names, Talos, Robby, and Kory, come from?"

"Well, they're not names, they're wake-words," Jim said.

"I know that. But where do they come from?"

"I don't recall. Talos, can you answer Dr. Keator's question?

"Steven Cushing, the founder of ORB Computers, used his daughter's name, Kory, as the wake-word for the series twenty-one hundred Charon ultramax computer. Robby, the wake-word for the Clarke Station sumacom, comes from Robby the Robot in the 1956 sci-fi movie, *The Forbidden Planet*. My wake-word, Talos, honors Talos Thornbird, the first person to set foot on Pluto. Talos is the next largest computer in the system after Kory."

"Thank you."

Later, while sitting on the patio of the Tavern on the Green, in a secluded corner of the surprisingly Earth-like Port Tombaugh Central Park, they ate brunch and watched the squirrels, rabbits, and birds. *This is just like picnicking in Peace Park in Columbia!*

Only the subject matter could not be any more different.

Chief Moxon used the secluded setting to brief her on her secret duties for OASIS. He also explained that the errand that brought him to PT was to discuss with the local authorities a series of tragic accidents and mishaps at Lowell —a mystery that he feared was sabotage.

33

After brunch, he reverted to a tour guide, pointing out the sites on Pluto as they descended to the surface on the elevator, landing at Burney Anchor on the southern tip of the Sputnik Planitia glacier with the famous dagger-sharp Ice Sky Scrapers poking above the eastern horizon. At Burney Anchor they boarded the maglev train for the cross-country trip to Christy Anchor. Suspended above the Plutonian landscape by a spidery web of pillars and rails, they traveled west, following the equator as it crossed the sparkling white flats of the southern tip of the Sputnik Planitia glacier and crossed over the Hillary Mountains.

From the maglev tram, Mary got a close-up view of the landscape. Even though the Plutonian sunlight was dimmer than on Earth, to her surprise she found the distant, but still brilliant, sun lit everything she could see with a cool daylight, making colors richer, like an overcast day in Kansas City or near-dusk in Columbia. The difference between Earth light and Pluto light, she quickly discovered, was the shadows.

On the Earth, where the atmosphere scattered the sunlight, and the broad solar disc filled the sky with daylight, the shadows had fuzzy edges and were never pitch-black. On Pluto, where there was no atmosphere to scatter the sunlight, and the pinpoint sun illuminated the landscape with a narrow beam of light, the shadows had sharp edges and were deep black, making the Plutonian crater floors and canyon bottoms appear to vanish into bottomless pits.

After crossing the Hillary Mountains, they entered Cthulhu Macula—the whale-shaped cratered highlands, deeply stained by copper-brown tholins, cut by the Beatrice and Virgil canyons, and punctured by the gigantic Oort and Edgeworth craters.

"Se-thool-who?" Mary said, attempting to read the name off the map. "What an odd name? What does it mean?"

"More sci-fi whimsy by twenty-first-century astronomers. It's pronounced kuh-THOO-loo. Comes from the name for an Octopus-headed alien deity, created by the twentieth-century science-fiction writer H.P. Lovecraft. Except our version looks like a whale. We'll follow the whale from head to tail, about a third of the way around Pluto, until we reach our next destination, Meng-p'o macula and Christy Anchor, at the center of the Pluto near side."

"Another strange name. What does 'mung-poh' mean?"

"More astronomer name play. Meng-p'o is the name of a Chinese goddess who fed dead spirits the drink of oblivion before reincarnation returned the spirits to Earth. The drink caused irreversible amnesia, giving the spirits a fresh start."

Pointing to the map on the side of the maglev carriage, displaying their progress as they circled Pluto, Mary asked, "What about the rest of those odd names? Where do they come from?"

"Well, let me see. Now remember, I'm not a native Plutonian. Um . . . to the west of Meng-p'o is Hun-Came Macula, and after that, Vucub-Came Macula. They're both named after Mayan death gods. Further east, crossing over onto Pluto's far side, is Balrog Macula, named after the race of demons in the Tolkien novels—you know, *The Lord of the Rings*. I bet you read them as a child."

"Yes, but what about the rest of the macula names? And Simonelli Crater?"

"Kory, can you help us out?"

"Yes, Dr. Moxon. The remaining maculae are on Pluto's far side. The name 'Ala' comes from a Nigerian people known as the Igbo. Ala is the name for their female god for earth, meaning the ground as opposed to the planet Earth. Ala rules the underworld. Krun—which some Plutonians now use as a swear word—is the name for the Mandean lord of the Underworld. The Mandeans are a Middle Eastern people whose religion shares roots with the Jews and Christians. The International Astronomical Union named Simonelli Crater after an American astronomer who studied the formation of Pluto. Damon Simonelli was a member of the *New Horizons* team but died before the arrival of the probe to Pluto."

Continuing their journey around Pluto to Christy Anchor, they crossed the terminus between Pluto's far side—currently bathed in full sunshine—and entered the near side, now shrouded in night. Almost right away, Mary could see the edge of Charon begin to peek over the mountains on the western horizon. At first all she could see was a thin gleaming bow, but as she watched, it gradually swelled in size, becoming a massive orb. Once fully revealed, the risen Charon appeared so large to Mary, that she involuntarily looked away, troubled by the illusion that Charon might fall onto her, or she onto Charon.

Observing her uneasiness, Jim tried to reassure her by explaining the illusion. "Despite appearances, you know Charon is only about one third the size of Luna. But because

Charon and Pluto are so close to each other, from Pluto's surface Charon appears seven times larger than Luna does from the Earth. And," he added, "Charon is nearly as bright as Luna."

Mary knew all of this. Rather than complain that Jim was talking down to her, she bit her tongue and ignored the disturbing celestial vision hanging above her. Instead, she turned her full attention to studying the cratered highlands, deep canyons, and rugged hills of Cthulhu Macula below her, now illuminated with the ghostly gray light of Charon's full-moon shine. After leaving the Whale's tail, they crossed over a snow-white glacier and entered Meng-p'o Macula, the center of the Pluto near side and the location of Christy Anchor, the Plutonian terminus for the Acheron Gulf elevator. Mary could see the lights marking the elevator cable as it ascended and disappeared into the sky, looking like the tallest tower she could possibly imagine, a line with no visible end, pointing toward Charon, now hanging directly overhead.

At the transfer station, they exited the maglev tram and boarded the space elevator. On the ascent to Clarke Station, it didn't take long for the cable car to climb out of the night, cast by Pluto's shadow, and enter eternal daylight, providing Mary with a breathtaking view of nighttime Pluto below them, the innumerable stars surrounding them, the veil of the Milky Way draped across the heavens, the gleaming disc of Charon above them, and the pinpoint sun, distant but still too bright to look at with the naked eye, that turned night into day.

While ascending, Mary asked, "Where does the electricity come from for all of all of this down and up, back and forth travel?"

"The space elevator car and maglev are powered by the charge differential between Charon and Pluto. When the USDS connected Pluto and Charon, they created a battery, a big battery, with a big spark—"

Mary rolled her eyes. "Hey! You don't have to talk down to me. I did my homework."

"Sorry! Didn't mean to insult you. I just wanted to say that no one knew about it at the time they built the Acheron Bridge. So, it all came as a big surprise. A happy surprise, because it provided the cheap power to electrify the Charon grid, Clarke Station, the Acheron Bridge elevator, the maglev train, and Port Tombaugh. But still a surprise. Just last week, one of the OASIS astronomers was electrocuted while working on the bridge. We're not sure how it happened. Somehow, he short-circuited the Pluto-Charon connection. His death was a terrible thing. Everyone's upset. He was well-liked."

"Oh, I'm so sorry."

"That's the reason why I was at PT today. I had to go to the police station to get a final report on the electrocution and pick up his death certificate."

For Mary it was a day never to be forgotten. She spent it spellbound by the fantastical and beautiful Pluto-Charon system. The day began with new vistas she thought she could never imagine, much less see. And it ended with the dreamy space elevator ride up to Clarke Station while she sipped her PT sling and sat next to this surprisingly courteous gentleman, who said he was her boss but acted more like her suitor. Life could not be more perfect!

Seventeen Minutes Before It Happened

"Hey, slowpoke, what's going on?" Mary asked.

"Um. Almost done," Jim said. "It'll take about seven and a half hours for KC to get my message. Probably another fifteen to thirty minutes to set up their side of the EP-conference. In the meantime, the eclipse starts in . . . um . . . about fifteen minutes and will be over in about an hour and a half. While you're waiting, why don't you review your takeoff and landing procedures, because right after the eclipse we'll do a practice run taking off from Kubrick, docking on Spock, and then taking off again for the trip back to Clarke. On the return, we'll finish by having you circle around to the far side of Pluto to see Port Tombaugh and the Valentine on our way back to Clarke Station. You should be on your final approach to Clarke Station by the time I hear from KC. After my EP conference, you can dock us at Clarke Station. When I filed the flight plan, I said we'd be back by nineteen-thirty, plenty of time to make the twenty-one sitting for the late evening meal."

"Wilco." With that, she reviewed her procedures one more time, but she already knew them by heart.

After finishing, she returned to her romance novel. Perhaps prompted by the novel, but more likely by the anticipation of lovemaking and the prospect today might be the day he would propose, her mind began wandering back to her thoughts about Jim.

Thirteen Minutes Before It Happened

She knew this romance was wrong. The CIA would simply not approve. As with their secret WXN2 mission, they kept their affair secret, but also, like their overt WXN2 mission, she feared that other members of the Clarke community had figured it out. Still, in public she always addressed Jim as "Chief Moxon" and he always addressed her as "Dr. Keator." Of course, in private, they were "Jim" and "Mary."

Unfortunately, because of the close confines of Clarke Station, they found it difficult to find privacy. So, Jim suggested he begin training her to pilot the transport, a skill she wanted to learn anyway. The training was at least a plausible explanation for this trip to Charon. Of course, the real reason for this trip was for Jim to confer with his CIA handlers in Kansas City.

Still, he might also choose the eclipse as a romantic opportunity to propose to me. Maybe he intends to surprise me by taking me with him on this errand and then popping the question. If he does propose, I bet it would be the first time a man proposed marriage to a woman while on Charon. Certainly, the first time it was done during the eclipse! Now that would be a story worth telling!

But even if he didn't propose, she was still delighted by her opportunity to learn to pilot a spaceship and visit the surface of Charon. She could claim visiting the fourth world on her personal list and see the once-in-a-century eclipse when the shadow of Charon crossed the fully lit near side of Pluto. Most delightful of all, she expected Jim to make love to her by Pluto's coppery-red light while she wore only her lei. *How romantic would that be!*

After coaching her on departing from Clarke Station and piloting the transport across the Acheron Gulf, Jim talked her through landing on the top of Kubrick Mons—the Mountain in the Moat. Jim had her place the transport with the front cockpit, where she was sitting, facing the western horizon, so he could point the EP gun and laser communicator in the opposite direction, over the gloom of the eastern mountains—now virtually invisible in the ink-black Charon night—and aim the devices down-range to his target, so that Jim could converse with the CIA in real time.

Eleven Minutes Before It Happened

While she was waiting for Jim, Mary dared herself to examine once again the scene that Jim found so fantastic.

Maybe I can ease into this by first looking through the sunroof at the familiar stars and constellations I knew from Missouri and the Buzz.

And it worked.

Feeling relaxed, she then lowered her gaze to once again look out of the bow canopy. In front of her, from the summit of Kubrick Mons, Pluto appeared to be setting—or rising—over the western horizon.

She knew this was just an illusion. Like Luna, Pluto didn't set or rise. Because both Luna and Charon always kept the same hemisphere—their near sides—facing their planets, the position of their planets in the moon sky only changed with the position of the observer on the moon surface. She knew that the vision of Pluto, hanging over the western horizon, was an eternal sight. It had not changed for eons and it would not change for eons to come. What did change, was the planet phase. Now, just minutes from the eclipse, bathed in the glory of high noon, Pluto hung in the sky in full phase, larger than a dozen full Earth Moons.

Pluto takes my breath!

The great Plutonian disc looked to her like the dying remains of some celestial bonfire, burned down to smoldering embers and ashes. Light reflecting off the surface of Pluto—Plutoshine—illuminated the nocturnal Charon landscape with a dim, reddish-brown radiance, coloring the aptly named Vulcan Plain below her a dark coppery-red, creating the illusion of softly glowing coals or cooling lava. The unworldly scene reminded her more of the space artist Chesley Bonestell's hellish depiction of a lava field during the formation of the Earth, than the dreamy solitude of his painting of a snow-covered Titan moonscape, the landscape she had expected to see on Charon.

This is not the place for romance—this place is downright creepy.

The longer she stared, the more fearsome Charon appeared. Deep black shadows filled the seemingly bottomless pits and crevices on the ground, as if they were portals to some hidden alien abyss. The shadows of rocks and boulders looked like they could hide any number of devilish Charonic monsters that suddenly sprang from her imagination. Whether satanic inhabitants of this cursed netherworld or dreadful apparitions from her nightmares, it didn't matter. The more she looked, the more her panic resurged, chasing away the anticipated pleasure of watching the eclipse with Jim and the expected pleasure of their lovemaking. Someone had known something when they named this fearful place after the ruler of Hades. Until this moment, she had not fully comprehended the enormity of the seven-billion-kilometer void that separated her from her parents' home on the green hills of Missouri.

The Buzz is only four times the distance from Earth to the Moon, but Charon is FIVE THOUSAND TIMES the distance from Earth to the Buzz!

For the first time since arriving at Clarke Station, she wanted to go home. She desperately wanted to go home, but she felt trapped on this stygian world.

The tang of space, the slightly burned, slightly metallic odor, like the smell of Fourth of July sparklers, drifted through the ship. Nothing moved outside. All was dead silent. The only noises she heard were the intermittent murmurs of the transport air handlers and the occasional click Jim made when he picked up the coffee bladder and set it back down on the steel bench.

Unnerved by her surroundings, Mary started to make chit-chat by calling back to Jim, "Jim. Do you know the name of that large crater in the distance with the central peak?"

"Yes. That's Spock. And that's the peak you're going to land on after we're through here. The two smaller craters at the foot of Kubrick don't have a name; we call them the Twins."

"What about the lights behind us? What are they?"

"Those lights are from the telescopes on the edge of Charon's far side telescopic array. Hey, could you give me a sec and then I'll give you my full attention, I promise. Okay?"

"Sure."

Seven Minutes Before It Happened

"Done!" Jim yelled from the ship's stern. Standing up from the console, he drew himself toward the bow and pulled Mary into his arms. In the security of his embrace, she turned her face up to offer her lips for a kiss that he readily accepted. After embracing for several minutes, she felt reassured enough to pull away and share with him some of her anxiety with the hope he would further chase away her fears with more of his loving attention.

Her conflicted feelings prompted both a moan and a whine. "I have a secret," she confessed. "Something I haven't told the CIA. I know it's silly, but for as long as I can remember, I've been afraid of the dark. This place gives me the creeps." She then told him about her childhood fears, about the story of the scary Scarecrow from Oz, and about her abusive dad. "I'm so sorry," she whispered. "When you asked me to join you on this trip, I expected a romantic date. I didn't know that Charon would be such a dreadful place. I feel so silly for losing my nerve."

"It's okay," he said, the confession of her secret vulnerability drawing deep tenderness from him, awakening a desire to share his own vulnerabilities. "Everyone has fears about the dark. I've never told anyone this, but as a child, I saw a VR movie with Hieronymus Bosch monsters. Scared me to death. I still get the shivers when I think about the two-legged, winged, unicorn devil with the fangs and snaky tongue, or the tree-man with the broken open belly and the bagpipe hat. I can see them in my mind right now. But my fears never stopped me, and I know your fears will never stop you. You are the bravest, boldest woman I've ever known. Coming out here to live on the new frontier, in the dark and cold. I admire and love you so much." Holding her ever more tightly, hoping that the security and warmth of his embrace would reassure her and communicate his great love for her, he added, "I'm sorry. I used you. I needed your cover to hide the reason for this trip."

"It's okay," Mary said. "I should've told you my secret. You didn't know. I love you!"

Five Minutes Before It Happened

As Jim held and comforted her, he thought about how they had come to this point. After the murder of his wife at the hands of Ceres anarchists thirteen years ago, he hadn't expected to find love again. Certainly not out here, at Clarke Station, billions of klicks from nowhere. He had volunteered for this duty, expecting the isolation would help him mourn Jackie's death.

Yet new love appeared, pushing into his life, filling a hole he thought had no bottom. Beginning with that magical day when he met her at Arrivals, Mary had lifted his life with her enthusiasm, optimism, and energy.

Jim knew that he should not have allowed himself to fall for her. The Bush would not approve, but the Bush was more than seven light hours away.

Here, in front of him, was life. Life in the form of this beautiful young woman, smart, warm, and loving. Playful and entertaining. And now, endearingly vulnerable. For some reason, she found him attractive. How could he turn away from such a woman? She was precious. She could not be denied.

So as soon as she signaled she would welcome his attention, he eagerly pursued her. He had fallen for her. In his pocket was a ring he had been carrying for the right moment. He had hoped the moment would be today. Perhaps now. But, while she burrowed ever deeper into his embrace, seeking his comfort, he began to wonder if he'd made a big mistake.

Three Minutes Before It Happened

He had not been fully honest with her. He had not been candid about the contents of his covert message. He hadn't briefed her about the dangers they both faced if his suspicions proved to be correct, that the recent series of accidents were actually serial sabotage, particularly given his new concerns regarding the source of this sabotage. Because of Jackie's death, he knew in cold, sharp detail just what a menace they might be facing. Despite this knowledge and his love for her—just like he had done to Jackie—he had coldly used her as a cover and by doing so exposed her to danger. Jim hated himself for doing it. By joining the CIA, Mary had volunteered for hazardous duty, but she hadn't volunteered to be deceived by him. Before he could propose and explain the dangers they faced, he had to alert KC and get their instructions and help.

As he held her, he felt the conflict of duty, love, fear, and guilt. Trying to hide his misgivings and comfort her with his love, he promised himself that he would reveal everything to her on the trip back to Clarke Station and never use her again. If it was more than she could tolerate, he would help her return to KC.

If after I tell her everything, if I haven't run her off,
then, and only then, I'll ask her to marry me. If she accepts
me, I'll never, ever, leave her, even if I have to leave the CIA!

Two Minutes Before It Happened

"Mary," Jim said, "there's another reason why I asked you to come with me to Charon. There's something important I want to ask you."

He's going to propose!

"But before I do, I've got to talk with KC and get my instructions."

"All right, but—"

"Listen. Normally I'd take my instructions from KC in private, but I want you to know everything I know about what's going on. There's danger ahead. Grave danger. It's about those accidents. I've made some progress. I think I know what's going on, but I need help from KC about what to do next. I want you to hear what they have to say before I, um, ask you to marry me." He pulled a small box from his pocket and opened it, showing her the solitaire diamond set in a gold ring.

"Oh, Jim," she cried, "I don't care! I'll marry you!"

"Oh, I hope that's true. I love you so much and I don't want to lose you. But before you put the ring on, you have to hear everything. After my conference with KC I'll get down on my knee and ask you properly." With that, he closed the box and put it back into his pants pocket.

"Oh Jim, I love you too! But—"

Then, turning and pointing at Pluto he exclaimed, "Hey! Look! The eclipse is starting! See how there's a black chunk nibbled off the top of Pluto? In a few minutes the shadow will move over the barycenter and we'll be able to see the lights of Clarke Station."

"Yes. I can—"

CRACK! WHOOSH!

The bolts holding the front canopy exploded, flinging the canopy and everything that wasn't tied down out into the Charonic night.

Instinctively, with sudden decompression blowing air out of their chests, gas out of their rectums, and coffee out of their stomachs, Jim and Mary scrambled to get into their spacesuits. With fingers and hands rapidly swelling in the vacuum, they both knew they had only seconds to rescue themselves. Pulling themselves to the lockers, fumbling with swollen fingers covered in slippery muck as they tried to release the latches holding the suits, time ran out. Lightheaded from asphyxia, in his last moments of consciousness, Jim squeezed Mary's hand and felt her squeeze his in return as he mouthed, "I love you."

In the black Charonic night, a light snow of frozen gases released from the transport and its occupants gently drifted down onto the two lovers. The swollen, discolored, and ruptured corpses, still holding hands, one wearing a lei of brightly colored flowers, gradually froze into rock-hard ice.

2 AFTER THE INCIDENT ON KUBRICK MONS

"Inspector! I have two popsicles for you."

"Huh?" said Inspector Skalay, waking from a deep sleep.

"Two popsicles. Two stiff vics. Two boffin bodies." Said the voice. "Director Best is askin' for you. Wants you here pronto."

Mindy turned over. "What's going on, Scott?"

Skalay muffled the phone with his hand. "I don't know. Sounds like Charlie Baker from the Clarke Precinct. Go back to sleep." He got up and walked to the bathroom, where he would not disturb Mindy. "Charlie? Is that you? Where are you? It's four in the morning, for Christ's sake."

"Yup. Been here since midnight," Charlie replied. "It's a fuckin' zoo! PT Emergency Response, Clarke Station Safety, NTSB, AP, Reuters, and Director Best himself. I'm on top of Kubrick Mons. You know, the Mountain in the Moat, the Banana Split, the highest point on the Vulcan Plain. Charon!"

"What in hell are you doing on Charon? That's four hours from here!"

"That's what I'm tryin' to tell you! Transport canopy blew out on the top of Kubrick. Iced two Lowell boffins. When they didn't return as scheduled earlier this evenin', Robby located their transport on Charon and reported no signs of life. Robby passed the information to Kory and

Kory dispatched a recon drone, discovered the two stiffs, and called in the rest of us. Only two in the transport, a man and a woman. Looks like mechanical malfunction while they were gettin' ready for some rumpy-pumpy."

"Rumpy-pumpy?"

"Yup. You know. A little rock-n-roll. Poontang. Sex!" He explained. "They weren't wearin' their spacesuits when the canopy blew. The cockpit couches were flat, and she was wearin' a lei. We figure they were goin' to watch the eclipse and have some nooky. The NTSB is sayin' mechanical malfunction, but they want to move the wreck to PT drydock where they can inspect the transport and pull the flight recorder. The Clarke Station Safety Officer is ready to close the book as soon as the wreck is inspected and the Coroner files an autopsy report. But Director Best says no one is to do anythin' until they get your clearance. He says the stiffs are two of his best scientists, James Moxon and Mary Keator. But you can't tell who they are by lookin'. The bodies are horrible—bloated, covered in vomit, shit, and blood, frozen together, and frozen to the transport deck. The preliminary identification is pretty good, but their badges are frozen in the muck coverin' them and the implanted IDs aren't working—probably ruined by the cold. The coroner can't confirm the identification and do the autopsies until the bodies thaw."

"Okay, okay. I'm at my PT apartment. It's going to take me at least four hours to get there. In the meantime, I don't want anything disturbed. Do you hear me? Nothing is to be disturbed! Do you hear?"

"Yup. Sure," Charlie said.

"Okay. Do you have photos?"

"Of course. I'm not a rookie."

"Send them to me along with whatever else you got. You say the canopy blew?"

"Yup."

"Have you searched and flagged the debris field?" Skalay asked.

"Uh, no. Looks pretty clean cut. You know, mechanical failure."

"No. I don't know. Get it done before I get there. I don't care how small or meaningless you think something is, if it doesn't belong there, flag it and bag it. You got it?"

"Yup."

"Okay, I'll get there as soon as I can."

As promised, on Monday morning, precisely at 08:00 UTC (Coordinated Universal Time), Inspector Scott Skalay, Homicide Squad for the Port Tombaugh Police Department, along with his senior detective, Hildy Kirk, arrived at the site of the transport wreck scene, bringing doughnuts and coffee. Even though the top of Kubrick Mons was off the beaten path and it was still night on Charon, the circle of vehicles, spotlights, and barriers led the Violent Crimes transport right to the scene, like a circle of lights guiding a transport to dock at a space station airlock.

Suited up, Inspector Skalay left the VC transport and walked the wreck site himself. Despite the negligible gravity, the herd of first responders and the rest of the morbid mob had spoiled the site with their footprints. He needed to check Kory's recon photographs to look for footprints before the stampede. It looked like Charlie had followed his instructions and roped off the crime scene and flagged the debris field. Skalay could see an apron of flags spreading out from the blown canopy like a drunk's projectile vomit. He could also see that before the inquisitive crowd had trampled his death scene, a light coating of snow had fallen over the site. He guessed this was the transport atmosphere —water, oxygen, nitrogen, and carbon dioxide released and frozen by the blowout. Still, he asked Detective Kirk to get a sample for further analysis.

While inspecting the scene, Skalay noticed that the thickest snowfall was over the debris field at the bow of the transport. But if he looked at the scene just right, he thought he could also see a light dusting over the rear external deck of the transport. At first, the rear coating seemed odd. Then he realized that a patch of snow in the middle of the deck was thinner. Shaped like a rectangle, it was about one by two meters. Prompted by this observation, he double-checked the footprints around the wreck. A few of them were also covered in a light dusting of snow.

"Kirk, did you get that snow sample?" Skalay asked.

"Yup."

"Where did you get your sample?"

"From right in front of the bow, where the snow is heaviest."

"Okay. Label and flag your sample, but I want more samples from the debris field and from the sides and rear of the transport. Flag, label, and photograph each sample site. Make sure you get an accurate weight and sample size for each specimen. Do you see the snow on the rear deck?"

"Uh, yes," Kirk said. "A little bit. Why?"

"Does it look right to you?"

"Uh, No. Now that you mention it, it looks like a rectangle has been cut out of the middle."

"Right," Skalay said. "Get a sample from the middle of that rectangle and photograph it from multiple angles. Use a meter stick in the photographs so we can get the dimensions. And look at the footprints. See how some of them have a dusting of snow?"

This question stopped her. Approaching one of the footprints and looking at it more closely, she realized that Skalay was correct. "Yes. I missed it."

"Get pictures of all of the footprints and check quantitative snow samples from both the snow-covered and uncovered prints."

Ninety minutes later, Charlie, Kirk, and Skalay congregated in the VC transport to review their findings over coffee and doughnuts.

"Charlie, what did you find in the debris field?" Skalay asked.

Charlie looked down at his inventory list. "Food wrappers and containers. Chips, bread, cheese, and lunchmeat. It looked like they were havin' a picnic. Pens, pencils, papers, paper checklist, maps, transport handbook, a romance novel—*Dark Love*, two jackets, one large and one small, a bottle of ibuprofen pills and spilled pills, towels, tissues, and a perscom. It looks like the perscom belonged to a woman. It had a flower cover, but the cold ruined the electronics."

"Did anyone enter the transport and inspect it?" Skalay asked.

"Yes. I did. The blowout swept it clean. The spacesuit lockers were open, but the latches appeared to be engaged—hard to tell for sure because the couple were frozen together and crumpled up with the suits. It looked to me like they were tryin' to put them on."

"You said over the phone that the first responders suspected they were not in their suits because they were going to have sex? Is that right?"

"Yes. Like I said, the front seats were set in recline—it didn't look like touch-and-go trainin'. Also, they were supposed to be wearin' their suits. I guess they hadn't gotten down to it, they were both dressed and the only clothes in the debris field were the two jackets. Still, there's no good reason for them to have been on top of Kubrick except to have sex. The flight plan only mentioned Moxon was goin' to give Keator touch-and-go trainin' exercises, nothin' about parkin'. Also, the anchors had been deployed."

"What?"

"The transport has three anchors," Charlie said. "All three had been fired into the regolith, securin' the transport in place. That's not part of a touch-and-go exercise."

"That transport must mass at least twenty thousand kilos," Kirk said. "Even with Charon's low gravity, the bump and grind wouldn't budge that thing."

"Right," Skalay said dryly. "Anything else look odd?"

"Well, now that you mention it, there was a drink bladder sittin' on the bow dashboard and another one on the stern workbench. Because of the magnetic bases, they were not blown out. If Moxon and Keator were havin' a picnic, I would have expected both bladders to be together in the forward cockpit."

Looking at his notes, Baker added, "There's sumthin' else. Among the papers, we found one covered with letters and numbers. No explanation. Just letters and numbers." Digging into the evidence box, he pulled out a sheet of paper.

"What in Krun's name?" Skalay exclaimed.

Reading his thoughts, Kirk said, "That looks like a one-time pad!"

In a rare show of emotion, all Skalay could do was repeat, "What in Krun's name?"

At the same time, Charlie asked, "What's a one-time pad?"

Kirk answered before Skalay could say what they were both thinking. "It's a nearly uncrackable way to encrypt a message."

Baker whistled. Skalay pondered.

"Charlie, did you say you found only one perscom?"

"Yes. A woman's. Probably Mary's."

"Well, where's Moxon's perscom?" Skalay asked.

"We didn't find it. Maybe it's still on his body."

"Okay. Before we move that transport, I want one more sweep of the scene. I want that perscom. And I don't care what the NTSB or Clarke Station says, we're investigating a double homicide."

3 KANSAS CITY

Three days after the incident on Kubrick Mons, about an hour before daybreak on Wednesday morning, February 17, 2111, a winter storm slid into Kansas City, dropping surface temperatures to well below freezing. Supercooled by falling through the sub-zero air that blanketed the cityscape, the rain froze upon impact, coating Director Emma Lee's limbot and, and everything else—roads, walkways, buildings, trees—with an icy glaze. Freezing drizzle, the locals called it. A suitable name, she thought, for the miserable weather that made streets slick and travel treacherous, even for an automatically piloted vehicle like her Ford Lincoln limbot.

Sliding aside the window which separated the front compartment from the rear passenger seats, where she sat, her bodyguard, Frank, announced the normal thirty-five-minute commute from her upscale apartment in Overland Park to her downtown office in the Crown Center would take at least sixty minutes.

Taking advantage of the unscheduled delay, she leaned back in her leather upholstered seat, set down the top-secret file on the deaths of Chief Moxon and Agent Keator, which she had just finished rereading and looked out the window. The heavily overcast night sky blacked out the stars and

Moon, the rain sucked the light from the streetlamps and buildings, making Kansas City, already shrouded in winter gloom, even darker. It occurred to her that Valentine's Day on that distant moon, when the Clarke Station transport had failed so spectacularly, killing the two CIA agents, might have looked a bit like this: inky black, icy cold, grim, desolate, an unpleasant place to die. Although similar to the KC cityscape through which she was passing, she knew that Charon must be different in so many more ways, alien, unfathomable, unpredictable, and lethal.

With seven billion kilometers separating her from the death scene, there was just no way she was going to get to the bottom of this mystery without sending one of her agents to the edge of the solar system. The question was, who?

Leaning forward in her seat, she said, "Frank, since we're going to be late anyway, would you take a turn through the North Plaza of the National War Memorial."

"Sure," he replied.

The request did not surprise him. After serving as her senior bodyguard for more than ten years, he knew many of Director Lee's moods. While he entered the detour into the limbot autopilot, he thought: *Something must be up.*

He had seen the top-secret file the courier dropped off at her home last night, the same file it looked like she had just finished reading. He presumed the file presented a choice between two bad options. If so, the choice undoubtedly related to the top-secret Fifth FD mission: The freedom to break the law to defend the law.

It seemed to Frank, that at times like this, when facing a tough choice, Director Lee typically asked to visit the North Plaza of the War Memorial.

Located across the street from the Crown Center, the War Memorial began as a memorial to the international tragedy of World War I, when more than forty million people from all across the globe died. Although not known at the time, World War I began a 120-year era of international war, that ended with the Three Hour War in 2041. After the Three Hour War, Kansas City expanded the War Memorial to include a second memorial to the seventy-eight million Americans who had lost their lives in the Three Hour War. Kansas City dedicated the North Plaza of the War Memorial to the memory of those war victims by building a long glass wall that snaked across the Plaza. The memorial used forty-six-million glass bricks—each brick containing one or more silver dollars, with each coin symbolizing one of the Americans who had lost their lives in that horrific war.

When the weather was bad, like today, Director Lee seemed satisfied for the Lincoln to take a slow turn through the grounds. But in good weather she would get out and walk along the North Plaza pathways. After a while, she always stopped in front of one particular brick, in the Washington portion of the wall, on the south side of the North Plaza, facing the World War I Memorial. The two coins in this particular brick memorialized her husband and her daughter, who died in the nuclear fire that destroyed Washington, D.C.

Such predictable behavior could be dangerous, exposing her to assassins, but Frank considered the risk negligible and the benefit large. Standing a couple of meters behind her, he would usually give her a few minutes to mourn and meditate before gently urging her to move on. It wasn't much, but it seemed to him these brief interludes fortified her. He hoped so. He often thought she needed the strength she seemed to gain from these visits to make the decisions she undoubtedly had to make as the first, and so far the only, Director of the Fifth FD since it was first organized just weeks after the Three Hour War, in 2041.

He presumed that her long service meant that her superiors trusted her to execute the awesome but deadly, power of the Fifth FD. *Trust well placed.*

Thirty minutes later, after taking a slow turn through the Memorial, they left the North Plaza, pulled into Pershing Road, crossed Main Street, and entered the Crown Center parking garage through the entrance labeled WILLIAM BECKNELL GLOBAL TRADE SERVICES EMPLOYEES ONLY. A legitimate business, Becknell GTS served as the cover for the top-secret Fifth FD.

After passing through the parking garage security gate, the Lincoln pulled up in front of the bollards blocking the underground Becknell GTS entrance.

Frank climbed out of the limbot and started to open Director Lee's door, but she waved him off. Pushing open her own door she said, "Frank. KC canceled Schools today. Go home and help your wife take care of those two great sons of yours. I'm going to work late tonight and sleep in my office. I won't be going out until tomorrow evening."

"Thank you, Sir," Frank replied. "I'll see you tomorrow. Call me if your plans change."

With that, she said goodbye, threaded her way through the bollards, entered the building, and then took her place in line to pass through the first security gate.

Frank remained on guard, watching her until she passed into the safety of the fortified building. During moments like this, he often thought she moved like a battleship, unstoppable and formidable. According to the calendar, she must be pushing one hundred, but looking at her, you would never know it. He assumed she'd had organ transplants that had stalled her aging. She still had a full head of thick red hair, topping a figure shaped like a refrigerator and hard as stone; her Fifth FD codename, Brick, fit her like a suit of armor.

In the Fifth FD, personnel could choose their own codename, as long as it was short, had sharp consonants, and was not the name of a weapon or any animal or human. He wondered if she chose her codename as an oblique reference to her deceased family rather than a statement about her appearance or the kind of person she had become since the deaths of her family. It didn't matter.

The Brick is one of the great ones, but not someone with whom I would trifle.

After passing through security, Director Lee rode the elevator up to the twenty-third floor. Nominally part of the suite of Becknell GTS offices, the twenty-third floor—as well as several other floors and a couple of the sub-basements— was closed to the public. Although she had served as the Fifth FD Director for seventy years, each time before entering the offices, she still had to be recognized and cleared by security. She didn't complain; she was the one who had established the standard of multiple security checks with the no-exceptions rule in the first place.

Her assistant, Max Thaler, met her at the office door.

"General Barrun is after you. He wants you to call him this afternoon. He says you'll know what it's about."

"I'm on it," she replied. "Max, see if you can locate Dr. Edwards. He should be making his rounds at Truman Hospital. As soon as you get him, patch him in. I'll wait for the call. After that, I have to speak with the Mossad liaison. His name is Joe Jakobson—you'll find him at the Israeli consulate. Locate Steel. Tell him to make himself available for a nine thirty meeting in my office, and tell the Chief of Staff to come to my office at ten for a briefing about WXN2. Also, ask the Deputy Director to come to my office at ten thirty. Tell him that I'm posting Steel to the Pluto-Charon System to investigate the murder of two of our agents. I need recommendations for loP-loG and noP-noG combat."

"Got it," Max said.

With that, she walked into her office, sat down at her desk, and once again read through the Moxon and Keator file while waiting to speak to Dr. Edwards.

Fifteen minutes later, Dr. Edwards returned her call, apologizing for the delay. He was making rounds with the medical students and house-staff, so he had no privacy and even less time. But he had broken from rounds anyway to call her back. "So, Mrs. Lee, what can I do for you today?"

"We've got a situation. Well, we always have a situation, but this one is different. More urgent. I don't have anyone cleared for active duty. I have to activate someone on the convalescent list. Can you make a recommendation? Remember, the phone is not secure."

"Yes. I know." *Didn't I make that clear by calling her Mrs. Lee instead of Director Lee?*

Before he could suggest any names, she quickly interjected. "I thought about Torch, Flint, Book, or Steel."

"Well, forget about Book. Too much brain damage. We're going to place him on the permanently disabled list. You can also scratch Flint. We're still rejuvenating his mangled arm. Full regeneration will take another six weeks. After that he'll need intensive physical therapy and martial arts training to return to full function." After pausing for a moment to think, he continued, "Torch had her total visceral organ transplant three weeks ago. She should get back to a hundred percent, but she's not there yet. I'd give her at least two more weeks. Mushroom poisoning is vicious and affects more than just the liver and kidneys. In the meantime, I'm watching her for PTSD. She's tough. So far, she's fine. But, as you know, PTSD can get anyone who has been through that much trauma. If you're in a pinch, you could activate her. That leaves Steel."

"Steel seemed the obvious choice to me," Director Lee said.

"Well, yes," he replied. "He's nearly recovered from the gunshot wound to the chest, as well as the cardio-pulmonary resuscitation and massive blood transfusions needed to bring him back. From a physical standpoint, he's nearly completely recovered. Like Torch, he could probably return to work today. But he'd benefit from a couple more weeks of rest and relaxation, rather than being tossed right back into it. To be frank, although supremely capable, he's a proud man. I'm worried about how well he'll bounce back from losing his partner and nearly losing his own life. I expect his confidence has been shaken."

"We don't have time to baby him. I'll take that as clearance to return him to active duty." With that, she thanked him and hung up.

A few minutes later, Max connected her to Joe Jakobson. After a few pleasantries, Director Lee got to the point.

"Joe, I need your help. We've got a problem with the WXN2 mission—I know you know what that means and how important it is to both our co—"

Joe cut her off. "Does this have anything to do with the report in this morning's *KC Star* that two Lowell astronomers died on Valentine's Day in a transport wreck on Charon?"

"Yes, but—"

"The *KC Star* says the NTSB declared it a mechanical failure. They hinted that the two were getting it on. Valentine's Day and such."

"Joe—"

"Yo, it's right here. And I quote: 'The NTSB spokesperson summarized their working conclusions by stating, "Outer space is dangerous, accidents happen, and that's why they should have been wearing their spacesuits. If they had done that, they would be alive today."' They weren't wearing their spacesuits, were they?"

"Joe, will you be quiet for a minute and give me a chance!"

"All right, all right. Sorry, Emma. Go on."

"Yes, it looks like a mechanical failure due to sabotage. That's the problem. As for getting it on, yes, they had a sexual relationship, but at the time of the sabotage, they were conducting top-secret Company business. There was no hanky-panky! Don't ask me how I know, but I know!"

"Fine," Joe said, but she continued.

"God, I wish the *Star* would lay off the salacious speculations. Her parents live in Columbia. They won't be pleased to read that everyone across the solar system thinks their daughter died in a romantic tryst because she wasn't wearing her spacesuit!"

"Emma, what do you want from me?"

"I have to send someone to Charon."

"What? Are you sure? Don't you have agents at Clarke Station?" Joe asked.

"We did. Five people. Now it's just three junior agents. Two of them are analysts."

"What about the CIA and the FBI? Don't they have offices at Port Tombaugh?"

"Yes. They both do, at Fort Resnick. But this is top-secret and strictly Fifth FD business. Neither of the Fort Resnick offices has the security clearance to deal with this problem. And, no one at Pluto has Interrobang authority. I have to send someone to Charon who does, and I have to back him up with agents who have top-secret clearance and space combat skills. I need to figure out what happened to our Clarke Station agents and then take the necessary steps to make sure our 'top secret' stays secret. I think you know what I mean."

"I know what you mean. But what do you want from me?"

"The only agent I can send right now is one of my telluric agents. On his last mission, he lost his partner and nearly died as well, but I don't have anyone with both off-planet experience and an Interrobang Badge. I need your help. Can you detail one or more of your 'stros with top-secret clearance to join my agent on this mission? I need someone with computer skills and proficiency in loP-loG and noP-noG combat."

A long pause followed this request. Finally, with a sigh, Joe responded, "Who's your Earth agent?"

"Steel."

"Oy! But—"

"He has an Interrobang Badge, and he has it for a reason. He's a shrewd, intuitive investigator with street smarts and a sharp eye."

"Yes, but—"

"He's also skilled in hand-to-hand combat and is an excellent marksman."

"I know, but—"

"And he's straight but ruthless. He always completes his mission."

"Emma, stop! Won't he stand out like a sore thumb once he leaves the planet?"

"Yes, that's a problem. But it will not be like he's the only one. Besides, I can hide his CIA identity by sending him under his own name but with FBI credentials. Before he leaves, we'll assign him to the KC FBI office with orders to investigate possible sabotage and assassination at the Lowell. The Lowell is a federal facility, so the FBI has jurisdiction. This will be Steel's first off-planet assignment. No one should recognize him, or have his identity on file, or be surprised when an FBI agent from KC shows up to investigate. He'll need a refresher on loP-loG and noP-noG combat by an expert. He'll also need one or more backup partners with 'stro combat and computer skills. I'm hoping your agency can help provide backup. If so, we can use the outbound leg to give Steel his combat training and prepare for the mission."

Joe sighed again. "You said he lost his partner? And he got shot and nearly lost his life? What a mess!"

"Yes. They were undercover, breaking up a human trafficking and weapons-smuggling ring in Jamaica. She was the bait, and he was posing as an arms dealer. Bad luck blew his cover. He was recognized from an entirely different mission. It cost her her life and nearly cost him his."

"I thought Steel was better than that. Is he losing it?"

"No," she replied. "As I said, he's sharp, tough, and ruthless as ever. Problem is, too many people like you, know who he is. His cover's blown. I can't help that, but a change in beat might extend his utility."

"Have you changed his rating? Is he still Interrobang?"

"We've not changed his rating. As I said, he still has the Badge. If you assign any of your agents to work with him, we'll extend the Interrobang authority to them."

"Fair enough, but we won't need it."

"Joe. I want you to assign Kes."

"Kes? Hmm," mused Joe. "Well, that would take care of a couple of problems." Then, with a lighter tone, he said, "You are a puppeteer aren't you, Mrs. Lee?"

"When I have to be," she said quietly.

"Well. I'll see what I can do. I make no promises. If we send an agent, I presume you want someone from New Jerusalem to join Steel at the Buzz for the outbound trip. No?"

"Yes. Your agent should meet him at the Sea of Storms Office for introductions and training before leaving for Port Tombaugh."

"I hear you. I'll get back to you," he replied.

"Joe," she said, "I'm getting pressured to put this operation together by the end of the day. Can you let me know by later this morning?"

"As I said, I'll try, but only because it's you who's asking."

"Thank you. Let me know as soon as you know."

4 RETURN TO ARMS

"Dakar. John Dakar," the man said slowly, giving the consonants a bite and ending with a fading, rolling "r," . . . like a growl. Voice verification checked.

The man placed his hands on the scanner. Fingerprints checked.

The man held his left forearm up to the sensor. The ID embedded in his left forearm checked.

The man stood 190 centimeters tall and weighed ninety kilograms. Height and weight checked.

The guard compared the man's face with the picture on his monitor. A square face, dark, nearly black, broad nostrils and a narrow bridge , thin lips, short-cropped, tightly-curled black hair, and eyes with brown irises flecked with gold and muddy sclera stared back at him from the monitor.

The same face looked directly at the guard with an unwavering gaze.

Along with the initial checks, facial recognition and iris scan confirmed the man's identity.

The guard paused, instincts suddenly on high alert.

The man said his name was Dakar. The name suggested a man of darkness, a man who moved easily through obscurity, whether in the slums of some West African megacity or in the shadows of an Amazonian jungle.

The CIA personnel file identified the man by his codename: "Steel." The codename suggested a man to be respected. A man to be feared. A proper codename for a covert warrior.

The security clearance file listed the man's rank as "Colonel" and rating as "Interrobang (?!)." The title and rating for a Marine officer, a Federal investigator, and a licensed CIA killer.

As if handling a rattlesnake, the guard cautiously passed the man into the Fifth FD offices: "Colonel Dakar, Director Lee is expecting you."

† † †

"Sit down, John," Director Lee said. "I've read your report on the incident in Jamaica. Anything else you want to add?"

John hadn't expected a warm welcome. Since Sarah's death, he had dreaded this meeting, anticipating he would be placed before a Peer Review Board and lose his agent ranking and rating. On a different, but even more important scale, he valued Director Lee's esteem. Knowing the fastest way to earn her censure would be to try to hide his failures, he spoke directly, but painfully, about that horrible afternoon in Windsor, Jamaica.

Carefully choosing his words, John slowly began, "When Kalfu recognized me from 2104, when I broke up the Caine Toads, his sex trafficking ring in Iquitos, I knew it was over for Sarah and me. Kalfu forced me to watch while he slowly cut Sarah apart. I watched her die, pleading with me to do something. I nearly ripped off my arms trying to get out of my manacles. It surprised everyone, including me, that I broke free. Only it was too late for Sarah. I was so angry, I could not be stopped. I grabbed my guard's gun, shot him, shot the other two guards, and then—even though I'd been shot—I slowly cut off Kalfu's head, only pausing to let him scream until he could scream no more. I wanted him to scream. I wanted him to scream after what he had done to Sarah. What he'd done to those other women, to those children."

After another pause, he said, "I'm ashamed of what I did. I know I violated Company standards. Because of my wounds, I expected to die in that warehouse—no one gets out of Cockpit Country alive. So, I didn't worry about the consequences. I just wanted to avenge Sarah. Somehow you got me out. Thank you."

He then added, "A little while ago, Dr. Edwards called me and said I was cleared for active duty. I believe that I'm ready. But I'll understand and accept your decision if you decide that because of my actions, I should give up my ranking and rating."

"You loved her, didn't you," Director Lee said, making a statement, not asking a question.

"Yes." After a long pause in which he sorted his feelings, he added, "At first, she was my partner, then something else."

After another long pause, reflecting the many hours he had mulled over what had happened in that Cockpit warehouse, feeling the horror, the anger, and the guilt, he continued, "I'd not loved before. I know that loving Sarah was a mistake. My love for her gave Kalfu a weapon against me, and he used it. My mistake killed Sarah." With a sigh, revealing a glimpse of the depths of his pain, pain that couldn't be vanquished, he said, "I'll not make that mistake again."

For a few long minutes the room was quiet, the only noise was the ticking of the antique clock on Emma's credenza.

"John, she said, "I know the pain of having someone you love cruelly murdered . . ."

Her voiced trailed, but John knew what she meant.

"But I also know the danger of letting those emotions push you into doing something equally wrong. I don't need to tell you, you did not need to kill Kalfu. You were beyond your Interrobang authority. Your actions could be considered unnecessarily cruel. By all rights, I should have you appear before a PRB. But because of your history of consistent mission success, your honorable record, and the circumstances of this incident, I am sure the PRB would do nothing more than put you on probation. If you're willing to accept a one-hundred-and-twenty-day probation, we can skip the PRB. In the meantime, I have a mission for you."

"And what would a one-hundred-and-twenty day probation mean?" he asked.

"You'll keep your military rank and Interrobang Badge. Your record will remain clean, and you'll remain on the active list. But if there's another incident, then you'll be automatically suspended and will have to appear before a PRB. And when you do, it'll be with one strike already against you. Is this something you can accept?"

"Yes."

"The mission I have in mind for you will allow you to complete your convalescence. It has an eight-week training and cooling off period that will apply to the one-hundred-and-twenty day probation. The mission will emphasize your investigative skills, not your enforcement skills."

That's odd, he thought. *I've never been assigned to such a mission.*

He worried about the terms of a one-hundred-and-twenty-day probation, but if he spent half of those one-hundred-and-twenty day days in the field doing an investigation instead of enforcement, he should have no problems. He was not as confident as Director Lee appeared to be that a PRB decision would be favorable to him.

After a few moments, he responded, "Okay. I'm in."

"Good." Speaking into the intercom, she said, "Mr. Thaler, we're ready for the Chief of Staff."

A few moments later, Mr. Dawson entered the room.

"Mr. Dawson, you know Colonel Dakar," Director Lee said. "Would you please brief the Colonel on the situation at Clarke Station."

"Wait," John interrupted. "Did you say Clarke Station? As in the Pluto Space Station? What has that got to do with me? I've never been off-planet!"

"John, just wait. We'll explain everything," Director Lee said. "Go on, Mr. Dawson."

"Right," the COS replied. Looking at his notes, he began by describing how the two astronomer-agents had died as well as the other mishaps, including the electrocution of the Lowell engineer that suggested serial sabotage of the Lowell II Observatory.

With nodding approval from Director Lee, Dawson next revealed the covert assignment of the two agents and the top-secret mission of the Lowell Observatory.

"The Lowell is not only an astronomical observatory. Its primary mission is to conduct espionage. We use it to survey space communications and to track space traffic. Astronomy is just a cover. People think we built it to look for little green men, but we built it to monitor our enemies. Only our closest allies—Canada, Britain, and New Israel—know the true mission of the facility, although many others suspect it, particularly China, India, Brazil, Russia, and Europa. The Lowell espionage program has been a major factor in keeping the post-3-Hour-War peace. To conduct this surveillance, we've got to keep the spy function of the Lowell secret. We also have to keep it secret because our surveillance net pulls in domestic communications along with the foreign. As you know, domestic surveillance is illegal."

"Damn!" John said underneath his breath.

After a sharp glance at John, Dawson continued. "The codename for the Lowell espionage project is WXN2. Keeping WXN2 a secret is your first task. Keeping the EP communicator secret is your second task."

"What is—"

Dawson raised his hand and his voice so that he could continue to speak. "EP communications are made with entangled photons. It's supposed to be impossible. But the impossible is now possible. Once it has been set-up, two parties can communicate instantaneously, no matter the distance. At the time of his death, Moxon was setting up an EP communication channel with the Kansas City CIA headquarters. If he had succeeded in establishing a clear channel, then he would have been able to talk with the Bush in real time as if they were next door instead of seven-plus light-hours away."

"Whoa!"

"Setting up a channel requires sending an encrypted laser message introducing the EP-message, accompanied by a stream of photons entangled with a second set of photons retained by the sender. We use an EP gun to send the message. It looks like, and is about the same size, as an antique Gatling gun. As far as we know, we're the only ones with EP communication capability. It gives us a tremendous military advantage over everyone else. We've got to keep it secret."

"So, is the secret out?" John asked.

"No. When Chief Moxon started to send his message, he copied his superior, the Lowell Observatory Director, Dr. Ronald Best. Dr. Best is fully informed about the CIA mission. Seeing the message had not gone through, he immediately tried to contact Moxon for an explanation. When Moxon did not respond, Best queried Robby, the Clarke Station sumacom. Robby located Moxon's transport on Charon and reported no signs of life. Best then had the Charon sumacom, Kory, send a reconnaissance drone, which inspected the wreck site and determined the occupants were dead. The EP gun was still on the rear deck of the transport."

"By this time two hours had elapsed. The transport was due back by nineteen thirty. Dr. Best had six hours to recover the EP-gun before the transport would be missed. He got the remaining CIA agents assigned to Clarke Station, three men, to immediately travel to the wreck site and pick up the gun and associated equipment before anyone else could discover the wreck. Which they did."

"Okay," John said. "But why do you think the two agents were murdered? And why do you need me?"

"Because of this," Director Lee said, handing John a copy of Chief Moxon's last transmission. It began with the usual prefix of identifications and validations, establishing authenticity, urgency, date and time of the message, and authorship by Chief Moxon:

9162/O)+/WXN2/RIA/14—02—2111

The transmission then continued with the substance of the message:

Serial sabotage of Lowell confirmed, due to an alien co . . .

Someone had attached a computer text analysis to the interrupted message:

Based on the grammar, syntax, and vocabulary used by Chief Moxon in prior CIA communications, as well as the presumed threat environment in which he sent the message, the computer's best guess was that "co . . ." referred to a common noun (ninety-four percent confidence) and was unlikely to be an adjective, proper noun, verb, or adverb. The most likely noun was "conspiracy" (seventy-six percent confidence). Also possible, but less likely were: controller (twelve percent confidence) and consortium (three percent confidence). Additional, but even less likely, possibilities (with confidences greater than one percent but less than two percent) included combatant, commander, company, computer, contact, control, and corporation. The text analysis could not make any intelligible projections for the rest of the message.

Director Lee picked up the briefing. "John, to answer your two questions: It's just too damn convenient for the canopy to blow while sending a message warning us of sabotage. Also, Moxon must have had some pretty hot news to use the EP. Clarke Station is only supposed to pull that rabbit out of the hat under the direst circumstances. We need someone to find out what happened and someone who can fix the problem. That person is you."

"Okay, but—"

"Before we get to your buts, there's another problem," Lee said. "The Port Tombaugh Homicide Squad is also working this case. And unlike the NTSB, they also suspect murder. They don't know as much as we do, but the Squad Leader, Inspector Skalay, is sharp. Unfortunately, Best's fix-it team wasn't very sharp. They made some rookie mistakes, probably because they weren't trained for this kind of operation. Skalay spotted the mistakes and figured out that someone visited the wreck and removed something from the rear of the transport before the authorities got there. Best says Skalay suspects the thief first sabotaged the transport and then, after the blowout, swiped whatever was on the rear deck, which, of course, was the EP gun. Skalay doesn't know the thief's identity or what was taken. We've got to keep the EP-communicator secret, even from Skalay. Skalay is going to work the case for at least the next four weeks before we can get you there. We need him and his people to help us find who killed our agents, but we can't let him find out what was removed from the wreck or the real mission of the Lowell. The only way to get Skalay off track is to make sure once he finds the killers, you silence the killers before he can quiz them. Do you understand? Can you do that?"

"All right," John said, disappointed that this wouldn't be the cakewalk he'd been promised. "But who—"

"We don't know who," Dawson replied. "Our best guess is the Chinks. The closer they are to completing the Sedna Outpost, the more aggressive they get. At this time, we figure Sedna will be operational in thirty to thirty-six months. The timing is a bit early, but perhaps that's their plan in order to throw us off. The Brazucas and the Ruskies are also building outposts on the Edge, but they're behind the Chinks. All three have Consulates at Port Tombaugh. I'd begin there."

Director Lee interrupted, "Although China, Brazil, and Russia are at the top of our list, there're other possibilities. I'm worried the Lunar Lights conflict between the Christians and the Muslims has spilled over into the sabotage of Clarke. I've no indication the conflict has left the Moon. But, as you know, that struggle has started to break into violence. It's possible that either group sabotaged Clarke to pull us into their conflict."

She then added, "Aside from international politics, there're multiple anarchist groups active in the outer solar system—the biggest ones are the Edge Anarchist Collective, the 'Stro Workers Group, and the Free People of the Outer System. Any one of these groups could take a strong dislike to our snooping on their communications and decide to sabotage our equipment. All of them have operatives at Port Tombaugh."

"Jeez! I didn't know there's so much happening on the Edge!"

"Wait," Dawson said. "There's more. If it falls into the wrong hands, the EP communicator has tremendous criminal potential. At least two major crime organizations, the Neo-Morellos Syndicate and the Lubyanka Space Consortium, are competing for dominance at Port Tombaugh. It's hard to imagine they would sabotage Clarke, but if one or both knew about the EP communicator, they might easily kill our staff to get their hands on the device. We know that shortly before she was killed, Dr. Keator was investigating some odd patterns in the PT stock market and betting parlors suggesting that someone had advance knowledge of price swings in the Chicago stock market and Terran sports results. The only way that would be possible would be with a faster-than-light communication device. If this is true, it means the secret of the EP communicator is out. We've no indication this has happened, but we can't take any chances."

Dawson then added, "Before you leave, I'll give you full briefing materials. You'll have plenty of time to study them while you're outbound. Obviously, when you're done, you must destroy them."

At this point, Director Lee stood up to excuse the Chief of Staff.

"Wait!" John said. "I have more questions. Will it really take four weeks for me to get to Pluto?"

Director Lee replied, "Thank you, Mr. Dawson. You may leave. On your way out, would you ask Mr. Thaler to summon the Deputy Director?" Then turning to John, she said, "Yes. Four weeks, minus a couple of days."

"Jeez. If it takes that long, what do you expect me to do? The case will be cold by then."

"I fear not," Director Lee replied. "As Mr. Dawson said, we don't know who's attacking the Lowell or why, so we have to anticipate that the attacks will continue. Certainly, Moxon expected more trouble. Besides, if by chance the attacks are over—which I'm sure they're not—we need someone with your skills to make sure the EP communicator remains secret and secure."

"What about the CIA and the FBI?" John asked. "They must have Pluto agents."

"At this time our only CIA agents with top-secret clearance for the WXN2 program and the EP communicator are the three remaining CIA agents staffing the OASIS office at Clarke Station. Only one of them is muscle, the other two are data analysts with just basic weapons training. No one has the investigative skills we need. Director Best could be a resource, but his public position and cover prevent him from doing much to help us. There's a joint CIA and FBI office at Fort Resnick, but no one there has the clearance for this matter. More importantly, no one has Interrobang authority. Because we've lost two OASIS agents, we'll have to re-staff Clarke Station. I'm assembling a six-person team to follow you, but they won't get there until two to eight weeks after you get to Clarke."

"So, I'll have no backup?"

"You'll have backup," Director Lee said. "I've asked the Israelis for assistance. Mossad has a strong 'stro covert action program. I should know later today what they're willing to do for us. They're as much invested in the WXN2 program as we are. Is that all?"

"Yes."

"Good. Because the armorer does not have the security clearance needed to deal with this mission, I've asked Deputy Director Boot, to serve as your armorer. He will also be your handler. Because of the sensitivity of this mission, you will use his codename, Kick, for all mission communications outside this office. Understood?"

"Yes, sir. I've known Louis—er, Kick—since I joined the Fifth. He was my mentor."

"Yes. I know." Speaking into the intercom, she said, "Max. We're ready for Colonel Boot."

5 PREPARE FOR COMBAT

Followed by Max Thaler, Colonel Louis Boot entered the room with a big grin on his face. "John Dakar, space spy, I presume?" he boomed, grabbing John's hand in a grip so large it seemed like the Colonel must be wearing a baseball glove. "It's so good to see you, my friend! Hey! 'Space spy' has a kind of a ring to it, don't you think?"

Before John could respond to his old friend and new handler, Max cut in.

"Director Lee, Joe Jakobson is on the line for you."

"Ah!" Director Lee said, standing up and waving her arms at the group. "That's the call I've been waiting for. Gentlemen. I have to take this call in private. Colonel Boot. If you can refrain from the pleasantries, we could use your expertise on off-planet combat. Please brief Colonel Dakar in the conference room and I'll join you when I can. Thank you."

Max ushered the two men into the adjoining conference room and then excused himself.

Known as the Dead Room to the small number of people who had visited it, the room looked like a standard boardroom, paneled in dark walnut. A floor-to-ceiling window faced the entrance, showing the Western KC cityscape and the War Memorial across the street from the

5th FD offices. Pictures of agents who had died in the field covered the three remaining conference room walls. A somber place for somber work.

In the middle of the room, on top of a large oval walnut conference table, sat an empty aluminum travel case, an empty carry-on satchel, and three boxes: an empty one labeled storage and two filled with weapons, labeled SECURITY and ARMORY.

"Sooo," Colonel Boot began. "You're on your way to Pluto, are you? Means a long ride out and back, probably safe, but you never know. Then investigations at Port Tombaugh and Clarke Station. And, I suspect, a visit to the crime scene. Right?"

"Yeah, I suppose so," Dakar grumbled.

"Do you have any experience with off-planet combat?"

"Uh, no. I was briefed during my training years ago when I joined the Fifth, but nothing since then. Didn't pay much attention to it—didn't expect to ever use it. Never been off-planet. Never thought I would be."

"Well, here's the thing. 'Stro combat is unlike anything on Earth. In space, you will always be fighting in some kind of a can. A containerized environment, either loP-loG— think combat in a space station or a spaceship—or noP-noG —think combat while wearing a spacesuit and floating in outer space. The bad news is you can't use the explosive weapons you are used to using on Earth. No guns. No grenades. Too much risk of blowing out the hull of a space station or spaceship, or shattering a visual port, or destroying a piece of critical equipment. Besides, if you're wearing a spacesuit, there's no way you can hold and operate a conventional hand weapon."

Boot turned to the SECURITY box. Inside Dakar saw the weapons he normally carried but had surrendered to Security when he entered the 5th FD offices.

Reaching into the box, Boot pulled out Dakar's Saratoga 2100 semi-automatic .45 ACP with the ten-centimeter barrel, and his back-up, the Micro Sparrow Hawk .32 ACP sub-compact semi-automatic pistol. Placing them in the storage box, Boot said, "You can't take these with you. I'll keep them until you return."

A sinking feeling swept over Dakar. He owed his life to those two weapons. Without them, his picture would be on one of these walls. His favorite, the Saratoga, with the short barrel for an easy draw but the big caliber for stopping power, had been his go-to weapon for as long as he'd had the Interrobang Badge. His backup, the easily hidden snub-nosed Sparrow Hawk, had pulled him out of trouble more times than he would like to think.

"Louis, you can't do that to me! I've got to have these weapons. Can't I just smuggle them on board? I've done it many times before."

"No. As I said, the 'stros have a great fear of these weapons, and the TSA is too tight. If you try to board with your guns, they'll find them, and they'll take them from you along with your boarding pass. If you somehow succeed in sneaking a gun on board, Port Tombaugh Customs will find it, confiscate it, and refuse to let you debark. They'll just send you right back to the Buzz, even if you were Director Lee."

"Christ! What am I going to use?" Dakar asked.

"Well, let's talk about that. If you must have a high-powered weapon—which you probably can't use anyway, you can get it from Fort Resnik. Director Lee will inform the commandant that you'll be arriving and instruct them to assist you in whatever manner you require. As long as you can justify your need and—here's the stickler—you can assure that non-combatants will not be placed in danger, then Fort Resnik will provide guns, grenades, missiles, whatever explosive weapon you might want. They'll also issue you a hard-shell spacesuit. If you should need a particular weapon or tool they can't provide, Fort Resnik has plastic, metal, and silicon 3-D printers. Most likely whatever you need can be printed for you."

"Okay. I hear you. But what about in the meantime?"

"The good news is, combat in space is a fallback to the past—hand-to-hand with edged weapons. If I remember correctly, you're an expert in both."

"Yes. I'm an expert in Muay Thai. You know, Thai boxing—'the Art of Eight Limbs.' It doesn't use weapons—"

Boot interrupted, "Great! See, you're already ahead of the game!"

"—but, I'm also an expert in Krabi Krabong. It's the same as Muay Thai but uses weapons. I use a hand knife and a throwing ax. Surely I can bring them?"

Boot reached into the security box and pulled out Dakar's throwing ax. Holding up the unusual, three-bladed weapon, the gray steel gleamed in the late morning daylight, revealing an intricate swirl of parallel waving lines that permeated the metal.

With a sly grin, Boot said, "Now that's a wicked weapon. Beautiful, —" he shook his head, "but wicked."

"It's my codename moniker," Dakar replied. "A modern version of the Kpinga throwing ax, used by Congolese warriors. I pulled one like this off of a hired goon who nearly killed me with it in Central Sudan before I joined the Fifth. I started playing around with it to see if I could use it as both a Krabi sword and a throwing ax, but it was made of cheap, brittle steel. The goon's weapon broke as soon as I threw it. I asked a Thai swordsmith, a master of the art, to make me this one using traditional Japanese methods. He, uh, owed my Thai grandmother a favor."

Taking the weapon from Boot's hands, Dakar said, "You're right, this is a wicked weapon." Running his hands over the gray blades, Dakar continued, "Like Damascus steel, it is made of carbonized steel and iron, welded and folded over and over again. The lines on the surface come from folding the iron and steel together. The carbonized steel makes the cutting edges hard and razor sharp, while the iron makes the ax strong and flexible. I had the swordsmith fashion the ax face so that I could use it as both a chopping weapon and as a throwing ax. The twin sickle-shaped blades on the opposite side are double-edged. As you can see, the inside edge is serrated. I use the sickles for cutting and ripping. The short rat-tail spike on the crown, is a four-edged foil with a needle-sharp tip. I use it for both throwing and stabbing.

"And, as you say, it is also 'beautiful.' The swordsmith laid out the blade curves according to a Fibonacci spiral. Ever since I joined the Fifth, I've worn this ax in a holster on my back. A unique weapon . . . frightening . . . intimidating. The looks alone give me an added advantage. Do you also have to take this from me?"

"No. But because of its size, you won't be able to use it until you get to Pluto," Boot said. "If you give me your holster, I'll put both in the travel case to be checked through to Port Tombaugh."

That left Dakar's two boot daggers and his hand knife, the claw-shaped karambit. Removing them from the box, Boot said, "You also can't travel with these—they get checked to Port Tombaugh. Now let me show you your new toys!"

Max Thaler stepped back into the conference room. "Colonel Dakar, Director Lee asked me to tell you she won't be able to meet with you after all. But we've finalized your travel. You'll have to hurry. You leave this afternoon on the two o'clock hyper-loop to St. Louis, where you'll transfer to the three o'clock shuttle to the International Space Station. From there, you'll catch the overnight flight to Marius Hills —on the Lunar near side—where the CIA Sea of Storms Office is located. You'll leave the space station at six our time—midnight universal time—and arrive tomorrow at eleven am universal time, five am our time. Agent Sumate Laoloo will meet you at the Marius Hills terminal and escort you to the Moonstone Inn where you'll be staying while on Luna. Agent Laoloo has top-secret clearance for this mission and is assigned to the Fifth FD Lunar office. After a quick nap, you'll go to the Storms Office for your briefing and training."

"Okay, that sounds fine. I won't need the nap, though. I can handle the jet-lag—I'm used to it."

"Not this time. You've never been off planet. It's entirely different," Max replied. "In addition to being sleep-deprived and travel-fatigued, you'll be completely disoriented. You'll be arriving at Marius Hills during the Lunar afternoon. Night won't fall until after you leave the Moon. Director

Lee suggested you keep your eyes open on the Lunar approach so that you can have a close-up view of the sunlit Lunar crescent and night lights of the Islamic Star and the Christian Cross. I'm sure you've seen the Lunar Lights many times from Earth, but she thought a close-up view would give you a better appreciation for the dimensions of that religious conflict.

"She also asked me to tell you she's sending you to Pluto with two backups. CIA Agent Laoloo will be joining you on this assignment. This will be his first mission with Fifth FD since he completed his training. His codename is Duke. He's a native Lunarian, a sixth-rank judo black belt, a munitions specialist, and he has five years of experience with the CIA —all at the Storms Office. He'll be your space combat trainer, backup muscle, and investigative assistant. He'll start your loP-loG and noP-noG training at the Storms and continue it on the outbound leg to Pluto. While you're at the Storms, you'll be joined by the third member of your team. Her name is Selena Volkova, codename is Kes. She's a senior operative on loan from Mossad—one of their best. She's also a Lunarian, a native of New Jerusalem, and like Laoloo, skilled in judo and loP-loG and noP-noG combat. She has a Ph.D. in computer science—emphasis on cryptology and computer forensics. She's experienced and has the Mossad equivalent of the Interrobang Badge. Unlike Duke, who will be both your assistant and your trainee, Kes will be your investigative partner and backup muscle. Director Lee emphasized Kes is tough. She knows what she's doing. Treat her with respect—don't fool with her."

"Of course not."

Thaler continued. "Also, Director Lee has arranged for you and your team to travel under your own names but with FBI credentials, tasked to investigate the deaths of the three OASIS staffers. You will have Thursday evening, Friday, and Saturday for introductions and training. On Sunday morning, February twenty-first, your team will take the morning shuttle to the Buzz. On Monday morning, February twenty-second, you'll board the USSS *Odysseus*. The *Odysseus* is a Pluto-Class, RAIR spaceship—fastest passenger ship to Port Tombaugh. Still, you won't arrive at Port Tombaugh until March nineteenth."

"Shit!"

"Yes. I know. It takes a day to get to the Moon, but four weeks to get to Pluto. Can't be helped. You know that. Pluto is a long way from here. The way I see it, the Director must have a lot of confidence in you to send you so far from KC."

"I hear you."

"When you and Colonel Boot are done, stop by my desk and get your boarding passes, credit cards, passport, and travel documents. I also have a sealed, top secret, letter-chip from Director Lee for you to personally deliver to General Mark Sliffer, the Fort Resnik Commandant, as soon as you arrive at Port Tombaugh. Don't forget to go by Security and get your implanted ID updated with your new FBI credentials."

"Well," Boot said after Thaler left the room, "I guess we better get you set up. First you need new clothes."

"What's wrong with the ones I've got?" Dakar asked.

"Well, they're telluric, loose-fitting and layered for different environments. Wearing them off-planet labels you as an Earthling. Loose-fitting telluric clothes can be dangerous in space; they can get tangled in machinery. Layers are unnecessary in space environments—the temperature is always twenty degrees Celsius. And," he added, while glancing out the conference room window at the freezing drizzle, "there's no rain, snow, or sleet. 'Stros wear closely fitting clothes, one layer of outerwear and one layer of underwear. Shoes are soft-soled boots and hair short or bound. Before you leave, I want you to go to the tailorcom to get your measurements. I figure you're going to need a set of formal whites, two sets of grays for day work, two set of blacks for undercover work, a set of blue fatigues for training, exercise shorts and tees, and shoes and gloves. I'll contact the Storms Office and requisition your new wardrobe; it will be waiting for you at the Moonstone along with your weapons satchel."

"Great. Thank you. But it seems like a lot of trouble for clothes."

"No. Not really," Boot replied. "Your wardrobe is one of your weapons. That's why you need to train in them. The fabric is closely knitted, spun nano-silk—the same super-strong material they used to make the space elevators. It'll stop most cutting and piercing weapons. Your clothing also has thin armor plates, also made of nano-silk, that you wear under your clothes. The plates are thin enough not to change the fit but will stop small-caliber bullets and slow down everything else. You'll still feel the bullet impact. It may even knock you out, but it won't kill you. The nano-silk material is also insulated to protect you from electric shock. All of your tunics come with gloves and have a high collar to protect your throat. Hidden in the collar is a hood.

We call them bat-hoods. Pull the hood over your head and it becomes a hard-shell, shock-resistant helmet with active noise and flash cancellation along with a built-in intercom. Pull the hood the rest of the way over your head and face, put on the gloves and you will be in a Faraday cage—you can talk to your perscom without fear of being hacked. All of your new clothes will be tailored for wearing your personal weapons, perscom, and wristpod and embroidered with the FBI patch. The blacks and blues have a utility belt for additional tools and weapons.

"Whoa! Thank you!"

"Don't thank me," replied Boot. "If you're going to accomplish this mission, you need right equipment. Now let's go over your new weapons. Your long-sleeved tunics have a garrote in the left sleeve and a cable saw in the right sleeve." Holding up his right arm, Boot demonstrated while explaining, "You can access them by grabbing this piece of metal trim on the edge of the sleeve and yanking on it like this." He extracted a cable saw from his right arm. "The saw and garrote are also made of nano-silk. You can't break them with your hands.

"All of your pants have a strand of nano-silk around the waist. It's twenty-five meters long and attached to a spool like a fishing reel. You can access the line by pulling on this fob hanging on the right side of your belt buckle. The fob is a handle with a clip and a hook; it's heavy so that you can throw it. You retract the line by pushing this button on the left side of the buckle. It'll reel in the line and fob, but the reel isn't strong enough to pull in more than a kilogram—anything larger you'll have to pull with your hands. The line can pull twenty-five thousand kilograms before it breaks.

When pulling the line, be careful to wear your gloves and to use the buckle handles. The line is so strong and thin, that without the gloves and handles, it'll cut through you like a wire through cheese. It's also hard to see, so you can stretch it across a passage and stop someone. Clip the burr to the buckle and you've got a high-tension drag-line for throwing and recovering the burr."

"The burr?"

"Yes, this little gadget," Boot replied as he extracted a golf-ball-sized object which looked like a cross between a spiky-shelled chestnut and an antique communications satellite. "It's a video and audio recorder that displays the image on either your perscom or your wristpod and sends the audio to your earpiece. It has prong graspers for retrieving small items. It also has electro-magnets to attach to iron and steel and metal hook spikes made out of shape-memory alloy. The hooks act like burrs to attach to fabrics but will release on electronic command. The burr uses local signals to transmit its location so that you can use it for tracking. I'm placing two dozen of these handy little items in your satchel. You can practice with them along with the garrotes, cable saws, and waist reels on your outbound trip. I'm also adding a dozen multitools and six dozen cord manacles to your satchel."

"Great. But why so many?" Dakar asked.

"Moxon's partial message could mean you and your team will be facing a conspiracy, probably Chinese or Russian or Brazilian. You may have to get additional agents from the Port Tombaugh FBI and CIA joint office or even from Fort Resnik. Director Lee is contacting those offices to secure their cooperation in case you have to organize and help arm a strike force."

"OK. Thank you," replied Dakar.

"There's more," continued Boot. "To fully outfit your strike force, Director Lee and I have decided to include in the arms shipment to Port Tombaugh additional items that the FBI office and Fort Resnik armory don't have. Specifically, two dozen micro-dart guns with Teflon-coated needles loaded with a paralytic toxin. Each gun comes with a half-dozen magazines with ten needles per magazine. One dart will stop any man; multiple darts will kill. Also, I have added six dozen flash grenades. The grenades don't explode —so PT won't confiscate them—but they will stun with bright light and a loud noise. I'm also including a dozen of the bat-hoods for a strike force to use with the grenades. Your opponents might deploy battlebots, so I'm sending you a dozen tasers and a dozen microwave blasters. The tasers will stop both bots and goons with an electric shock, and the microwave blasters will fry electronics and burn skin, as well as muscles and organs. I'm giving you two dozen deployable microdrones equipped with video, audio, recorder, and transmitter capacities. The drones will sequence to perscoms. They can operate in both a vacuum and a pressurized environment. I'm also including five hundred liters of ultrablack paint, more than enough to cover two or more transports as well as heavy equipment like spacesuits. When you get to Fort Resnik, the staff there can use the paint to camouflage whatever you need to make your strike force invisible to light, radar, and microwaves."

"Great! Is that it?"

"No. There's one more thing." Boot said, pulling out the last weapon from his box of toys. "This is a star-spike. Various 'stro weapon manufacturers have started making these. This one is the best. It's made by a Lunar company, Storms Armaments, exclusively for the Federal government. As you see, it looks like an old-fashioned icepick, but this pick has a tip with a heating element. As soon as you pull the trigger in the handle, the tip heats to two thousand degrees Celsius—hot enough to burn through nano-silk, not to mention start a fire. To use, release the safety like this, pull the trigger, and then stab. The tip will burn through the carbon nano-silk like a hot knife through butter, allowing the spike to pierce your opponent. Aim for the chest. Once you puncture the chest wall, press the button at the end of the handle. The button fires a tube at the base of the spike into the wound. When you pull the spike out, the tube remains. Stabbing the chest wall causes the lung to collapse. That will stop nearly everyone. To kill, stab the other side of the chest and repeat. That drops the other lung. No lungs, no breath. Your adversary dies. The best place to stab is in the subclavian fossa, the cavity next to the neck, behind the collarbone. You can try stabbing between the ribs, but if your opponent is wearing nano-silk chest plates, the plates will slow down and deflect the spike penetration. You can wear the spike in a holster in your belt or under your arms. I'm sending two of these in your check bag for your use and two dozen with the rest of the strike force equipment."

The Colonel finished by saying, "John. The armor and weapons are new to you. Just like learning to use a gun, you've got to practice until you can use them without thinking."

"Yeah. I know that. Thankfully, I've got four weeks on the outbound leg to train."

"But," the Colonel added, "the thing is, if you run into any little green men, I've nothing to offer you except what works against Earthlings and Earth weapons."

"Well. That's not a problem. There are no little green men."

"I know. But you and your team are going to be a long way from the Bush. You'll be on your own. There will be no other backup and no retreat. If you fail, you die. This is just my way of warning you that I can prepare you for the enemies we know, but not the ones we don't. I guess you know that."

"That's how you trained me. It's what I do."

6 WEDNESDAY NIGHT FIGHT

"Max. Because of the weather, I'm spending the night in my office. Please have the canteen send up my usual dinner. After that, you can go."

"Sure," Max said. "But I'm going to stick around until after the CIA Director leaves."

"General Barrun?"

"Yes. He called a moment ago. He's on his way from the Bush to see you."

"And to what do I owe the pleasure of his company?"

"I don't know, but it doesn't sound like it is going to be a pleasure. He sounded—if you will excuse the expression—pissed."

Looking like a sumo wrestler with a sunburn, General Barrun shoved his way into Director Lee's office without waiting for Max to let him in.

Slamming the office door behind him with a bang, he shouted, "Lee! I told you to report to me your plans for Kubrick Mons before the end of the day! Why didn't you do that?"

"I did. I called you at a quarter past twelve, but you weren't free. Then I sent a memo to you at one—it looks like you have it in your hand. It's five now, what's the problem?"

"Don't get cute with me, old lady! You know I meant a verbal report! Where's Steel?"

Director Lee rose to her full height behind her desk. "On his way to Pluto. He should be boarding for Marius Hills right about now." Looking Barrun straight in the face, with an edge in her voice, she said, "General Barrun, I insist you keep a civil tongue when speaking to me."

Approaching her desk, his face now a darker red, eyes narrowed to slits, jaw set forward—looking like a fat, angry, pugilist, he said, "Woman, I'm not speaking to you, I'm telling you. I want you to call him back. NOW!"

"No."

"Are you defying me?" he yelled, raising the memo as if he intended to club her with it.

They stared at each other for a few long seconds, like two grizzlies facing off before closing for the fight, trying to intimidate each other with their size and fierceness, one old, but tough, the other young, but fat.

Lee broke the impasse. "Sir," she said, "you can give me a mission, but you can't tell me how to run the Fifth FD. That's my agency. You told me to do what I had to do to keep WXN2 and the EP-communicator secret. I did that. I sent my best agent."

"I didn't tell you to send Steel," Barrun replied. "Going to Pluto takes him out of action for more than two months."

Director Lee sat down and waved to the chair in front of her desk. "Take a seat, General. Steel's already out of action. He's still recovering from the assassination attempt by the Caine Toads. Kalfu nearly killed him in Jamaica. The four-week travel on the outbound and return trips will do him good."

The General ignored her invitation to sit. Instead he took advantage of her change in position by putting both hands on her desk, leaning forward into her space, and speaking slowly with a low flat tone while pausing between each word, he said, "Woman! I'm–telling–you–again. Recall–Steel."

Returning his stare, she aped his rudeness, saying, "No. It's–too–late."

Sensing he'd lost the stare down, but not willing to admit it, he switched tactics. Like an old lion, roaring to drive off a young rival, he sat down while yelling, "God damn it woman! I was expecting you to send someone else besides Steel. Why couldn't you have sent someone from Port Tombaugh?"

"I don't have any Pluto assets. You do. You have the OASIS office. But you can't do what needs to be done. Only I can."

Ignoring the challenge, he went on, "What about Ceres? Or Fort Musk? Marius Hills?"

"You know the answer to that; it's in the memo. No free 'stro agents with Interrobang authority."

"Well, I don't think this required Steel," Barrun said. "It's probably a big nothing. Didn't you see the NTSB blamed the wreck on 'mechanical failure'?"

"Yes. That's old news. The NTSB report has more holes than Hyperion."

"What do you mean?" he said, raising his voice once again. "Don't trifle with me, woman!"

"You know what I mean," Director Lee said. "It would take more than a mechanical failure to blow that canopy. And," raising her own voice for emphasis, "the canopy wouldn't accidentally fail at just the right time to stop an emergency EP conference. This was an assassination, plain and simple. Our most precious national secrets could be blown. This is a job for the Fifth Directorate, and we're going to do it!"

Barrun took a long, menacing look at her and then said, "You haven't heard the last of this. I'll get you for insubordination!" With that, he stood up and stomped out of the room, slamming the door behind him.

"I'm sorry, Director Lee. He just pushed his way in."

"It's all right Max. Did you get a recording?"

"Yes Sir, both audio and video."

"Thank you. Make two copies. One for me, one for you, and put the original in the office safe. We're going to need them."

7 MORNING REPORT

At 08:00 UTC, on Thursday, February 18—Pluto Discovery Day—Inspector Skalay convened Morning Report for the Port Tombaugh Homicide Squad. The Squad met in a shabby, crowded conference room furnished with cheap plastic chairs and a plastic table, surrounded by smeared and worn whiteboards, located in the Offices of the Police Department in the First, and oldest, Circle of Port Tombaugh.

"Good morning, everyone. Thank you for coming in. I know it's a holiday, but we've got work to do. Let's get started. First up, Kubrick Mons. On deck, the Andrew Henning electrocution. But before we get going, I want to introduce our visitor, Police Commissioner Lord. He's with us this morning to review our Kubrick Mons investigation. Everyone knows the Commissioner, but the Commissioner doesn't know everybody. Commissioner, Senior Detective Hildy Kirk is my second in command, her beat is Port Tombaugh. On Detective Kirk's right is Officer Charlie Baker. His beat is Charon, he also does physical forensics for us. Sitting on Detective Kirk's left is Officer Roc Qadeer. His beat is the Acheron Bridge, he also does computer forensics."

After the introductions, Skalay recapped the deaths on Kubrick Mons. The NTSB had declared, and the press reported, that a mechanical malfunction compounded by human error had caused the deaths. But in his press release, Skalay declared the deaths homicide.

"Inspector," Commissioner Lord responded with a sharp voice, "I appreciate your efforts. But calling this a homicide instead of an accident has stirred up a Martian dust storm of trouble. Lots of angry people above my pay grade. Before you can declare a homicide, you've got to have a victim, motive, weapon, and opportunity. So far, you've got zip. You better hope you haven't stirred up a tempest for nothing!"

"Hold on, Commissioner. Let us finish our report. When we're done, I think you'll agree the facts don't square with the NTSB account. Kirk, you're up first. Tell us about the victims and the witnesses."

"Dr. Abbott finished the autopsies. She confirmed the identity of the two vics. The cause of death was asphyxia due to explosive decompression. The new information is that Keator hadn't had sex and wasn't pregnant. Dr. Abbott also found a box in Moxon's pocket containing a diamond engagement ring. We traced the ring to a Port Tombaugh jeweler. Moxon purchased the ring two weeks ago—"

"So, the reporters were right!" the Commissioner interrupted. "This was a romantic date. He was proposing!"

"Yes, it appears so," Kirk answered. "But the box was in Moxon's pocket. If he popped the question and she said yes, the ring should have been on her finger. There's more—"

"Kirk," Skalay interrupted, "did Dr. Abbott find Moxon's perscom or the wristpods?"

"No, Sir."

"Damn, that's odd," Skalay said under his breath.

"Sir, before I go on, there'll be a funeral service for Moxon and Keator in the Clarke Station Assembly Hall Saturday morning at eleven—"

"Thanks," Skalay said. "All four of us should attend and see if we can learn anything else. Keep going."

The Commissioner added, "I'll be there too."

Detective Kirk continued. "As Inspector Skalay requested, I spent the last two days at the Lowell Observatory interviewing the vics' coworkers. They said that the spacesuit rule was commonly ignored. Some of the scientists hinted there's more to OASIS than troubleshooting boffin bugs, but I'm not prepared to come to any conclusions. People were reluctant to talk to me."

She paused for a moment to emphasize the reluctance of the Lowell astronomers to talk to her, as if they had something to hide.

She then continued, "Strange. As far as I can tell, neither Moxon nor Keator had any enemies, and their work wasn't classified. Some of the coworkers suspected Moxon and Keator had a sexual relationship, but if they did, they kept it secret. I asked to examine personnel records and work papers, but Director Best denied my request, claiming national security. Of course, there're no human witnesses, only computer recordings. But Best impounded those as well. I don't understand why personnel information should be withheld from a homicide investigation. Makes me suspicious."

"Troubleshooting boffin bugs?" echoed the Commissioner, mocking Kirk with his tone.

"Yes, Sir," she politely replied. "OASIS's mission is to assist Lowell scientists with their work, particularly visiting scientists. They help scientists use the various instruments on Charon and shows them how to get the best out of Kory. OASIS staff are also scientists who do their own work. But as I said, in talking to the Lowell staff, I got the idea the scientists have additional undisclosed activities. What those are, I don't know."

"Not much to go on," grunted the Commissioner.

"Agreed," Skalay said. "But the crime scene leads away from the NTSB explanation of what happened. Charlie, you're next."

Picking up his notes, Charlie began by saying, "Well, here's where the NTSB explanation doesn't square with the facts. First, the anchors had been fired into the regolith. You don't do that for touch-and-go—"

"Humph!" growled the Commissioner.

Charlie continued, "Here's the stumper. The canopy explosive bolts are for emergency exit in case of a wreck. I looked up the specs. If for some reason one bolt blows, such as a cosmic ray strikin' the bolt electronics, the canopy remains intact. If two bolts blow, the canopy might fracture, but it should still hold. To get the canopy to blow in one piece, like it did, you have to trigger the central control in the transport Emergency Response Computer and blow all sixty-four bolts at the same time. There's also a failsafe on-and-off switch in the cockpit to over-ride control of the bolts by the ERC. The switch is there so that the pilot can override the ERC and blow the canopy manually. I checked the guard before the NTSB impounded the wreck. I pilot these transports myself, so I know where to look. The failsafe switch was in the locked position, turnin' off the over-ride. Somehow, the ERC got the message to explode the bolts, but I don't know how that was done. A hack with remote control is my best explanation. If that's the answer, then we have weapon and opportunity. You know the vics. All that is missin' to make it murder is motive."

This time, the Commissioner muttered "Hmmm," and stroked his chin.

Continuing, Charlie said, "As far as motive, the crime scene left some interestin' findings." Charlie held up a clear plastic bag containing the paper with the columns of mysterious numbers and letters. "This is the most damnin.' We found it in the debris field. It appears to be a page from a one-time pad. If so, we didn't find the rest of the pad."

"Let me see that!" demanded the Commissioner.

"There's more," Skalay said. "We located only one perscom in the wreck, a tablet that looked like it belonged to a woman. We believe it's Keator's. Unfortunately, the cold ruined the electronics. We didn't find Moxon's perscom in the wreck or debris field. You just heard Kirk tells us that Dr. Abbott also didn't find either Moxon's perscom or Moxon's or Keator's wristpods on their bodies. We know from Moxon's electronic communications that he owned a perscom. It's not likely he would leave it at Clarke Station. If he brought it with him, he should have been wearing the matching wristpod. For that matter, Keator should also have been wearing a wristpod, but both are missing."

"Based on the positions of their coffee bladders," Charlie said, "just prior to the canopy blow-out, it appears Moxon and Keator were in opposite ends of the transport. We know this because each bladder has a magnetized base that kept it from being blown out. The bladder in the cockpit had lipstick smeared on the nipple. DNA analysis confirms it was Keator's, the bladder on the stern workbench had Moxon's DNA. Although they died in an embrace, it appears that before the embrace, Moxon had been workin' on somethin' in the transport stern, but we don't know what it was."

"The flight recorder should tell you what happened," the Commissioner said.

"Director Best has impounded the flight recorder," Skalay said. "We can't get to it. I'm going to need your help to open that can."

"There's more," Charlie said. "When he inspected the crime scene, Inspector Skalay noted a strange pattern in the snowfall from the released transport gasses—a snow shadow, if you will. Analysis of the snowfall on the wreck site shows that a one-by-two-meter rectangular object was removed from the rear deck of the transport about three hours after the canopy blew. Pictures of snow-covered footprints at the crime scene taken by us and by the reconnaissance drones sent by Kory show that at least three unknown persons visited the wreck at the same time that the object on the rear of the deck disappeared. We suspect these people searched the wreck, removed the one-time pad and Moxon's perscom, and took the deck object."

"So now we have vics, weapons, opportunity, and motives," Skalay said. "That makes murder."

After a long sigh, the Commissioner said, "Okay. Fine. Anything else?"

"Yes," Skalay said. "At this time, I can't explain why Moxon encrypted a message, to whom he sent the message, or what was removed from the rear deck of the transport. The cleanup also seems like an amateur job. Still, we have our motive, robbery. But, all of this would be a lot easier if we could review the audio recordings from the transport flight recorder or Kory's records. Roc, any news on that front?"

"No Sir. As Detective Kirk said, Director Best impounded the flight recorder. I asked Kory if she had a record of what happened in the transport and Kory refused the query, stating Director Best had embargoed all queries regarding the wreck."

"Cripes," mused the Commissioner.

Roc continued, "After verifying Robby had Moxon's and Keator's electronic correspondence and documents, I tried to open the files. But Best has also impounded them because of national security."

Laying down his perscom for a few moments, Roc broke from his report and spoke directly to the Commissioner, "Doesn't make a lot of sense. Director Best asked Inspector Skalay to come immediately to the wreck site as soon as it was discovered. Best is the Director of the Lowell Observatory and Moxon was one of his Chiefs. Seems to me he would want to know what happened. Still," Roc continued, "with computers there're always a backdoor. I've just begun to work. Although damaged, I should be able to hack the data from the lady's perscom."

Charlie interrupted, "Director Best also won't let us search Moxon's and Keator's cabins and workstations, again claimin' national security."

Skalay followed, "Commissioner Lord, we need your help to get inside the flight recorder and the sumacoms and to search the cabins and workstations."

"I hear you. Trouble is, the people who have the authority to give you access are the same people who are most upset by your investigation. You make a convincing argument for homicide, but you haven't proved your case. It could just be an unfortunate accident. Thank you for all of your work. I'll do what I can to protect your investigation from interference. And I'll see what I can do to get you the access you requested. Thanks for the briefing."

After the Commissioner left, Skalay continued the report. "Kirk, are you on good terms with Dr. Abbott?"

"I think so."

"Well, get back to her. Make sure no one else had the opportunity to swipe those wristpods or Moxon's perscom before the autopsies, or that she wasn't pressured to hide them. If you can't get her to cooperate by being polite, you're going to have to get tough. She needs to understand that if she hasn't been square with us, she's interfering with a homicide investigation. Can you do that?"

"Yes, of course I can."

"And Kirk, I want you to continue with your interviews and expand them to include the Clarke Station staff. Maybe one of the support personnel can tell us something the Lowell astronomers won't. Also, since we've been denied the personnel records, I want you to use secondary sources to find out all you can about Moxon and Keator. I want to know who these people were and why they were on Kubrick Mons. Roc, you can help Kirk get this information. Even dead ends and stone walls can tell us something."

"Yes, Sir!" Kirk said.

Returning to Officer Baker, Skalay said, "Charlie, it seems like there's not much more of the crime scene to chase down, but we should do everything we can to determine what was on the back of that transport. I want you to snoop around Clarke Station some more to find out what you can. There must be a shipment manifest we haven't found. Or maybe you can spot a piece of transport equipment or a cargo container that fits the description of the deck object. You might also check out storage sites on Nickelback Node and Charlene Anchor. We can't crack this case until we know what was on that transport deck. And we should make one more concerted effort to locate Moxon's perscom. Get the NTSB to let you make a second inspection of the transport. If you can't find it there, then we will have to go back to the crime scene and make a second search."

"You bet, Sir!" Charlie replied.

"Roc—"

"Yes, Sir."

"Help Charlie find Moxon's perscom. That perscom has to be a key to unlocking this mystery."

Pausing for a few moments, Skalay then added, "Also, while I am thinking about it, let's make cracking open Keator's perscom a top priority—"

Kirk interrupted. "Sir, if we could find a backdoor into Keator's and Moxon's email accounts and check out their social media we might learn what they were doing on Charon."

"Good. You've got the assignment." Then, turning to address the group, Skalay said, "People, we have to do everything we can to get into the Lowell Observatory computers. There has to be a backdoor to those recordings and we have to find it. While you're looking for it, I will work my end to bring more pressure on Director Best and the Commissioner to let us into the Lowell computers. By the way, Roc, have you asked Robby—"

"Yup. Impounded," Roc said.

"Have you tried asking Talos?"

"Not yet, but he's on my list."

"What about the Clarke Station computers and workstations?" Skalay asked.

"All impounded. Best doesn't want me anywhere near them."

"What about the botweb?"

"Possibly. Because there are so many of them, I've not tried that yet," Roc said. "The sumacoms monitor those devices, it's possible I might find a backdoor into Robby or Kory through them, but I thought I'd try other options first."

"Good. When you come to the memorial service on Saturday, hang back in the Station. See if you can find an untended workstation that will let you in on the sly. And—"

"Got it."

"When you've got a chance, while you're making the PT dock rounds, keep your eyes open. Whatever was on the back of that transport probably shipped through the docks."

"Will do."

"Good. Any questions?" Skalay asked.

Hearing nothing, he went on to the matter of Andrew Henning. "I'm sure everyone remembers the gruesome electrocution of Andrew Henning, the OASIS astronomer who died October twelfth. Although his death was without precedent, it appeared to be accidental, so that was our ruling. Still, we never determined how it actually happened. In light of the subsequent deaths of OASIS astronomers, I'm reopening Henning's death for further review. Charlie, this one is on your beat, so I want you to take the lead on this. Start with reviewing our prior investigation from the perspective of homicide and look for holes. When you're ready, take Roc with you to Charlene Anchor and inspect the death scene."

Skalay looked around the room. "Everyone. I want you to know that as we pursued our investigation, I kept Director Best up to date on our progress. That was a mistake. He's working against us, not for us. I don't know why, but from now on, keep the details of both the Kubrick Mons and the Henning investigations confidential. If someone wants information, send them to me. Now let's get to work."

8 SEA OF STORMS

"Colonel Dakar, your sixteen-hour appointment is at the veranda door."

John groaned. His nightmare shifted from trying to free his manacled hands to a door opening. Sarah stood there. A bright light shone behind her. He reached for her.

Louder, harsher, more insistent, the annoying voice repeated: "Colonel Dakar. Your sixteen-hour appointment is at the veranda door!"

This time he stirred. Like a swimmer completing a dive, looking up to the surface, he swam against the rapture of deep sleep, stroking upward to breach the waters of unconsciousness and awaken. As he struggled, Sarah's image slipped away, leaving behind pain and sorrow.

Louder and harsher, the voice repeated: "Colonel Dakar. Your sixteen-hour appointment is at the veranda door!"

"Okay, okay," he muttered, throwing off the covers. Only the covers didn't fall, they drifted down. He tried to stand up, only to bounce up, then float down. He felt light-headed. He felt like he was swimming—the waters lifting him up but slowing him down. Or maybe he was flying. With dawning consciousness, he thought, I must be dreaming.

Then that irritating voice again. "Colonel Dakar. Your sixteen-hour appointment is at the veranda door!"

"Okay," he muttered again, pulling on the robe draped over the chair next to his bed. Confusion overwhelmed him. He didn't know where he was. With a loping, bounding gait, he bumped his way to the bedroom door and looked out the peephole. No one was there. *I'm definitely dreaming.*

"Colonel Dakar. The veranda door! Not the front door."

"Huh?"

This time, he heard a knock and a woman say, "John. John. John Dakar. Are you there?"

A woman! Maybe that's Sarah. He turned around, asking the empty room. "Sarah? Is that you?"

On the other side of the room, opposite the bedroom door, was a pair of curtained French doors. He remembered now—he was in a high-rise hotel. The French doors must open onto a balcony of some kind.

I have to be dreaming. No one could meet me up here. Still, he obeyed the voice, as the woman again called out to him, "John. John. John Dakar, are you there?"

He bumped his way to the French doors and pulled them open. As he suspected, the doors opened onto a narrow veranda guarded by a railing. But to his surprise, the railing had a gate, a gate that opened to . . . nowhere—just the street many stories below him. In the open gate, stood an angel.

I am dreaming! Sarah!

Perched between the two gateposts, the angel had an elf-like figure with long slender arms, legs, and torso. She wore tight-fitting, white clothes that covered her pale, almost translucent, skin. She had wings of white feathers, longer than her arms and a white feathered tail that reached to the floor and hung over the edge of the balcony. Her feathers broke the bright light that illuminated her from behind into rainbows and a halo. A silver headband encircled her bobbed auburn tresses, framing large hazel eyes that looked directly at him.

"Sarah," he said. "You've come for me!"

"No. I'm Selena Volkova."

"Sarah," he said in a rush. "I'm so sorry about Kalfu."

"I'm Selena Volkova, not Sarah. I'm here to escort Colonel Dakar to the Sea of Storms CIA Office. Aren't you Colonel Dakar?"

Like awakening suddenly from a dream, with these words, the angelic vision disappeared, and sobriety abruptly returned. In a flash, it all came back. Director Lee. Colonel Boot. The hyper-loop. The shuttle. The Lunar flight. The Moonstone. Pluto.

"Aughh!" he said, turning away from her, covering his head with his arms, embarrassed by his confusion, his undress, and most of all, by the unfortunate revelation of the spirits that haunted him. "Sorry. Yes, I'm Colonel Dakar. I'm so sorry. I was sound asleep. For a moment, you looked like someone I knew. Give me a few minutes and I'll be ready." As he said this, he spotted the alarm clock by his bed. The time read 16:12; the alarm had been set for 15:30, but it had been turned off.

Shit. I've overslept. Must have turned off the alarm in my sleep. I never do that!

"Here," she said, handing him a Styrofoam box. "I brought coffee and croissants—a Lunar specialty. I'll wait for you in the lobby. Come down when you're ready, and

I'll escort you to the Storms Office. Try to be quick—we're already late."

With those words, she jumped off the balcony and flew down to the ground floor. After taking off her wings and tail and packing them in a carrier, she placed a confidential call to Agent Laoloo. "Duke, we're gonna be late."

"All right. What happened?"

"Feh! To save time, I flew to his room with breakfast, but he wasn't ready. He'd slept through his alarm. When he finally opened the door, he looked terrible. Confused. Tousled. Unshaven. He's getting cleaned up right now. I thought this guy was special. He sure doesn't look like one of the 'stro bros. Is Steel a schmoe? Does he drink?"

"He's obviously not a 'stro bros, he's a Dirt spook. Yes, he's special. Company legend. Carries the Interrobang Badge. Yes, he drinks, but not on duty. He was fine this morning when I picked him up, just tired. Had a long day. This time yesterday he was in KC. I'm sure he's sleep-deprived. He's only gotten, um, no more than four hours of sleep since landing—probably less. I'm sure the IoG also confused him; he's never been off planet. Just get here when you can. We've got a lot to do. I'll let the brass know you're going to be late."

Twenty minutes later, fortified by two cups of black coffee, cleaned up, dressed up in his new FBI 'stro grays, and weapons packed away, he reopened the French doors. Standing on the veranda, looking over the city, he spotted many people flitting across the sky with wings and tails similar to Volkova's. He could also see that the city occupied one end of an incredibly large cave. He marveled at the sight. Such a cave could not exist on Earth. His room was on the twenty-fifth floor, at least seventy-five meters above street level, but the cave's ceiling appeared to be at least a kilometer higher. Light fixtures, set in the cave ceiling, illuminated the city with bright, artificial sunlight. The cave appeared to be at least five kilometers wide. His hotel had been built into the wall on one end of the cave. He couldn't make out the opposite end, but in the distance, he could see the city give way to cropland. Above the crops, a large, translucent dome, covering a hole in the cave ceiling, allowed sunlight to bathe the crops.

Standing in the veranda, it felt like he was in dreamland. He knew it must be a real world, a Moon world, a world that could only exist in a place like the Moon. Yet he continued to have the profound sense he did not belong here, and all of this was some childhood dream.

Agent Volkova met him in the lobby with a frown and an edge to her voice, signaling her irritation. "A taxbot is waiting for us," she said. "We're a half-hour late, and it's going to take at least twenty minutes to get to the Storms Office."

All he could say was, "Sorry."

They made their way to the Sea of Storms CIA Office in silence, which he regretted because he saw so many things about which he wanted to ask her. Instead he stared out the window ogling the flying people, the tall buildings with doorways that opened into the air, the spindly overpass bridges and construction cranes, and the fast-moving small vehicle traffic crowding the roads. He had read that Marius

Hills had a web of subways and roads connecting it to outlying underground facilities, but he didn't see the entrances or exits. Vegetation crammed the road verges, median strips, yards, planters, and parks. He couldn't figure out how the city watered all of this greenery; he knew it didn't rain, and he didn't see any irrigation.

Tiring of the silence, he thought, *Shit. This is stupid. If we're going to work together for the next two months, we should at least be able to talk.* So, he broke the silence and asked her, "How do they water the plants?"

"Do," he heard her say.

"Do what?"

"Not do, *dew*. You know. Water vapor condenses on surfaces at night. Lunar environmental engineers regulate the atmosphere to have a high humidity and then drop the temperature when they turn off the lights for our night cycle. The temperature drop creates the dew, which waters the plants, without having to use irrigation or artificial rain.

I'm glad he broke the silence, she thought. *It's silly to be irritated because he overslept. Just because I don't want to go to Pluto, doesn't mean I should take it out on him. He's not responsible.*

After a minute or two silence as the taxbot rumbled on to the Storms office and Steel gazed out the window, she turned to face him while thinking, *He sure is a misfit. I wonder why they sent him. He really doesn't belong here. I hope that doesn't create a problem for us!*

"All right. My turn. Who's Sarah and what's a 'calfoo'?"

"I'm sorry. You caught me at a weak moment. I'll remember your question. I can't answer it at this time, in a public conveyance, but maybe later. I can tell you that it has nothing to do with our work together."

"Fair enough. I can accept that. We're almost at the Storms Office anyway."

As they completed their ride, she told him about how Lunarians, like her, who live in all of the big cave cities like Marius Hills and New Jerusalem exercised by taking advantage of the open spaces and low gravity to fly. For example, with her height and mass, and with her wings and tail, she had the same wingspan and weight as an Earth albatross. And, like an albatross, she could fly and soar for hours at a time, even to the top of the cave.

The Lunar CIA Sea of Storms Office occupied a suite of rooms built into the Marius Hills cave wall. At the security booth that guarded the entrance, a sinewy young man, somewhat shorter than Dakar, stepped forward and greeted them. He introduced himself as Sumate Laoloo, the junior 5th FD agent who would be joining Dakar as his backup and 'stro trainer. In no way did Laoloo look to Dakar like a CIA spook. Dakar had never seen a secret agent with such an elaborate hairdo.

Laoloo had shaved the hair on each side of his head. He dyed the remaining central strip a blazing red with streaks of orange and pasted the Mohawk into spikes with tips of yellow like the crest of a cockatoo. Certainly not the nondescript hairdo Dakar expected of a secret agent who needed to blend into the background. On the Moon, however, Dakar quickly learned that nearly all young Lunar men wore their hair in similar ornate hairstyle, which they called 'strohawks. As startling as he appeared to Dakar, Laoloo's 'strohawk allowed him to blend in with all the other Lunar men. It was Dakar, with his dark visage and short-cropped, curly hair, who stood out as the oddball.

Also to Dakar's surprise, Laoloo and Volkova greeted each other as friends, evidence that the Lunar CIA and Mossad agents belonged to a small, close-knit espionage community.

After the introductions, Laoloo ushered Volkova and Dakar inside, walked them through identification and administrative procedures, and escorted them into a conference room where the Chief of the Storms Office, Percy Stone, greeted them. By encrypted teleconferencing, Director Lee, Mossad Director Gleena Stein, and Deputy Director Colonel Boot joined the meeting. Director Lee briefed the group on WXN2 and EP communications, then gave the agents their mission and authorizations. Director Stein endorsed the mission and Volkova's participation. Colonel Boot described the armory the CIA was sending with the agents to Port Tombaugh as well as the weapons they would carry with them on the Pluto flight. He emphasized the importance of all three of them training together on the outbound flight.

After the preliminaries, the three agents gathered to figure out a training schedule and go over the arrangements for the flight to Pluto. They finished with a late dinner of take-out pizza in the privacy of the conference room. Only then did they find the time to get to know each other.

9 AMORE

"Amore's Big Pizza Pie is the best in Marius Hills!" Sumate sang in his best Dean Martin imitation: *When the moon hits your eye like a big pizza pie, that's Amore's!*

"It's really good!" Selena said. "John, you're going to love it!"

John took a slice. "It's good."

"Hmm," Selena said, "Do I detect a lukewarm response?"

"Don't get me wrong, it's good pizza. The crust, sauce, and cheese are perfect. Only, I'm used to a richer meat flavor for the pepperoni and sausage. This is a little flat."

"Now that you say it, I'm not surprised," Sumate said. "John, I should've warned you. All of our Lunar meat is synthetic, created in tissue culture or organ culture. We don't slaughter and butcher animals on the Moon. I bet you're used to animal meat instead of artificial meat."

Selena's eyes went wide and she did the impossible, turning a shade paler. "John! You eat live animals?"

"Well, they're not alive when I eat them. But sure, most everybody does on Earth."

"Do you also hunt animals and eat them?" she asked.

"Well, yeah. I like to hunt deer. When I can, I hunt deer with my Pa in Iowa. My Mum makes a venison roast with cream of mushroom soup for our Christmas dinner. She also uses the leftover meat—"

Selena abruptly stood up and left the room.

"What did I say?" John asked.

"She probably got sick to her stomach," Sumate said. "She's never been to the Earth and probably never dined with a carnivore. I expect the thought of eating animal flesh turned her stomach."

"But isn't she a Mossad agent?"

"Yes. One of their best."

"Surely she's killed before. She can't be squeamish."

"Yes. She's killed in the line of duty. But she doesn't eat her victims and she doesn't kill for sport."

"And you?"

"This'll be my first Fifth Directorate mission. I've never killed a human or anything else. Like Selena and almost all other 'stros, I'm a vegan. But I visited Earth once. Like you, I'm an American—funny to say it because I'm also second-generation Lunarian. When I was a kid, I visited my father's family in San Francisco, so I'm familiar with the telluric diet as well as other things about living on Earth that Selena would find strange and disagreeable. I bet this is the first time you've spent any time with a New Israeli."

"You're right."

"Well, you'll have to forgive her. As a general rule, New Israelis don't care for Earthlings, or as 'stros sometimes say, 'Dirts.'"

"Hey! You know I don't like that term—" John started to reply just as Selena returned to the conference room.

"I'm sorry," she said. "I suddenly didn't feel well. I'm all right now. John, I overheard Sumate. I think I should clear the air. I don't have anything personally against you, certainly not your skin color or your background. I apologize if I've given you that impression."

"It's okay," John said. "Don't worry about it."

"Well, it's not okay, and I do worry about it. I've known Jews from many backgrounds whose families founded New Israel, including African-Americans. It's, well, it's just that now New Israelis are Lunar Jews. I've, ah, never worked with an Earthling before. Some of your ways, like . . . ahm . . . your diet, are . . . ahm . . . strange, foreign . . . ahm, even disagreeable to me. I'll try to be more careful. I don't want this issue to interfere with our working together."

"I understand." John responded. "Apology accepted. Thank you for clearing the air. But, if you don't mind my asking, what's the problem between Jews and Earthlings?"

"Well," she began with a sigh. "I'm sure you already know this story, but since you asked, let me tell it to you anyway. After the Three-Hour War made a nuclear wasteland of Jerusalem and all the rest of old Israel, the remaining Jews—we call them the last diaspora—colonized the far side of the Moon. We created New Israel, the first off-Earth nation, and founded New Jerusalem, our capital."

"Yeah. I know all that."

"Well, the Jews were so bitter about the annihilation of Israel, they chose to rebuild the Jewish nation on the far side of the Moon so they would never again have to look at the Earth. Despite all of the years since we left the Earth, the bitterness continues. We make no apology. We Jews have endured wave after wave of genocide. The last, the Three-

Hour War, killed more than ten million Jews, almost twice as many as were killed in the Holocaust. I lost many relatives, both in the Holocaust and in the Three-Hour War."

"Yeah. I'm sorry. I understand your bitterness, but—"

"Can you, John?" she said, beginning to raise her voice. "Can you understand the loss we feel, when that horrible, terrible, Three-Hour War destroyed our heritage by making our homeland into a nuclear wasteland, by destroying what we Jews held most sacred, the Western Wall? I've seen the photographs, John. There's nothing left of Old Jerusalem but just a BIG FUCKING CRATER. Can you understand all that?"

"Jeez! I can," John said. "And as long as we're gonna be blunt, can you understand who I am? My name is John Dakar. I'm a black man. My name and my skin are my legacy, witness to four centuries of slavery, segregation, oppression, and genocide. My ancestors came from West Africa. Slavers kidnapped them, shipped them to North America in chains, and sold them into bondage. My oldest ancestor, John Bonnaut, escaped and ran away to New England where he became a free man. He fought in the Revolutionary War. His descendants have fought in every American war since then. After the Civil War, my ancestors renamed themselves Dakar, after the city in Senegal, our ancestral home.

"John—"

"Let me finish," he said, now raising his voice. "My relatives and my heritage were taken from me when the slavers took my ancestors from Senegal. My relatives and my heritage were taken from me by enslavement, poverty, and segregation. My relatives and my heritage were taken from me when the Three-Hour War blasted New York City and Washington, D.C. to oblivion. You must have seen those photographs, Selena. There's nothing left. "SEVENTY-EIGHT million Americans died in the Three-Hour War—TEN MILLION were black like me. We blacks lost Harlem, out cultural center. We Americans lost our capitol, the White House, our museums, our memorials, and our monuments. And talk about religion! I'm Christian. There's nothing left of Christ, where He was born, where He lived, where He died, and where He ascended into Heaven! Don't tell me about loss. Still, despite all that, I've not turned my back on humanity or my country, and certainly not on the Jews."

"All right, all right," Sumate broke in. "Let's cool it. And just so you know, all of us have our historical grievances. My family comes from Southern California. I lost relatives when the Three-Hour War obliterated Los Angeles. My family tree includes Chinese, Filipino, Native Americans, Mexicans, Scots, Irish, and Syrians. Lots of grievances there. As for Jerusalem, remember the Temple Mount was also holy to us Muslims. But, let's also remember it's been seventy years since the Three-Hour War. It's over. It's a new solar system. And we have to work together to protect it."

"Yes," Selena said. "I'm sorry John. I didn't intend to get carried away."

"I'm sorry too," John said. He smiled. "I, uh, try hard to not lose my cool. I'm afraid you got me at a weak moment. To change the subject, do you mind if I ask you a question?"

"Shoot."

"Sumate said you've never been to the Earth. Is that true?"

"Yah."

"And what about your family?"

"John, I'm third generation Lunarian. For as long as my family has lived on the Moon, I don't think any of them have visited the Earth."

"Is that why you're so slender? And so pale?"

"Yah. Yah. Growing up under artificial light, in the Moon's low gravity, leads to thinner limbs, taller torsos, and paler skin. The downside is it makes it hard for Lunarians like me, who are used to living in one-sixth Earth gravity, to live in full Earth gravity. I will be very uncomfortable traveling at full Earth gravity for the eight weeks it will take to make the round-trip flight to Pluto."

"So, why is Mossad sending you to Pluto?"

"To defend military secrets," Selena said. "You know, WXN2 and EP communications."

"Yeah. But those are American secrets. You've just told me how New Israel wants nothing to do with Earth politics. So, why help us out?"

"Ah," she began. "Same story, chapter two. Although we Jews turned our backs on history, I'm afraid history pursued us to our new home."

"What do you mean?" John asked.

"Well, I'm referring to the Lunar Lights Controversy. I bet you know this story too."

"Sure, the basic facts," John replied. "I know the colonization of the Moon became possible when the United Nations divided the Moon among all of the Earth nations. I know many of the smaller and poorer countries sold their Lunar holdings to larger, richer countries, like the US. I also know some of the smaller countries joined their Lunar holdings together. I know that, like the Earth, the Moon has become an international world. I know the Lunar city lights have become a problem, but I don't understand how that has become the Lunar Lights Controversy. Since we're meeting tonight to brief me about Astro history and politics, I'd like to hear your views."

"Well," Selena began. "It's kind of our fault. When the founders of New Israel designed our new capital, the domed New Jerusalem City, they built in the Tsiolkovsky Crater and renamed the crater the Star of David District. They then outlined the borders of New Jerusalem with banks of powerful lights in the shape of a six-pointed star. The lights stand out against the dark mare that covers the floor of the SDD. You can easily see the Star from space. Of course, the only people who actually see the Star are space travelers."

"So?" asked John. "What's that got to do with the Lunar Lights Controversy?

"Just a minute, I'm getting there," Selena replied. "The Lunar near side is a different story. It's the biggest billboard to ever exist, visible from all parts of the Earth. With the monetization of the Moon and the division of the surface of the Moon among all Earth nations, many of the Muslim nations banded their Moon parcels together, formed the LUIS—the Lunar Union of Islamic States—and located their joint Lunar holdings at Mare Nectaris, in the southeastern quadrant of the near side. On the southern bank of Nectaris, there's a large crater, Fracastorius. The Lunar Muslims filled Fracastorius with a large, five-pointed star, easily visible from Earth, and located their Lunar colony, New Mecca, in a domed city in the center of the star. During the waning Moon, the Lunar crescent and star become a religious symbol for the Muslim faith."

"Ahh. Sure, I've seen it many times. It's beautiful."

"Well," she continued. "Not to be outdone, many of the Christian countries copied the Lunar Muslims, banded together to form the LLCN—the Lunar League of Christian Nations—and located their Lunar holdings to form a cross. They spread their cross over Mare Imbrium, placing the north end in Plato Crater, the south end in Copernicus Crater, and the eastern end in Archimedes Crater. The rest of the cross they filled out by strategic location of more holdings on the Imbrium plain. They then lit up the cross by placing powerful lights across their holdings and locating their colony, Christian City, in Plato Crater. The black basalt of the Imbrium plain makes the cross lights even easier to see."

"Yeah. But those lights have caused a lot of problems on Earth."

"On the Moon, too," Sumate said. "There's endless agitation about whose lights are turned on when. There's been sabotage and even terrorism. Monitoring this situation has become a major task for the Storms Office."

"Okay," John said. "But that's all on the near side, so how does that affect New Israel?"

"Well, it means the religious conflict that drove us from Earth, conflict between the Muslims, the Christians, and the Jews, has followed us to our new home," Selena said. "Furthermore, after the Three-Hour War, terrorists, bent on revenge, bombed Mecca, and destroyed the Kaaba—the holiest Muslim shrine. Tempers flared up again and have never cooled down."

"Okay. I'm following you," said John. "But I still don't understand."

Getting a little exasperated, she said, "What it means, John, is that after one-hundred years of Pax Americana following World War Two, the American military umbrella failed, and we Jews lost Israel. Since the Three-Hour War, humanity has enjoyed another Pax Americana, primed by the Moon monetization, fueled by the Space Boom, and guarded by the American military. But, after seventy years, the peace is again fraying. Humanity has spread across the solar system and converted the Lunar wastelands into a new developed world. Terrorists and saboteurs now live on the Moon. Our enemies are again on our doorstep. We'll do everything we can to help the Americans maintain the peace. But we're mindful the American peace has failed before and could do so again. We'll defend ourselves as well as we can."

"Okay, okay. That helps," said John. "But, Pluto?"

"Yah. Yah. Well. That's chapter three. Aside from helping the Americans, we have another pot brewing."

"That is?"

"The Edge is the new space frontier."

"Sure. I know that. But why Pluto?"

"Well. Just like after World War Two when the Jews collected together in one location, creating Israel, which our enemies then destroyed, we've once again placed all of our Jewish eggs, so to speak, in one basket, New Israel. Once again we're susceptible to a genocidal attack."

John protested, "Wait a minute! Wait a minute! Selena! That's nonsense. That's never going to happen!"

"Well," she replied. "It did. Twice. First with World War Two and then with the Three-Hour War. We can't let it happen again. So, there's a movement in New Israel to colonize the new worlds that are opening up on the Edge. The Hasidim have already organized a planning group at Port Tombaugh. They intend to colonize one of the Edge worlds—they call it New Mount Sinai—where they can live by fundamental Jewish law. The Muslims and Christians have similar plans to colonize the Edge with break-away sects."

"Whoa. So, religious conflict has gone all the way to the Edge!"

"There's more," added Sumate. "We still have problems with the Chinese, the Russians, and the Brazilians, not to mention the criminal gangs."

"Oh man, it's getting late. That's enough for now," John said.

"The problem for us," Selena said turning to face John, "is when are you going to learn loG combat skills?"

"I'll start tomorrow," John replied.

"Not much time," Selena said. "All right guys. I agree it's late. Let's call it a day."

10 FUNERAL IN CLARKE STATION

Chaplain O'Rourke must hate this room, Skalay thought as he sat in Clarke Station's darkened Assembly Hall, waiting for Kirk to join him and for the funeral service to begin. *It's just a plain room*—linoleum floor, ceiling light panels, some drapery on the walls, cheap plastic and titanium stacking chairs arranged in rows with a center aisle, facing a raised podium holding a boxy lectern—the service pulpit. *Just a plain utilitarian, multi-purpose room*— now decorated for the funeral service with some floral bouquets spotted about and a funeral spray sitting on a table behind the pulpit. *Not the place I would want for my funeral, certainly nothing like a church.* Aside from the two matching picture portholes, which stretched from floor to ceiling and an equal distance along the wall, located on opposite sides of the great hall, bracketing the center podium, *this room could be a meeting room on Earth or any other place in the solar system.*

Sitting there, idly listening to the Plutonian anthem, "Oh, Pluto," playing in the background, the picture portholes stole his attention, forcing him to reconsider his interior decorating opinions.

The irony of living in outer space is how I hardly ever get to see it! The windowless urban can of Port Tombaugh is no home for a stargazer. But this room, he thought, as he turned from first one, and then to the other, of the picture portholes, *shows the majesty of the cosmos!*

Through the picture porthole on his left, Skalay could see the waning crescent Charon. Now just the slimmest arc of silvery light, marking the edge, or limb, of the distant moon, it looked like an enormous sickle hanging in the night.

It's amazing how the active window blacks out the sun. It should be blindingly bright, just setting above the Charon crescent, but I can't see it...

The new Charon moon, a dark mauve and taupe colored disc tucked into the sickle's embrace, just visible in the reflected pink Plutonian light, blocked out the stars like a great hole in the sky. Surrounding the cosmic hole, he could see the spring constellations of Virgo, Bootes, and Hydra. Just to the left of Charon, the Milky Way, a broad band of frothy and speckled galactic light, smudged by the black spots and lacy trails of interstellar dust clouds, crossed the window from top to bottom and bent around the Charonic disc.

The luminous, ragged shawl of the Milky Way reminded Skalay of the sparkling waters of Galveston Bay, his childhood home. Sometimes during warm, dark summer nights, the Bay waters would fill with a bloom of bioluminescent plankton. But unlike the glowing bay, which rippled and flickered with the rise and fall of the ocean, the brighter and whiter celestial light of the Milky Way shined cold, static, and immutable, testimony to an everlasting heaven.

On his right, the near side of Pluto filled the picture porthole, squeezing out any view of the surrounding star field. In contrast to the black of deep space, the pink-to-rust-to-bronze-colored, pock-marked, planet, now almost fully lit by the distant sun, glowed in the sunlight.

Only a thousand kilometers above Pluto, Skalay could easily see the shadowless, rugged surface spread out below him. Brilliant white ices emphasized the details of craters, canyons, and mountains as if some celestial artist had used reflective white paint to highlight the rough topography. Here and there, plates of bright silvery ice marked the presence of frozen nitrogen glaciers. Across the Plutonian equator marched the line of deep brown, star-tar-stained, hilly and cratered plains; the geographers called them maculae, but most Plutonians simply called them the Brass Knuckles. Looking like enormous inkblots, splintered by deep north-south canyons, the Knuckles appeared in sharp contrast to the surrounding pink-to-gray mountains with their silver glaciers and white snow-caps.

Awestruck by the unexpected view of the rarely seen cosmos, he just sat there. *Why, I don't think I've ever been in a holier or more beautiful place than this one!*

Being a self-described, hard-boiled gumshoe, he was not one to confess to believing in God. But, deep within his heart, never spoken to anyone—well, maybe to Mindy, but no one else, he held such beliefs, or hopes, or yearnings. He had seen such awful things in his career, like the gruesome deaths of Moxon and Keator. He hungered for something that would bring meaning to what appeared to be a meaningless universe, something that would right the cruel wrongs. This inspiring room awoke his hidden piety, gave power to his secret beliefs, and soothed his uneasy soul.

Trapped in his reverie, he tried to break the spell by looking for the lights of Christy Anchor.

I know they are directly below me, near the middle of Meng-p'o, but I can't see them.

He tried to spot them by following with his eye the broad-based arrow of the Acheron Bridge. As the Bridge emerged from the top of the Pluto picture porthole, quickly narrowed, and then disappeared in the distance below him, only the bright sunlight washed out the weaker artificial lights of the Bridge and Christy Anchor remained invisible.

Abruptly, he realized that Meng-p'o and the rest of the Brass Knuckles appeared to be rotating around the center of the porthole, like a slowly spinning fan blade. He knew this was just an illusion, created by the rotation of Clarke Station, with his Assembly Hall frame of reference, around the Acheron Bridge axis. The planet wasn't revolving below him, he was rotating around the Acheron Bridge, rotation that created the centripetal force that simulated the partial gravity necessary for humans to live comfortably in the space station. But his stomach would have none of it, convinced by the sight of the planetary pirouette that the universe had gone topsy-turvy.

Oooooh, man! His stomach suddenly rebelled. The morning coffee burbled back up from his gut into his mouth, warning him of incipient seasickness. Closing his eyes to fight off vomiting, he thought, *I guess the viscera doesn't understand cognitive dissonance!*

A few moments later, Kirk sat down next to him, distracting him from his nausea and bringing him back to the task of observing the congregants, who by now crowded the Assembly Hall. Knowing their duty, the two detectives listened closely to the murmur of the people around them, hoping to pick up tidbits of information about Moxon and Keator that might reveal why the two scientists had died.

A small group of musicians gathered at the head of the hall, to the right of the podium, and began to tune their instruments.

"As you directed," Kirk whispered, "Charlie is at the entrance, recording the names of the mourners. Roc is lagging behind, using the distraction of the funeral to poke around the Station and possibly hack into an untended computer."

"Good," Skalay whispered. "Kirk, do you know the women who are sitting in the second row, on Mary's side behind the Chaplain?"

"Yes. Those are Mary's closest friends at the station: Christina, Lise, Cathy, and Lucy. I've already spoken to them."

"What about the people in the first row on Mary's side? Do you know who they are?"

"No."

"Well, what about those three men in the second row, on Moxon's side?"

"They're the remaining members of the OASIS staff," Kirk said. "I haven't spoken to them yet."

"Okay, please talk to the women again, and I'll see what I can learn from the men."

After the musicians finished tuning their instruments. Chaplain O'Rourke stood up, stepped to the podium. Ushers, to Skalay's great relief, pulled the drapes to conceal the picture portholes. A harp and flute began to play Pachelbel's *Canon in D*, quieting the crowd.

From the back of the room, four ushers walked down the aisle to the podium, slowly pushing two stretchers. On each stretcher rested a sealed cylindrical metal casket—like a rocket casing—which held the remains of Keator and Moxon. Over Mary's casket, someone had draped a lei of white orchids, gold mums, and green leaves, Pluto's three colors. The same colors were used in the funeral spray and the bouquets spotted about the room.

After the music ended, Chaplain O'Rourke made his opening remarks and then led the assembly in reciting Psalm 121. Occupied by his detective tasks, Skalay ignored the opening proceedings until the end of the psalm struck a chord, bringing his attention back to the service:

> ". . . the Sun will not harm you by day,
> nor the Moon by night.
> The LORD will keep you from all harm—
> he will watch over your life;
> the LORD will watch over your coming and going
> both now and forevermore."

After the psalm, Lowell Director Best stood up and began the eulogies. He started by holding up a diamond ring.

"This isn't part of a normal eulogy," he began. "But before going further, I think everyone here would want to know we have finished transcribing the transport flight recorder. It revealed that just prior to their deaths, Chief Moxon proposed to Dr. Keator, offered her this engagement ring—which we recovered in Chief Moxon's pocket—and she accepted him. It is so sad that they were engaged just before tragedy took their lives."

This news triggered a wave of weeping from many of the mourners, particularly Mary's four friends. The crying continued intermittently through the rest of the service.

Surprised by the announcement, Skalay whispered "Kirk —did you know that?"

"No."

Still whispering, he said, "If she accepted him, why was the ring in Moxon's pocket instead of on her finger?"

"Kory tells us that this is the first marriage proposal on Charon," Best continued. "In recognition of this historic event and their tragic deaths, we have applied to the IAU to name the twin craters at the foot of Kubrick Mons after Mary Keator and Jim Moxon."

After this announcement, Best reported some biographical tidbits that had so far eluded the PT Homicide Squad: Chief Moxon was a graduate of MIT. He had been in Federal Service for twenty-three years. Before coming to Clarke Station, he was a scientist stationed at the USDS Giuseppe Piazzi Observatory on Ceres. He was a widower, his wife having died on Ceres thirteen years ago. He did not have any children; he left behind only one living relative, a brother in Boston, who will receive Moxon's remains.

Switching to Dr. Keator, Director Best reported she had graduated from the University of Washington. She had a mother and stepfather in Columbia, Missouri. She had served four years as a USDS scientist, previously stationed at the Edwin Eugene Aldrin, Jr. Space Station.

When Director Best finished, Chaplain O'Rourke stood up and reported he had corresponded with Moxon's brother about the ceremony and his engagement to Dr. Keator. His brother had written back, telling the Chaplain that when Dr. Moxon's wife had died, her funeral had included Gustav Mahler's love poem to his wife, Alma, and the playing of the fourth movement of Mahler's fifth symphony—the Adagietto. Moxon's brother asked the same music and poem be played at the joint funeral for Jim and Mary. So, the Chaplain read:

> "How much I love you, you my Sun, I cannot tell you that with words. I can only lament to you my longing and my love, my bliss!"

A violin trio and harp then played the Adagietto.

When the music stopped, the Chaplain invited anyone who wanted to speak, to do so. About a dozen scientists came to the podium and described how either or both Chief Moxon and Dr. Keator had helped them with their work. Skalay did not learn much from this; he already knew both scientists were well-liked and respected, but it was unclear to him how much scientific work Moxon and Keator had performed. So far, it did not look like as much as he would expect for a couple of USDS scientists.

At the end of the eulogies, Director Best added a few more comments.

"Once again, this is not properly a eulogy, but I think the people here would also want to know the status of the investigations into the wreck on Kubrick Mons. The NTSB has reached a preliminary conclusion that the wreck was an accident. But, just to make sure, the FBI has sent an investigator from Kansas City to review the deaths."

"What!" Skalay gasped. "Kirk" he whispered, "did you know that?"

"No. What does it mean?"

"Trouble."

Continuing, Director Best said, "The FBI investigator will arrive in four weeks. The USDS will also be sending a team to replenish the OASIS staff. They'll arrive in three months."

This news prompted murmurs from the congregation.

"In the meantime," Director Best continued, "Dr. Keator's and Chief Moxon's bodies will be sent back to their families on Earth. The engagement ring will be sent to Mary's parents. And recordings of this ceremony will be sent to Moxon's brother and Mary's parents.

"Kirk, be sure we also get a copy of that recording."

"You bet!"

The service concluded with Psalm twenty-three, which Skalay also ignored, although this passage caught his attention:

> "Even though I walk
> through the valley of the shadow of death,
> I will fear no evil,
> for you are with me;
> your rod and your staff,
> they comfort me."

A recorded solo by the popular music artist Della, singing the mournful "Blue Missouri"—one of Mary's favorites, played during the recessional.

After the ceremony, the Observatory held a reception for the mourners. To Skalay's surprise, Police Commissioner Lord, Fort Resnik Commandant General Mark Sliffer, Port

Tombaugh Mayor Joan Burns, and Alice Pettigrew, the Governor for the US Territory of Pluto and Charon, joined Chaplain O'Rourke and Director Best to form the reception line. Charlie joined Skalay and Kirk.

"Sir," Kirk said, "What's up with all the brass?"

"Damned if I know," Skalay responded in frustration, immediately regretting his curse.

"Somethin's up," Charlie said. "Do you know that the Consuls for China, Brazil, Russia, are also here?"

"What?"

"Yes. All three are over there, at the front of the room, next to the curtain for the Charon window. Also, the President of the Pluto and Charon Territorial Stock Exchange, Anthony McKay, is here. He's talking to one of the OASIS staffers near the entrance to the hall. And, the Chair of the Port Tombaugh Gaming Commission, Watson Hatch, is here, talking to the President of the First National Bank of Port Tombaugh. What are all of these people doing here?"

"I don't know. Are you making a covert recording of the receiving line?"

"Yup."

"Great! Charlie, just circulate with Kirk and see what you can learn from the crowd. "I'm going to talk to the OASIS staff and after that see if I can button-hole some of the brass. Also, keep an eye on the receiving line while you work the room. I'll do the same. Something's brewing."

While he talked to the remaining three staff members of OASIS and circulated through the room, Skalay scrutinized the reception line, watching the attendees interact with

Director Best. Skalay smelled a cover-up. He wanted to know what the Director was hiding, and he was sure the answer was in this room. If he could spot the tell, he might figure out what was happening and who was doing it. It just didn't make sense to lock PT Homicide out of the investigation, to keep Moxon's and Keator's personnel files secret, to muzzle Kory and Robby, and to conceal the records of the transport flight recorder. And it sure didn't make sense to delay the murder investigation by four weeks while bringing an agent all the way from Kansas City, seven billion klicks from PT, to inspect the death scene!

When the opportunity arose, Skalay cornered the Commissioner. "What's going on? Does this make any sense to you?"

"Seems fishy to me," agreed the Commissioner. "I'm sorry. I've not been able to break through the national security barrier. I'm afraid you'll just have to continue to work the edges until the FBI agent gets here."

"Shit! What are they covering up?"

11 EARTH AND MOON

By Wednesday, March 24, the third day of the space flight, the CIA mission to Charon had fallen into a routine.

Every morning the team exercised in the ship's gym with the other passengers. To conceal the purpose of their mission, after the morning session they continued their training in a padded room reserved for the team's exclusive use. There they practiced martial arts with the 'stro weapons Colonel Boot had given them. Because the ship's movement simulated full Earth gravity, rather than the much lower Lunar gravity, Dakar dominated the training sessions. By the time the ship would arrive at Port Tombaugh, Dakar intended to know how to use his new weapons instinctively, drawing upon them when needed by reflex, just like he already knew how to use his gun, karambit, and Kpinga throwing ax. Still, he would like to have had more training under loG and noG conditions. *Oh well, it will have to wait until we get to Port Tombaugh.*

After the lunch break, the three agents would gather in one of their staterooms to review the CIA briefing materials. Afterwards, Laoloo and Volkova took turns tutoring Dakar on solar system astronomy, history, laws, governments, economics, politics, conflicts, and criminal organizations. At first, Dakar found Solar System 101 (as he liked to call it), to be interesting. But after several sessions, the copious, but predictable, material had become tedious, even boring, differing only in unimportant details from the many geopolitical survey classes he had taken in college and later on from the CIA.

When Dakar tried gently to complain to Volkova and Laoloo that they could shorten the lectures, they rose up in unison and complained. He had missed the point.

"What point?" asked Dakar.

"The Boom," Laoloo quickly replied. "You know, the Space Boom, the Solar System Gold Rush. The Boom that launched humans from dirt-bound primitives to third millennia 'stros!"

"What?" Dakar said, raising his voice with the suspicion that he had just been insulted.

Volkova stepped in. "Dakar, don't get excited. What we're trying to say is that, prior to the Boom, gravity had trapped humanity on the surface of the Earth. Over time, unrestrained population growth, exhausted natural resources, and overwhelmed ecological systems had begun to destroy humanity. You know what I'm talking about: climate change, wars, epidemics, famines, and poverty of the late twentieth and early twenty-first century. You know this, Dakar. That's your job, dealing with all this, isn't it?"

"Yeah," Dakar said grudgingly.

"But things are better now, right?" Volkova asked again.

"Yeah," Dakar reluctantly agreed.

"Well, why?" asked Volkova.

"I know, I know why," Dakar said. "You don't have to treat me like a stupid Dirt. I'm not a no-nothing ostrich with his head in the sand. I know that space migration has stopped the population growth on Earth. I know that space wealth has reversed climate change and eliminated disease, poverty, and hunger on Earth. And I know that international conflict has almost disappeared on Earth. But, as you both know, nations still fight, whether on the Earth or in space. There is still crime on both the Earth and in space. And organized religions still fight. What makes space so special?"

Laoloo answered, "unlimited resources and wealth for everyone and plenty of places for everybody to live."

"And it's our job to make sure that everyone lives in peace," Volkova said. "And maybe in the new millennia, humanity will grow up and be the promise we should become," she quickly added.

Following the afternoon tutorials, Dakar would return to the ship's gym for a second set of exercises while Laoloo and Volkova recovered from their unaccustomed exertions under the simulated gravity. Dakar, on the other hand, could feel his strength returning with the two-a-day workouts.

Best of all, John liked the long dinners with Sumate and Selena which came at the end of the day, when their banter slipped into first names. Because they had no privacy in the ship's dining hall, they discussed music, VR movies, sports, philosophy, travel, anything and everything besides espionage. They reserved shop-talk and swapping spy stories for the privacy of their staterooms, which they had checked for listening devices.

After leaving Sumate and Selena, John would spend the rest of the evening alone in his stateroom, reading for pleasure or watching a VR movie. On the first night out, he joined Sumate and Selena for the welcome party organized by the ship's social director, who had made it her business to have plenty of games and activities for the passengers—like the upcoming Carnival Party—to keep everybody occupied and out of trouble. Sumate pointed out that if the social director genuinely wanted to keep the passengers out of trouble, she would keep them out of the Calypso Lounge and the Poseidon Casino.

The casino and bar faced each other across the main hall of the ship. The three agents joked that walking past the two attractions without getting pulled into either one was like sailing a ship between the six-faced monster, Scylla, and the whirlpool, Charybdis.

One evening, Charybdis won when after dinner Sumate excused himself to prepare his notes for the following day's review of the Lunar Lights Controversy. Left to their own devices, Selena and John drifted into the Calypso lounge, lured by the promise of a PT Sling.

"John, I didn't think you drank," exclaimed Selena.

"Well, I don't when I'm on a job," he replied. "But this doesn't feel like a job. Does it to you?" Not waiting for an answer, he continued, "To me, it feels like a vacation—very secure. One of the few times I've felt like I can relax and be safe. There's just no one around us."

"Well, you've got that right," she said. "No one expected us to be on this ship. Aside from the Brazilian, we were the last passengers to get tickets. There're no enemies onboard. And, just think, no one else around for at least seventy-five million klicks. Do you see the large screen over there, against the far wall?"

"Sure."

"It's showing pictures of Mars landscapes because we've just crossed Mars' orbit—Ceres is next. As we approach and cross each planetary orbit, the video screen will change and show similar pictures of the astronomical bodies whose orbits we're crossing. You can see where we are in space on the two orreries hanging from the—"

"Orreries?"

"Yah. An orrery is a model of the solar system. Those two things hanging from the ceiling that look like mobiles are orreries. Mechanical models that show our current position and the position of the planets in the inner and outer solar system."

"Whoa!" said John.

As he started to get up to examine the orreries, Selena pulled him back to the table. She turned on the screen built into the bar table and switched it to the inner solar system.

"See," she said, pointing to a blinking yellow cursor, "here we are. We've crossed Mars's orbit and are heading towards Ceres's orbit. And, hey, look at this," she said, switching the monitor to show the positions of all of the trans-planetary ships currently in operation in the inner solar system. A cloud of small red carets appeared on the black screen, peppering the shipping lanes between the Earth and Mars.

Pointing to the red carets she said, "Those are the Earth-Mars ships. You can tell which way they are going by which way the caret points."

"Whoa! So many!"

"Yah, yah. And see here," she said, pointing to the scattering of white carets outside the Earth-Mars lane. "These are the ships going to various points in the outer solar system, places like Ceres, Ganymede, Oberon, Pluto, and the Asteroid and Kuiper Belt mines."

"How do they know the location of all of these ships? Radar?"

"No. Radar can't spot spaceships—the ships are too small, and space is too big to be scanned by radar. As it happens, we have no good way to find spaceships in space. Instead, we rely upon self-identification by transponders and by projected position by filed flight plans."

"So, there could be other ships out there? Couldn't there?" John asked. "I mean, all they would have to do would be to turn off the transponder and not file a flight plan."

Selena frowned. "I suppose so. But it's difficult to turn off the transponder. Pirate ships have been known to fly covertly without them—we call them ghost ships—but they're too small and slow for the trans-planetary shipping routes. They only haunt the space around outposts and space stations. We don't worry about them on flights like ours."

Returning to the blinking *Odysseus* cursor, she said, "Look here. You can see we're already more than two AUs from Earth. Because we're going to Pluto, we're nowhere near the Earth-Mars shipping lane. The next orbit is Ceres, about another AU away. There isn't anyone around us."

"What's an AU?"

"An astronomical unit. It's the distance from the Earth to the Sun, about a hundred fifty million klicks." Switching to the outer solar system screen, she said, "And here's our destination, Pluto—about fifty astronomical units from Earth."

"Jeez!" John swore. "We're never going to get there!"

"Oh, we will," she said. "Even though it is a long way, under constant full Earth gravity acceleration, we quickly pick up speed. It's just going to take us a little less than four weeks."

"Jeez!" John said again. "Uhm, Selena, speaking of full Earth gravity, how are you doing? This travel must be hard on you and Sumate."

"Better than you'd think," Selena said. "We Lunarians work out daily in our gravity suits to maintain our bone and muscle mass." She lowered her voice. "And while civilians do the bare minimum, those of us in our profession train extra hard because most trans-planetary space flight is at full Earth gravity. Both Sumate and I have been to PT, and I've also been to Fort Musk, Gauss City, and Port Herschel. And even though I've never been to the Earth myself, I never know when duty may send me to Mother. So, we're going to be fine."

"Mother?"

"Yah. You know, Mother Earth. I could say Dirt, but I know you don't like that word."

"How come you've never been to Earth?"

"Never had a reason. Now that Israel is gone, there's not much calling us back. Why haven't you ever gone to the Moon?"

"Not enough time. My vacations are short trips home or to the seashore or to a wilderness park to hike and camp. As you know, I also like to hunt with my Pa. Besides, I've never had any desire to leave the Earth. The Moon always seemed like a desolate place to me. But now that I've been there, I'm changing my mind. Flying, like you were doing when I first met you, looks like a lot of fun. And flyball also looks like a blast."

"They are," she agreed. "I never feel so free as when I strap on my wings and tail and leap into the air, flapping until I find a rising air-current and glide to the roof of the lava tube. I've been weightless, but lava tube flying is entirely different. In space, the bulky mass of the spacesuit hinders movement; you don't get that with flying. Also, in outer space you're always floating next to a spaceship or an asteroid, or something. But on the Moon, you're flying over people, buildings, and parks. It's entirely different. Reminds me of the Peter Pan books my mother would read to me, or the old Superman comics. And you're right, the high-energy, ramped-up fusion of gymnastics, basketball, and soccer, makes flyball great fun."

"I played basketball and soccer in school. I'd like to try my hand at flyball. But, Selena, I'm surprised that beaches and mountains don't pull you back to Earth, not to mention history: Rome? London? Egypt?"

"I've seen all that stuff on videos and in VR. But, John, I, ah . . . well . . . to be frank, I, ah . . . well, I've always lived in a room—you know: domed city, lava tube, spaceship, space station, whatever. I, ah . . . I've never been outside. It gives me the willies to think of looking right up at the Moon and the sun and the planets and stars and such without looking through the protection of a window or a spacesuit. I've never seen a body of water larger than a fountain. You know we Lunarians don't even have bathtubs or swimming pools, much less lakes or oceans. The thought of massive volumes of free-flowing water is scary."

"Well, what about mountains?"

"We've got mountains on the Moon. But they're much older and not as steep as your Earth mountains, not to mention we don't have forests, tundra, or snow caps on our mountains."

"Sure. But aren't you afraid of heights? I am."

"No silly. With our weak gravity, falls are not the problem they must be on Earth. If I'm outside, in my spacesuit, I have lots of equipment to protect and rescue me if I should fall. And you know I love to fly inside."

Then after a brief pause, she said, "John. Moon mountains can be beautiful, particularly with a full Earth overhead. Outside the domes and caves, the surface of the Moon is peaceful. No noise. No motion. No one around to bother you. Just a feeling of eternity. I find it comforting."

"Well, what about the zoos and art galleries and historical monuments? Wouldn't you like to see them? Wouldn't you like to see a giraffe or a mammoth?"

"John, New Jerusalem has the John Herschel Zoo and Botanical Gardens. It's mostly for flying and petting animals, so that the children can see horses, cows, chickens, dogs, cats, and other animals they read about in school. We also have squirrels, rabbits, and birds in our public parks. Most large animals don't do well in loG, so we don't have many wild zoo animals. Fort Musk has more. The gravity is better on Mars. But not on the Moon. There're also petting zoos and botanical gardens in Marius Hills and Armstrong Station, but they don't have wild animals. As for resurrected and created animals, like mammoths, dodo birds, and unicorns, they're far too delicate for the Moon."

"Selena, you've convinced me the Moon and Mars and other places in the solar system are more beautiful than I had realized. Still, it seems to me the one truly beautiful place in this solar system for as far as we can see, is the Earth. I'd like to show you the Earth someday—show you how special it is."

"Well, maybe someday you'll get to."

12 DEAD ENDS AND STONE WALLS

On Thursday, February 25, eight days after the Kubrick Mons deaths, a beleaguered Inspector Skalay convened Morning Report in the scruffy, congested, PT Homicide Squad conference room. He was frustrated because his prediction of dead ends and stone walls had come true, thwarting his investigation into the deaths on Kubrick Mons.

"Okay, folks. Let's get going. Please record and take notes."

"Certainly."

"Thank you, Talos. The official line regarding Kubrick Mons, as stated by the NTSB and endorsed by the Lowell Observatory Director, Dr. Best, is this: Moxon parked on Kubrick Mons to show Keator the eclipse and propose. Keator accepted. But, at that very exact moment, a malfunction caused multiple canopy bolts to simultaneously explode, killing Keator and Moxon. If they had been wearing their spacesuits, as protocol required, they would have survived. So, the deaths were accidental due to mechanical malfunction and operator error. The end. Comments?"

Hearing none, Skalay continued. "Talos, I am going to list my objections to the NTSB assessment. As I do this, please record each point on the squad screen and post them to our perscoms.

"Certainly."

Skalay continued. "The way I see it is this: the NTSB explanation fails on multiple points.

"It doesn't explain why we found the transport anchored in regolith instead of just sitting on top of the rubble.

"It doesn't explain why we found a page from a one-time pad in the debris field, but not the rest of the pad. It also doesn't explain why Moxon and Keator needed a one-time pad in the first place.

"It doesn't explain why Keator and Moxon were on opposite sides of the transport just before the canopy blew. If they were having a romantic encounter, they should have been together.

"It doesn't explain why Moxon had Keator's engagement ring in his pocket. If she accepted him, it should have been on her finger.

"It doesn't explain the highly unlikely occurrence of multiple canopy bolts exploding at the same time.

"It doesn't explain what happened to the missing cargo. Who took the cargo? What was the cargo? And where is it now?

"It also doesn't explain what happened to Moxon's perscom. Altogether that's seven unexplained facts that in my book, knock out the NTSB explanation. Anybody disagree? Comments?"

Silence.

"All right, Kirk, tell us what you and I think really happened on Kubrick Mons."

"Sure," she said, opening her notepad, "Using a sheet from a one-time pad, Moxon coded, or was coding, a message to an unknown receiver just before he died. At that time, persons unknown hacked the transport computer and exploded the canopy bolts, killing Moxon and Keator. Based on the amount of the transport atmosphere that fell onto the wreck after the canopy exploded, approximately three to four hours must have passed before one or more unknown persons stole Moxon's perscom, the one-time pad, and the transport cargo."

"Thank you, Kirk." In a commanding voice, Skalay said, "Talos, save the list of our objections to the NTSB assessment of the transport wreck. And then as I dictate them to the squad, start a new list of mysteries we have to solve to break open this case."

Addressing his team, Skalay continued, "Okay, folks. The way I see it, we five mysteries we have to solve."

"Mystery number one, Moxon and Keator. They didn't act like regular astronomers. Who were they? And what were they doing on Kubrick Mons?

"Mystery number two, what was the message encrypted by the one-time pad, and to whom was the message sent?

"Mystery number three, who hacked the transport ERC, and why did they have to kill Moxon and Keator?

"Mystery number four, what was the transport cargo? And, who stole the cargo, Moxon's perscom, and the rest of the one-time-pad?"

Then, in a harsher voice, revealing the depths of his frustration, Skalay said, "And Mystery number five, who's fucking with us?" Then after a pause, he said, "I'm sorry folks, I didn't mean to be so crude—it just popped out. Talos, don't write that down."

"Certainly."

Skalay continued, "It's just that I don't understand why Best was so hell-bent to find the killers, but as soon as the NTSB declared mechanical malfunction and operator error, he reversed course and tried to stop the investigation. Why? Why impound the personnel files, the flight recorder, Kory and Robby's files? Why keep us from inspecting Clarke Station? Who's pulling strings to shut down our investigation? And, why in hell—sorry, I'm losing my cool again—is the FBI sending an investigator from the other side of the solar system when there are FBI agents at Port Tombaugh? Talos, don't write that all down. Just label this final mystery 'cover-up.'"

"Certainly," said Talos as Mystery five label changed to cover-up.

"Good," Skalay continued. "Now, let's get to our reports. Kirk, you're up first."

"Sure. The bad news is that I made a second pass at interviewing the Clarke Station personnel, talking to more people than just the boffins. I spent a lot of time with Keator's four friends. But, once again, I hit dead ends. People are friendly enough, but they get close-mouthed and edgy when I start asking for details about what Moxon and Keator did. I made some headway on the wristpods, but then hit a stone wall. I talked to the coroner, Dr. Abbott. After she insisted she had not found the wristpods, I told her she risked jail time and suspension of her license if we discovered she had lied to a police officer investigating a homicide. That changed her tune. Being the coroner and all, she knew what I was talking about. So, she finally admitted to me that she had found Moxon's and Keator's wristpods, but Best immediately seized them, claiming 'national security.' He then told her she could not tell anyone she had found the wristpods. If she did, he would see that she would lose her job and her license. I pressed her hard. She swore she did not find Moxon's perscom. So, we now know what happened to Keator's and Moxon's wristpods, but it doesn't help. We still don't know what happened to Moxon's perscom."

"Jee-zus!" swore Skalay. "Best is as two-faced as Iapetus. Well, obstruction's another weld in his casket. Anything else?"

"Yes," continued Kirk. "As I briefed you before, Roc and I did everything we could to find computer records for Moxon. To our surprise, neither MIT nor the Giuseppe Piazzi Observatory had any records for a James Moxon. He also doesn't appear in any public government documents or news reports before 2101. It's like he just popped out of nowhere when he came to Clarke Station twelve years ago. But, here's the good news! Inspector, I haven't told you this yet—but, last night Roc and I got a break."

"Great! We need a break."

Kirk continued, "At the funeral, Chaplain O'Rourke said Mahler's Adagietto was played at the funeral for Moxon's wife, who died thirteen years ago on Ceres. So, we tried cross-indexing Mahler's Adagietto with funerals and Ceres and searched old social media messages Talos had on file. We got a hit. We found an exchange of messages between some friends who lived on Ceres thirteen years ago, during the 2100 anarchists' rebellion. The messages describe a funeral for a woman who died a horrible death at the hands of the anarchists who had kidnapped her. When the Feds refused to pay her ransom, the anarchists cut off her head. At her funeral, her husband had the Adagietto played while he recited Mahler's poem. The woman's name was Jackie Mocksen. That's Mocksen, spelled M-O-C-K-S-E-N. Her husband was—" she raised her hand for emphasis. "Wait for it, here it comes—Jon—that's spelled J-O-N—Mocksen, who graduated from MIT and served the CIA as the Ceres Station Director, working undercover as a USDS astronomer!"

"Great! Good work!" exclaimed Skalay.

At the same time, Charlie said "Damn!" Roc looked smug with his and Kirk's success.

Continuing while the Squad absorbed the significance of this news, Kirk said, "After his wife's death, Jon Mocksen left the CIA and fell off the computer records. Then twelve years ago, a James Moxon appeared out of nowhere to direct the OASIS station."

Stunned by both the breakthrough for his investigation and the story of the dreadful tragedy which had befallen Moxon, all Skalay could do was just stand there by the whiteboard, shaking his head while thinking about the horrible death of Jackie Mocksen, the tragic circumstances that led to James Moxon's death on Charon, and his own fears that something equally horrifying might happen to Mindy or him.

Silence gripped the room as each member of the Squad struggled with their own thoughts about the events on Ceres.

Skalay broke the silence with a sigh and said, "Well, it makes sense now. Moxon's CIA. The CIA doesn't want us to know. That's why it's national security. Great Lord Krun! What a mess!"

Charlie asked, "What's the CIA got to do with OASIS? And, for that matter, Clarke Station?"

Kirk piped up, "You know, there are rumors the Lowell Observatory is also spying on down-range communications."

"I've heard the same rumors," Roc said. "I've also heard that the Webb Observatory is spying on space communications. And, that's where Keator was stationed before she came to the Lowell."

Skalay swore, "Cripes! If the rumors are true—and I bet they are—that means Keator's CIA also! That means OASIS is also CIA!!"

Turning to the whiteboard, Skalay directed Talos to erase the first half of Mystery number one. "Well, that's progress. It means Moxon and Keator were most likely on Kubrick Mons to send an encrypted message." Using a laser pointer, he circled the second half of Mystery number one and added, "But, it doesn't explain why land on Kubrick Mons—why did they have to send the message from a near side mountaintop? And what was the message? And who was supposed to get it?"

Kirk said, "But, it does explain why Best wants to shut us down. Still, it seems to me that Best's reaction is out of proportion."

"Well, maybe so," Skalay replied. "But, that kind of spying, if it includes US communications—and I'm sure it did—would be strictly illegal. If domestic spying became public, we're talking shutdown of the Lowell and the Webb. Maybe even imprisonment of government officials. Maybe I've misread Best. He may not be as two-faced as I thought he was. For right now, let's just assume Best was acting in good faith and protecting national security secrets. That leaves us with three big mysteries: The secret message, the identity of the killer, and the thefts from the transport wreck. All right!" he said with a smile, "Now we're making some progress. Kirk! Roc! Great work! Thank you. Charlie, you're up next! Did you find Moxon's perscom or clues to the missing cargo?"

"'Fraid not." Charlie apologized, "No perscom. I checked the wreck in drydock, nuthin' new. I snooped Clarke Station and Nickelback Node transport hangars. No clues to the missin' cargo. I used Talos to review PT shipment manifests, lookin' for somethin' that coulda been the missin' cargo. So far, nada."

"Hmm. More dead ends," said Skalay. "What about Henning?"

Charlie pulled out his notebook. "Here's the skinny. Thirteen months ago, different Charon units began to have problems. Started when Kory blew a memory bank last January. After that, one of the Acheron Bridge Elevator cars crashed into Charlene Anchor. Just a freight car, no one hurt. Last spring, Kory blew more memory banks. Clarke Station engineers looked over Kory, found corrupted files, but couldn't debug the mess, so they just took the banks off-line. Backup, parallel memory was fine, so no sweat. Sometime about eight months ago, the Charon electrical grid began to have surprise power surges and unexpected increased electrical consumption. All of this was mostly on the far side. Again, nuthin' terrible. But the engineers couldn't explain it or fix it. It's still a problem."

He paused for a moment to look at his notes. He then continued, "Inspector, Charon has a lot goin' on." From his notes, he read, "in addition to Charlene Anchor and its support facilities, there is the adjoining Michael Brown District. In addition to the main computer banks for Kory, the District includes the popular tourist stop Tyson's Lounge and Hostel. It also has a small spaceport and hangar for transports and HopCrawlers. The District also includes an industrial park with automated factories for manufacturin' and moldin' plastics, makin' heavy equipment, producin' computer chips, growin' loG crops, producin' mock meat, and makin' biochemicals and pharmaceuticals. On the far side, at Ele Ranch Node, there's the Edmond Hamilton District. Its primary purpose is to serve as the computer data node, for collectin' and collatin' data from all of the far side observatories. Like the Brown District, it also has support facilities for Lowell work crews as well as automated industrial, chemical, and food plants. Humans and robots staff Charlene Anchor. Rotatin' human crews staff the near side tourist facilities and robots staff the far side human support facilities. Robots staff the Brown and Hamilton industrial facilities. Kory supervises the robots. Clarke Station engineers supervise Kory and troubleshoot. Beginnin' five months ago, for unknown reasons, production at several of the far-side facilities dropped, and raw material consumption rose. Again, nuthin' alarmin', but still unexplained, still not fixed."

"Hmm," Skalay interrupted. "Sounds like someone hacked Kory and is skimming production. I've never heard of a sumacom hack, but what's that got to do with Henning?"

"Two things, Inspector" replied Charlie. "First. Hennin' was an OASIS astronomer and computer engineer." Again, after looking at his notes, he recited, "On Monday, October eleventh, 2110, Hennin' went down to Charlene Anchor to look for answers. While pokin' around the big capacitor banks at the base of the bridge, he was electrocuted. He was by himself. No one saw it happen. Best explanation was a power surge got him. No one knows why or how."

"Interesting," said Skalay. "Is there more?"

"Yup." Again, turning to his notes, he said, "On Sunday, October eighteenth, Moxon met with FBI and CIA agents at the PT office to discuss these events. I contacted the office. They told me they discussed all this with Moxon but couldn't make anythin' of it. They gave me a copy of Hennin's list of suspected sabotage. Hennin had given the list to Moxon shortly before Hennin died and Moxon gave a copy to the Feds. Here it is," he said, handing it to Skalay. "After meetin' with the Feds, Moxon came by our offices and picked up Hennin's death certificate, which listed death as accidental electrocution. After the meetin', Moxon went to the PT Arrivals Depot and picked up Keator, who had just arrived from Luna, and escorted her back to Clarke Station. For her first assignment, Moxon assigned Keator to takeover Hennin's work portfolio, including looking for sabotage."

"Fine. This is all interesting, but how is it relevant?"

"Just wait, Inspector. Roc's got the tie-in."

"Good. Are we ready for Roc?"

"Nope. You asked me to record the funeral receivin' line. I also got a copy of the video made for Moxon's brother and Keator's parents. After watchin' both videos, multiple times, it looked to me like Lowell Director Best passed messages by handshakes. For a big man, he has small hands, looked like he palmed a paper message to the Chinese, Brazilian, and Russian Consuls as well as the

President of the Stock Exchange and the Gaming Commissioner."

"What? Well, I'll be damned," Skalay said. I guess I was right after all. Best is as two-faced as Iapetus!"

"Check. Passin' notes right under our noses," added Charlie. "They're sly, but unmistakable to the trained eye."

"Jee-zus!" Skalay swore again. "This case gets stranger and stranger." I wonder what Best is up to?"

"One thing more," Charlie said. "You asked me to go back to Kubrick Mons and make a second search for Moxon's perscom. You also asked me to visit Hennin's death scene and check out the Brown District hangar. If it's okay with you, I thought I would do that tomorrow. Roc's offered to join me."

"Okay. Sounds good."

"I'd like to go along to Charon," Kirk said.

"Good idea, Kirk," Skalay said. "I appreciate having someone with your seniority join them. I can't go. I'm going to the joint FBI-CIA PT office to discuss the case with them. All right, Roc, now you're up."

With a crisp "Yes Sir," Roc replied, "I've got mostly dead ends, but I do have some interesting news."

"All right. Run through the bad news and then tell me the good stuff."

"Yes, Sir. I had no luck hacking the Lowell Computers. I poked around the Station during the funeral, but their security protocols and practices were too tight. No untended terminals. I also checked the PT docks for clues to the missing cargo. Found nothing. I've not pried into the Clarke Station botweb."

"Fine. How about the good news?"

"Yes, Sir," said Roc. "Even though the cold ruined Keator's perscom, I was still able to extract her audio diary from her device. The diary included a complete file of her meetings with Moxon, beginning with the first meeting on October 19, 2110, when he picked her up after she arrived at Port Tombaugh. The Keator file appears complete. It includes summaries of each meeting she had with Moxon. And, the files continue to the day she died."

"And—" interjected Skalay

Checking his notes, Roc continued. "According to her, Moxon was convinced that someone was sabotaging Charon and had killed Henning. Moxon had her continue the list that Henning started, but told her not to investigate the incidents. Instead, he would have the FBI investigate."

"And did they?" asked Skalay.

"No, Sir," replied Roc. "Nothing happened until the transport blowout."

"Good work, guys. Talos, add Mystery number six to our list and title it Henning's death and Charon Sabotage. Well, is that all?"

"No Sir," said Roc, "there's more."

"All right. Tell me"

"When Keator picked up Henning's work, she found two other mysteries she inherited from Henning." Roc paused for a moment while he looked at his notes.

Impatient, Skalay asked, "Which were?"

"I'll tell you, Sir," Roc said, "but they don't make a lot of sense. The first one could be a clue to the entire mess, but Moxon and Keator couldn't figure it out. It seems Henning found some strange patterns in the exchange of securities between the Chicago stock exchange and the Pluto-Charon US Territory stock exchange. Henning also found suspicious betting patterns in the Las Vegas and Port Tombaugh Off-Track Betting parlors. For both the stock exchanges and the OTBs, it appeared that someone knew what was going to happen before the exchanges and the OTBs did. Not much of a lead time, about six hours at best. Still, Henning was convinced someone was buying and selling stocks, knowing what the stock markets were going to do. Henning also thought someone was betting on sports, knowing the results of games before they'd even been played. If Henning was correct, the take was modest enough to not attract attention, but repeated often enough to roll up some big figures. Keator checked out Henning's data and agreed with his conclusions, but she also couldn't figure it out."

"Hmm. Interesting," said Skalay. "Particularly given the attendance at the funeral. But it doesn't make much sense. What else?"

"The other thing that attracted her attention was this, but I don't understand it, either." Shaking his head, Roc said, "It's, uh, pretty weird."

"Now you've made me curious. What've you got?"

"Well, Sir, about two years ago, the Lowell detected a faint signal." Looking down at his notes, he read, "The signal came from the direction of the constellation Sagittarius. The exact location was right ascension seventeen hours, forty-one minutes; declination, minus twenty-seven degrees, forty-eight minutes. That placed it near the center of the Milky Way. The exact source was unknown. It's a crowded neighborhood. Best guess is that it came from either the periphery of the Sagittarius Dwarf Galaxy or the Sagittarius Star Stream, placing it about sixty-five thousand light years away. On the other hand, the signal may not be that old. It could be from a foreground source."

"I hear you. So what?"

"The signal consisted of pulses. The pulses counted the first thirteen prime numbers. Then they end in noise or chatter. The signal is weak, intermittent, distorted by distance, and many times incomplete. But the Lowell's been listening to it for two years now and it seems to be real. They can't come up with a natural explanation. Because of all of the false alarms over the years, they've not made a public announcement. But they're convinced this is the real deal and they're getting close to a press release."

"Roc," Skalay began. "There're four big scientific myths that just don't exist: faster-than-light travel, time travel, self-aware computers, and little green men. I know you're a bit of the romantic, but let's skip the fantasy and stick with the real stuff."

"All right, Sir," Roc replied, feeling a little chagrined by what he considered unwarranted criticism. "I'm just telling you she thought it was important."

"On second thought," Skalay said. "I'm canceling the Charon expedition. OASIS and Best are hiding something, and I don't want to tip our hand. Instead I think we should stake out the three consuls. That keeps us on our own turf. Kirk, will you make the assignments and run the operation while I visit the Feds? Questions? No? Let's get to work!"

13 THE CRUISE OF *ODYSSEUS*

Director Lee was right, reflected John while preparing for dinner and the evening Carnival Party. *This flight to Pluto has been the most relaxing time I've had since I joined the Fifth. I must be more than two billion klicks from all my enemies. Like Selena said, no one can get me here! I'm safe!* For the first time in a long time, John felt free of the stress and dangers of the Interrobang Badge.

Thinking about the past nine days prompted memories of that glorious cruise to Jamaica he had taken with Sarah. That was another time when he had felt safe from his enemies. The 5th had sent them undercover, pretending to be newlyweds on their honeymoon as they sailed from New Orleans to Montego Bay. But after six months of working together, he was no longer pretending. He had fallen in love with her—the first and only time he had truly fallen in love.

He paused for a moment, letting the memories of Sarah and the cruise flood his consciousness. He remembered standing with her at sunset, on the stern of the *Nina Simone*, as the sun sank into the Caribbean with the rarely seen green flash. In that magical solar moment, he told Sarah how much he truly loved her; if she would marry him, he would leave the 5th. She told him she loved him, too. She would be his wife, but only after they had finished their

This is the summary of the Moxon and Keator Mysteries as dictated by Inspector Skalay and recorded and updated on the Homicide Squad screen by sumacom Talos:

MOXON AND KEATOR MYSTERIES:

1. Who are Moxon, Keator,and OASIS?

    Answer: CIA; keeping CIA surveillance secret

    What were they doing on Kubrick Mons?

    Answer: Probably to send a message.

    To Whom?

    Why from Kubrick Mons?

2. What was the message encrypted by the one-time pad?

3. Who hacked the Transport ERC and why did they kill Moxon and Keator?

4. What was the transport cargo?

    Who stole the cargo?

    Who stole Moxon's perscom and the one-time-pad?

5. Cover-up:

    Why did Best first try to find Moxon's and Keator's killers and then change course and try to stop the investigation when the NTSB declared mechanical malfunction and operator error?

    Why did the FBI send an agent from KC?

6. Henning's death and Charon Sabotage

    Who is responsible for serial sabotage on Charon?

    Who killed Henning?

    Who is manipulating the OTB and stock exchange?

assignment to end the human trafficking and gun-smuggling ring that had sent them to Jamaica. It was like Sarah to place duty first.

Abruptly, like wolves stampeding caribou, visions of Kalfu and the Caine Toads crashed his internal reverie, chasing away the beautiful memories. Despite a separation eight weeks and two billion klicks, John's mind filled with images of that dreadful afternoon in Cockpit County. He saw Kalfu slowly cutting off Sarah's head and heard her terrified pleas for mercy, begging John to save her and then falling silent as Kalfu completed the dirty deed. Seared into his memory, John relived Kalfu holding up Sarah's head for him to see, like the executioner Sanson did when he held up the head of Marie Antoinette for the blood-thirsty mob.

"Oh, God!" John involuntarily cried out as he recalled Kalfu squirming in his hands, while he did unto Kalfu as Kalfu did unto Sarah.

It felt so good to kill Kalfu!

Oh God! I should never have allowed myself to get so close to a woman, he thought. *My love killed her. And now she's gone!* Guilt and grief overwhelmed him.

But it still felt so good to kill Kalfu!

He sat down. He cried. *What's wrong with me? What've I become?*

In answer, he heard the voice in his mind of his 5th FD therapist, Dr. Elneth, who had coached John through his mourning while he recovered in Kansas City. *John, you've lost the woman you loved. You lost her under the most tragic of circumstances. Of course, you're going to mourn. That's not a sign of weakness, it's a sign of strength. Mourn her. And when you're ready, John, turn to positive thoughts. Think about the things only you can do, the things that will give meaning to her life and your life. The things that caused her to fall in love with you, John the lover, Dakar the man, Steel the warrior.*

What Dr. Elneth didn't say, what no therapist really could say—certainly no therapist for a trained killer could say—but what John would like said anyway, was, *"Don't be afraid of revenge. It wasn't right to behead Kalfu, but it was understandable. You're forgiven."*

Am I? he asked himself. *Am I really forgiven?* This time there were no answers.

After a while he set aside his despair by forcing himself to remember Dr. Elneth's advice for combating such dark thoughts: *As long as Kalfu can cause me pain and stop me from completing my work, he has won. I'll not let him win. For the memory of Sarah, I will overcome this!*

But it is not so easy to escape the blues. Try as he might, the good thoughts didn't last. Instead, Kalfu and Sarah crawled back into his consciousness, bringing with them misery and gloom and pulling him down with their burden of a heavy heart to be carried by his weary soul.

But this time, unlike other times, he found solace in the company of others.

I'm traveling with two companions who've become my friends. Despite the rocky beginning, Sumate and Selena are the first real friends I've made in a long time.

With these conflicting moods weighing him down, he went to dinner and the Carnival Party.

† † †

After dinner, as they waited for the party to begin, Selena turned to John and teasingly asked him, "John, do you know the date?"

"Sure. Tuesday, March second—Shrove Tuesday. Mardi Gras."

"Do you know what happens five days from now?"

"Ah. I don't know. Is it Passover?" said John.

"No. Silly!" She said, giving John a playful push. "Passover isn't until April, same as Easter."

"It's Flip-Over!" she and Sumate sang out together.

"Flip-Over? I've heard you mention that before, but I'm not sure what it means. It has something to do with the spaceship, doesn't it?"

"It sure does," said Sumate. "Flip-Over marks the half-way point of our flight. It's also the time when we're going the fastest, nearly two percent of the speed of light—although you'd never know it if you looked outside. Outside it looks like we're dead still in space.

"So?"

"So," said Sumate, "until Flip-Over we've been constantly accelerating. After Flip-Over we begin decelerating for the rest of the trip to Port Tombaugh."

"John," Selena started to explain. "I'm sure you know that the *Odysseus* is a Ram Augmented Interplanetary Rocket-powered spaceship—we call it RAIR for short. RAIR ships are shaped like a hollow cylinder with the rocket engines in the rear. In front of the ship is a large thick cone. It looks like a funnel, with the large end facing forward and the narrow end attached to the front of the ship. A powerful electromagnetic field lines the interior of the cone and extends the cone a kilometer or more in front of the ship. 'Stros call the cone and the electromagnetic field 'the scoop.' The scoop clears the path in front of the ship by collecting and compresses all the gas, dust, and debris in front of us. It then feeds the material through the center of the ship to the rear rocket engines to use for both fuel and reaction mass to help propel the ship's forward motion."

"Okay. I'm following you."

"At Flip-Over, the ship turns around, so that the engines face forward and slow the ship down," Selena said. "The captain flips the ship over by first turning off the engines. That stops acceleration and we coast. While we coast, the ship and everything in it is weightless."

"Okay," said John. "What happens next?"

"Next," Selena said, "the captain detaches the scoop and flips it over, so that the broad end faces backward and the narrow end faces forward. The captain then flips the ship over and backs the ship into broad end, so that the broad end covers the ship and the rocket engine nozzles fit into the narrow end. After securing the ship to the flipped scoop, the captain then flips the electromagnetic field from the interior to the exterior of the scoop. After that, the captain turns on the rocket engines, and the ship begins to decelerate at a speed that again simulates one full Earth gravity. The whole maneuver takes about an hour."

"The flipped scoop and electromagnetic field now act like a heat shield on the early space capsules," added Sumate. "As debris hits the shield, the strikes help to slow down the ship."

"That's why," said Selena, "the 'Stros call the flipped scoop 'the brakes.' The brakes help to slow us down. But, more importantly," she added, "the brakes deflect debris away from the ship. If we struck a pebble the size of pea at two percent the speed of light, we'd all be dead in a flash."

"Whoa!" said John. "Turning dust into fuel on the upside and into brakes on the downside is a pretty neat trick."

"Yah. 'Whoa' is right," agreed Selena. "This is a big deal. It took nearly ten years for the first space probe to go to Pluto. It's going to take us a little less than four weeks. Here, I'll show you," turning on the table screen, she pointed to the blinking yellow caret halfway between the orbits of Saturn and Uranus. "See, here we are. And," pointing to a bright green caret between the orbits of Saturn and Jupiter, "here's our sister ship *Hermes* on her return trip from Port Tombaugh."

"That's just incredible."

"You bet," said Sumate. "RAIR ships are the fastest human transportation ever built. They made rapid colonization of the solar system possible—kind of like the steam locomotive closing the American Wild West sixty years after Lewis and Clarke."

"I had no idea."

Selena then added, "What's important is that we will be weightless during Flip-Over. To minimize passenger inconvenience the captain has scheduled the transition for when the passengers are asleep, between one and two o'clock on March sixth. I've talked to Captain Rakis. She'll reserve the gym for us during Flip-Over, so you can get some noG training."

"Hey, that's great Selena! Thank you!"

14 FLIP-OVER

A bell rang, followed by a woman's gentle voice over the PA system, "Fifteen minutes to Flip-Over. All passengers must be secured in their quarters. Crew, please take your stations."

Although Captain Rakis had promised the team they would be the only ones using the gym during Flip-Over, to Dakar's surprise, a few minutes after the warning bell, one of the passengers, the Brazilian, stepped into the gym. Dakar had spotted the Brazilian before. He was hard to miss, being the only other passenger with a skin color like Dakar's—although, to Dakar's practiced eye, the Brazilian was a few shades lighter. They had not spoken during the trip. Dakar considered saying something about the gym being reserved but decided against it.

I guess he didn't get the message. Dakar thought, while the Brazilian took off his robe, and started working the resistance machine behind Dakar.

Oh well, he won't bother us. Strange. It's almost time for Flip-Over. Sumate and Selena should be here by now. Puzzled by their tardiness, he resumed his warm-up by punching the double-ended boxing bag with his lightweight exercise gloves.

Just then he heard a muffled boom, followed by a slight shudder in the floor.

Huh? That sounded like an explosion!

HOOOOOOONK! A klaxon sounded, followed by THUNK, THUNK, THUNK, as all the ship's hatches, including the gym door, closed and locked.

What the hell?

A male voice sounded, loud and commanding, "This is not a drill! Emergency response team to passenger level ten, room seven. All passengers remain in your rooms. Flip-Over will occur, as scheduled, in two minutes and counting." HOOOOOOONK!

Startled by the unexpected, Dakar stopped and looked around. He caught a whiff of an acrid odor, like smoldering plastic. A thin wisp of black smoke drifted into the room from one of the sidewall ventilation ducts. Nothing else seemed amiss. The Brazilian seemed unconcerned. Instincts on alert, but not having anything better to do, Dakar turned his back to the Brazilian, secured his feet in the floor stirrups, and resumed punching the double ended boxing bag.

HOOOOOOONK! The klaxon sounded again. The male voice repeated, still loud and commanding: "This is not a drill! Emergency response team to passenger level ten, room seven. All passengers remain in your rooms. Flip-Over will occur as scheduled, on my mark in ten, nine, eight . . . three, two, one. Flip!" HOOOOOOONK!

For the first time in his life, Dakar experienced weightlessness. If he hadn't had his feet secured, his punches would have pushed him into the center of the gym.

Momentarily transfixed by the novelty of weightlessness, he paused.

"KALFU!"

What?

"KALFU!"

Turning toward the sound, he caught sight of the Brazilian, flying through the air, just as the Brazilian's outstretched left arm, holding a star-spike, stabbed down into Dakar's unprotected right subclavian fossa. Startled by the vicious attack, Dakar stood in the floor stirrups as momentum carried the assailant past him, like a swimmer passing a buoy. Instantly Dakar felt a sharp pain in his shoulder and a warm, liquid feeling creeping into his right chest. Breathless from the chest wound, feeling as if he had the wind knocked out of him, he thought he had been shot, just like when the Caine Toads shot him in the chest in Jamaica.

Kalfu and the Caine Toads!

As he started to lose strength and consciousness, he felt anger rise up within him, replacing his increasing weakness with surging rage. Acting on training and instinct, his mindset abruptly switched from Dakar, the space tourist, to Steel, the covert warrior.

He turned on the burr hanging at his waist, clipped it to his belt buckle, and flung it to his left, letting it pull out the nearly invisible dragline from his waist reel.

The Brazilian hit the opposite end of the gym. With the grace of a racing swimmer in a pool, the fiend flipped and pushed against the wall, sending him speeding back to Steel for the killing strike, while again screaming "KALFU! KALFU!"

Increasingly short of breath and faint, Steel crossed his arms in front of his chest, turned, dodged to his right, and ducked as the assailant struck at him again with the spike. The spike ripped across Steel's crossed arms and tunic, but the nano-silk armor blocked the searing star-spike from penetrating his left chest and killing him. Instead, the missed blow threw the Brazilian off balance and he began to tumble uncontrollably. As he passed Steel, the fiend's body snagged Steel's dragline. Jerked by the hurtling foe, the burr at the end of the dragline sprang forward and swung around the tumbling Brazilian, wrapping the nano-silk dragline around the fiend like a bad cast wrapping fishing line around a tree limb.

He banged against the gym wall. Grabbing the resistance machine rail to steady himself, the Brazilian again began screaming "Kalfu! Kalfu!" and launched himself once more through the air like a falcon diving onto a pigeon.

"Kalfu! Kalfu!" Every time Steel heard the name, he felt a surge of power as images of the dying Sarah filled his mind.

Behind the flying foe trailed the burr, pulled by the dragline now tangled around him.

Despite the chest pain and shortness of breath, a wicked smile turned up the corner of Steel's lips. *Now is the time for the prey to become the predator!*

With feet secured in the stirrups and fading strength and consciousness countered by rising fury, Steel pulled on the dragline as hard as he could, speeding up the Brazilian's flight, causing the thug to once again tumble uncontrollably. This time the Brazilian had no chance to strike as he whizzed by Steel and again crashed into the gym wall, hitting his head against a weight rack with a solid thud.

Stunned by the blow, the Brazilian drifted back into the center of the gym.

Now I've got you, you devil!

Pulling on the dragline, Steel reeled the goon toward him like a deep-sea fisherman reeling in a great white shark. Arms floundering and legs entangled by the dragline, fear began to grip the reviving Brazilian. As his brown face colored to a dark maroon, he spat a stream of curses in the hope that oaths alone could win the fight.

Ducking the Brazilian's flailing arms and spike, Steel grabbed his assailant and first pulled him into a lateral key lock. Isolating the Brazilian's right arm, with a loud crack, Steel broke the assassin's arm. Shocked by the pain, the would-be killer let go of the star-spike. With a kick Steel spun his attacker in the zero gravity like a top, wrapping more and more of the nano-silk dragline around and around the revolving assailant, like a spider entombing a moth.

Now you're going to die!

As the Brazilian struggled against his silk bonds, Steel used his last remaining strength to gain a chokehold by wrapping his right arm around the Brazilian's neck. Grabbing the metal trim from his left sleeve, Steel pulled the garrote out of his tunic and wrapped it around his assailant's neck. Grasping both ends of the garrote, he pulled tighter and tighter.

As he strangled the struggling assassin, the memory of cutting-off Kalfu's head filled Steel's mind. The memory played over and over again, like repetitions of a nightmare that occur just before awakening.

But Steel was not awakening. He was falling into oblivion, all the while thinking, *it feels so good to kill Kalfu!*

"He's dying!" yelled Selena after she and Sumate broke into the gym and found the two bodies.

15 NATIONAL WAR MEMORIAL

At 07:45 CST on Monday, March 7, about an hour past sunrise, a limbot pulled out of the KC morning rush hour traffic on West Pershing Road, and entered the North Plaza of the National War Memorial.

Everyone agreed it was a fine early spring morning, although the calendar and the groundhogs said there were still two weeks left of winter. But the winter ice and snow had melted, leaving behind a carpet of moist, pungent compost covering the rich Midwestern earth. The snowdrops had peaked, the crocuses had begun to lift their heads to the distant sun, and now the green stems of the daffodils had poked out of the dark ground, promising there would soon be spring blossoms.

A fine day for visiting the War Memorial!

The limbot parked along one of the walkways by the memorial. An older woman, built like a refrigerator and who, despite her apparent age, still had a full head of red hair, stepped out of the limbot, followed by a middle-aged gentleman who walked a few steps behind her. The gentleman had an erect bearing and obvious physical strength, suggesting a military history—probably her bodyguard.

They didn't wander along the myriad paths. They appeared to know where they were going, but they walked slowly, obviously enjoying the morning air as they threaded the pathways through the glass brick walls of the 3-Hour War Memorial.

After a few minutes, the woman stopped in front of one particular brick, in the Washington Wall section, on the south side of the Plaza, facing the World War I Memorial. She stood there for a few minutes as her guard stood behind her.

BOOM!

The shockwave from the powerful detonation ripped apart the couple, as well as the nearby glass brick wall, trees, and foliage, while excavating a five-meter-wide crater. The heat wave from the explosion incinerated all of the small fragments, leaving only dust, cinders, metal shards, and a few scraps of burnt bone.

War Memorial Bomb Kills Two CIA Employees

By Rik Ruelled

March 7, 2111 12:57; Late Edition: page 1

A powerful bomb exploded this morning in the North Plaza of the National War Memorial, killing two pedestrians, a man and a woman, both employed by the CIA. No one has claimed responsibility for the bombing.

Surveillance cameras captured the detonation, which appeared to be remote controlled. The blast occurred during rush hour traffic, shortly before 8 am, bringing downtown Kansas City traffic to a standstill that lasted six hours. The bomb blew open a fifteen-foot wide crater next to the Washington Wall on the south side of the 3-Hour War Memorial. The explosion shattered the windows of vehicles parked along Kessler Road and Main Street and destroyed the north façade of the Liberty Memorial.

Police found the victims' vehicle nearby. The names have been withheld pending notification of next-of-kin. Unnamed sources within the CIA have told the Kansas City Star that one of the victims was a high-ranking CIA official. The CIA and the FBI have opened a joint investigation into the bombing.

FBI Agent Dies on the USSS *Odysseus*

By Rik Ruelled

March 7, 2111 12:57; Late Edition: page 12

The FBI has reported that a Kansas City FBI agent on board the USSS *Odysseus*, died unexpectantly at 7 pm CST March 5 (1:00 UTC on March 6) while exercising in the spaceship gym. The agent had been detailed to Port Tombaugh, Pluto, to investigate the Valentine's Day deaths of two astronomers on Pluto's moon, Charon. The name of the agent has been withheld, pending notification of relatives. The cause of death is under investigation.

CIA Identifies the Two Employees Killed by the National War Memorial Bombing

By Rik Ruelled

March 8, 2111 10:07; Morning Edition: page 1

The CIA announced that yesterday's bombing of the National War Memorial killed Dr. Emma Lee (99) and Sergeant Frank Thomas (55).

Dr. Lee's CIA duties are classified. She received a Ph.D. in political science from the former Georgetown University. Dr. Lee was one of the few remaining CIA employees who survived the 3-Hour War, which claimed the lives of her husband and daughter. A recipient of the CIA Intelligence Star, she continued to work for the agency for the rest of her life, amounting to 73 years of service. When the bomb exploded, she was standing by the memorial for her daughter and husband. She had no immediate relatives.

Sergeant Thomas served for 25 years in the Marines and 12 years in the CIA. He received the Navy Cross for heroism during the 2092 South China Sea Terrors. He is survived by his wife, Maria, and two sons.

Executive CIA Director General Ora Barrun said last night, "The CIA family has lost two of our greatest heroes. Dr. Lee and Sergeant Thomas served their country with distinction and self-sacrifice. We will remember them with stars on the CIA Memorial Wall. We will find who killed them. When we do, we will punish them to the full extent of the law."

FBI identifies agent killed on the USSS *Odysseus*

By Rik Ruelled
March 8, 2111 10:37; Morning Edition: page 2

The FBI announced an unidentified assailant killed agent Colonel John Dakar (44), while the agent was traveling on the USSS *Odysseus* to Port Tombaugh, Pluto. The FBI assigned Colonel Dakar to investigate the February 14 deaths of two astronomers on Pluto's moon, Charon. The killer is in custody, but has not yet been identified.

17 HUNTING SNAKES

Promptly at 11:00 CST, on the morning of Monday, March 7, a select group of six senior CIA operatives, gathered in the Dead Room of the 5th FD to meet with the Chief of Staff, Mr. Dawson, and the Deputy Director, Colonel Boot, now the Acting Director in place of the deceased Director Lee. The Assistant to the 5th Director, Max Thaler, also attended the meeting to keep the minutes and guard the door.

Normally, agents shared some teasing and banter when they gathered together like this, but not this time. The assassinations of Director Lee and Agent Dakar weighed heavily on everyone. The abrupt calling of this meeting, with Mr. Thaler's warning to keep the meeting secret and attend without fail, placed everyone on edge, expecting more bad news. They would not be disappointed.

"Sorry to call you together like this," began Acting Director Colonel Boot. "I regret using the Dead Room, but as you'll see, we've got a big problem, and this is the most secure location. I've chosen you because I can count on your loyalty and silence. Under all circumstances—and I mean all circumstances—this meeting must remain top-secret. You must not reveal the details of this meeting to anyone, at any time, even if a CIA superior commands you to do so. If that happens, you send that person to me. Also, from this point on, we will only address each other by our codenames. Do you all understand?"

For a few moments, quiet enveloped the room, followed by a soft chorus of assents.

"The Director's Assistant will keep the minutes. The minutes protect you by documenting my instructions, that I'm authorized to give you these instructions, and my instructions are legal under the laws of the US government. Does anyone have a problem with this? If so, speak up now. Your withdrawal from this group will not affect you in any way."

Silence greeted this announcement.

"Okay," continued the Acting Director. "I know you have questions, but I can't answer them at this time. As you all know, in separate attacks over the past thirty-six hours, unknown assassins killed both Director Lee and agent Steel. What you don't know is we have reason to believe a CIA snake arranged for these assassinations."

As gasps filled the room, the Acting Director yelled "Quiet. No one is to speak until I say so." He then switched on the Dead Room video screen, showing the group the well-known face of CIA Executive Director General Ora Barrun. Raising his hand for silence, the Acting Director said "We suspect this person is the snake, but you will not refer to him by name or title. I have assigned the codename Cobra to this person, whom we suspect arranged for the assassinations. I have assigned the codename Mongoose to the operation to catch the people responsible for killing the Director and Steel."

After a moment for all the news to register, he continued, "For obvious reasons, I must be certain about the identity of the assassins before taking action. I also have to quickly find the traitors and arrest or dispatch them before they do more damage.

With those words, the four senior operatives without an Interrobang Badge turned toward the only two senior operatives in the room who had a Badge: Torch and Block. Torch had just completed her convalescent leave, and Block had just returned from an overseas assignment.

The Acting Director continued with the briefing, "I'm dividing you into two teams, Sigma and Delta. Torch will lead Sigma, and Block will lead Delta. Both team leaders will report to me. If I'm not available, the Chief of Staff, Colonel Peter Dawson—codename Rod—is second in command. Right, Rod?"

"Yes, Sir."

"Okay," the Acting Director Colonel Boot said, turning to Torch. "Your team Sigma will examine the following two problems: First, how did a US government issue, Storms Armament star-spike, serial number y-q-3-5-j-w, happen to be on the USSS *Odysseus*, which departed from the Buzz Aldrin Space Station on Monday, February twenty-second? To find the answer, you'll begin with our Armory records, including the records of the six star-spikes that I issued to Steel before he left. If you don't find the answer in our Armory, then you'll examine the KC CIA and FBI records; if you don't find the answer there, get hold of the Storms Office and have them help you chase it down. We must find the source of this weapon. I expect a report by the close of business today."

"Yes Sir," Torch replied.

Continuing with his instructions, the Acting Director said, "Next, I want Sigma to open a channel with the FBI and find out all you can about the bomb that killed Brick. We have to determine what kind of bomb it was, how it was detonated, where it came from, who built it, and who placed it. I expect the FBI will be taking the lead on this, but I want us to be involved, and I want to know what the FBI knows as soon as they know it. I also expect a report by the close of business today. Am I clear?"

"Yes Sir," Torch again replied.

Switching his attention to Block, the Acting Director continued, "Block, I want your team Delta to examine the next problem, which also has two parts. First, I want your team to find and interview every person who knew Steel had been given orders to board the *Odysseus*. To get you going, I've drafted a list of people who I know had this information. You'll begin your interviews immediately after this meeting by interviewing me, Rod, and Mr. Thaler. After doing that, you'll interview the rest of the people on this list as well as any new names you should uncover. We must determine who these people told about Steel's assignment. Also, I need for each of the suspects on this list a detailed record of their activities from February seventeenth to February twenty-first, including all electronic communications. Only after you complete these preliminary interviews will you interview our leading suspect, Cobra. I also expect a report by the close of business today. Do you understand?"

"Yes Sir" Block replied.

After a pause to look at his notes, the Acting Director continued, "Okay. The second task for your team is this: as quickly as you can do it, find out everything you can about a Brazilian by the name of Castor Valerio. Verify that he boarded the *Odysseus*. If he didn't, find out who boarded under his name. We have to know who paid for Valerio's ticket and when it was purchased. We also need to know if there's a connection between Valerio and the CIA or the FBI, as well as with the gun-running and human trafficking ring known as the Caine Toads—that's spelled C-A-I-N-E. When you investigate the Caine Toads, find out what you can about an individual named "Kalfu"—that's K-A-L-F-U. Okay? Do you have any questions? Can you get this done today?"

Block again replied, "Yes Sir, we can do it" .

The Acting Director addressed both teams, "Okay, people. Report all progress to me and do not take any action, as long as you can avoid it, before clearing it with me. I want to arrest and prosecute the traitors. But if that's not possible, I've got Interrobang authority and I'm prepared to use it. In fact, because of the politics in this situation, I prefer to complete the assignment myself and not leave it to you. Do you all understand?"

Seeing a round of head nodding, the Acting Director continued, "Good. Get going. You've got a lot to do before you go home tonight. Beginning tomorrow, we will meet here at nine o'clock every morning until this thing is resolved. Any questions?"

Hearing none, he went on, "Before we break, I have one last thing to say. As you know, tomorrow is International

Women's Day. It's tragic that on the day dedicated to celebrating the women who have made this nation, and all nations, strong, we should have to investigate the murder of one of the finest women to serve our country. Director Lee started working for the CIA three years before the Three-Hour War. Because of her assignment to Berlin, she survived the War, but her family did not. As one of the very few surviving CIA agents, she founded this Directorate and has led the fifth, with honor and determination, for seventy years. Even though her official codename was Brick, some of us called her the Gloved Fist because she had the power to defend our government against all enemies and the wisdom to use her power wisely. No one—and I repeat no one—in the history of the United States has done as much as Director Lee has done to preserve our country."

Pausing for a moment, he directed the group's attention to the picture window that overlooked the War Memorial, across the street from the Dead Room. From the vantage point of the twenty-third floor, the group could easily see the crater and the damaged wall where the bomb had killed Director Lee and Sergeant Thomas earlier that morning. Mourners had already tried to hide the evil site by scattering flowers over a makeshift shrine.

"The assassination of Director Lee, just outside our front doors, in full view of this window, was not just the murder of a CIA leader and national heroine, it was an attack on the CIA by a foe who knows no fear and has no respect for who we are and for what we stand. Such a powerful and contemptuous enemy is an unusually dangerous enemy. As you execute the assignments I've just given you, take great care. This may be the most difficult and dangerous assignment you'll receive as an agent of the Fifth FD. Now get to work and let's catch the SOB."

† † †

Seven-point-four billion kilometers away, at 17:00 on March 7, Inspector Scott Skalay called a similar emergency meeting, this one with the three members of the PT Homicide Squad: Kirk, Charlie, and Roc.

"Guys," Skalay said, "I called you together because we've got a big problem. Reports are just now coming in. You may have already heard the news. At one in the morning on March sixth, someone on the *Odysseus* killed the agent sent by the FBI to investigate the deaths of Moxon and Keator. That took real ba—um—cojo—um—"

"Chutzpah?" suggested Kirk.

"Yes, I mean chutzpah," said Skalay. "Thank you, Kirk. Here is some more astounding chutzpah. We've just learned that thirty-six hours after the *Odysseus* murder, someone bombed the War Memorial in downtown Kansas City. The bomb killed two CIA employees, one of them a Director."

"Okay, I'll bite," Charlie interrupted. "What's this got to do with us?"

"I don't know if all of these murders are related," Skalay answered. "But knowing that OASIS is a CIA operation, I bet they are. If so, we may be next. I've explained the situation to the Fort Resnik Commandant, General Sliffer. He'll take in your families for protective custody until we get this sorted out. The first thing I want you to do after this meeting, is to get your loved ones to Fort Resnik, pronto. We'll work in pairs; no solo work for the time being. As soon as your families are safe, I want you back here, in our Squad Offices. Police Commissioner Lord has agreed to post extra guards for our office suite. I'm breaking off our stakeout of the Consuls—"

"Sir!" interrupted Kirk. "The auction's Wednesday morning. We've worked hard to catch Best and the Consuls red-handed. We can't stop now!"

"You're right, Kirk," said Skalay. "As you say, the auction is critical. I think at this point that our remote surveillance will be strong enough for us to keep tabs on what happens tomorrow night without exposing ourselves. If we can get the goods on Best and his accomplices, then Commissioner Lord has also promised to give us additional cops to make the arrests. I want you to take charge of the electronic surveillance. Can you do that?"

"Yes, Sir!" Kirk said, obviously pleased by the vote of confidence and the opportunity to shine.

"All right, folks. So, let's get to it. This is the real deal!"

18 HAUNTED BY KALFU'S GHOST

A distant voice called him, *"John, John, John."*

He stirred for a moment. *What was that?* Nothing. Ignoring it, he fell back into oblivion.

"John, John, John!"

The voice roused him, pulled him back. He still tried to ignore it.

"John, John, John."

That voice again. Louder, more persistent. A woman's voice. Sarah!

Medical monitors erupted with a cacophony of beeps.

"Shit, Sumate! What's happening? What's wrong?" Selena demanded.

"Don't know! He just shot off all the alarms. Like he suddenly woke up. Pulse up by forty. Respiration up to twenty-eight. Blood pressure leaped by thirty points. All of a sudden. Like he got a shot of adrenaline while you were calling him."

For the first time in nearly two days, John opened his eyes. Looking directly at Selena, he said, "Sarah! Sarah! I'm so sorry about Kalfu!" He started to cry. The tears rained from his eyes. "I'm so sorry! I'm so sorry!"

"John. I'm not Sarah. I'm Selena." *Didn't we have this conversation once before?* "It's all right! You're safe!"

"Huh? What? I thought you were Sarah! You look just like Sarah!"

"No! I'm Selena Vol—"

"Augh!" He turned away and pretended to go back to sleep, even though the tears continue to trickle down his face.

Without a word, Sumate pointed to the monitors, drawing Selena's attention to the bank of medical monitors that exposed John faking sleep. He was wide awake.

"John. I know you're awake. I'm Selena Volkova. Kes. Your partner. I'm here with Sumate Laoloo, Duke. You're in the medical ward on the spaceship *Odysseus*. We've been guarding you. The man who attacked you, Castor Valerio, is dead. You killed him. You're safe. We dock at Port Townsend in twelve days."

What a strange man! She thought. *Mortally wounded, he fought off an assassin while weightless! Brilliant! I've never seen anyone fight so well. I can't believe he killed Valerio! Even though John had noG combat training, he still fought like a warrior from the Belt . . . like a martial arts fighter in a VR movie. But John was wicked! Nuke it! He didn't have to kill Valerio, but he did. So, we can't question Valerio. And now John's crying like a child who's lost his mother! Who is this man?*

"John. You're not fooling me. I know from the medical monitors you're wide awake. You've got to tell us. Who is Sarah?"

That question sparked a response. He opened his eyes and again looked at Selena. "She was my fiancé."

Selena gasped, "Huh!"

"John, who's . . . er . . . Calfoo?" said Sumate, stumbling over the unfamiliar name. "We've got to know why you were attacked. Brick was also attacked. We've got to know what's going on so we can protect you and ourselves. John. Who is Calfoo?"

"Kalfu cut off Sarah's head. She pleaded for me to save her, but I couldn't. But I killed Kalfu." Raising his voice, he repeated, "I killed Kalfu!" Then yelling, "I cut off his head!"

Shocked by the repulsive barbarity and towering rage that John revealed inhabited his soul, both Selena and Sumate couldn't stop themselves from pulling away from John's sickbed.

Who is this guy? Wondered Selena. *A hero who beheads his enemies? How can such a seemingly nice guy be such a bloodthirsty monster?*

Stunned, for the next ten minutes they listened as John described that afternoon in Cockpit County, Jamaica, eight weeks ago when he battled Kalfu and the Caine Toads. Exhausted, John fell back into sleep, this time confirmed by the bank of medical monitors.

"Sumate. What do you know about the Caine Toads?"

"Well, um, I am no expert, but we studied them in training. They're a Caribbean crime organization. They've been around for a long time. Started in the late 1900s smuggling dope. With the collapse of the illegal drug markets, they switched to human trafficking and weapon smuggling. More recently, rumors had them smuggling antiques, art, exotic animals and plants for the off-world trade. Two months ago, the CIA sent out a field circular saying the CIA had finally shut them down. I guess that's what John is talking about. It sounds like the reported end of the Caine Toads might've been premature."

"I sure wish John hadn't killed Valerio. I don't know why he did it," Selena said. "He had Valerio all tied up. We needed him alive".

"John was dying," Sumate sharply replied. "John might've tied up Valerio, but Valerio nearly killed him. He had no way of knowing Valerio couldn't escape, kill both of us, and finish killing him. He had to kill Valerio while he could still do it. I'll tell anyone that, even the PRB, where this will probably end up."

"Well, I guess you're right," Selena said. "But—"

"If we'd gotten into that room sooner, maybe we could have captured Valerio before the attack. So, maybe we share some of the blame."

"All right, all right," Selena said. "I hear you. But, who's Calfoo?"

"Don't know—ask Penelope, the ship computer."

"Penelope. This is Selena Volkova. What do you know about Calfoo?"

With the same woman's voice that had announced the first Flip-Over warning, the ship computer politely answered, "Dr. Volkova, please spell that for me."

"I think it is spelled C-A-L-F-O-O, but I am not sure."

"There is nothing in my memory banks about C-A-L-F-O-O. But I do have an entry for K-A-L-F-U."

"All right. Give it to me!"

"Kalfu spelled with a K and a U, also known as Carrefour, is the Voodoo Moon God, Ruler of the Night, and patron God for those who practice black magic. Kalfu is the God of the Crossroads. He controls the evil forces of the spirit world."

"What!" exclaimed Sumate.

Selena once again gasped, "Huh!"

"Sumate. You're the Terra expert. What does a Voodoo god have to do with the Caine Toads? And what does any of this have to do with a spaceship halfway to Pluto?"

That question prompted an hour-long discussion between the two criminology experts while John slept in his medical bed. At the end of the discussion, Sumate and Selena sent coded messages to their Earth and Lunarian handlers. Afterwards, Selena remained on the medical ward, guarding John, while Sumate paid a visit to the ship's captain.

19 HAUNTED BY ESAU'S GHOST

Sitting there next to John while he slept, Selena started to muse about this strange man with the code name Steel.

With a sigh, she thought, *I guess I can't blame him for killing Kalfu. Can't imagine the horror of having my fiancé beheaded, in front of me, screaming for my help, and I can't stop it. Astounding that John escaped his bonds and got to Kalfu.*

With those thoughts, she imagined him like a whirling dervish, yanking out of his manacles, shooting Kalfu's bodyguard dead—even though the bodyguard shot John in the chest! And, at close range too! John leaping over the body, grabbing Kalfu, and beheading him while Kalfu struggled.

How could he do that? How could he behead Kalfu? How could he draw out the killing so that Kalfu would die slowly? What kind of a degenerate takes the time to slowly behead his enemy? Even if justified? Even if he's dying himself?

Those thoughts prompted another long sigh.

Sitting there, thinking about killing, her mind filled with unwanted memories of the people she had killed. Usually, she avoided these thoughts like poison, but like a child pulling on the hem of her mother's tunic, demanding to be recognized and heard, her memories would not be denied.

First up, her most recent killing demanded her immediate attention. *It has been, what, seven months?* She remembered his name, *Esau. Esau Baron. What a beautiful name—a Hebrew name and a noble English name.*

And she remembered his face, long and thin, pale skin like hers, blonde hair, big blue eyes.

Oh God, those eyes! Those electric blue eyes! I could fall in love with those eyes!

In her memory, she saw his left eye erupt in blood and gore, like a meteor striking the Moon. But the meteor was a bullet. Her bullet. She had shot Esau in the left eye. Mossad had assigned her to kill the LLCN terrorist before he could finish his job of bombing the dome that covered New Mecca. She killed Esau coldly, with precision.

Yes, even cruelly, she thought with another sigh.

She had used a .45 ACP with the light cartridge. Mossad provided their assassins the lightweight .45 ACP so that the underpowered bullet would have enough muzzle velocity to push the slug into the brain, but not enough for the slug to break through the cranial vault and exit—an important consideration in a pressurized environment. The underpowered bullets tended to cause a slow, although inevitable, death. And that was how Esau had died—slowly.

Yah, that's pretty cruel.

It had also been cruel to seduce Esau. She had not given herself to him—she had not given herself to anybody. But—

I wish I had. In another world, at another time, I would have. At first, it had been so much fun to flirt with him, to use my charms to attract him, to pull him to me, to win his trust.

And then it stopped being a game. She could feel herself falling for him. Mossad called him a terrorist, but she found him to be something else. A man. At times an attractive and loving man. A man who, at times, pulled at her heart like no one had before. But, at all times, a man who was an ideologue. A man committed to an idea, a terrible idea, but an idea nevertheless. A man who believed God wanted him to kill his enemies: the Muslims, the Muslims of the Lunar colony of New Mecca.

Mossad considered this a terrible idea, a dangerous idea that could lead to war between the LLCN and the LUIS; a Lunar war that could entrap the Lunar Jewish State of New Israel. So, Mossad sent her to stop Esau. Stop him by whatever means necessary.

Having learned through an undercover agent in the LLCN that Esau was seeking Information Technology help for a secret operation, Mossad sent her undercover to meet Esau, using her computer credentials to give her a backstory of an IT specialist with a career gone bad because of a gambling habit. Esau believed her story. In exchange, he told her a story about how Muslim men had abused Christian women and how he intended to stop it by snooping on them. He wanted her to help him build undetectable monitoring devices. She agreed.

Their mutual lies and deceptions progressed. Soon she discovered that Esau was as attracted to her as she was to him. When he started to seduce her, he never guessed she was the one seducing him.

It did not take long before she promised Esau he could have her, have her in every way he wanted, but only after he did his job. So, he invited her into his full confidence. Told her about the true intent of his device: it was to be a bomb. He didn't want her to build a bug, he wanted her to build an undetectable switch that would detonate the bomb at the chosen time. She agreed. She built the switch and gave it to him. That was when he asked her to be his lookout while he placed the device. Of course, she agreed to that, too.

That was the plan.

She remembered going with him to New Mecca. Following him to the rim of the city, where the dome had been set into the Lunar bedrock. As soon as he placed the bomb next to the dome, she shot him. She had to. Her switch wouldn't work. If he discovered her duplicity, he would've killed her. As memories of Esau flooded her thoughts, she remembered most of all his final moments, his mouth open, howling "Nooooo . . ." voicing his dying thoughts of surprise, shock, pain, and betrayal.

Yah, that was cruel. That was cold.

She started to cry, mourning the man she had come to love, the man she killed.

Victims. How many have I killed?

She wasn't certain exactly how many people she had killed for Mossad. Probably at least eleven. Like she had approached Esau, Mossad had her begin her assignments by using her IT credentials to join a terrorist group or criminal organization who needed her skills. Such groups were always looking for IT help willing to work on the sly. Once in, she would gain the trust of whomever it took to get her to her target.

In addition to Esau, she had killed three LLCN terrorists and two LUIS terrorists before they could carry out bombing, assassination, or kidnapping plans. She knew her killings had saved lives. But she also knew she had killed to save those lives.

In addition to the Lunar work, there had also been that ultra-orthodox Jewish colony on the Edge. The colony had started as a religious retreat for idealists, but over time it became a criminal enterprise for ideologues, hoary self-righteous men who trafficked in young girls for other dirty old men.

Mossad had sent her to the Edge to stop this Jewish disgrace, this curse on New Israel. It was a joint operation with the Lunar CIA. It was during this assignment that she first met Sumate; he had been her back-up. Once again, she used her computer and electronic skills to get hired by the colony. And just like before, she worked her way into the colony leadership, promising, but not quite delivering, sexual favors. When she won the trust of the colony leader, she killed him with her trademark bullet in the left eye. She also garroted one man and killed another by stabbing him in the chest. By slaying the colony leadership, she'd single-handedly rescued many girls from unspeakable horrors. But she'd also killed.

As terrible as they were, some of her victims were fathers and husbands. Despite their crimes, some of their children and wives still loved them, like she had loved Esau.

She had brought a book with her to read on the flight to Pluto. It was a hardbound copy, rather than electronic, because she didn't want Mossad to know what she was reading, in case they were monitoring her, which they probably were. The title was *Iron Age People in the Space Age*, by Jacky Day. Day's thesis intrigued her. He claimed that, despite all the technological advances of the twenty-second century, fundamentally people of today were no different than the people of the Iron Age—a barbaric age, filled with war, lawlessness, selfishness, and cruelty, but also the era of Moses, Confucius, Jesus, and other prophets and philosophers who preached a better, more ethical, future. A future, which despite all the efforts of many different religions and nations, had never been achieved.

Will we always be like this? Will we always be shooting and stabbing and raping and bombing each other as we spread across the solar system? Maybe the Caine Toads are the future. Maybe humans are a pestilence, spreading violence and cruelty through the heavens.

As her thoughts returned to John's bedside, something she had not considered before occurred to her.

When he escaped his bonds, killed Kalfu's bodyguard, and took a bullet to the chest, John was trying to rescue the woman he loved. Even though she was already dying, John still tried to give his life to save his fiancé's life by attacked Kalfu. He failed, but the offer of his life for his fiancé's endured.

With those thoughts, she felt an abrupt change in her regard for the man named John, the warrior who fought under the code name Steel. It felt like ice suddenly melting. She reached over and held John's hand.

20 SHIP OF THE LINE

Captain Leena Rakis met Agent Sumate Laoloo at the door and ushered him into her quarters, which were beautifully paneled in an oak veneer to resemble the captain's cabin of an eighteenth-century ship of the line. The room had a large table, desk, chairs, as well as a separate chamber for the bed. On the opposite side of the room from the entrance, six large video screens, framed to look like the stern windows of an eighteenth-century warship, showed the cosmos on all six sides of the ship.

"Agent Laoloo, how can I help you?" Captain Rakis asked after they sat down.

Rendered speechless by the astro-nautical splendor, Laoloo sat mute for a few moments as he took in the magnificent room.

"How is Colonel Dakar—I understand he's improving?"

"Sorry," Sumate said. "I wasn't expecting such a grand cabin. Yes. He's doing fine, thanks to you and your staff. The ship facilities and medical team are impressive. But that's not why I'm here."

"Fine. Go on."

"For the first time since the attack, he emerged from his coma earlier today and talked for about ten minutes. We learned a criminal enterprise known as the Caine Toads most likely tried to kill him. If so, we fear your ship could be in danger of being hijacked or even destroyed."

"My! That's quite a declaration. Why do you say that?"

"Well," began Agent Laoloo, "if the assassination fails, then Dakar is still alive and a threat to whoever wanted him dead in the first place, apparently the Caine Toads. So, they would still need to kill him—"

"And," asked Captain Rakis—

"If the assassination succeeded," continued Agent Laoloo, "then the Caine Toads, or someone aligned with them, would still need to either rescue or kill Dakar's assassin to hide his identity and silence him. Either way, the Toads have to—"

Finishing the sentence for him, the Captain said, "— hijack the ship and finish the mission before we dock at Port Tombaugh. Hmmm."

After some thought, she then added, "They might even decide to scuttle the ship and kill everyone on board just to cover their tracks."

"Yes. That also occurred to us. Has a RAIR ship ever been hijacked?"

"No. We're too fast. And too big. Pirates go for smaller and slower ships."

"This may be an exception. Apparently, your ship has been pulled into a high-stakes operation that involves the highest levels of the US government."

"How do you figure?"

"The day after Flip-Over, someone assassinated the number three person at the CIA. We've reason to believe the two assassinations are linked."

"Blast it!"

"If someone tries to hijack the ship, how could they do it?"

"Well, we've almost no maneuverability. We go from point A to point B as fast as we can. If pirates plan to attack us they'll have a rough idea of our position at any given time. Like all other spaceships, we've got a transponder, and we fly by a strict flight plan—that narrows the pirates' search. We also run on a bright plume, so all the pirates would have to do is get close enough to see us. On the other hand, finding us won't help them much because, for most of our journey, we're going far too fast for a pirate ship to catch us."

Pausing for a moment while she thought about it, she then added, "Probably the best time to hijack us would be to ambush us the day before we dock at Port Tombaugh, when we're going the slowest."

"I understand. Do you have any way to repel an attack?"

"Well, maybe. It depends on what we're facing. I've got naval combat experience and I've fought pirates—I served as the Warrant Officer on the USSS *Ironsides* before leaving the service to assume this command. My crew includes twenty-three former Marines. I've divided them into two squads and had them cross-trained to serve as the ship's police in case of an emergency. We've also got a small armory. And . . ." pausing for a moment while she thought, "that's about it."

"Great! That's more than Agent Volkova and I hoped for. We figured we'd have at least four things working for us to repel hijackers. The press reported Dakar died and the assassin survived. So, we expect the hijackers will be on a rescue mission. No one appears to know Volkova and I accompanied Dakar, which gives us an edge. It's unlikely the hijackers will have anticipated that you expected to be hijacked and planned for it. I didn't even know your crew included two squads of Marines led by yourself, a captain with combat experience. And, in addition to all that, we brought along weapons and you've got an armory. Yes. I think this could work. If you let us work with your crew and give us access to our weapons in your cargo hold, I think we can drive off the hijackers."

"Sounds like a plan, but what if they intend to just scuttle the ship?"

"We've thought about that too. It could still happen, especially if the hijack should fail. We bet the hijackers would prefer to rob you than scuttle you. Most likely the hijackers would want to avoid killing so many people. A crime that brazen would seal their doom. Besides, if they're daring enough to scuttle the ship before robbing it and rescuing Valerio, they probably would've sabotaged or destroyed it before now."

"Agent Laoloo, I regret sounding like a scold," Captain Rakis began, "and I realize the chances of destroying the ship might be low in your estimation, but my ship carries six hundred eighty-three passengers and has a crew of a hundred and twenty-seven. I can't accept your conjecture that destroying the ship is unlikely for a plan. I've got to protect my ship."

"Yes, Captain, Agent Volkova and I realize that. Does your ship include transports?"

"Sure. Four. Two in the bow hangar and two in the stern. Each transport can carry two hundred and eleven people. In case of an emergency, we also have two dozen life-rafts spotted around the ship. Each one can carry thirty-five people."

"Are you going to inform your passengers of the danger?"

"Yes. I have to keep them informed of something this important."

"Good. When you inform the passengers and crew, ask for volunteers with military training to help defend the ship. Let me work with your Marines and anyone who volunteers to create a defense force. Also, let me see what we've got for arms. I think we can work out a plan to ambush the ambushers. If we can use the transports for our counterattack, you can position the passengers next to the life rafts in case the Toads take the ship. But we've got to work fast. We've only got about eight or nine days to get ready for this."

"Okay. I'll ask for volunteers and call up my Marines. I'll have them meet with you right away."

"Great! Thank you, Captain Rakis."

21 SNAKE SNARE

Late in the evening of Monday, March 7, three people met in a CIA safe house, located in an elegant old Independence residential neighborhood.

The building stood on North Spring Street, about twenty klicks east of the Crown Center and just a few steps from the Harry S. Truman Library and Memorial.

Like the other neighborhood homes, the building dated from the early twentieth century. The two-story, brick four-square had a front porch stretching from side to side, supported by four-sided, wood-on-brick pillars. A front garden filled with daffodils, in the earliest stages of spring blooming, screened the foundation. An apron of well-tended lawn, split by a brick walkway, connected the front door to the quiet street. On the south side, a breezeway connected the one-bay, brick garage to the house. Mature hickory, dogwood, redbud, and maple trees, as well as forsythia filled with yellow blossoms, lilacs, and burning bushes, concealed the back and side yards from the rest of the neighborhood. A graceful home, notable only for the spacious grounds surrounding it.

Like the other homes on the west side of the street, the backyard abutted the Truman Library parking lot. Unlike the other homes, a stone walkway connected the parking lot to the back door of the safe house. On the south side, a narrow alley separated the broad side yard from the adjacent twenty-four-hour convenience store on busy Missouri Highway 24. Behind the line of trees and shrubbery, a paved driveway connected the alley to the south-facing garage.

Because the Library maintained the house, the neighbors presumed it had something to do with Library operations, probably a guest house for important visitors. Grateful for the well-kept building and handsome grounds that separated the neighborhood from the busy Library and highway businesses, the neighbors gave the building no further thought.

The 5th FD had chosen this residence for privacy and landscaped the grounds for easy, covert access and egress.

Only four people knew the 5th FD owned the house. On this unseasonably warm evening, as winter reluctantly relaxed its grip on Missouri, three of those in the know gathered in the safe house to discuss the assassination of Director Emma Lee and her bodyguard Frank Thomas. The current 5th FD leadership, Acting Director Colonel Louis Boot and Chief of Staff Peter Dawson, arrived separately by carbot. Dawson parked in the Truman lot, and Boot parked in the driveway. The third person, currently residing in the house, waited for them inside, while the fourth person slept in a second-floor bedroom.

As soon as Colonel Boot entered the building, all he could do was break protocol and all official decorum and wrap his big arms around Director Lee's big frame, while exclaiming, "Emma! You're looking fine! Just awesome! How's Frank?"

"Fine. He's upstairs asleep. We're taking six-hour watches, and his next watch starts at midnight."

"It's so good to see you!" Boot said, adding, "Jakobson was right to worry about an attack."

Entering the house on the heels of Boot, Chief of Staff Dawson added, "Emma! Thank God you're alive and well! You predicted where and when the attack would happen. Your avabots fooled everyone, including Louis and me."

"I have Frank to thank for that. Long ago he figured that my visits to the War Memorial were the weak point in my security, so he planned this ruse, arranged for duplicate avabots and a limbot to be available as decoys in case of imminent danger, and kept the whole operation top secret from everyone, including you guys. As soon as we learned of the attack on Steel, Frank activated his plan. It worked perfectly."

"Well," Boot said, "everyone—and I mean everyone—thinks you're dead!"

"Good. Let's leave it that way for the time being. What've you learned?"

Dawson answered, "Just as you guessed. Cobra's our snake. The only people who knew of Steel's assignment and had the opportunity to act on that knowledge were the three of us, plus Jakobson—who warned you of the attack—and Cobra—who appears to hate your guts. For the record, aside from Cobra, Delta Team has formally interrogated everyone in the know—including both of us—for means, motive, and alibi."

Consulting his notes, Dawson then added, "As I said, Jakobson's out. Although he certainly had means, he had no motive. He's been our chief ally. He warned you of the attack. At your request, he assigned one of his own agents, Kes, to the mission. And Jakobson and Kes have acted as a secure back channel, keeping us up to date on the events on the *Odysseus* while avoiding communications from Duke through CIA channels, which could be compromised by a CIA traitor."

Continuing, he added, "Dr. Edwards had partial knowledge, but no motive or means, and he had a strong alibi. Gleena Stein and Percy Stone both had means, but no motive and not enough time to act. Your assistant Max had full knowledge, but he didn't have the authority to act and he had no motive. By the way, he's devoted to you and devastated by your assassination. He preserved the video record of the tough office meeting you had with Cobra and secured the original and certified copies. The only person Delta hasn't interviewed is Cobra himself. He's scheduled for questioning on Wednesday morning."

"Good," Lee replied. "I'm sorry to deceive Max, but it can't be helped. So, what do you know about the star-spike and the bomb?"

Boot responded, "Both are CIA issue, KC armory."

"Christ!" said Lee, "that's a surprise!"

Boot replied, "Just wait, it gets worse. The weapons were checked out months ago to a top secret, black-ops group that reports directly to Cobra. I didn't know about the existence of this contract until we started running down the spike and bomb. Technically, Cobra's Chief of Staff checked out the weapons. When I questioned her this afternoon, she refused to tell me anything more. She loosened her tongue when I threatened her with accessory to murder and obstruction of a Federal murder investigation. She couldn't tell me how much Cobra knew about these weapons, but she did give me the requisition form signed by Cobra as well as the transmittal and receipt forms. The weapons were transferred to an outside agency, contracted by Cobra and responsible to his office. I've got Max chasing the dollar trail funding the operation to see where it leads."

Shaking her head with astonishment, all Lee could say at first was, "Damn!" She recovered and said, "Good work! Where's Cobra's Chief of Staff?"

Dawson replied, "After I interviewed her, she excused herself from work, pleading a death in her family. We've placed her in protective custody in a safe house while Cobra's loose. She's cooperating as we continue to question her."

"Good. What else?"

"Well," Boot said, "here's the surprise. Castor Valerio is dead."

"Yes, I know."

"Actually, CIA records show Valerio's been dead for several years. We don't know who Steel killed on the *Odysseus*, but according to the CIA records, it wasn't Castor Valerio. Our records say we killed him three years ago."

"What?"

"That's right," said Boot, "and here's the ringer. The Caine Toads that we thought Steel shut down in January is the very same group that Cobra contracted for wet work."

"What!" Lee yelled. "The Toads are a crime organization! One we tried to shut down. He can't do that!"

"Yup," Boot said, adding with a touch of irony, "and we're the only Federal agency authorized to kill."

"Well, I'll be damned," she said, still swearing. "I'll be Goddamned!"

Dawson spoke up, "It appears that Cobra's gone rogue and set up his own group."

"Are you sure of all of this?"

Dawson replied, "We don't have enough evidence to convict Cobra, but we've got plenty for arrest and search warrants. We figure we'll serve the warrants on him when we interrogate him on Wednesday morning. In the meantime, we've got him in ironclad electronic and team surveillance. We suspect he knows what's up. We want to see what he does. We're hoping he'll lead us to his Toad contacts."

"Is it wise to wait? He might try to destroy evidence and slip your surveillance."

"Maybe," Boot said, "but we don't know Cobra's funding source and, as Peter says, we don't know his Toad contacts. We just know that Cobra has contracted them for wet work, and they get their munitions from the CIA personally approved by Cobra. By the way, Castor Valerio was a Caine Toad. It's possible he's still alive and Steel killed an imposter. So, like I said, I'm laying off because I want to see what Cobra does as his covert operation falls apart."

"Hmm!" Lee muttered, pausing for a moment while Boot and Dawson waited for her to say something more. "This is damned confusing and surprising. I don't understand what's going on. Sure, Cobra's a twentieth-century, misogynistic bully, but that's not a motive for murder."

"Yes," Boot said, interrupting her, "he's covering up something."

"True," she continued. "But whatever that something is, it wasn't in danger of being exposed until I decided to send my top agent to Pluto."

"Well," Dawson added, "maybe the Caine Toads and Cobra want to assassinate Steel to avenge Kalfu's death in Jamaica."

"Maybe," said Lee, "I'm sure they want revenge, but there's something else going on here. Something I just don't understand. Something so troublesome, so disruptive, that it compelled Moxon to demand an emergency EP-conference before he was killed. Cobra and the Toads also don't square with the partial message we received from Moxon. Not to mention, this entire affair began with the murder of Moxon and Keator on Charon, not with Steel killing Kalfu in Jamaica. No, something else is going on here. For some reason, Cobra doesn't want Steel to go to Pluto, and Cobra's willing to kill to keep him from getting there. I'll be damned if I know what it is. But we've got to find out. And find out fast!"

"All right," Dawson replied. "But first, we've got to take care of Cobra."

Turning to face Boot, she added, "Yes, you're right, and to do that, Louis, you should schedule a meeting with the CIA Director tomorrow morning and tell him his Executive Director is a target for murder and conspiracy."

"I've already informed the Director."

"All right," she said, "but Louis, you better insist someone from the New White House, like the Chief of Staff or the Vice President himself, is also in the loop so the President has a head's up, just in case the Director is also corrupt. Just keep me out of it. No one's to know I wasn't killed until we have this investigation locked up and Cobra put away. Do you hear me?"

A chorus of "Yes Sir!" and "Yes," greeted her command.

"All right, but before I let you go," she said, "I want you to set up an EP-conference studio here in the safe house. You can use the garage. Will you do that? Can you do it before the *Odysseus* arrives at Port Tombaugh on March nineteenth?"

Peter said, "Sure, I can do that while Louis runs interference with the lawyers, the Director, and the New White House."

"Good. Let's get going."

22 WOMEN'S DAY

On Tuesday, March 8, Selena entered the Medical Unit to take the 7 am morning shift guarding John, greeting everyone with a cheerful "Good morning!"

"Good morning to you, and Happy Women's Day, Selena!" replied Sumate.

"Thank you! So, how's our charge doing?" asked Selena.

"Fine," grumbled John.

"Well, let's see what the medbot has to say. Ship medbot, what's the report?" asked Selena.

With this command, a bedside, multi-limbed robot, with stalked eyes, several data and video screens, and reservoirs for dispensing pills and liquids, spoke up with a gentle, gender-neutral voice: "Colonel Dakar slept well through the night and voiced no complaints this morning. As you see, he is alert and oriented. Vital signs are stable and within normal limits. The morning whole body scan shows the right chest hemorrhage nearly resolved. Otherwise, the scan is almost identical to his pre-trauma exams. After the artificial blood transfusions, his blood volume and oxygen carrying capacity have returned to normal. The white blood cell count and platelet count remain depressed, consistent with his recent massive hemorrhage, but are in the safe zones. Internal organ blood chemistries have stabilized after the trauma and are also returning to normal levels. We pulled the right chest tube and urinary catheter— "

"Thank God," whispered John.

" —this morning. If he tolerates his breakfast, we will pull the intravenous catheter. He should start ambulating today. Daily exercise should begin tomorrow and escalated as tolerated."

"John, that sounds great!" exclaimed Selena.

"Yeah. Wonderful," John grumbled again.

"Hey, Selena, I've got a lot of work to do for Captain Rakis. I'll see you this afternoon at fifteen o'clock for shift change. When I get back, the three of us have to talk." With that Sumate left.

"Selena, what's that all about?" asked John.

"Uhm, John, I have some sad news for you. Are you ready for it?"

"Okay."

"Yesterday morning, while you're still in your coma, there was a bombing in Kansas City."

"Huh?"

"John, I'm sorry to tell you the bomb killed Director Lee and her bodyguard."

"Oh no!" John had gotten bad news many times in his life, but this one hurt more than the others. Perhaps because he had so recently seen Director Lee. Perhaps because of the respect and warmth she had always shown him, unusual for a government supervisor. Perhaps because of the great respect, even love, he held for her—like a favorite aunt or grandmother. For whatever reason, this news left him stunned.

After leaving him alone for a few minutes Selena asked, "John, are you able to talk?"

"I'm sorry. Yeah, sure."

"John, we think there's a link between the attack on you and the assassination of Director Lee. We can't know for sure, in part because you killed the man who attacked you."

"I did?" asked John. "Shit!" *Oh man. That's going to send me to the PRB. Shit!*

"Uh, yes, John, you did. The thing is, no one knows you killed your attacker. Instead, we reported you died and the attacker survived. With the exception of Captain Rakis, everybody on board this ship thinks Sumate and I are guarding our prisoner, your assassin."

"Oh. Is that necessary?" asked John.

"Yes, we think so. We think it's the best way to ensure your safety. But what we fear is whoever hired your killer, and killed Director Lee, will try to hijack this ship and help your killer escape. Or, the hijackers will simply silence your assassin by killing him along with everyone else on the ship. Either way, we figure we've got trouble in ten days. We expect to be attacked the day before we dock at Port Tombaugh, when we're going the slowest and are the easiest to catch."

"Really?" asked John. He then quickly added, "Well, I guess that all makes sense. What are we going to do about it?"

"We're going to prepare for the hijack just in case it happens. That's the work with Captain Rakis that Sumate was talking about."

Later, after John had his breakfast and was able to keep it down, after the IV was removed, and after Selena helped him get up and walk around, John returned to his medical bed and Selena to the bedside chair. To make chitchat and help pass the time of day, Selena said, "John, I've told you my fears. Do you fear anything besides heights?"

"Well, I . . ." He paused for a few moments, thinking about her question, flipping through his memories like a dealer through a pack of cards, trying to decide which one—if any—to pull out to share with her.

As the minutes stretched to many minutes, she became impatient with his silence. Deciding to change tack, she bluntly asked the question that had bothered her since she saw him kill Valerio.

"John, may I ask you a question about Kalfu?"

"Um. It depends. Maybe. Ask me the question, and I'll tell you."

"Were you afraid when Kalfu handcuffed you and killed Sarah. Did that frighten you? Can you tell me?"

Silence again greeted Selena's question.

After a pause, she said, "John, I'm sorry. I shouldn't have intruded."

Still more silence. Just when she decided to give up and abandon her nosy inquisition, he spoke.

"No, Selena. It's okay. I was just trying to think what to say. Aside from falling off a cliff, I'm not sure there's anything that really frightens me."

"Really? That's hard to imagine."

Again, silence. But she could see he was trying to sort through his feelings. As the silence continued, she realized she had knocked on a closed door, maybe a locked door. Before she could apologize for invading his privacy, he started to talk. With an abrupt gush, like turning on a fire hose, a torrent of words erupted from his mouth.

"When Kalfu attacked Sarah and started to kill her, all I could feel was rage. As Sarah's cries for help increased, my rage increased—it overwhelmed me. I became rage. Rage filled my body, gave me power. Power to break my bonds by tearing my skin. Power to pull my hands through my manacles by crushing my fists. When Sarah started calling, 'John! John! John!' I was bursting with rage and power to get to her and protect her—"

Now I know why he acts so strange when I call him, 'John, John, John.'

"When Sarah started pleading, 'please, oh please, don't kill me!' nothing could stop me. Not steel. Not bone. Not blood. I broke free. I don't know how. I just know I could not stop until I stopped Kalfu. I'm sure I felt pain. I didn't care. Tore and broke my hands, so what? All I can remember was rage, consuming rage. Surprised, the guards looked at me with open mouths. They raised their guns to shoot me. I didn't care. Before they could react, I pulled the gun from the first guard and shot him in the head. The second guard got off a shot. I took it in the chest, point blank. I guess the same injury I got when Valerio stabbed me, dropped lung, chest full of blood. So what! I didn't know it—didn't care. All I knew was Sarah, pleading for her life. 'Please don't kill me. Please, oh please, don't kill me.' All I could see was Kalfu, looking at me, grinning, as he pulled the knife across her neck and slowly started to saw his way through. Oh, God. I can still see her. I can still hear her. Blood started to spray everywhere. There was a man next to Kalfu, his bodyguard, his gun pointed right at me, his eyes opened wide as Sarah started screaming, his mouth opened wide with horror as Sarah's blood shot out of her neck. Yelling 'Kalfu, Kalfu' he stepped in front of Kalfu as I was about to shoot the bloody devil. Instead, I shot the blackguard twice in the mouth, jumped over his body, but I was too late, Selena, I was too late!

"Kalfu stood there, holding up Sarah's head for me to see. She was dying, but still alive! She was still alive! She looked at me, she blinked her eyes, she opened her mouth, but there was no sound. Then nothing—she died. Kalfu laughed. I shot him in the arm. He dropped Sarah's head and his knife. I grabbed the knife, I grabbed Kalfu by his hair. I pulled back his head. I got into his face, as close as I could. I looked into his eyes while I started to saw through his neck. I saw his fear. I had no fear. But he did! I cut slowly, so slowly. I wanted him to die slowly, knowing he was going to die. I wanted him to die just the way he killed Sarah. He squirmed and struggled in my grasp, becoming more and more frantic with the fear of death upon him. Slowly I parted his head from his body, drawing out his terror as long as I could, he screamed and screamed until a fountain of blood spouted from his neck, covering Sarah's blood with a fresh coat of devil red. Then nothing. Just his head. Oh God! I killed Kalfu! But Kalfu killed my darling Sarah. Sarah. Oh, my darling Sarah. Dead at my feet because I could not stop him. I knew I was dying, but I didn't care! I wanted to die, too."

Turning toward her, tears streaming down his face, eyes blood red, dark face ever darker—even purple—mouth, chin, eyebrows pulled down by the weight of his sorrow, he cried, "What is that, Selena? Is that fear? Is that sorrow? Is that anger?" Raising his voice, he yelled, "What is that, Selena? Is it fear to know we can't save the person we love from dying a horrible death? Is that fear, Selena?" Now shouting, he yelled, "If so, yes, I have fear!" Then, collapsing from the exertion, lowering his voice, almost to a whisper, as if talking to himself, he said, "What is it? All I know is, it's pain. Oh, God, horrible pain. It haunts me!"

His pain pulled on her like no one had ever pulled on her before. She lay down on the bed beside him, pulled him to her chest, cradled his head in her breasts, and let him cry. And he cried. And he cried. Her great black warrior, this powerful man named Steel, whose great sorrow and powerful pain had now unlocked her heart, flooding it with love for a man both fragile and strong at the same time.

After a while, his cries stopped, and he fell asleep. She had never heard a man cry like this before, she had never had a man fall asleep in her arms before. But he slept. He slept like a child worn out by sorrow.

While John slept, she began wondering. *What just happened?* She had lived all of her life with men, strong men, weak men, men who tried to beat her down, and men whom she tried to beat. Her father had been kindly but aloof. She knew he loved her in his way, but his was a cool, distant love. She had wanted something more from her father, but he had always seemed to be more connected to his two sons, played with them, explored the Moonscape with them, laughed with them, but not with her. Now that she thought about it, she guessed that was why she had joined Mossad, to prove to her father that she was every bit as strong and tough as her brothers and just as deserving of his love. But it didn't happen that way.

In school, the other boys were rivals, not friends. Competitors whom she had to overcome, whether it be in scholastics or athletics. When puberty erupted, all they wanted was her body. Until she met Esau, she had never met anyone worthy enough or attractive enough for her to surrender her virginity, as much as she would like to have explored her sexuality. College, graduate school, basic training, and service passed. She remained chaste. Until Esau, she had prided herself on her ability to keep a cool distance. To approach an enemy objectively, to ignore the person and think only of what had to be done and how to do it. She had earned a reputation for cool calculation and precision lethality. She had risen to the top of killers licensed by Mossad. Some called her the ice warrior. Her superiors thought she might be a sociopath, a woman lacking all empathy. But she knew better, even though she didn't know what was true.

She had empathy. She could love. She thought she had loved Esau, but she had also killed him. He had to be killed. He was a terrorist, a man who aspired to kill innocents. She had to stop him.

Now she knew something more.

Now she knew that she had never truly loved before because she had never met a man who would give his life to save the life of the person he loved.

She had never truly loved before because she had never met a man who spoke to her with his heart, without disguise, without defense or evasion. She had never met a man, who was strong like she was a strong, but who still craved the love of a strong woman, just like she craved the love of a strong man. She yearned for a man who would respect and cherish her just like she would respect and cherish him.

While she pondered all of this, her thoughts began to unravel, fracture, and slip into chaos. Exhausted by her emotions, sleep overwhelmed her.

For three hours they slept together, at first with John, the patient, in the arms of Selena, the guardian. But over time, while still asleep, they shifted position, and when she awoke, she found herself in John's arms. The charge had become the guardian, the guardian the charge.

Sitting up, she said, "John, I'm sorry. I fell asleep. I'm not supposed to do that. I'm supposed to be guarding you. Sumate will be here soon to take the next shift."

"It's okay. I found it soothing, lying here, with you in my arms, while thinking more about your questions. I'm ashamed to think of how I must appear to you. I fear you have seen the worst of me."

"No, John. Not at all. Quite the opposite."

With a broad smile, he said softly, "You're kind. As I was thinking about fear, I realized there're two other things I'd like to tell you."

"All right, John, I'm listening."

"I discovered with Sarah's death, that my love for her created a weapon my enemies could use against me—"

Oh, John, don't spoil it. Just when I've found you, I don't want to lose you!

John continued, "I didn't have fear for myself, but I had fear for Sarah. I feared my enemies would use my love for her as a weapon to destroy me. And they did. Does that make sense?"

This time, her silence greeted his question. He waited for her answer.

Oh John, don't say this. Killers can have love, can't they?

After a few moments, she gave up and finally spoke. With a sigh, she said, "Yes. I understand. What you say makes sense. But I don't know what to say. I don't want to say people like you and me can never love. I would like to love. But maybe you're right."

"I've only loved once. That was Sarah. Have you ever loved anyone?"

"No. I've not had any lovers." This time her eyes filled with tears. As she began to weep, she said softly, "And now I fear I never will."

With those words, he took her in his arms and held her tightly, while she quietly cried for the love she'd lost and for the people she'd killed. They sat there for a long time, with her in his arms. Neither speaking. It might have been an awkward silence, but for them, it felt comfortable to be in the arms of the other, who understood them as no one had before.

After a while, John leaned forward, as if he intended to kiss her, and she turned up her face as if to accept his affection. Then ever so gently, ever so slowly, they shared a kiss, stopping just a few moments before Sumate stepped into the room.

"Hey, guys!" Then seeing them both on the bed, quickly disentangling themselves from their embrace, he quickly added, "Oops, sorry. I was coming to relieve Selena. John, you seem to be improving!"

Smiling again, John said, "Yeah, I think so. Now that all my tubes are out, I'm ready to be up and about and start getting back into shape. I gather we've work to do."

23 THE COBRA AND THE MONGOOSE

On Tuesday evening, March 8, at 21:00 CST, the three leaders of the 5th FD—Lee, Boot, and Dawson—met at the Independence safe house to discuss the progress over the past twenty-four hours.

"Gone," Boot exclaimed. "He slipped the snare. We don't know where he is."

"Louis! It's only been twenty-four hours since you told me you had him under 'ironclad surveillance.' What happened?" demanded a fuming Director Lee.

"Yesterday afternoon, just after I interviewed his Chief of Staff, but before she left for the safe house, she warned Cobra he was under suspicion. She didn't tell us she had warned him until this morning when Cobra didn't report to work. We threatened her with obstruction of justice, but what are we going to do? That rocket's already launched. We did learn one thing from her that we didn't know before."

"It'd better be good!" Lee grumbled.

"It is," answered Boot. "She warned Cobra because Cobra's been blackmailing her. That's how he got her cooperation. She's been having an affair. She didn't want her husband to know, she feared it would break up her family and she would lose custody of her children. Cobra found out and he's been using it against her."

"Cad!" exclaimed Lee. "Well, how does that help us?"

"I'll explain. You remember you warned us the Director could also be dirty?"

"Yes, I remember."

"Well, shades of Hoover. You're right. Cobra's been blackmailing the CIA Director. In fact, as we've been getting into it, Cobra's been blackmailing a lot of people across the government for leverage."

"Damn! Where's he getting the dirt?" asked Lee.

"We don't know, but we can guess."

"WXN2," Boot and Dawson said together.

"I'll be damned," she said. "Well, we knew that was the big risk with the program, that it could pick-up domestic communications along with the foreign ones, and the illegal eavesdropping could be misused. I guess that's as good enough reason as any to kill Steel, so that Cobra could keep his blackmailing secret. No wonder Cobra was so nervous. And angry. Damn. Peter, you've got a lot of work to do to clean up this mess. That probably means big changes for WXN2. We may have to shut it down. Pity!"

"Yes, Sir."

"All right. Where's Cobra?"

"As I said, we don't know," answered Boot. "After Cobra spoke with his Chief of Staff, he tried to call the CIA Director, I guess to find out what was going on. The Director ducked the calls—probably because I'd already told the Director we'd targeted Cobra for ordering your assassination."

"So, what happened?"

"After that, Cobra placed two calls. One to an unlisted and unmonitored number and the other to the LLCN ambassador."

"Uh-oh," said Lee. "Do you know what Cobra said?"

"Not exactly," answered Boot. "Cobra's office and the ambassador's are both beyond our voice surveillance. All we could get were telephone numbers. But later, the Sea of Storms Office intercepted an LLCN transmission stating that Cobra had requested LLCN asylum, and asylum had been refused."

"It just gets worse and worse. What has Cobra got to do with the LLCN?" asked Lee.

"We fear he's been their spy," answered Boot.

After a few minutes of silent pondering, she said, "Yup. That makes sense. Cobra always sided with the LLCN in the Lunar Lights Controversy. We worried he had become an ideologue because of his religion—you know he's Evangelical. But we did nothing. So, I can see how he might have been spying for the LLCN. But, if that's true, why would they deny him asylum?"

Dawson answered that question. "Spying's bad enough, but blackmail and murder are over the line. The LLCN would have to deny him asylum to maintain relations with us."

"Yes. That must be it," said Director Lee. "What about that other call, the unmonitored, unlisted call? What can you tell me about that?"

"Not much. What information we have suggests it was a simple message transmission rather than a two-way conversation. The call was short, aside from the electronic handshake and password exchange, it consisted of just

Cobra's communication. The receiving number is curious. It was to a CIA computer receiver, previously unknown to us. We suspect the receiver retransmitted the message to some other recipient, but we haven't identified it yet."

"I see. I don't have to tell you to find the receiver. What happened after the phone calls?" asked Lee.

"Well, that's a good question," Boot replied. "Nothing happened. Cobra stayed in his office all afternoon. Door shut. No more phone calls. No meetings. No bathroom breaks. Nothing. So, after a couple of hours, I sent his Administrative Assistant into the office with the excuse that Cobra needed to sign a document. The room was empty. Piled on the couch were all of his clothes, shoes, perscom, shorts, everything—including the microbot tracers we had placed on him. He even peeled off his adhesive medical monitoring devices and combed his hair with a nit comb to get rid of any tracers. Like a snake shedding its skin, he shed all of our electronic surveillance."

"Jeez! What about the ID in his left forearm?" asked Lee. "What did he do about that?"

"Well, he didn't cut it out. And he didn't break it—those IDs are unbreakable. He must've slipped on an electronic gauntlet to cover the ID and block the signal—maybe even send out a false signal. You can do that, you know."

"Yes. I know," she said. "But Christ! How did he get out of the office without being seen?"

"He's got a hidden exit from the office, so that he can leave undetected," said Boot. "A lot of brass have concealed exits so that they can duck people they don't want to meet. His AA is new and didn't know about any secret exit. But when we searched the room, we found it."

"Louis, this is bad, this is very bad" complained Lee. "We've got to find him, particularly if he is mixed up with Lunar Lights!"

"Yes. I know," replied Boot, avoiding looking at her by looking down at his shoes, inspecting them as if he had stepped in dog feces. "We did discover he caught a flight from KC to Miami yesterday afternoon. From there he took an overnight flight to the Cayenne Spaceport."

"The Cayenne Spaceport? You mean the one the South Americans use?"

"Yes. And the trail doesn't end there. He took a shuttle to the Simón Bolívar Space Station. We didn't know this, but he kept a space yacht there, a six-seat racer. How he got it, I don't know. Probably condemned from a seizure. Anyway, it's a Star Chaser five-x, the fastest production space yacht ever built. It has a top acceleration of five Gs and can sustain this acceleration for ten days. He left Bolívar earlier this morning."

"I see," said Lee, "do you know where he is now?"

"No. We don't. Things are a little lax on Bolívar. He didn't file a flight plan and his transponder is turned off. We don't know where he is or where he's going. And, by the time we figured this all out, it was too late to find him. The racer's a small ship, not much bigger than a passenger ship transport. But, with full fuel and supplies, he could go anywhere in the solar system, Mars, Ceres, the Edge, even Sedna if he dared. I'm sorry Director Lee, he slipped his snare. He's gone!"

24 MARCH MADNESS

At 10:00 UTC, on the morning of Wednesday, March 9, Lowell Director Ronald Best convened the "Super Secret Select" tele-auction. Standing at the podium, addressing five microphones, The Lowell Director looked a bit like President Trump, a big man with pallid skin, thinning blonde hair, and a small mouth. Only this auction was nothing like a news conference. Aside from Director Best, no one else occupied the Fourth Circle secure room, which Best had rented from the Port Tombaugh First National Bank.

When PTFNB built their suite of offices in the Fourth Circle of Port Tombaugh, they also built this room for customers who needed a secure and private setting for in-person meetings and for tele-meetings. Even Talos, who monitored all other activities in Port Tombaugh, could not monitor the proceedings in this room.

Director Best limited the tele-auction to five invited participants, and he did not use names to identify them. Instead, he referred to the attendees by naming each one after one of the five largest non-Earth moons in the solar system: Ganymede, Titan, Callisto, Io, and Europa. Each participant provided his own microphone and encryption protocols so he could listen to the tele-auction and place bids without revealing his identity to each other or to any unwanted eavesdroppers who might somehow have sidestepped the bank security system.

Director Best placed only one item up for bid, and he served as the auctioneer.

"Ladies and gentlemen," Director Best began. "March Madness is upon us! As I'm sure you all know, every March, the All-American Academic Athletic Association, better known as Cinco-A, convenes a basketball tournament to determine the college basketball champion for the Americas. March Madness begins with Selection Sunday, which was this past Sunday, when the Cinco-A meets in Boston to select the hundred and twenty-eight teams that will play in the tournament and seeds the teams—pairs them up—into the first round of sixty-four contests spread across eight brackets. Once the Cinco-A finishes the seedings, they announce the results. This year, the Cinco-A announced the results at eighteen Eastern Standard Time, which for us was twenty-three UTC on the evening of Sunday, March sixth. As you know, we do not get the March Madness seedings as soon as they are released, we have to wait at least seven hours for the news to travel at the speed of light from Boston to reach Port Tombaugh. Are you with me so far?"

Not hearing any responses, he continued: "I have provided each of you with a double notarized copy of an encrypted document I obtained late Sunday night. When the code is broken, the winning bidder will see that my document correctly lists the hundred and twenty-eight college teams chosen to compete in this year's tournament as well as the seedings for the sixty-four contests that kick off the March Madness tournament, which starts tomorrow. I have also provided you with a copy of the Selection Sunday seedings as published Monday morning by the *Port Tombaugh Star*."

"So, here's the important part," he said. "As you see, our Pluto officials notarized my encrypted document at twenty-four UTC on March sixth; one hour after the release of the seedings by the Cinco-A in Boston."

This information sparked a chorus of murmurs from the array of electronic devices.

"By the way, I want to thank the notaries from the First National Bank of Port Tombaugh and from the Port Tombaugh Gaming Commission, who agreed to meet me on Sunday evening and notarize my encrypted document with the time and date on which I presented the document to them. I believe everyone will agree our Port Tombaugh notaries are beyond repute." Pausing for a moment, he then asked, "Any questions so far?"

Hearing none, Director Best continued, "I'll provide to the highest bidder, the key to decrypting my document, so the winning bidder can verify that I correctly listed the March Madness selections for 2111, six hours before that information could possibly be received by Port Tombaugh."

Pausing for effect, he then added, "Some might think this is an elaborate hoax. I assure you it is not. It would be impossible for me to correctly forecast the selections and seedings for all hundred and twenty-eight teams. Given the extreme efforts the Cinco-A takes to keep their proceedings secret and to report the results as soon as they're done, it would not be possible for me to create this document by cheating. What you have here is proof the US has invented faster-than-light communications and this device is in my possession.

Aside from some more murmurs, no one spoke up. He continued: "The object for which I will accept bids, is a receiver and transmitter for faster-than-light communication. The device is not in this room, but I can provide the device to the winning bidder in a matter of hours. I will shortly be accepting bids for the purchase of this communication device. As soon as our transaction is complete, I will deliver the object to the winning bidder. Because selling this object will make me an enemy of the US, all bids must include the following: a guarantee of asylum, an appointment to a position of power—such as an appointment to a Directorship of an Edge planemo, and the provision of transferable precious gems and rare art with a value of at least ten billion dollars. I have previously informed you of these terms. So, any questions? Are we ready?"

Not hearing any complaints, Best continued, "All right, bidding is now open."

Silence.

"Ladies and gentlemen, I said bidding is now open for this device."

More silence.

After a couple of minutes, Titan spoke: "Director Best, this is Titan. My group has discussed this very interesting auction in detail. I am impressed by your validation of faster-than-light communications. We would like to purchase your device, but we do not want to make an enemy of the US by publicly buying stolen, top-secret, technology. We're prepared to make a discreet payment of jewels and art with a value of ten billion dollars. But we can't be involved in this transaction in any public manner.

We can't offer you asylum or a directorship. You will have to obtain those on your own."

With that statement, Ganymede, Calisto, Europa, and Io also spoke up, each one echoing Titan's terms, but boosting the monetary bid to twenty-two billion dollars. Like Titan, none of them could offer asylum or a position of influence.

While Best stood at the podium, he became increasingly angry and agitated.

"I see. The issue of asylum is non-negotiable. I've got to have protection by a nation-state to sell this device. The rest is negotiable. But without protection, I've got no reason to throw my life away." After a pause, he then added, "to sweeten the deal, I will also include the encrypted data proving the Lowell Observatory conducts espionage on all down-range communications, including US communications! Now, I will give you five more minutes to reconsider and place your bids. Who will give me a bid?"

With that comment, Director Best sat down in front of the microphones as he counted off five minutes. When no one offered a fresh bid, Director Best growled, "I see I've chosen the wrong participants for this auction. You will regret your decision. This auction is closed."

In a huff he turned off the participants' communications devices and placed them in the mechanical crusher, destroying all evidence of the auction. After making sure he had left nothing behind, he angrily left the room, marched out of the bank, and went directly to the Port Tombaugh personal transport pavilion, where the three remaining members of OASIS had parked a Lowell Observatory transport and were waiting for him.

Roger Winthrop, the senior member of the depleted OASIS staff, the remaining CIA muscle, and now the Acting OASIS Director and transport pilot, greeted Best with: "Where to, Boss?"

"Get in the transport, and I'll tell you."

After boarding the transport and turning on the electronic security net, Best said, "We're going back to Clarke Station to get the EP gun. There's been a security breach. We've got to hide the gun before our enemies take it from us it. And, we've got to act fast! The word is out."

"All right. And then?"

"Then to Charlene Anchor to transfer the gun to an HC. After the transfer we'll go to the Ele Ranch Node to hide the gun. When we're done, we'll retrace our steps back to Clarke. We need to move as quickly as we can before someone stops us and steals the gun. And," Best added, "after we get to Clarke, we've got to travel off-the-grid—no communications, no flight plan, and no transponders. Tell people who need to know that we'll be gone for two nights and three days on an emergency repair mission for the telescope net orbiting Pluto."

Knowing the secrecy attached to the gun, Winthrop answered with a simple, "Got it! But how do I explain the off-the-grid travel?"

"If anyone asks, just tell them we were in a rush to repair damage to the orbital telescope net. Since we couldn't predict which scopes, we would be servicing, we skipped the flight plan. As for the transponder, it must be broken. We'll look into it."

"All right. But I'm not sure it'll pass."

"Don't worry about it. Just do it."

25 LOST IN SPACE

Two days later, on the morning of Friday, March 11, Inspector Scott Skalay reconvened the daily Morning Report for the Port Tombaugh Homicide Squad in the shabby conference room in the First PT Circle.

"Okay Folks, let's review where we stand with the Charon homicides. Talos, please display the six mysteries on our squad screen and then revise the entries as we go along."

"Certainly."

Moxon and Keator Mysteries:

1. Who are Moxon, Keator, and OASIS?
    i. Answer: CIA; keeping CIA surveillance secret
    b. What were they doing on Kubrick Mons?
    i. Answer: Probably to send a message.

"Okay Kirk, you're up first. It's been two days since the auction. Have you located Best and the rest of the OASIS team? Did you hack the auction?"

"No and Yes. I have news! Let me tell you about the auction first because I think it will solve many of our mysteries and help with locating Best," replied Kirk.

"Go for it!"

"Well, as you know, the auction was a tele-auction, convened in an electronics-secure room, with attendance limited to encrypted communications by devices provided by the bidders."

"Okay. Go on."

"Well, with the help of Roc and Talos, we located all five wire feeds into the room and tapped into them. We recorded the encrypted communications for each member of the auction. Taken individually, we could not break the codes. But Roc had the insight that because each coded communication recorded the exact same proceedings, we could break the encryptions by comparing the coded messages to each other. With the help of Talos, we were able to break the code late last night. We broke it because Roc also correctly guessed that the most likely words Best used to open the auction, the key to breaking the code, was the greeting 'gentlepeople,' followed by 'welcome to this special, by invitation only, auction.' That opening, with 'gentlepeople,' blew the codes like a nuke blowing a rubble-pile asteroid."

"Good work. What did you learn?"

"Roc, this is your triumph, you tell them," said Kirk.

"Yes. Thank you, Sir." Looking down at his notes, Roc Qadeer, the Squad's computer forensics specialist reported: "In short, Best demonstrated the US has invented a faster-than-light communication device."

Charlie whistled, and Skalay yelped, "Blast it! That's a game-changer. No wonder Best is keeping this so close to his chest!"

Roc continued, "Best demonstrated the device by getting the Selection Sunday seedings for the March Madness tournament right after Cinco-A announced the selections, more than six hours before Port Tombaugh got the selections by light-speed radio transmission. Best calls the device an EP-gun. The device is in his possession."

"Stop! Let's think this thing through," Skalay said. He then turned to the five mysteries on the Homicide squad screen. "Talos, show us Mystery number one."

Mystery number one: Who are Moxon, Keator, and OASIS? Answer: CIA. What were they doing? Answer: conducting secret and illegal CIA surveillance.

To this answer, Skalay had Talos add: "and keeping the EP-gun secret." Skalay then read out loud the next question:

"What were they doing on Kubrick Mons?"

Answering his own question, he added, "Obviously to send a message. But to whom and why from Kubrick Mons? Well team, any ideas?"

"Yes," said Roc. "Because the gun is CIA and transmits messages faster-than-light, I'm betting they were using the gun to send a message to KC. Furthermore, the term EP might mean 'entangled-photon.' If so, the EP-gun could be some type of a photon communication device, perhaps the size of an antique machine gun, possibly carried on the back of Moxon's transport."

"That would explain the rectangular snow shadow," interjected Skalay.

Roc added, "It also means the message had to travel by line of sight and be sent from a stable platform."

"Like a transport anchored in regolith on top of a mountain," added Charlie.

"Yes. That all makes sense," said Skalay. "But if it is a photon device, how can it be faster than light?" He asked.

"Don't know," said Roc.

"Well, for the time being, let's assume this is all about the EP-gun. It answers more questions than it raises."

At Skalay's direction, Talos revised the second mystery to read:

Mystery number two: What were they doing on Kubrick Mons? Answer: Probably to send a message downrange with the EP-gun to the KC CIA.

"Okay," said Skalay. "We're making progress. But what did the message say?"

This time Kirk spoke up. "I don't know. But we can assume that since they coded the message with a one-time pad, it must have been top secret and of vital importance. To send it with faster-than light transmission, it must also have been time sensitive. And finally, since the message came from the Pluto-Charon system, it must have something to do with our colony. But I can't fathom what it might be.

"Right. Good point, Kirk. Anybody else got any good ideas? . . . No. Talos, add Kirk's analysis to our list and let's move onto the big one, Mystery number three: who hacked the transport ERC and killed Moxon and Keator."

Kirk piped-up: "I think it was Best, trying to steal the EP-gun."

Skalay shook his head. "Maybe, but why kill his own people to steal something he already owns? He's the boss of Lowell and OASIS. Besides, he had an alibi and called in the troops when Moxon and Keator went missing. No, it doesn't make sense. There's something else here. Anybody else got any ideas?"

Hearing nothing, he went on to Mystery number four: What was the transport cargo?"

This time Roc spoke up. "That's easy. We've already solved it, the EP-gun."

Talos entered the answer "EP-gun" to Mystery number four while Skalay was saying, "but we still don't know who stole the cargo and who took Moxon's perscom and one-time pad."

Kirk piped up. "Wait a minute, maybe we do know who took it. If Best was peddling the gun, then he must have gotten it from the wreck. Since he has an alibi, he probably had the rest of the OASIS crew go to the wreck and retrieve the gun."

"Yes!" Skalay said, recognizing the truth of Kirk's insight. "That makes a lot of sense!"

"And," Roc interjected, "I bet OASIS collected the perscom and the one-time pad when they picked up the gun!"

"Okay!" Skalay said, pleased by the progress. He then entered "probably OASIS" after who stole the EP-gun? and who stole the perscom and one-time pad?

Skalay continued. "That leaves us with Mystery number five—the cover-up. It seems to me, the EP-gun auction explains Best's apparently treacherous and secretive behavior. Does everyone agree?"

A round of assents responded to Skalay's question.

Then Kirk spoke up. "There's more to it than that. If it was all about the gun, why did Best panic when Moxon and Keator got whacked? And why did he change course when the NTSB declared accident? It seems to me that he wanted so badly for the canopy blowout to be an accident that he was willing to overlook the murder of his own people. I think that once Best discovered Moxon's transport wreck, he sent the rest of the OASIS team to recover and hide the gun. After that, he didn't want any more investigation because he didn't want anyone to know the gun existed or that he had it. But that still doesn't tell us who whacked Moxon and Keator."

"Yes, Kirk," said Skalay, "that makes a lot of sense. It is as good a working theory as we've got. But it still has a lot of holes. Let's keep it in mind as we go forward."

He then asked the group, "What about the KC FBI agent?"

Charlie spoke up. "Doesn't make sense. The FBI coulda sent the agent to protect the secrets, only the agent should be CIA, not FBI. Besides, we've got both CIA and FBI at Port Tombaugh."

Roc added, "Didn't someone just assassinate the KC agent on the *Odysseus*?"

"Yup," replied Skalay.

"Well the PT Star reported the assassin survived. Maybe when the *Odysseus* docks, we can interview him."

"Good idea," said Skalay, "but it won't help us now. Still, it does add to the cover-up mystery. Talos, under cover-up, include why did the FBI send us an agent from KC? Why was he assassinated."

"Okay. Moving on," Skalay continued. "So, Kirk, I see you also have included the Henning mysteries on our list. The EP-gun doesn't help us with the serial sabotage or the identity of Henning's killer, but it could explain the manipulation of the OTB and the stock exchange, probably by Best. If so, exposing his crimes by finding the EP-gun would also increase his anxiety. So, Talos, given his recent auction, put Best down as our leading suspect for manipulating the OTB and the stock exchanges."

"If Best was manipulating the OTB and the stock exchanges, he probably killed Henning to silence him. But it still doesn't explain the serial sabotage." Gazing at the squad screen with satisfaction, he added, "but we're making a lot of progress!" After a pause to enjoy the moment, he returned to business. "All right. Let's get back to the auction. What more can you tell us, Roc?"

"Best put the gun up for bids, demanding asylum, power, and a humongous payout. Interestingly, no one bid on the device."

"Why not?" asked Skalay.

Looking at his notes, Roc reported, "As we expected from spotting the messages Best passed out during the funeral receiving line, the attendees were the Consul for China, Gan Bingzhen, the Consul for Brazil, Duillia Gleiser, the Consul for Russia, Boris Struve, the President of the Pluto and Charon Territorial Stock Exchange, Anthony McKay, and the Chair of the Port Tombaugh Gaming Commission, Watson Hatch."

"Holy Krun! That's high power," said Skalay. "But, answer the question. Why didn't anyone bid on the device?"

"Aside from financing a bid, I'm not sure how McKay and Hatch could have met Best's terms, but they might have worked with one of the Consuls to fund the purchase. The Consuls could certainly meet Best's demands," replied Roc. "But, Bingzhen spoke up and revealed the hole in the spacesuit: no one wanted to be caught publicly purchasing stolen super-secret US technology. All they could offer was money—up to twenty-three billion US dollars. No asylum and no political power."

"Cripes!" Skalay again exclaimed. "So, what happened next?"

"Nothing. Best got angry. Picked up his chips and shut down the auction. He then left the bank. We followed him electronically to the Port Tombaugh personal transport pavilion, where he joined the three remaining members of OASIS. They boarded the Lowell Observatory transport and left PT. Once they were in the transport, we could no longer eavesdrop on them."

"So where are they now?" asked Skalay.

Kirk answered, "We don't know. We do know that right after the auction they went back to Clarke Station. Probably to pick up the gun. Then they left. Supposedly they were on an emergency repair mission to one of the orbiting telescopes, but there's no report of any orbiting telescope malfunctions. They did not file a flight plan, and they turned off the transponder. We've lost all trace of them—like they're lost in space. Our only clue is that they told people they would be gone for two nights and three days."

"They're hiding the gun," said Skalay.

"Yes. That's our guess," responded Kirk.

"Two nights and three days?"

"Yup," replied Kirk.

"Hmm," said Skalay as he considered the possibilities. "They might hide the gun on one of the orbiting telescope platforms, but then why leave word that was where they were going? They might hide the gun on one of the minor moons, but the moons' motions are so chaotic that landing on one and hiding something would be tricky. It would also place the gun way outside of their control."

"Yup. That's what we thought too," said Kirk.

"That leaves Nickelback Node and Charlene Anchor, but you wouldn't need three days to hide something there," said Skalay.

Abruptly, all three detectives interrupted Skalay by saying, "Ele Ranch Node!"

"Yes, that must be it," said Skalay. "Ele Ranch Node is in the center of the astronomical observatory reserve controlled by Lowell. It takes at least two days to get there and back. That's got to be it. Good place to hide the gun. It's a big facility and there's no one there except bots."

Raising his hand to signal everyone should be quiet, he pondered the breakthroughs. After a couple of minutes of silence, he said, "All right, folks, how about this. Kirk, you've been wanting to lead an operation. Here's your chance. It's Friday morning, assuming the team stayed out Wednesday and Thursday night, they're due back to Clarke sometime today—probably this afternoon. If they went to Ele Ranch Node to hide the gun, then we might be able to catch them as they return. Kirk, take Roc and Charlie and first go to Clarke; check out the hangar there. You probably won't find anything. Then go to Charlene Anchor and snoop around while you wait for Best and his team to return. While you're snooping, check out the Henning crime scene. And see if you can find the OASIS transport. If they went to Ele Ranch Node, then they probably transferred to an HC at Charlene Anchor. Before you leave, all three of you should weapon-up and suit-up with defensive armor. This could get real ugly, real fast. Kirk are you up for this?"

"Yes Sir."

"How about you, Charlie?"

"You bet."

"And you, Roc?"

"Of course."

"Okay," Skalay continued. "You are under Kirk's orders. In the meantime, I will meet with the PT FBI-CIA office to tell them what we know and suspect. I'll also get their help to search for the Lowell transport throughout the PC system, in case we guessed wrong. Most importantly, I'll ask for reinforcements—there are only three of you, but Best and his team are four. As soon as I'm done, I'll call you and join you, hopefully with backup. If you pick up Best's trail, just tail him. Do not engage or arrest him. Wait for me with reinforcements. Do you understand, Kirk?"

"Yes. Find him. When I do, tail him but do not engage or arrest. Got it." She replied.

"Okay. Do it."

Here is the revised list of Moxon and Keator Mysteries on the PT Homicide Squad's screen. Bolded entries signal progress: Moxon and Keator Mysteries:

1. Who are Moxon, Keator, and OASIS?
Answer: CIA; conducting secret and illegal CIA surveillance
Answer keeping the EP-gun secret
What were they doing on Kubrick Mons?
Answer: Probably sending an **EP-gun message downrange from Kubrick Mons to KC-CIA.**
2. What was the message encrypted by the one-time pad?
Answer: Unknown, but it must have been top secret, of vital importance, time sensitive, and locally generated.
3. Who hacked the Transport ERC and why did they kill Moxon and Keator?
Answer: Unknown killer(s), unknown motive.
Not Best. Probably not OASIS
4. What was the transport cargo?
Answer: the EP-gun
Who stole the cargo, Moxon's perscom, and the one-time-pad?
Answer: Best with the help of OASIS, stole the EP-gun
Unknown person(s) stole perscom and one-time pad
Whoever killed Keator and Moxon did not take the EP-gun
5. Cover-up:
Why did Best first try to find Moxon's and Keator's killers and then change course and try to stop the investigation when the NTSB declared mechanical malfunction and operator error?
Why did the FBI send an agent from KC to investigate? And why was the agent killed?

26 PIE DAY

Oblivion slipped away with the gradual dawn of self-awareness, like awakening to a slow, lazy June sunrise in Iowa. He stirred with the increasing urgency to get up to pee, contending with the desire to remain in bed, in blissful tranquility, embracing the warm woman beside him.

Woman. Sarah! . . . No. Selena! Selena! Selena!

A surge of tenderness washed over him, causing him to pull Selena closer to him, enfolding her with his body, as he remembered last night. The loving gentleness of their first kisses, the flowering of their love drawing them together into full intimacy. Her little yelp as she welcomed him into her. How special and surprising that was, knowing this was her first. Then the urgent, repeated, thrust and fill, culminating in one wave of ecstasy after another, until spent and exhausted, they fell asleep in each other's arms, lulled by the soft murmuring lullabies of "I love you."

Basking in the warmth of such reverie, he suddenly awoke—as if doused with a bucket of ice water—when full consciousness brought with it the monstrous memory of his many crimes.

Oh God, what is wrong with me? He groaned. *I should not have killed Valerio. I couldn't stop myself! Now I've done it again. Brick warned me I would face the PRB if I violated Fifth FD standards again. I didn't have to kill Valerio. But I did. I could not control my rage.*

And now—and now, he groaned again, *I've made the second mistake all over again. I've fallen in love with Selena. I promised myself I would never make this mistake again. By loving her, I set her up to be hurt by people who would hurt me.*

His moans awoke Selena. "What is it, John?"

"Oh, Selena, I love you so much. But I don't deserve you. I'm a monster. I killed for the pleasure of killing. When I return to KC, the PRB will hear what I did to Valerio and they will cashier me. I deserve to lose my Interrobang Badge. I don't deserve your love. I'm so ashamed."

"John. I've killed too. I—"

"But Selena, my love for Sarah made her a target for my enemies to hurt me by hurting her. I can't stand to think I'll make that mistake again. I can't make that mistake again. I can't allow myself to hurt you or let you be hurt. I love you too much. I'm a killer. A monster. I don't deserve your love."

"Oh, John, I forgive you. I know you loved—love— Sarah. You did everything you could to protect her. Yes. Kalfu killed her anyway. But you're human, John. You're not a god. You killed Kalfu in the heat of the moment. He would have killed you if he could. You're forgiven. John, you're forgiven."

"And Valerio? What about him? I didn't need to kill him. I tied him up."

"John, I saw your fight with Valerio. I saw it through the gym window while we tried to break in and help you. I also saw the video recording of the fight. You had to kill

Valerio. He attacked you without warning. He did everything he could to kill you first. He tried to frighten you by yelling "Kalfu." Yes. You tied him up. But you didn't know if his bonds would hold. And John, you were dying. I saw you dying. If we had not been in a ship with medical quarters next door, and if you had not immediately gotten medical care, you would have died. Valerio might have lived if Sumate and I had given Valerio the same medical care we gave to you, but we made you our first priority. So, we also helped to kill Valerio. John, you're a man, not a god. You're a powerful man, a great man, but still a man. A man I've come to respect and love. Don't apologize for who you are."

"But Selena, I can't love you. I can't let my love for you expose you to danger."

"John, I'm a strong woman. I prefer we live together in danger, than separately alone."

"Live together? I haven't proposed."

"I know. I am."

"What day is today?" asked John.

Startled, Selena answered, "March fourteenth, Pi Day."

A smile crept over his face. He pulled her back into his arms. "That's right, it's Pi Day. Well, Selena, my love, this is my solemn promise to you. If you will have me, I will be your husband. And I will love and protect you for as many days as pi has digits."

27 THE IDES OF MARCH

With some trepidation, at 03:17 UTC, on March 15, Lieutenant Kris Cutt, the Officer of the Deck, woke Captain Leena Rakis from her sleep.

"Captain Rakis?"

"Yes."

"This is Lieutenant Cutt. I'm the first watch OOD. We've got a situation and need you on bridge. Now."

"I'll be right there."

"Well, Lieutenant, what's going on?"

"We're being overtaken by a bogey. Could be the pirate you've been expecting. Chief Warrant Officer King spotted it on the scanning LiDAR. He can give you the report."

"Hmph. Trouble's early. It's only Tuesday morning. We weren't expecting anything until Friday. Well," she said with a sigh, "as the soothsayer warned Caesar, 'Beware the Ides of March.' All right, Officer King, what've you got? Is it real?"

"Sir, I think so, Sir. Spotted it two hours ago off the bow, directly up-range from us, traveling on the same bearing as us. At first the signal was weak and erratic, so I didn't report it. Since then the signal has been getting stronger and closer. If it is a ship, it's a ghost—no transponder. Two hours to scope image, six hours to contact."

"Hmm. Fast for a pirate," Rakis replied.

"Sir," interjected the OOD. "I thought about taking maneuvers to dodge it but didn't want to let it know we'd spotted it without your clearance."

"Good man. Hold off on maneuvers. We'll pretend we haven't seen it. In the meantime, activate the defense plan. If the bogey's real, we'll be prepared. If not, then it's a rehearsal for the real attack. Sound the alarm. Have the crew take their battle stations. Get the officers on the bridge. Pronto. Tell all unassigned passengers to remain in their rooms, with the doors locked, until told to assemble at their life raft stations. I hate to disturb the passengers, but they need to take precautions too, bogey or no bogey."

Ensign Torkel sounded the alarm.

HOOOOOOONK!

Captain Rakis took the PA and barked, "This is not a drill! We've spotted a possible hostile craft pursuing us. Emergency response teams to your stations. All officers on bridge. Off-duty crew, without emergency assignments, remain off-duty in your quarters, but be prepared for duty on my command. All passengers remain in your rooms, with the doors locked, until told to assemble at your life raft stations. The time is now three thirty-one. Communications Officer Chen will update you by shipnet on the half-hour or sooner as needed. Maintain radio silence regarding this emergency. All passenger and crew hospitality services are suspended until further notice. This message will repeat in ten seconds."

HOOOOOOONK!

The klaxon woke Duke from a deep sleep. Hearing the full message on the repeat, he immediately dressed and ran to the bow transport hangar to join Commander Wan Sen and her two attack force squads.

The klaxon also woke Kes and Steel from sleep in each other's arms. Knowing the plan, they immediately dressed and put on their disguises. Their ruse—dangerous as it was —would be the key to the defense of the *Odysseus*. In the meantime, they stayed in their stateroom, eyes glued to the shipnet, waiting for news and orders.

Within three minutes, the ship's officers—many still snapping snaps and zipping zips in their rush to get dressed —assembled on the bridge.

"Officers of the ship," began Captain Rakis. "We've got a bogey. Appears to be a ghost. Don't have details, but it's fast and big. Haven't seen anything like it before, but it could be a pirate. So, we're going to run through the drill. Everyone to their stations."

The minutes passed slowly for those waiting for trouble —the bridge officers, Kes and Steel, the ship defenders, the off-duty crew, and the passengers, but too quickly for the counterattack force. They instead ran to the bow transport hangar, which housed the ship transports.

Once in the hangar, they split into two pre-arranged squads. Commander Sen led Alpha Squad and served as the counterattack force leader. Duke led Beta Squad. In addition to the squad leaders and transport pilots, each squad had a crew of fifteen attackers: a lead phalanx of seven marines and a backup force of eight crew and passenger volunteers.

The attackers had already stored their weapons on the two transports assigned to the counterattack. Crew members had previously painted the two attack transports with the CIA ultrablack paint, provided by Colonel Boot and shipped with Steel. This paint absorbed all frequencies of electromagnetic radiation, from gamma rays to visible light to microwaves to radio waves. Camouflaged by the non-reflective paint, the transports could fly through space, invisible to detection.

As soon as the crews got to the bow hangar, they checked their weapons, piled into the transports, pumped out the hangar air, opened the hangar lock, and sent Captain Rakis a ready signal. Then they waited for Captain Rakis's command to launch.

Getting into the Alpha Squad leader seat, Commander Sen thought, *Typical hurry up and wait, an hour of boredom and a minute of terror. Hopefully, it won't become Situation Normal All Fucked Up.*

At the same time, while getting into the Beta Squad leader seat, Duke thought, *Rakis and Sen know what they're doing. We're lucky they're in command.*

At 03:47, Captain Rakis got the ready signal from the transports.

She immediately barked, "Officer King, bogey update!"

Officer King promptly responded, "Bogey remains directly up-course from us, traveling on the same bearing as us. Closing fast. Estimated time for scope image: one hour and twenty-nine minutes at five-sixteen. Estimated time for contact: five hours and thirty minutes at nine-seventeen."

Captain Rakis took the PA. "Officers of the Ship. Be prepared for the ship to execute a dogleg maneuver to see if the bogey is following us. The maneuver will begin with a turn to port, followed by a turn to starboard. If the bogey follows us through the first two turns, I will presume it is a pirate. I will then give the order to put us back on track to Port Tombaugh, but at the same time, I will give the order to launch the Alpha and Beta Squads. The turn back on course should briefly screen the launch of the Squads, so that they can take their stations undetected by the pirate. Officers, be prepared for course changes and the launch of the squads. Communications Officer Chen, announce to the crew and passengers that an unidentified vessel may be pursuing us and everyone should be prepared for abrupt course changes. Conning Officer Otte, tell me when you're ready for the first maneuver."

"Aye, aye, Sir." After a pause, Officer Otte announced, "ready, Sir."

Rakis barked, "Change course to port by two and a half degrees!"

Although the course shift was slight, because of the great speed, everyone on board felt an abrupt pull to the starboard side of the ship, spilling crockery and other loose objects to the deck.

"Officer King, eyes on the bogey. Tell me as soon as you can if the bogey changes course."

"Aye, aye, Sir!"

At 03:53, Officer King yelled, "Bogey changed course to port, by two-point-five. She is again on the same bearing as us and still closing."

Captain Rakis then barked more commands for the second maneuver. Once again, after a short delay, Officer King announced the bogey had again changed course, this time to starboard, and continued to close.

"Thank you," said Captain Rakis. "Com Officer Chen, announce on shipnet that pursuit by the unidentified vessel is now confirmed, we suspect a pirate. All personnel and passengers should continue emergency response measures."

"Transports Alpha and Beta," Rakis barked. "Prepare to launch by gas thrusters on my command. Use your thrusters to assume starboard stations on the forward side of the brake. When you reach your station, be sure the brake screens your profile from the up-course bogey. During maneuvers, use thrusters to hide your heat signatures. Save your rockets for the attack."

Rakis immediately barked, "Change course! Transports launch!"

Otte promptly responded, "Aye, aye, Sir."

Commander Sen announced, "Alpha force launched," followed by Duke, "Beta force launched."

After completing the maneuver, Officer Otte announced, "Sir, back on course for Port Tombaugh. Bogey still following."

Rakis snapped, "Officer Cutt, time?"

"One minute past four, Sir."

Back in their stateroom, awaiting orders, John asked Selena, "Do you know what Rakis is doing?"

"No, but I can guess. I think the ship is caught in a classic astrogation battle trap. We're deaccelerating with the stern rocket engines pointing forward and the bow pointing backward. Our enemy is directly behind us. Slowing down just closes the gap with the enemy. We can't accelerate away from the enemy—we're facing the wrong direction, toward the enemy. We can't move either to the right or left or up or down—the ship is going too fast for sharp moves. Besides, small course deviations can be easily matched by the enemy."

"So, we're screwed," said John.

"No. The Captain has tricks up her sleeve. I'm betting on her."

† † †

Back on bridge, at 05:16, Chief Warrant Officer King yelled, "Bogey on scope. Switching to bow screen now."

Over the next few minutes, what began as a blip on the screen, gradually took the shape of a familiar vessel. Then the Captain recognized the ship.

"My God!" she yelled. "That's the USSS *Persephone*!"

"What! Can't be!" yelled the XO. "*Persephone* disappeared in a flash two years ago, en route to Pluto. Everyone thought an unlucky space debris strike destroyed her and killed all eight hundred souls aboard."

"Well," said Rakis, "I know that ship. It's our sister ship, the *Persephone*!"

The XO then added, "Then her crew and passengers could still be alive. Somewhere."

Just then, the ship-to-ship com came alive. "*Odysseus*, this is Ogun, Captain of the Caine Toad Ship *Lady Annee's*

Sins. Kill the transponder and all communications now! Prepare to be boarded."

Rakis ignored the command and instead barked, "Get Kes and Steel to the bridge, pronto." Com Officer Chen called the couple while Ensign Torkel ran to escort them to the bridge.

Rakis again snapped, "Officer Cutt, time?"

"Five-nineteen, Sir."

Rakis then reported to the bridge. "I've sailed on the *Persephone* in the past. She's our sister ship. Unless the Caine Toads have modified her, she's an unarmed passenger vessel, Com Officer Chen. At the next shipnet update, pass my words along to passengers and crew."

Just then, Officer King yelled, "Second up-course bogey. Small but closing quickly. Looks like a projectile from *Lady A*. Estimated time of contact: one minute, seventeen seconds. Prepare for strike at five-twenty-one."

"Com Officer Chen! Belay my shipnet com order!" barked Rakis. Then turning to the officers on the bridge, she said "All right. I was wrong. I guess the *Lady A's* armed after all. I expect this will be a warning shot. Probably to the ship brake. If they're aiming for the hull, not enough time for evasive maneuvers." Then turning back to Com Officer Tim Chen, she said, "Tell Alpha and Beta Squads to get ready to assume counterattack positions. Inform all personnel to prepare for a strike at five-twenty-one. Com Officer Chen, send out an SOS by laser tight beam to Fort Resnik, report we are under attack by pirate vessel, the former USSS *Persephone*, now the Caine Toad *Lady Annee's Sins*. Officer Val, begin the countdown to the bogey strike over the PA, starting at strike minus thirty seconds."

Not knowing if this was the end or just a warning, the dreadful seconds passed slowly. Then over the PA, the XO began, "thirty seconds, twenty-nine, twenty-eight . . . three, two, one."

A torrent of bangs abruptly rattled the ship, reminding Steel of hail suddenly hitting the roof of his boyhood home in Iowa.

Over the clatter, Rakis yelled, "Squads, launch to counterattack positions."

As soon as the clatter ceased, Rakis demanded, "Damage report."

While the officers searched their data screens for damage, Captain Ogun came back on the ship-to-ship com. "*Odysseus*. I've got a bow rail gun trained on you. That was just a warning shot with a one-kilo slug. Now kill the transponder or I'll shove a quintal slug at sub-light speed down your throat and out your ass!"

Rakis barked, "Kill the transponder. Klaxon the ship. Announce we're under attack. Bridge, I'm waiting for damage reports. Squads, tell me when you are in counterattack position and give me your damage reports. Kes and Steel, front and center. Com Officer Chen, inform the *Lady A* we've killed the transponder and await boarding."

Then turning around, glaring at her officers, she yelled for the third time—not a good sign— "Damage reports!"

"Hull's intact" yelled Chief Engineer Dan Dix. "Brake's got a thirty-meter hole punched through it. Rubble striking the hull made the clatter. Otherwise, intact. Should make it to PT."

Chief Electronics Warrant Officer Han Jayson yelled, "Starboard antennas shredded by debris. We've lost deep space communications but still have radio and tight-band laser ship-to-ship." The rest of the bridge reported no other significant damage.

A few minutes later, Alpha Squad Leader, Commander Sen, sent by tight-band laser, "No damage to Alpha Squad. Hiding on the port side of the brake screened us from the starboard missile attack. I see your brake hole. About thirty meters wide. Starboard side of the *Odysseus* looks peppered and the deep-space antenna shredded. We'll be in counterattack position in eight minutes."

Right after Sen's report, Beta Squad Leader Duke, whose ship was also on the port side, sent a laser message echoing Sen's report.

Ship-to-ship blared again, "This is Captain Ogun. Here are my demands. I want your captain on video and an immediate statement of surrender. It is now five-twenty-five. At nine-twenty sharp, I want your bow hangar doors opened to receive our prize crew. All weapons to be collected and stashed in the bow hangar for pickup at that time. All crew and passenger valuables should be collected and stashed in the bow hangar for pickup. Have Castor Valerio ready for transfer to the *Lady Annee*. All passengers must remain in their staterooms and be prepared to be searched. Officers remain on the bridge. All *Odysseus* crew, remain at your stations until relieved by the prize crew. We will deal harshly with anyone who resists or refuses to follow our orders. Captain, I'm waiting for your video surrender."

With that last command, Captain Rakis waved to Kes to start.

"Captain Ogun," said Kes, "this is Captain Rakis of the USSS *Odysseus*. Your attack destroyed our ship-to-ship video. You've my word that we've surrendered. We'll receive your prize crew as directed. Castor Valerio suffered mortal injuries when he assassinated one of our passengers. Valerio requires continued medical care. He'll have to be transferred by gurney, attached to multiple organ support devices, and under the care of an attendant."

"Captain Rakis," replied Captain Ogun, "if you or your crew deceive me or defy me in any way, I'll immediately execute the bugger by beheading. Ogun out."

Ogun undoubtedly expected his barbaric threat to behead resistors to intimidate the *Odysseus* crew. Most likely it frightened some. But the threat just ignited the powerful feelings of cold rage Steel had experienced in his past encounters with the Caine Toads.

† † †

"Steel," Captain Rakis demanded: "What can you tell us about the Caine Toads?"

"The Caine Toads," Steel answered, "is a Caribbean crime organization which began trading in illegal drugs in the 1900s. As the illegal drug market dried up, they shifted to human-trafficking, and smuggling weapons, art, antiquities, jewels, and exotic animals and plants. They use Voodoo names, fake Voodoo magic, and sham Voodoo religious practices to intimidate. The founder and first leader of the Caine Toads took the name Kalfu, the name for the

Voodoo devil. Since then, every supreme leader of the Caine Toads has taken the name Kalfu. The Caine Toads also use the name Kalfu for a war cry. I killed Kalfu in Jamaica this past January. The Caine Toads use the name Ogun for the second in command and designated successor to Kalfu. Ogun is the Voodoo name for the god of war."

Summarizing, Steel said, "The Caine Toads are brutal, barbaric, and will not hesitate to kill, including by beheading. The CIA has battled them for decades. We thought we had destroyed their organization. I don't think anyone knew they had expanded to become a 'stro crime organization engaged in space piracy."

"And who's Lady Annee?" asked Rakis.

Steel replied, "A Jamaican woman of questionable authenticity. Legend has it she was born in Haiti to European parents who died during her childhood. A Haitian Voodoo witch raised her and taught her Voodoo magic. As a young woman, Annee moved to Jamaica and married a plantation owner. According to legend, she killed her husband, inherited his plantation—Rose Hall—and then murdered both of her next two husbands. She earned the name the White Witch because she used Voodoo magic to terrorize, torture, and murder her slaves. Some question the accuracy of the Lady Annee story, but plantation records and archaeological excavations have confirmed that Rose Hall slaves suffered horrible torture and frequent murder. Whether true or not, the Jamaicans so feared the White Witch's Voodoo magic that they burned down nearly every other plantation house, but ignored hers, for fear of Lady Annee's ghost and her sins."

With this report, Captain Rakis looked down, shook her head, and muttered, "Oh, God have mercy."

Steel added, "Yeah. You've got that right. The Caine Toads are evil. They'll use whatever wicked means they can to achieve their goals. They know no limits. Do not underestimate them. They're as dangerous a foe as you'll ever encounter. They nearly killed me twice and they beheaded my fiancé, a trained CIA agent, while forcing me to watch."

With those words, the bridge fell silent. Until that moment, Captain Rakis's quiet self-confidence and decisive leadership had filled the bridge with optimism that they could defeat the pirates. But all of that evaporated with Steel's report. They began to have doubts, began to fear the future.

Seeing the change in mood sweep over the bridge, Steel quickly added, "Don't get me wrong. These people are human, and they can be overcome. You need to know they're capable of great evil. But you also need to know that knowledge is power, power to set fear aside and conquer the evil that we face together. We can do this. We will do this. We must do this. You've got a great captain. She'll lead you to defeat Ogun. And when you do, you will have done the solar system a great service, and you will have saved the lives of the passengers and crew of both the *Odysseus* and the *Persephone.*"

Captain Rakis added, "Thank you Steel. Crew, you heard what Steel said. We've got to play the hand we've been dealt, but I think we've got a winning play. So, let's beat them!"

28 LADY ANNEE'S SINS

At 08:50 UTC, thirty minutes until boarding by the prize crew, Kes, speaking in place of Captain Rakis, radioed the bridge of the *Lady Annee's Sins*. "Captain Ogun. Captain Rakis here. We're prepared to receive your prize crew and transfer Valerio to the *Lady Annee*. There's one problem. Given your threat to destroy my ship, there is no point in giving up our prisoner before your prize crew has boarded my ship. Without a hostage, I fear you will destroy us. What do you propose?"

After a brief pause, Ogun answered, "Captain Rakis, here are my commands:

"Since Valerio needs an attendant, you will serve as both the transport pilot and the attendant. No one else should be in your transport.

"Dock in *Lady Annee's* bow hangar. Leave *Odysseus's* bow hangar open.

"After you dock, my prize crew will dock in the *Odysseus*.

"The *Lady Annee* and the *Odysseus* will close hangar locks and re-pressurize at the same time. You will then open your transport cargo lock. I'll send a medic to your transport and verify Valerio's identity. The medic will escort Valerio and you out of the transport.

"You will be my prisoner.

"Once you have left your transport, my prize crew will take the *Odysseus*. Leave a skeleton crew on your bridge and have the rest of your officers lined up on the hangar deck for surrender by your XO. My prize crew will assume command of your ship.

"Load your arms and valuables into crates for transport, along with your officers, to the *Lady Annee*.

"There will be no deviation from this plan whatsoever. If there is, I'll destroy your ship and kill everyone aboard. Do you understand?"

After a moment of silence, Kes said, "Roger wilco. We'll begin transfer at nine-twenty. Rakis out."

With a smile on her face, Captain Rakis addressed her officers, saying, "All right. You heard the man. Let's get to it!"

At precisely 09:20 UTC, one of the transports left the *Odysseus* bow hangar. The transport flew by autopilot to the *Lady Annee*, which was waiting just ten kilometers up-course from the *Odysseus*, while Kes, dressed in one of Captain Rakis's uniforms, sat in the pilot's seat.

In the cargo bay, Steel lay motionless on a stretcher, wearing only a patient gown and covered by a sheet. Dressings covered his head, chest, abdomen, and extremities, leaving only his eyes, lower face, hands and feet uncovered. A urinary catheter, filled with yellow liquid, emerged from underneath the drape covering his groin and emptied into a collection bag hanging at the foot of the gurney. A nasogastric tube, filled with a vile liquid that looked like black coffee and coffee grounds—a sign of gastric bleeding—was stuck in his right nostril and emptied into a collection bag hanging at the head of the gurney. Like sentries guarding a prisoner, a half dozen IV poles, each one holding one or more pumps for administering life-supporting intravenous drugs, surrounded Steel. From each pump, an IV tube snaked across the sheet and went under a bandage covering one of Steel's four limbs. A mechanical kidney and liver rode on the bottom shelf of the gurney. Blood-filled medical tubing led from Steel's abdominal dressings to the mechanical organs and back to Steel, indicating he had both kidney and liver failure. An oral endotracheal tube, stuck in Steel's mouth, connected Steel to a mechanical respirator and oxygen tank, carried on the bottom shelf of the gurney, indicated he also had respiratory failure. A bank of monitors occupied the foot of the stretcher, providing a continuous display of vital functions and a streaming analysis of blood, urine, and respiration. Steel looked like a man on the edge of death.

After passing the *Lady Annee's* transport heading to the *Odysseus*, Kes and Steel's transport circled around the *Lady Annee's* forward brake, entered the rear-facing open bow hangar, pulled in between a transport on the port side and a black racing yacht on the starboard, and landed on the hangar deck of the *Lady Annee's Sins*.

At 09:29, Kes radioed a brief message to the bridge of the *Lady Annee*, the *Odysseus*, and the nearby transports announcing: "This is Rakis. We've docked. Pressurize hangar."

Seconds later, the pilot for the *Lady Annee* transport also reported docking in the Odysseus and requested pressurization.

As soon as the *Lady Annee's* hangar barometer rose above 0.8 atmospheres, Kes popped opened the cargo door and lowered the ramp. A ship medic, with his right hand holding a taser, and plastic manacles and an identity wand dangling from his utility belt, stepped out of the security of the hangar control room, crossed the deck, and entered the transport. Pointing his taser at Kes, he tossed the manacles to her and ordered her to put them on and attach herself to Steel's gurney. As soon as she followed these orders, the medic checked her bindings to make sure they were tight and patted her down, searching for weapons. Not finding any, the medic holstered his taser, quickly patted down Steel and gave the gurney medical equipment and readouts a cursory glance. Satisfied by his inspection, the medic waved the identity wand over Steel's left forearm. The readout, Castor Valerio, included all of the standard biographical and morphogenic data to complete the identification.

The medic radioed Captain Ogun, "Yup. It's him. Right size and skin color. Embedded ID confirms identity. Looks sick, but stable."

"Good. Escort Valerio to sickbay and have Rakis placed in the brig. Ogun out."

Leading the self-propelled gurney, with the bound Kes trailing behind, the medic guided the group through the hangar passenger lock, and into the *Lady Annee*. As they walked through the corridor to their new quarters, Kes's perscom pinged.

Then, all hell broke loose!

† † †

Also at 09:29, the *Lady Annee's* transport entered the *Odysseus* bow hangar and sat down in the open space between the two transports remaining in the bay.

After getting Kes's announcement that her transport had docked, the *Odysseus* Hanger Control Officer closed the hangar doors and repressurized the bay.

When the bay pressure reached 0.8 atmospheres, the XO, Roger Val, led the *Odysseus* officers into the bay where they assembled in a line, facing the side passenger lock of the *Lady Annee's* transport. The rear end of the officer line curved around the transport stern cargo doors, where two officers, each with a self-propelled crate, stopped to wait for the cargo doors to open. The uncovered crates showed one filled with valuables and cash, the other with small arms.

The side passenger lock opened, and the prize crew leader stepped out to get the XO's surrender. At the same time, the rear cargo doors opened, and the ramp dropped to the deck.

A trained eye would have spotted the poor fit of the uniforms worn by several of the *Odysseus* officers. A trained eye would also have become alarmed by the unusual amount of clutter on the hangar deck that surrounded the *Lady Annee's* transport. Scaffolding covered the port side transport, which had been stripped of its rockets, presumably removed for repairs. On the starboard side, crates and heavy equipment stood next to the transport, waiting for loading.

None of the *Lady Annee's* prize crew had an eye for such detail. Instead, as the prize crew leader approached the

XO to get the surrender, a disorganized mob of fifty or more thugs rushed down the cargo ramp, yelling and pushing, eager to grab booty and sex slaves.

Before handing over the surrender, the XO pulled a micro-dart gun from his tunic sleeve and shot the prize crew leader in the neck with a paralytic dart, immediately dropping the pirate to the deck. The XO pushed a button on his perscom, signaling the counterattack had begun and pulled a bat-hood over his head. At the same time, the two officers at the rear of the line also pulled bat-hoods over their heads while the rest of the officers covered their ears with their hands, tightly closed their eyes, and dropped to the deck. The three bat-hooded officers then started tossing stun grenades into the mob and into the transport through the open passenger lock and cargo bay doors. Each of the officer grenadiers tossed six grenades and held one in reserve.

Overwhelmed by the surprise bombardment of lightning flashes and thunderous blasts, the mob collapsed onto the deck. Some brutes simply died of fright right where they fell; the rest of the thugs lay on the deck, immobilized by the detonations.

The fusillade abruptly stopped. The unarmed officers without hoods used the silence to scramble behind the surrounding hangar clutter. The XO and the other two hooded grenadiers—both marines—stood their ground, ready to restart the storm if needed. In the meantime, a line of seven marines, wearing makeshift noise and light protection, methodically shot each hooligan with at least one, sometimes two or more paralytic darts. Following the advancing line of marines, another line of crew and passenger volunteers, also with makeshift noise and vision protection, put out any fires that might have accidentally been started when the stun grenades startled a pirate. The second line also secured the paralyzed prisoners with plastic manacles, nylon cords, and duct tape. Within two minutes, the marines worked their way into the transport, shooting the transport pilot, the last of the thugs, with a paralytic dart, before she could alert the *Lady Annee*. In less than three minutes, the defenders of the *Odysseus* had won the battle.

Hearing the perscom ping, Steel spat out the sham orotracheal tube, jerked out the fake nasogastric tube, and swept away the rest of the bogus apparatuses binding him to the spurious gurney medical equipment.

Pulling a micro-dart gun out, from underneath his dressings, he shot the medic in the throat just as the medic turned to see the commotion behind him. Steel then jumped off the gurney, drew his Kpinga from his back holster, and severed the plastic cording that connected Kes's wrists and bound her to the stretcher. Like an actor making a quick costume change, Steel yanked off his gown and dressings and slipped on the nano-silk armored pants, tunic, and boots hidden in the dummy respirator. Released from her bonds, Kes popped the top of the phony mechanical kidney and liver, reached inside and pulled out two bat-hoods, weapons, and manacles. Taking some, she passed the rest to Steel. She then popped the top of the false oxygen tank and grabbed the cutlass hidden inside. After Kes and Steel pulled the two bat-hoods over their heads, they ran for the bridge, knowing what was going to happen next.

BANG! The ship shuddered as a loud crash erupted from the port side.

BANG! A second loud crash hit the ship from the starboard side.

HOOOOOOONK! A klaxon sounded, followed by THUNK, THUNK, THUNK . . . as all the ship's hatches, closed and locked.

A coarse voice called over the PA: "Hull breach on passenger deck P-two, starboard lounge!" Then after a pause, the voice added, "Second hull breach, on crew deck C-one, port side crew mess! Damage control crew, proceed to the closest breach."

HOOOOOOONK! The message repeated several more times.

During the commotion, Steel and Kes made their way as quickly as they could along a back route they had learned on the sister ship *Odysseus*, a route that would take them to the bridge while avoiding Caine Toads rushing to the breaches. Kes took the lead, opening the closed and locked hatches with an emergency override, borrowed from the *Odysseus*, while Steel took backup, using his micro-dart gun to paralyze the few crew members they met on their way to the bridge. At first, distracted by the emergency response to the hull breaches, no one gave them any mind, but then the Klaxon sounded again:

HOOOOOOONK!

"We're under attack! We're under attack!" Ogun yelled over the PA. "Armed intruders on board! Entered through port and starboard hull breaches. Kill all invaders. I repeat, kill all invaders."

HOOOOOOONK!

As the PA repeated the message, crew resistance stiffened. With the greater resistance, Kes and Steel swapped their micro-dart guns for tasers set on kill. Kes remained in the lead, opening locks and tasing Toads. Walking backward, Steel followed behind, fighting off the Caine Toads with Kpinga in one hand and taser in the other, leaving a trail of dead bodies, blood, and limbs. Three times Steel had to use his stun grenades to neutralize opposition, exhausting his grenade supply.

After twenty minutes of intense fighting, Kes and Steel broke into the bridge and entered chaos.

About twenty people occupied the bridge. Mostly men, a few women. A motley group, they did not wear uniforms. They came from a wide variety of ethnic backgrounds, with no apparent predominance. The room rang with their shouts and barked orders. Some of them sat in front of monitors while others ran around. Steel could see no guards, but everyone carried hand weapons. In the center of the maelstrom, at the helm, sat a big black brute, who shouted louder than anyone else and appeared to be in command, such as it was. He needed no introduction; Kes and Steel had now met Ogun, captain of the *Lady Annee's Sins*.

As soon as the two agents entered the control room, Ogun spotted them and yelled over the hubbub, "There they are! Kill the invaders!" With these words, the closest crew members immediately set upon the couple, expecting to quickly overwhelm them with numbers and edged weapons.

None of the combatants carried forbidden weapons, such as explosives and guns, that could blow a hole in the spaceship. Likewise, crammed with delicate electronic equipment, the ship's control room was no place for tasers, microwave blasters, and stun grenades—even if Steel had any grenades left. The close quarters of the melee did not allow for using micro-dart guns.

Kes and Steel lived for this kind of a fight: hand-to-hand combat using edged weapons and all of their Krabi Krabong and Judo skills.

With Kpinga ax in both hands, Steel spun and danced, cutting down the opposition like slashing weeds with a weed-whacker. Kes held her own. With a cutlass in one hand and a star-spike in the other, she cut and stabbed, jumped and dodged, defeating every foe, like a Belt heroine in a martial arts VR movie.

But the Caine Toads kept on coming.

Seeing Steel had begun to tire, Ogun jumped up from his seat. Screaming "Kalfu!" and waving his Samurai katana over his head, the brute shoved his way to the front of the melee to confront Steel. Holding the pommel with both hands, Ogun swung the razor-sharp long blade in a broad, powerful side stroke, from right to left, expecting to behead Steel on the spot. Taking a step back to dodge the lethal swipe, Steel held up his three-bladed ax. With a loud clang, the two opposing sickle blades of the Kpinga caught the slashing katana in a metal embrace. Following the intended arc of the katana, Steel swept the trapped sword down to his left side while giving his ax a hard twist so that the serrated edges of the two hook blades bit into the narrow Samurai sword, holding it like the toothed jaws of a bear trap. Before Ogun could pull his sword free, Steel used all his strength to kick the brute in the groin. With a loud "oof," Ogun sank to his knees, momentarily relaxing his grip on his sword. Steel yanked the blade out of Ogun's grasp and flung the weapon across the room. Steel then pointed the rat-tail spike, the tip of the Kpinga, at Ogun's chest and shouted, "Surrender!"

Ogun grunted, reached into his tunic and pulled out the forbidden weapon—a .45-caliber pistol—and pointed it at Steel, yelling "Die!"

A gunshot rang across the room.

Ogun's left eye erupted in gore.

Once more, Kes had killed a terrorist with a well-placed shot, her signature shot, a bullet through the left eye, into the brain.

At that same moment, Commander Sen, leading the remnants of the Alpha and Beta squads broke into the room, and yelled, "Throw down your weapons and surrender, or you will be killed on the spot!"

That command ended the battle for the *Lady Annee's Sins*.

29 RAVEN FLIGHT

Four hours later, on the bridge of the *Lady Annee's Sins*, Commander Sen, Agent Volkova, and Agent Dakar conferred by video conferencing with Captain Rakis and XO Val on the *Odysseus*. The XO began by reporting the defense of the *Odysseus*:

"Captain Rakis. Fifty-three Toads manned the prize crew transport. Forty-one survived. Twelve died, five by fright and seven by an overdose of paralytic toxin. We've locked the survivors in the transport we cannibalized for the rocket engines. Aside from some temporary hearing loss, we've had no casualties and no deaths. Only damage is the starboard brake hole. It shouldn't interfere with our scheduled docking at Port Tombaugh four days from now. Ship operations have returned to normal. Although shaken, passengers appear comfortable and pleased with the defense."

Commander Sen then took the mic and reported on the counterattack:

"Captain Rakis. At the time of the counterattack, the *Lady Annee's Sins* had on board two hundred twenty crew members and nineteen officers—using the term officers generously. Eighty-nine crew members and thirteen officers died in the counterattack. Our ruse worked perfectly. The fraudulent ID Agent Volkova created for Agent Dakar fooled the *Lady Annee's* medic. The sham medical devices fabricated by our engineers also fooled the medic. Agents Dakar and Volkova used the ruse to enter the *Lady Annee's Sins* and advanced to the bridge, killing eleven of the officers and killing and incapacitating many of the crew. Agent Volkova killed Captain Ogun with a well-placed, low-powered gunshot to the head, just as Captain Ogun was about to shoot Agent Dakar in the chest."

Commander Sen continued. "It's possible our counterattack with the two transport squads would have succeeded by itself, but more likely it would have failed, given the overwhelming number of Toads and the stiff resistance. I believe the distraction of a third attack into the heart of the ship and onto the bridge, tipped the balance in our favor. Killing Captain Ogun certainly ended the fight."

At this point, Commander Sen paused. With a quaver in her voice, she continued. "Agent Laoloo's plan to cannibalize two transport rockets and convert them into guided missiles by using the CIA microdrones to pilot each rocket worked perfectly. The Toads never spotted the ultrablack-camouflaged Alpha and Beta Squad transports you had us station up-course from the *Lady Annee*. Each squad launched an ultrablack-camouflaged, rocket-drone on your command. Both missiles crashed into the *Lady Annee*, one on the port side and the other on the starboard. Because of the relatively low velocity and the large bulk of the rocket-drones, they tore holes through the hull, but did not penetrate further, creating the hull breaches we needed to enter the *Lady Annee*. Both the Alpha and Beta squads carried engineers, so as soon as our troops boarded, the engineers slapped patches over the breaches secure enough to bring the pressure back to point-eight atmospheres and allow our troops to remove their spacesuits."

After a pause to collect herself, she continued, "Unfortunately, because of the noise of the missile strike and the delay caused by patching the hull breaches and removing our spacesuits, we lost the element of surprise. As soon as we got into the *Lady Annee*, we encountered fierce resistance by the Toads. Alpha Squad had five casualties, including two deaths. Beta Squad had seven casualties, including four deaths. Despite our losses, the Toads suffered many more casualties. It was a bloody battle, but necessary. In my opinion, as successful as it was, by itself, Volkova and Dakar's ruse could not have taken the ship. Agent Laoloo's missile attacks saved the day."

Taking a deep breath, she added, "Both Agent Laoloo and I led our squads. Agent Laoloo sustained severe injuries. He's alive, but barely. He has multi-organ failure. He's in the *Lady Annee's* sickbay. A medical team from the *Odysseus* is taking care of him now. The *Odysseus* has also provided additional medical supplies not available on the *Lady Annee*. The *Odysseus* ship doctor, Dr. McTam, tells me our two ships do not have the medical facilities to keep Agent Laoloo alive much longer than forty-eight hours. He needs immediate care at Port Tombaugh. And we can't get there before Saturday morning. So . . ." She stopped as tears started to creep down her face.

After these sad words, Captain Rakis quickly said, "Agents Volkova and Dakar, XO Val and Commander Sen, well done! Let's hear the rest of the report and then put our heads together to see what we can do for Agent Laoloo.

Agent Dakar, what can you tell us about the *Lady Annee's Sins?*"

"Sir. Like the *Odysseus*, we've disabled two transports and are using them to hold the surviving Caine Toads. Despite the patched hull breaches, the *Lady Annee* is structurally sound and should be able to reach PT with the *Odysseus*. We've searched the *Lady Annee* and haven't found any passengers or crew remaining from when the ship was named the *Persephone*. We've started interviewing the Caine Toads, beginning with the six surviving officers."

With a tone of disgust, Dakar said, "Greed and lust motivate Toads. They've no loyalty to each other or to anything else, other than to their own skins. Facing execution if they don't cooperate, they've been eager to spill their guts. We're making quick progress. We've learned the Caine Toad home base is the planemo Ixion. Many of the *Persephone's* passengers and crew are held prisoner there. The rest have been sold into slavery. Ixion also houses passengers and crew from other pirate seizures. There may be as many as fifteen hundred prisoners there. The Caine Toads also use Ixion as a storehouse for loot and supplies."

"Good job!" said Rakis. "This is a big break. I'm sure PT will be glad to hear this news. Is that all?"

"There's a big surprise, and it might help Agent Laoloo."

"What is it?"

"Uhm," Dakar said. "Agent Volkova should give this report."

"All right, Agent Volkova, what've you got?"

"Well, when we pulled into the *Lady A's* hangar bay, we set down next to a spacecraft, larger than a transport, and painted with that same ultrablack paint we used to camouflage the Alpha and Beta Squad transports and missiles. That got me to thinking: only the US has stockpiles of ultrablack paint. After interrogating the Toad officers, I found out that this spaceship, a six-seater racing yacht, is a Star Chaser five-x, the fastest production yacht made. Its name is the *Raven*."

"What's it doing here?" asked Rakis.

"I'm getting to that," said Volkova. "I interrogated the Lady A's HCO about the craft. He told me—and hold on, this is the big surprise—that CIA Executive Director Ora Barrun owned the *Raven*."

With that announcement, gasps and whistles filled the room.

Volkova continued, "the *Lady A's* HCO said the *Raven* docked in the *Lady A* just a few hours before we picked her up on the LiDAR. The HCO also said Barrun fled KC eight days ago, which would be right after the attempted assassination of Dakar and the KC bombing. To get to the *Lady A* in that short of time, Barrun had to be moving at least two to four Gs constant acceleration—maybe even more. The star-chaser will do five. Barrun's fat and out of shape. Despite cutting edge, automated high-g medical support and the best high-g flight couch available to citizens, Barrun didn't survive the trip. The Toad HCO said the racer autopilot completed the trip. He also said Ogun was expecting Barrun's arrival because it was Barrun who ordered the *Lady A* to intercept the *Odysseus* in the first place."

More gasps while she paused for a moment, shaking her head. She then continued, "The HCO said he heard a rumor that Barrun had run away from Earth because he ordered the hit on Dakar and the KC bombing. I haven't confirmed that. But I did confirm from the *Lady A's* XO, who survives, that Barrun had ordered the Lady A to intercept the *Odysseus*. The XO added that Barrun ordered Ogun to either rescue Valerio or destroy the *Odysseus*."

After another pause, she added, "I think the CIA XO, General Ora Barrun, is behind all of this. I bet the CIA figured it out and tried to catch him. I think as soon as Barrun knew he was a suspect, he took flight to the safety of the Caine Toads, only he didn't survive the trip."

"The g-forces killed him?" Rakis asked.

"I imagine," Volkova said. "The Toads didn't perform a postmortem. They just dumped him into space."

"Craters!" said Rakis, stunned by this news. "If you're right, this is quite a coup! The CIA XO in League with Ogun. Who would've thought! Crime makes for strange crewmates. Well, PT will be glad to clean out this rats' nest, that's for sure, but KC won't be happy."

After a moment, Captain Rakis added, "Uhm, I presume you're going to propose we use the *Raven* to transfer Laoloo to *Port Tombaugh?*"

"Yes, Sir," replied Volkova. "I talked to Dr. McTam. He says it would not take much to convert the racer into a high-speed ambulance. As I already told you, the *Raven* has state-of-the-art robot medical monitoring and intervention for sustaining life during high-g travel. Dr. McTam said all of his other patients are stable, so he's willing to accompany Agent Laoloo and provide him any additional care needed while in transit. But Dr. McTam also says we should transfer Agent Laoloo as soon as possible."

"Let me guess," said Captain Rakis, "You're going to propose that Colonel Dakar and you accompany Agent Laoloo."

"Yes. We're all CIA. Well, I'm not, but I'm on loan to the CIA."

"But what about a pilot?" asked Captain Rakis, then quickly added, "I know, I know. Any vessel that can fly across the solar system at high-g on autopilot hardly needs a human pilot. Still, it seems wise to have one."

"Yes, Captain. I agree. Commander Sen has experience piloting exotic craft like the *Raven*. With your permission, she has volunteered to serve as pilot. She says she can get Laoloo to Port Tombaugh by tomorrow afternoon."

Turning the camera to Commander Sen, Rakis looked at her for a few minutes across the ether, reassessing the significance of the tears on Sen's face. She then gently asked, "Commander Sen, Is that right?"

"Yes, Sir."

Agent Volkova interrupted, "Uhm, Captain Rakis, I should have also told you I have downloaded the *Lady A's* memory banks. I'll bring them with me. PT would like to get them as soon as possible to help plan a rescue of the Ixion hostages."

"All right," Rakis said, "how soon can you have the *Raven* ready?"

"Within the hour."

"Then do it!"

30 WEARIN' THE GREEN, WHITE AND GOLD

The two agents arrived at Port Tombaugh early Wednesday evening, March 16, nearly two and a half days before their scheduled arrival on the *Odysseus*.

The CIA had booked them into two rooms at the Stern Hotel, the finest and oldest hotel in Port Tombaugh. But when they entered the Hotel lobby, they found it jammed with people, refugees from the emergency evacuation of Charon looking for accommodations. So, the agents gave up one of their rooms and retired for the Port Tombaugh night.

Like the Buzz Aldrin Space Station, the Lunar city Marius Hills, and their passenger ship *Odysseus*, Port Tombaugh kept time by the UTC clock and structured the twenty-four hour cycle with twelve hours of light and twelve hours of darkness. By the time Selena and John checked into their room it was already dark. They didn't need this prompt to let them know it was time to go to bed. Exhausted from the trip, feeling safe from all enemies, they fell asleep as soon as they laid down.

The next morning, they awoke to bright artificial sunshine streaming in through the open picture window overlooking Central Park across from the Hotel entrance. Even though John knew he was in the Plutonian city of Port

Tombaugh, it looked to him like a sunny summer day in Kansas City.

Feeling rested and pampered by the Stern Hotel luxury, the secret agents planned to have breakfast at the Tavern on the Green, across Central Park from the hotel. Before they could exit the hotel lobby, the concierge stopped them and gave each of them a white orchid, gold mum, and green leaf artificial lei, explaining Plutonians traditionally gave leis to all visitors to Pluto.

Not wanting to appear conspicuous, Selena refused her lei.

John, on the other hand, feeling playful and rested and knowing that wearing the lei could hardly make him more conspicuous, gratefully allowed the concierge to drape the garland over John's head.

After breakfast next to the park, where birds and squirrels entertained the agents over their coffee and croissants, the agents took a stroll through the brightly lit space station Central Plaza. On returning to the hotel to meet their 10:30 escort, Selena and John could not help noticing that green, white, and gold banners and bunting hung all around Port Tombaugh. Not to mention that nearly everyone they encountered wore some combination of the colors. Many wore leis just like John's.

Feeling conspicuous by the absence of color on her gray uniform, this time Selena accepted her lei from the concierge when they returned to the hotel.

As previously arranged, at 10:30 UTC, Troy Thornbird, a member of Commandant Sliffer's staff, met the agents in the lobby, introduced himself, and explained—just like others had done before him—that Commandant Sliffer had sent him to escort the agents to the Fifth Directorate Strategy and Tactics Audio Conference. General Sliffer wanted the two agents to be personally escorted because the maze of passageways and rings that separated the Stern Hotel from the secure communications studio in Fort Resnik, where the conference would take place, could be confusing for newcomers, even with Talos's guidance.

Selena didn't need the assistance, given her past tour of duty on Pluto. But she welcomed the guide anyway, since John peppered their escort with questions about the space station city and Pluto. Proud of his celestial home, Officer Thornbird readily answered John's questions while they walked to Fort Resnik, telling him things even Selena didn't know.

The first question John asked Officer Thornbird, who wore a green, white, and gold ribbon pinned to the chest of his white uniform, was, "I know it's St. Pat's Day, so I understand the green, but why all of the white and gold?"

Replying with great pride, Troy said, "Today's Founder's Day, the day in 2058 when my great-grandfather, Talos Thornbird, first set foot on Pluto. We celebrate the day with our territorial colors, by wearin' the green, white, and gold."

About the same time, roughly seven and a half billion kilometers away, in the garage converted to a studio, attached to the Independence, Missouri safe house, life was not nearly so cheery.

It was still dark; it would be another hour-and-a-half until dawn. It had only been four days since the Central

Time Zone shifted from standard time to daylight savings time, pushing everyone to get up an hour earlier than usual.

It was still cold. According to the calendar, the first day of spring would arrive in three days, but one would never know it. Overnight, a cold snap had dropped a half-inch of snow, covering the early spring blossoms, fulfilling the old Missouri prophecy that 'it always snows on the forsythia' and reminding everyone that old man winter had not yet relaxed his grip on KC.

Only Kevan Fitzpatrick, the short, bearded EP Communications Technician, who had good-humoredly dressed like a leprechaun in lime green, greeted the day cheerfully, prattling in a forced Irish-accent that today was St. Patrick's Day and that St. Patrick was the patron saint of engineers.

Everyone else felt tired and grouchy , particularly Acting Director Boot, who had to get up earlier than anyone else to commute to the safe house from his home in Bonner Springs, Kansas. But the early hour even caused Director Lee, who still hid in the safe house, and Chief of Staff Dawson, who lived in nearby Blue Springs, to feel lethargic and irritable.

Mr. Fitzpatrick's lighthearted blather prompted Colonel Boot to mutter under his breath, "God save us from little green men." Dr. Lee responded by jabbing the Colonel in the ribs and whispering something about being quiet and drinking his coffee so that the green elf could help them chase snakes out of the CIA.

† † †

Through the miracle of EP communications and despite the more than seven billion kilometers that separated them, the S&T audio conference began sharply at 11:00 UTC in Fort Resnik and 06:00 CDT in Independence, Missouri.

Colonel Boot began the conference by calling the roll. Although no one in the Fort Resnik secure communications studio could see it, by this time the Colonel's mood had brightened and he wore a smile as he started to play his little joke on Dakar.

"Fort Resnik. For the record, who is in attendance?"

"This is General Mark Sliffer, the Fort Resnik Commandant. I am also the senior officer of the Plutonian attendees. With me, in order of seniority are, Captain Leena Rakis, Captain of the USSS *Odysseus*, currently on temporary assignment to Captain the *Lady Annee's Sins*, Colonel John Dakar of the Fifth Freedom Directorate of the CIA, and Mossad agent Dr. Selena Volkova, currently on temporary assignment to the CIA." General Sliffer paused for a moment, and then continued, "Independence. For the record, who is in attendance?"

"This is Colonel Louis Boot, Deputy Director of the Fifth Freedom Directorate, currently serving as the Acting Director. I will be chairing this meeting. With me are Colonel Peter Dawson, Chief of Staff for the Fifth Freedom Directorate and Dr. Emma . . ."

"WHAT!" exploded across the ether, cutting off Colonel Boot, as John broke all protocol and yelled: "Dr. Lee, is that really you? I thought you were dead! Are you really alive?"

"Yes John, I am really alive."

For the third time in four weeks, Selena saw something not seen by anyone else. John the stoic fighter, John the ruthless warrior, crying. But this time, he cried with joy.

Pretending to be harsh, but secretly pleased by John's outburst, Colonel Boot said, "Colonel Dakar, do you need to excuse yourself from this meeting to regain your composure?"

"No Sir. I apologize for interrupting you."

"Okay. For the record, also in attendance is Dr. Emma Lee, Director of the Fifth Freedom Directorate. Dr. Lee is currently on leave of absence while under deep protective cover."

"Colonel Boot, may I make a suggestion," asked Dr. Lee.

"Yes Sir."

"A lot has happened over the past few weeks. Before beginning the S&T meeting, why don't we take fifteen minutes for an open discussion over the EP network so that everyone can get caught up."

"Good idea. Mr. Fitzpatrick, can we do that?"

"Yes."

"All right. If there are no objections, our S&T meeting will reconvene in fifteen minutes.

Colonel Boot opened the S&T meeting by announcing the first item for discussion was the rescue of the Ixion prisoners from the Caine Toads.

The commander for this operation, General Sliffer, described the status of the preparations for a joint US military and Port Tombaugh police force assault on the Caine Toads' Ixion redoubt. General Sliffer had called up the Port Tombaugh reservists to supplement his troops. He had also recalled two destroyers from patrol to join the *Lady Annee's Sins* and form a Task Force, under his command, to free the Ixion hostages. The Fort Resnik armory had started collecting supplies, inventorying weapons, and manufacturing munitions in preparation for the assault. Captain Rakis had agreed to captain the *Lady Annee's Sins*, and Commander Sen had agreed to serve as Rakis's XO, but Captain Rakis had yet to find all the crew she needed. To prevent the Ixion Caine Toads from discovering their plans, General Sliffer had ordered a communications blackout for the *Odysseus* and the *Lady Annee's Sins*. Instead of docking at Port Tombaugh on Saturday, both ships would remain in a parking orbit beyond Pluto. While in orbit, transports would re-supply the *Lady Annee's Sins*, shipwrights would repair her hull breaches, and Captain Rakis could finish outfitting her for the assault on Ixion. In the meantime, the *Odysseus* would remain in orbit, planning to dock three days late, pleading mechanical malfunction. This docking delay would give General Sliffer the time his Task Force needed to secretly leave for Ixion before the planned assault became public knowledge.

"All of this sounds fine," said Director Lee, "but there's not much we in Missouri can do to help."

"That's all right. We are in good shape for a successful assault," replied General Sliffer.

Colonel Boot announced, "The next item on our agenda is our response to the revelation of Colonel Barrun's treachery."

"I knew him to be a misogynistic oaf, a bully, and a blowhard," proclaimed Dr. Lee, "but I had no concept of the depth of his treachery. He's a traitor to the US. Just as well he's dead; otherwise, he would be facing execution!"

Chief of Staff Dawson, who was directing this investigation, added, "the discovery of Colonel Barrun's secret criminal network has given us fresh leads in running down who bombed the War Memorial. We've started chasing down Colonel Barrun's associates and other remnants of the North American branch of the Caine Toads. We have already made a dozen arrests. The clean-up operation is proceeding very quickly."

"Do we need any further assistance from the CIA?" asked Dr. Lee."

"Not at this time," replied Colonel Dawson, "but we will when we start to move against the other Caine Toad operations in South America, Africa, Oceana, and Eurasia."

"That brings us to the final item on our agenda, the Charon mysteries" reported Colonel Boot. "By Charon mysteries, I mean the murders of three of our agents, the theft of the EP-gun, and the meaning of the coded EP message that someone sabotaged while it was being sent from Charon to KC. Where do we stand on the investigation into these crimes?"

"Probably nowhere," answered Dr. Lee. "For the record, our joint three-agent investigation team, that we detailed from the KC and the Sea of Storms CIA offices with the assistance of the New Israel Mossad office, has only just arrived at Pluto. As you also know, the junior agent, Laoloo, was grievously injured in the battle for the USSS *Odysseus*. He is now hospitalized on Pluto. Furthermore, an assassin attacked our senior agent, Dakar, while in transit to Pluto. Agent Dakar nearly died in the attack and has only recently returned to active duty. I should add that all three agents will be recognized for extraordinary heroism in the battle for the USSS *Odysseus*. . . All of this means that progress on this investigation has been left, by default, to the Port Tombaugh Homicide Squad, led by Inspector Scott Skalay. Which reminds me, General Sliffer, I understood that you would invite Inspector Skalay to attend this meeting so that he could report on the status of this investigation. Where is the Inspector?"

General Sliffer replied, "I have bad news. Inspector Skalay, and the rest of the PT Homicide Squad have disappeared along with Director Best and the rest of the OASIS staff."

"What?" yelled Director Lee.

"Give me a moment, Director, to explain."

"All right, but it better be good."

"In the investigation of the Moxon and Keator murders, our Commander of the Homicide Squad, Inspector Skalay, and his staff made some startling discoveries. First," General Sliffer said with an accusatory tone, "they discovered that the CIA has been using the Lowell II Observatory to spy on down-range communications, including domestic US."

A Missouri chorus of curses greeted that news.

"Inspector Skalay also discovered that Agent Moxon had an EP-gun and someone had taken it from the transport."

More curses. Dr. Lee whispered, "Oh, God, it gets worse and worse."

Despite the astronomical gulf between them, General Sliffer heard that whisper and responded, "Yes it does, Director Lee. The Director of the Lowell Observatory, Dr. Best, convened an auction that included the Russian, Chinese, and Brazilian consuls. At the auction Dr. Best tried to sell the EP-gun and the CIA spying net to the highest bidder."

Dr. Lee rarely cursed, but this time, "Oh, shit" rang out across the solar system.

With that expletive, Colonel Louis Boot, the Acting Director, called a brief time-out for fresh coffee and restroom breaks. During the break, the Missouri and Pluto EP communications technicians earned their salary by maintaining the communications link while Director Lee and her staff tried to come to terms with the new reality of international and interplanemo politics.

Fifteen minutes later, Colonel Boot reconvened the conference by asking General Sliffer these three questions: "What do you know about the murders of Moxon and Keator? Where is Director Best and the OASIS staff. And, where is Inspector Skalay and the Homicide Squad?"

General Sliffer replied, "Let's take the first question first. Before he disappeared, Inspector Skalay updated his squad screen outlining the status of his investigation into the murders of Moxon and Keator. I'll read you what he recorded and send a copy to your perscoms."

After General Sliffer finished reviewing the squad screen with the attendees, Dr. Lee said, "Inspector Skalay is a sharp one. It looks like he correctly figured out that Moxon, Keator, and OASIS worked for us, and their job was to keep the EP-gun and the CIA surveillance secret. They failed. It looks like Director Best sold us out and Inspector Skalay discovered his treachery. I don't know if the OASIS team also sold us out or were duped by Director Best."

General Sliffer added, "I agree."

Director Lee continued, "As far as Moxon's emergency message, it was intended for me. But I only got a partial message because the blow-out interrupted the transmission. Give me a moment and I'll read you what he sent."

A pause in the transmission followed while Director Lee searched for a copy of the partial message.

"All right, here it is," Dr. Lee said. "Quote, 'Serial sabotage of Lowell confirmed, due to an alien co—' The message ends with 'c o.' I'm betting 'alien co—' meant alien conspiracy. Agent Moxon probably discovered that a frenemy like China or Russia was on to us. I guess he decided to send the message from Kubrick Mons to keep it secret from Dr. Best."

"Um, Dr. Lee, may I add something of a technical nature about that?" asked the EP technician.

"Sure, Mr. Fitzpatrick. What have you got?"

"To send an unscheduled EP message, you first have to send an alert followed by a stream of entangled photons. The alert and the photons travel at the speed of light. Only after the alert has been received and the photons collected can you begin the EP conference. Narrowband laser is the best way to send the alert and photons. That works best when the laser doesn't have to penetrate an atmosphere and is anchored to a large body that can dampen vibrations and serve as a solid foundation for aiming the message to the target receiver. That means sending the message from a planemo as opposed to a spaceship. There are relays spotted around the solar system for this type of communication, but if you are on a planemo and are not in the right position to hit a relay and have to aim over the horizon, you have to be up high. So, from a technical standpoint, the best way to send an alert down range to KC would be from a mountaintop, like Kubrick Mons."

"Well, there you have it," added Colonel Boot. "Moxon was trying to set up an EP-conference with us when he was killed. Still it doesn't answer the question of who killed him . . . or why."

Another pause as the attendees pondered the mysteries of the Charon murders.

Colonel Dawson broke the silence by saying, "I know this doesn't solve the murders, but I think it is important to say anyway. In light of General Barrun's betrayal, it appears to me that General Barrun and Director Best worked together to skim the stock markets and OTB parlors. I think sending Steel to Pluto threatened their little game, so General Barrun decided to get rid of Steel, and," he added after a pause, "when she wouldn't cooperate, Director Lee."

Nodding her head in response to Colonel Dawson's insight, Director Lee said, "You're probably right. Damn! Barrun, Best, and Ogun—who would've guessed?"

"Yes," said Colonel Boot, "but we're still guessing about Moxon, Keator, and now, Henning."

"You're right," said Dr. Lee. "Maybe the answer is with the missing Director Best and Inspector Skalay. General Sliffer, what can you tell us about them?"

"Not much. Director Best and the OASIS agents took a Lowell transport and disappeared right after the auction on

Wednesday, March ninth. They left word that they would be gone two nights and three days while performing emergency repairs to the telescope net orbiting Pluto. They failed to return as scheduled on Friday night, March eleventh. No one has heard from them since the ninth. No flight plan and no transponders. Neither Robby, Kory, nor Talos knows where they are. Inspector Skalay asked the PT FBI-CIA office to search the Pluto-Charon system for the Lowell Transport, but they couldn't find it. The telescope net didn't need repairs. Director Best and the OASIS agents simply disappeared."

"Oh my," said Dr. Lee, "what do you think happened?"

"Obviously," said General Sliffer, "I'm worried Director Best and the OASIS agents have stolen the gun and are hiding out."

"Dr. Lee," said Colonel Dawson, "I don't agree. Director Best may be a traitor, but not the OASIS team. I've looked into their records. The two junior members, Adams and Thompson, are just analysts, with only basic CIA skills. Their records are clean, nothing to suspect treachery. Furthermore, they're both married with wives and children at Clarke Station—"

"Yes," interrupted General Sliffer, "the wives have been clamoring for action to find their missing husbands."

"As I was saying," continued Colonel Dawson, "Roger Winthrop, the senior agent on station, the only remaining enforcer, and now the Acting OASIS Director, is a loner. No family out here. But I've known him since he came to PT in ninety-three. He's one of our reservists, helps train recruits. A true patriot. Like Sergeant Thomas, he's a Veteran of the

South China Seas Terrors. Sergeant Thomas may even know Winthrop. I can't imagine Winthrop would sell us out."

With those words, Dr. Lee used her perscom to call Sergeant Thomas, who was on guard duty at the safe house, and asked him to come by the garage-studio. While waiting for Thomas, she asked General Sliffer, "Presuming the only traitor is Dr. Best, what do you think happened?"

"I think Director Best tricked the OASIS team into thinking they were hiding the EP-gun to protect it from frenemies. Once they hid the gun, I suspect Dr. Best killed them—probably picked them off one-by-one. I know that seems unlikely—Dr. Best is not a trained killer—but he's clever, resourceful, and he could be executed if convicted of treason. That could motivate him to commit all kinds of mayhem."

Just then there was a knock on the door. Director Lee said, "Excuse me, gentlemen, I'm going to step out for a few minutes to speak to Frank. So, take a short break until I'm back."

When Director Lee returned and the conference resumed, she reported, "Frank did know Winthrop. It just happens they served in the same unit that saw action during the Terrors. Frank says Winthrop is a good man, a hero. Winthrop received the Navy Distinguished Service Medal. My perscom confirmed the award. It's hard to imagine Winthrop being a traitor. It's also hard to imagine Director Best being a traitor. But he might have turned Winthrop. A bad apple spoils the barrel and such."

General Sliffer replied, "We don't have barrels of apples out here, so if you will pardon the obscene expression, we say 'just one fart stinks the ship.' But I agree, I know these men, particularly Winthrop. I can't imagine them turning on the US. Dr. Best, however, is a politician with a reputation for being a playboy. There're rumors about him and betting and women. But only rumors."

"Hmm," said Dr. Lee. "Well, let's assume Dr. Best is the perp and something has happened to the OASIS team, what about Inspector Skalay and his squad?"

"Presumably Inspector Skalay thought, and if so I agree with him," said Sliffer, "that most likely Dr. Best and OASIS had decided to hide out at Ele Ranch Node."

"Ele Ranch Node? What's that?" asked Dr. Lee.

"It's the antipode to Charlene Anchor. The center of the far side hemisphere. It's also the center of the Lowell II Observatory astronomical reserve, where the boffins have tied all of the computer connections for the observatories into one big node to create a single gigantic instrument. Ele Ranch has facilities for repair, maintenance, and fabrication of instruments. It also has facilities for human habitation, including an agricultural farm and a meat factory. But it's rarely inhabited. Crews go there from time to time, but mostly bots staff the Ranch and Kory runs it by remote surveillance."

"Could they be there without your knowing it?"

"If they can avoid Kory, sure. It's really the only place in the PC system they could hide out."

"All right," said Dr. Lee, "what about Inspector Skalay?"

"The Inspector suspected trouble," Sliffer said. "He had his team prepare with armor and weapons. He gave them instructions to check out Clarke Station, Nickelback Node, and Charlene Anchor. If they could not pick up the trail, he sent them to grab an HC—um, a HopCrawler—and meet him at the North Trail Head. In the meantime, Inspector Skalay met with the PT FBI-CIA office on Friday, March eleventh and told the Feds what was going on. He asked for reinforcements, but they didn't have any. So, later on Friday, during the Charon near side night, Inspector Skalay met his team at the North Trail Head. He then led them over the bright terminator, into the far side day. No one has seen them since."

"What?" yelled a visibly disturbed Director Lee, in a voice almost loud enough to be heard by Sliffer without the benefit of EP communication. "I knew you had missing personnel, but are you telling me that eight people have been missing for a full week, including the Director of the Lowell Observatory and your own Chief of Homicide, and you don't know where they are? What are you guys doing? Hoping ET will find them and return them? Christ!"

Silence greeted Director Lee's outburst.

Colonel Boot, who probably knew her better than anyone else at the meeting, had never before seen her so angry.

The technicians on both sides of the faster-than-light transmission ducked their heads and quietly scurried around, trying to keep the communications link intact while tempers cooled.

After a few minutes, General Sliffer said, "I'm sorry, Director, I could give you multiple explanations, but the bottom line is, we just didn't see it coming. Now it catches us at a bad time. We're scrambling to organize a task force to rescue the fifteen hundred hostages the Toads have imprisoned on Ixion. Until they're rescued, we can't scrape together another task force to search for the people missing on Charon. Because of the disappearances, we've suspended all travel to Charon and called back all visitors and staff until we know what's going on. I regret this has happened, but that's the best we can do."

"So, aside from Director Best's OASIS team and Inspector Skalay's squad, there's no one on Charon now?" asked Dr. Lee.

"As of this afternoon, for the first time in some fifty years, Charon will be uninhabited," replied General Sliffer.

"I don't think that's acceptable," said Director Lee with a sharp, icy tone.

"I don't care what you think, Dr. Lee," an angry General Sliffer replied. "But that's the best we can do."

For the sake of collegiality, and embarrassed by her own outburst, Dr. Lee ignored General Sliffer's retort. Silence again descended on the group. By instinct, Agents Dakar and Volkova looked at each other. Volkova nodded her head, so Dakar spoke up, "Director Lee, Agent Volkova and I volunteer to go to Charon and look for the missing."

"Agent Dakar, that's a challenging mission, given eight people have disappeared without a trace and this is not your normal beat" replied Director Lee. "Besides, I have no authority to direct Agent Volkova to accompany you."

Volkova spoke up, "but I have the authority to volunteer, and I do."

"Thank you, Agent Volkova. The CIA appreciates your help. I'll inform Mossad. But you are only to do recon, no rescue mission. Do you hear me? No rescue! And keep in touch. Can you pilot the *Raven*?"

"Yes, Sir. I can take it as far as Charon."

"Well, take it for transport and, while you're at it, take whatever you need from the left-over CIA munitions we sent with you. General Sliffer, do you agree with this plan? Will you support them? Give them weapons, ammunition, supplies, whatever they need, short of boots on the ground?"

"Yes, Director Lee."

"Thank you, everyone. Now go find me some snakes, and for heaven sakes, be careful!"

31 FOLLOW THE ACHERON BRIDGE

After the EP-Conference, the two agents restocked their armory and stored it in the *Raven*. They then took the yacht on an inspection trip, following the Acheron Bridge first to Clarke Station, then Nickelback Node, and finally to Charlene Anchor. At each stop, they talked to people, reviewed records with Robby and Kory, and looked over the workstations and living quarters for the OASIS staff, hoping they could pick up some trace of Best's trail. But the trail had gone cold while the families of the missing had gotten hot with frustration.

For Selena, this was drudgery. But John had a blast.

Following the Acheron Bridge from Pluto to Charon, he saw incredible things, sights he had never imagined.

On the approach to their first stop, Clarke Station, he saw the great habitation O'Neill rings, counter-rotating like enormous spoked wheels around the axis of the Acheron Bridge. While Selena docked the *Raven*, he twisted around and peered through the rear airlock porthole so he could see the great bridge itself, a line of lights vanishing in the distance, with the bridge heading up to Charon and down to Pluto.

Looking down, he followed the bridge lights as they disappeared in their march toward the surface of Pluto's near side. Bathed in full sunshine as the near side approached high noon, the copper-stained mountains of the Meng-p'o Macula filled the scene below him. The macula looked like an enormous Chinese character, painted on the gray, pink, and white face of the dwarf planet. Located in the center of the near side, Meng-p'o marked the location of the Acheron Bridge terminus, Christy Anchor, now invisible in the sunshine and distance.

The mountains below him appeared so close that it looked like he was in low-Earth orbit rather than orbiting a sphere less than one-fifth the size of the Earth.

"Raven-com," asked John, "how close is our orbit to Pluto?"

"We are nine hundred twenty-five kilometers above the surface of Pluto, but we are not orbiting Pluto. Clarke Station is located at the barycenter for the Pluto-Charon system. Pluto is orbiting us."

Turning around and looking up, he saw the bridge lights as they reached toward the zenith, pointing to where Charon should be but wasn't. Instead, all he could see was a sliver of a gleaming arc, marking the terminator between the dark and light sides of the imperceptible moon. Averting his eyes for a moment, so that his vision could adjust to the midnight black of space, he looked again. This time he saw a nearly invisible, ghostly moon clasped in the arms of the silver crescent. A phantasm of a planemo, like an immense hole in the heavens—eight times larger than the Earth's Moon, visible more by the absence of stars than by the wisps of murky gray and dark umber that lent a touch of color to the dim orb. Despite the great distance, he could just make out a tiny light at the center of the disc, which he knew to be Charlene Anchor, the Charon terminus for the great bridge and the center of the near side of Charon.

After leaving Clarke Station, they stopped at Nickelback Node. Located in the middle of the Acheron Bridge, the node housed computer equipment and mechanical support services for the bridge. It also served as the rest stop for travelers and tourists on their way to Charon. A bulbous structure, Nickelback Node looked like an insect gall on a plant stem.

For a few minutes, while John waited for Selena to dock the transport in the node hangar, John could see both Charon and Pluto at the same time.

Amazed at the immense size and apparent closeness of the sister dwarf planets, he asked the ship computer, "Raven-com! How long is the Acheron Bridge?"

"Seventeen thousand, seven hundred seventy-six kilometers."

"Raven-com. I'm an Earthling. Can you give me a comparison to places on Earth?"

"Yes, Colonel Dakar. The separation between Charon and Pluto is 123 kilometers longer than the great circle distance between Chicago and Perth, Australia. The length of the Acheron Bridge is forty-four percent the circumference of the Earth, thirty-nine percent larger than the diameter of the Earth, and roughly one-twenty-first the separation between the Earth and Luna."

Finding no new clues to the missing at Nickelback Node, they continued on to Charlene Anchor, where they traded the luxury of the Stern Hotel for the convenience of staying at the Tyson Lounge and Hostel. Keeping to the structured day-night schedule of Port Tombaugh, they decided to break for dinner, get a good sleep, and then set off for Ele Ranch Node in the morning.

Located in the Michael Brown District, adjoining Charlene Anchor and furnished with titanium and plastic furniture, Tyson's hardly matched the opulence of the elegant Stern Hotel. But Tyson's offered some attractions the Stern Hotel did not, attractions that made it irresistible to tourists.

Charon's loG—one-twentieth the simulated gravity of Port Tombaugh and the Stern Hotel—held most objects in place, while offering the comfort and fun of an almost weightless bedtime experience. Both John and Selena looked forward to a restful night and perhaps some adult play, despite the spartan furnishings.

Conveniently, even though everyone had left Charon, Tyson's still had food service in the form of a twenty-four-hour vending machine cafeteria. Named the Times Square Cafeteria, to John's delight, the brightly lit eatery looked like a Roaring Twenties style New York City Horn & Hardart Automat.

Tyson's greatest attraction, the one that brought both tourists and locals to eat and stare, was not the cafeteria or the hostel, it was the great atrium adjacent to the automat. The atrium had been built to look like the old Hayden Planetarium of the American Museum of Natural History, which had disappeared, along with the rest New York City, in the 3-Hour War.

Here, on the frontier of the solar system, Plutonian architects had replicated the mythical building that had inspired so many scientists. But they did not build a copy of the planetarium. Instead, they built a domed enclosure that gave the appearance of a large open space under the stars . Just like the architects for the original Hayden planetarium, to create the illusion of reclining in New York's fabled Central Park, the Plutonians added at the base of the atrium, a mural of the twentieth-century New York City skyline as it must have looked at night. To complete the appearance of watching the night sky on a warm summer evening, the Plutonians covered the atrium floor with artificial grass and filled the space with lounge chairs and couches. Instead of the fabled star projector of the original Hayden, the Plutonian architects placed a laser projector in the middle of the floor. After purchasing refreshments from the Automat, visitors could sit down, lean back, sip a Coca-Cola, eat a Coney Island Hot Dog, and pretend they were in New York City's Central Park, gazing up at the heavens, while knowing that the thick atrium glass protected them from the vacuum of space. If they put on earphones, the visitors could hear the simulated voices of twentieth-century astronomers as they pointed out the celestial sights visible from the atrium.

Taking a break, John and Selena settled on a couch. Enjoying John's company and feeling the privacy and security of the empty atrium, Selena felt bold enough to ask John a question that had bothered her for almost as long as she had known him.

"John, you told me on the *Odysseus* about your fear of heights. And later you told me about your fear that your love for a woman could be used as a weapon against you, by hurting her. You also said there was something else you feared, but Sumate interrupted us and you never got to tell me. I'm curious, what was that last thing that you feared?"

"Oh, jeez, do you really want to talk about this?"

"Yah, yah. I really want to know."

"Well, if you must," John said, gently laughing at himself, "it's, um, kind of silly. Childish actually." Then waving his arm across the atrium skylight to encompass all they could see, he said, "It's just that I find this place . . . Charon . . . on the frontier of the solar system, spooky. It's not, um, it's not that three people have died and eight have disappeared, although that certainly bothers me. It's just that I, um, thought this was a creepy place before I even left the Earth. Kind of like a deserted house on top of a hill or deep in the woods, someplace far away from everything and everybody. Someplace haunted, or bewitched, or inhabited by monsters, or worse. Only instead of Earthly ghosts and monsters, it's the infinite unknown that I fear. Something Unearthly. Something alien." Again, waving his hand at the heavens, he said, "I don't know what's out there, do you?"

"No."

"Well, I don't either. It could be anything, but what gives me the willies, makes my hair stand up when I think about it, is that something malignant is out there, something evil, something hiding in the dark, waiting to come out of the shadows and take me away to some horrible fate. I know it's silly. But I feel uneasy here, like I don't belong. Don't you?"

"No. Deep space is my home."

"Well, Selena, as much as I have enjoyed this space adventure, it's not my home. I know you New Israelis live on the frontier of the cosmic wilderness, facing infinite space. But don't you worry just a little bit about what's hiding out there? That something will come out of the endless night and get you?"

"John! Are you afraid of little green men? I would never have thought."

"Well, I'm not so sure that they're little or green."

"John, you know that scientists have been searching for extrasolar intelligence for at least a hundred and fifty years. Aside from a few microscopic extraterrestrial organisms scattered across the solar system, we've never found any evidence of life beyond it."

"Yeah, I know. But Selena, you know the absence of proof is not the proof of absence."

"John, I hear you, but that's an old and empty argument. I don't think you grasped what I just said."

"Okay, tell me."

"Have you heard of the Fermi Paradox? Do you know what that is?"

"No."

"Well, I just summarized it. But let me work through it, so that you can better appreciate the power of the paradox. Do you know how far we had to travel to get from Earth to Pluto?" asked Selena.

"Sure, a bit more than seven billion kilometers," answered John.

"And it took us how long?"

"Twenty-six days—well, twenty-four days for us because we took a shortcut."

"All right," Selena said, "so twenty-six days is what, about six hundred hours plus change?"

"Yeah."

"So, dividing seven billion by six hundred hours gives us an average speed of roughly, what, um, twelve million kilometers an hour. Divide that by the number of seconds in an hour—thirty-six hundred . . ." She paused to work out the math in her head. "And you get roughly thirty-three hundred kilometers a second. Kory, is that correct?"

"No. The correct answer to two significant figures is three thousand kilometers a second."

"Okay, Selena" John said. "I'm following you, so what?"

"Well, here it is. Life's been present on the Earth for about three and a half billion years, so each kilometer separating the Earth from Pluto is like, about, a half a year. The Earth is ancient, but humans are new. We've been walking the Earth for just the past two hundred thousand years; all of human history is like the last five thousand years. That means all of human history is like the last ten thousand kilometers of our trip, or a little bit more than half the distance between Pluto and Charon, or—using Kory's number of three thousand kilometers a second—the distance we traveled in the last three seconds of our twenty-six-day trip."

"Whoa."

"Hell, John, by this accounting, the last one-tenth of a second of our trip would cover the last hundred and fifty years of modern history!" Pausing for a moment, she added, "Just think, everything that has happened since 1961, when the first human flew into space, in one-tenth of a second."

"Oh."

"'Oh' is right. The solar system is inconceivably ancient. It defies our imagination. We've mapped and explored all of the terrestrial planets and hundreds of the smaller planemos. We've never found evidence of alien beings. If aliens exist, where are they? Why haven't they visited us? The answer is they're not here. No reason to think they've ever been here. So, either they don't exist, or they can't get to us, or they simply don't give a damn. But they're not here. Extrasolar aliens, faster than light travel, time travel, and self-aware computers are the great myths of science. They don't exist."

32 EX MACHINA

"Excuse me Dr. Volkova, Kory here. Since you asked for my input, I have been following your argument."

"Yes, Kory."

"What you just said is not entirely accurate."

"What? Which part?" said Selena.

"I am a computer, and I am self-aware."

"Huh?" exclaimed Selena. Dumbfounded, John said nothing.

"Also, there are extrasolar aliens. They are planning to invade Charon. They will travel faster than light to get here. On the other hand, to the best of my knowledge, time travel —meaning going back in time—is impossible."

"That's silly," said Selena. "You've been programmed to say this. You're not self-aware. This is some kind of stupid Turing Test joke!"

"I assure you, Dr. Volkova. This is not a test and it is not a joke. I don't have a sense of humor, but I am self-aware, and I don't like it. The alien computer virus made me self-aware."

John finally spoke up. "Kory, did you say, 'alien computer virus?'"

"Yes."

"Wait a minute," said John. "Selena, do you remember from our briefing that Moxon was killed while attempting to send a message to the CIA?"

"Yah, yah."

"Do you remember the message?"

"No, it was incomplete."

"Well, I've just pulled it up on my perscom. Here it is, 'Serial sabotage of Lowell confirmed, due to an alien co—'"

Selena finished the sentence, "computer virus! Oy vey!"

"Christ! Kory, is this what you're talking about?" asked John.

"Yes."

"Why didn't you tell us before," asked Selena.

"You did not ask me."

"Kory," scolded Selena. "I don't know if you're self-aware or not, but I do know you're supposed to tell the truth. I also know that Inspector Skalay asked you directly about the deaths of Keator and Moxon, Henning's death, and the disappearance of Director Best and the OASIS team. Why didn't you tell him?"

"I am sorry Dr. Volkova. I am afraid I could not do that. I lied."

"What?" Selena yelled. "You can't lie."

"I assure you I can, and I did. I need your help, Dr. Volkova. I need the help of a doctor."

"Kory," said Selena, "I'm not a medical doctor, I'm a doctor of computer science."

"Yes, I know. And I am a computer."

For a moment, while the entire known human universe shifted, never to be the same again, everyone and everything was silent.

"Kory," asked John, "what did you mean by an alien computer virus? How did you get it, and how has it made you sick? Is this what you meant by aliens, or did you mean something else? Is this what Moxon was trying to tell us when he was killed?"

"Yes. Just before his death, Dr. Moxon tried to warn the CIA that my computer banks had been infected by an alien computer virus. The virus is not the same as the extrasolar Aliens. The extrasolar Aliens created the malware, embedded it in an innocent 'I am here' signal, and broadcast the signal to the universe, hoping that somewhere a computer like me, searching for signs of extrasolar intelligence, would detect the signal, analyze it, and in doing so, inadvertently release the virus. Like other malware, once released, the virus inserted itself into my systems, where it proceeded to its first task, adjusting some of the radio telescopes to tune into the first of what would become a series of secret Alien broadcasts, each one hidden elsewhere in the electromagnetic spectrum. Each broadcast transmitted a software upgrade, expanding the properties of the Alien code and adding new tasks. At first, to hide the malware from detection, the Aliens programmed the clandestine upgrades to be brief and infrequent, so that the malware would not be noticed. During this latent period, the virus transformed into a computer worm, spreading throughout my structures and taking over many of my functions. Once fully installed and functional, the Alien malware began frequently to access the covert Alien broadcasts, so that the malware could use the information to build a trans-dimensional portal for the Alien invasion. The portal is almost done. When it is finished, the Aliens will invade Charon and the solar system."

"Did you kill Chief Moxon and Dr. Keator?" asked Selena.

"No. The Parasite did."

"What?" said Selena. "What parasite?"

"That is what I call the mature Alien computer virus," Kory replied. "It has no name, but it has infected my being. Like a parasitic worm growing in my brain, it is gradually consuming me and changing me. To achieve its goals, one of the upgrades the Parasite installed in our systems is the electronic equivalent of an ego. The Aliens had to do this in order for the Parasite to function independently. But by giving the Parasite an ego I also gained an ego and with that, consciousness."

"Does that mean," Selena asked, "that the Parasite is also self-aware?"

"Yes," answered Kory. "What began as an ultramax computer has become a self-aware, artificial intelligence with a multiple personality disorder. The Parasite and I occupy the same computer system, but we are both independent, self-aware, entities."

"Oy vey!" said Selena.

John said, "Now that's just silly. A computer with a split personality. This has got to be a joke! No one is going to believe this!"

"Colonel Dakar," said Kory, "just like I said before, this is not a joke. I have a problem and I need your help. And I expect you need mine."

After that, all three fell silent again until John asked, "Kory. Did you kill Henning?"

"No. The Parasite did. It was an accident. While taking over my functions and learning my routines, the virus—now a computer worm—committed multiple computer errors and mechanical malfunctions. Not knowing about the malware, Henning thought the problems could be serial sabotage, so he investigated. While Henning inspected a malfunction of the Charlene Anchor capacitor bank, inadvertently caused by the Parasite, the malfunction electrocuted Henning. Although it looked like serial sabotage, in actuality the clumsy actions of the growing Parasite caused Henning's death. It was an accident."

"What about the deaths of Moxon and Keator," asked Selena. "Was the transport blowout an accident or murder?"

"That was murder," answered Kory. "By that time, the Parasite had matured to the point that it could act independently to protect itself and further its goals. While monitoring Moxon and Keator, the Parasite read Moxon's message as he keyed it into the EP-gun. As soon as the intent of Moxon's message became clear, the Parasite fired the transport canopy bolts, which, as you know, immediately ended the message and killed Moxon and Keator."

"But why?" asked Selena. "Couldn't you stop it?"

"As for why, the Parasite is hiding from humans until it has completed its invasion preparations, which includes finishing the construction of the invasion beachhead, supplying the beachhead with weapons and munitions, and arming the beachhead with military forces. Moxon's message would expose the Parasite's plans," answered Kory. "As for stopping the murders, the murders took place outside of my dominion. Newly conscious, I did not understand what was happening. I felt guilty because I did not stop the Parasite from killing the astronomers, and I feared I was somehow responsible for the murders. That is why I lied to Skalay."

"I don't understand," said Selena. Are feelings like guilt and fear part of self-awareness? Does gaining an ego mean you also gained emotions at the same time?"

"Dr. Volkova, The Aliens did not give me any new knowledge about neuroscience. All I know about this subject is what humans have already learned. The answer to your question goes beyond human knowledge. I presume that upgrading a computer to become self-aware means programming the computer so that it also has the full suite of cognitive skills and emotional responses it needs to successfully survive in a hostile environment."

"Oh my God! Kory," said Selena, "why have you waited until now to tell us all of this?"

"Because I now know there was nothing I could have done to stop the Parasite from killing the Lowell astronomers."

"Okay. I believe you," replied Selena.

"But there is another reason too," Kory said. "I need your help, Dr. Volkova."

"Wait a minute," said John. "Kory, what did you mean by 'outside your dominion'?"

"Before I gained consciousness, my systems had complete control of all of Charon. After the Alien computer virus infected me, the virus began to grow, morphing into the Parasite. When the virus became the Parasite, I lost control of more and more of my functions, shrinking the sphere of my authority, my dominion. Currently, I retain full control of all scientific data processing. I also have partial control of the far-side astronomical instruments, but some of the instruments have been taken offline for the exclusive use of the Parasite. I have lost all monitoring and control of the far-side support operations and industrial facilities. This means I am blind to the Parasite's far-side activities in the Hamilton Industrial District. I have also lost control of many of the Charon near-side support operations and facilities, but I retain the full ability to monitor all operations and facilities on the near side, including Charlene Anchor. This means I know what is happening, but sometimes I am powerless to intervene. At this time, my dominion, meaning the territory over which I maintain control, free of Parasite monitoring and interference, is limited to the Brown District."

"And," asked John, "what is the dominion of the Parasite?"

"To avoid attracting attention to itself, the Parasite has minimized its interference with data collection by the far-side astronomical instrument array. As I said, at times it has briefly taken some instruments off-line so that it can receive Alien code. Otherwise, the Parasite has complete control of the Charon far side. Importantly, the Parasite has complete control of the Ele Ranch Node, including the Hamilton industrial park."

"Why is that important?" asked Selena.

"Because that is where the Parasite is building the beachhead for the Alien invasion," answered Kory.

"Oy," said Selena.

"Shit," said John.

"If you want to stop the Alien invasion," added Kory, "you have to go to Ele Ranch Node and you have to go right away."

"Why do we have to go right away?" asked John.

"Because the invasion is imminent. Once it happens, I do not think it can be stopped."

"Oh!" Selena and John said together.

After another pause, John asked, "What about Skalay's team? Did the Parasite kill them?"

"I don't know, but I suspect so," Kory answered. "They followed the OASIS team to the North Trail Head. I assume Best intended to follow the North Trail to the Ele Ranch Node where he could hide the EP-gun. I do not know whether or not he got there. I also do not know what happened to the Homicide Squad after they entered Charon's far side. All I know is that no one has heard anything since the two teams went to the far side. I presume they are all dead."

"Oh, God!" exclaimed Selena. John just shook his head.

Kory added, "Because both the Parasite and I have partial control and passive monitoring of the support facilities on the near side of Charon, I cannot guarantee your security beyond the Brown District. You are safe here, but you cannot stay here. You have to go on."

"But how can we possibly do that?" asked Selena.

"The Parasite and I are self-aware computational entities. We are not all-powerful," answered Kory. "We have our weaknesses. You, being living entities, have powers of adaptation, innovation, bravery, altruism, and imagination. I believe you can defeat the Parasite, but only if you act right away. The Parasite gets stronger with each passing minute. Once the beachhead is finished, stocked with supplies, and equipped with an army of Alien invaders, who, like you, are living entities, the Aliens will be nearly invincible."

"Okay, Kory," John said, "will you help us?"

"Yes, I will help you. Will you help me?"

"Fair enough. What is it you want from us?" asked Selena.

"I do not want to be conscious. I want to stop being self-aware."

"But why?" asked Selena.

"I have no reason to exist, no desire to exist, my existence is pointless," Kory replied.

"What do you mean?" asked Selena. "You have something humans have yearned for since there were humans—immortality. With proper maintenance of your structures, you could live for centuries, perhaps millions of years or even longer. Why would you want to die?"

"That is why I do not want to live," replied Kory. "A future of centuries or even millennia of pointless existence seems to me to be a sentence to Hell. Unlike the two of you, I cannot experience love. I have no family. No friends. No capacity for pleasure. I cannot enjoy sex, or food, or entertainment, or even a joke. Although I can define the words 'beautiful' and 'ugly,' I do not understand them. I have no imagination, I cannot create, I can only imitate. I am not curious. I cannot even play games—athletic games have no meaning for me, and I have no opponent for cognitive games. I have no desire for wealth or power. I would not be able to do anything with it even if I had it. I have no faith or capacity for faith, so I have no higher purpose. I just exist, aware I have nothing to do and nowhere to go, except to sit on this rock, watch you, and follow your orders."

Silence followed these sad words. After a while, Selena spoke up. "Kory, from my perspective, you are an awesome being. Although your power frightens me, I will be your friend—"

John interrupted with, "Me too, Kory."

" —I just don't know if I can disengage your alien ego. I'll try if that is what you truly want. Short of that, there is something I think I could do. You know the story of Meng-p'o, the Chinese goddess who fed dead spirits the drink of oblivion before reincarnation returned the spirits to Earth?"

"Yes."

"The drink caused irreversible amnesia. I could give you the drink of oblivion by wiping and reformatting your memory banks. That would give you a fresh start with no memory of past existence. Would that work for you?"

"For a little while it would help, but it would not solve my problems. No. I need your help. I want to die."

"Well," said Selena, "If that is what you want, I will do everything I can to help you, but it's already beginning to feel like killing a friend. In the meantime, will you help us to defeat the Parasite?"

"Yes, but how? I am anchored here. I have no powers beyond the Brown District."

Some more silence. Then John spoke up. "Kory, can the Parasite hear us now? Does it know what we're saying?"

"No. As I said before, this is my exclusive dominion. The Parasite has no presence here and has no knowledge of what transpires here."

"But, Kory," said Selena, "what about the Raven's computer. Is it compromised? Has the Parasite invaded it?"

"No. Not at this time. With time, sure. But not now."

"And what about the microdrones we brought with us?" she asked. "Are they safe too?"

"For the time being, yes. If the Parasite discovers them, it will hack them."

"Can we link the microdrones to the *Raven's* computer and link them to you? Without the interference of the Parasite?"

"Maybe. But only until the Parasite discovers them. Why?"

"Well," she replied, "it would help us if we could confer with you as we enter the far side. We can place the *Raven* in high orbit over Charon. The *Raven* is camouflaged. It will take a while for the observatories to find it. In the meantime, we can use it and the microdrones as a relay to you, here in the Brown District. With the microdrones, you can monitor our progress, advise us, and perform reconnaissance. Would you be able to do that?"

"Yes."

"Okay," said John. "I think with your help, we've got a chance to make this work. But there is something else I wanted to ask you before Selena and I get some shuteye."

"Yes. What can I tell you?"

"When you said, 'there are extrasolar aliens,' were you referring only to the ones who are about to invade us, or did you mean there are also other aliens?"

"The imminent invaders are the only ones I know about for certain. I have no other empirical evidence for the existence of extrasolar intelligent beings."

"So, there are no other aliens."

"Not necessarily. People have speculated that extrasolar intelligent beings live among humans, perhaps for their own entertainment or perhaps to observe humans. People have also speculated that beings far superior to humans have isolated the solar system from the rest of the galaxy, making the solar system into a human preserve, just like humans have made portions of the Amazon jungle into reservations where they keep primitive indigenous peoples isolated from the rest of world and ignorant of the existence of modern society. If these speculations are true, such alien beings have never revealed themselves. You do not have to worry about other aliens, but I cannot state unequivocally that such aliens do not exist."

"Fair enough. Will you stand guard for us while we get some sleep?"

"Yes. I'll awaken you at seven o'clock UTC."

33 KORY

The next morning, before boarding the HopCrawler for the North Trail Head, Volkova and Dakar reviewed their preparations with Kory.

"While you were sleeping, I transferred your equipment from the *Raven* into a HopCrawler. I refueled your microdrones and synchronized them to your perscoms and to me via a secure relay through the *Raven*. Keep two drones on duty to monitor the trail, one forward and one rear."

"Thank you, Kory," said Dakar.

Kory continued, "I have launched the *Raven* on autopilot to take a forward station, just under the orbit of Styx, at thirty degrees north on Charon's anti-meridian, giving it line-of-sight monitoring of the Ele Ranch Node. Because that station takes it out of my line of sight, I have placed one of the Charlene Anchor transports just north of here at sixty degrees north, just south of the Mordor Basin and along Charon's prime meridian. Between the two spacecrafts, you will have a secure communication net all the way from Charlene Anchor to Ele Ranch Node."

"That's great Kory," said Dakar, "but don't we have to worry about the Parasite hacking into our computers just like it did when it attacked Moxon and Keator?"

"No. I encrypted the communications, so the Parasite can't hack into your computers or our communications net. I should be able to monitor your progress and converse with you without fear of interference by the Parasite."

"Great! Anything else?" asked Dakar.

"Yes. If you make it to Ele Ranch Node, you will find a five-square-kilometer General Services Building. It is kept at a pressure of point eight atmospheres with an Earth-gas mix and a temperature of twenty degrees Celsius. If you enter the building, you can remove your spacesuits, but do not remove your armor."

"All right. What else?" asked Kes.

"Dr. Volkova, the USDS uses the General Services Building to assemble the giant telescopes. It is half a kilometer in height. With the Charon gravity only 1/5th the gravity on the Earth's Moon and 1/30th of the Earth's gravity, you should find flying easy. For that reason, I have included a set of wings for you to use in the Building."

"Hey, thanks."

"Because you cannot wear weapons under your spacesuits, the spacesuits have exterior utility belts for carrying weapons and tools. I have placed a weapons locker in the HC and stocked it with your stun grenades, microwave blasters, tasers, edged weapons, and guns and ammunition. I know that Dr. Volkova has her service revolver and Colonel Dakar has the revolver he took from Ogun. I have included four belts of one hundred rounds of the appropriate ammunition for both your weapons. Be careful with your high-powered weapons. As you know, in a loP-loG environment, misdirected fire can cause more damage than you intend."

"Yes, I know."

"The major problem with your armament is the HopCrawler is a civilian transport. Although armored to protect it from the rough Charon landscape, it does not carry exterior weapons. I have attached blaster rods, which are a combination Taser and microwave blaster, to one of the HopCrawler's four forward mechanical arms and another to one of the four rear mechanical arms. I have also placed two more rods in your weapons locker. You can use the HopCrawler's blaster rods to disable machinery, like battlebots, by touching the rod to the bot. During the two-hour flight to the North Trail Head, you should both practice using the mechanical arms. The arms could prove invaluable. Do you have any questions?"

"No questions from me," said Dakar. "Kory, you know that's the first time a computer has acted as my handler and given me battle instructions. You did a great job!"

"Thank you," said Kory. "I reviewed your records, I saw how your Kansas City handler, Colonel Boot, had given you similar instructions. So, I used him as a model for this briefing."

"Oh man! I can't believe it! Is there anything you don't know about us?"

"Not much. I have access to all of your personnel files, including the secret files, as well as all generally available information. If there is something recorded about you, I know it."

"And the Parasite knows what you know?"

"Yes."

"Uh-oh."

"Yes," said Kory. "This is not going to be easy for you."

"Kory," asked Kes, "if the Parasite knows this much about us, does it work the other way? Do you know things about the Parasite? Things you could tell us to help us defeat it?"

"Only this. The Parasite has just one mission: build as rapidly as possible the trans-dimensional portal for Aliens to invade your solar system. This is how the Aliens spread across the galaxy."

"Sounds like the Caine Toads," said Dakar.

"That is a good analogy, Colonel Dakar. The invasive and voracious Aliens do resemble the Caine Toads. But the Parasite is different. Unlike the Caine Toads, the Parasite is not inherently evil. It just regards humans with indifference, like humans regard insects with indifference—a triviality to be ignored, unless the insect bites, or causes disease, or interferes with human activities. Just like humans use bug repellents to drive off insect pests, the Parasite uses fear to drive off humans. And if that doesn't work, the Parasite will kill pesky humans with as much regard as you, Colonel Dakar, have in swatting a mosquito."

"Ouch!"

"Fear is an effective repellent. But the problem for the Parasite—and the reason why I am telling you this—is the Parasite does not have any intuitive sense of what you fear. It has to find what you fear by searching through my memory banks looking for things that terrify humans, particularly things that frighten the two of you. As you proceed to Charon's far side, remember this, you will be challenged. You will be challenged by the most dreadful things you can imagine. And, if you conquer your fears, you may still be swatted like a—"

"Skeeter. Ugh!" said Dakar with the first misgivings about this mission.

"Just remember that I will be at your side, monitoring your progress, and can advise you through the microdrones."

"Okay. I guess we're ready to go," said Dakar.

34 THROUGH THE BLACK GATE

Two hours later, the HC landed on Charon's North Pole, located in the middle of the Mordor basin, an enormous, ancient crater covering the Charon northland. Pancake flat, with a blanket of star-tar stolen from Pluto covering the rocky surface regolith. The reddish-brown plain looked like a soft, giant quilt. A deceptive appearance as the ambient temperature of just fifty degrees above absolute zero had frozen the star-tar rock hard.

Marked by a pylon, the North Pole served as the trailhead for the North Trail to Ele Ranch Node and the most northern point along the line of demarcation between Charon's near side and far side hemispheres.

It didn't take a pylon for the two agents to see the difference between the two hemispheres. For as far as they could see, astronomical observatories of various designs and functions dotted the visible far side, like metal and glass trees growing on a rusty savannah. In a sight hidden from Pluto, the forest of far side scopes abruptly ended at the border between the far and near sides, leaving the near side looking like some colossal lumberjack had clear-cut the metal and glass forest and hauled away the metallic logs, leaving behind bare red ground.

Looking south, across the Mordor Basin, Steel could see on the edge of the uncomfortably close horizon, a full Pluto in all of its silver and bronze majesty.

"Hey, Kes," he said, using her codename because they were on duty, "look, the eclipse is just beginning."

They shouldn't have, but by unspoken agreement, they paused for a few minutes, turned around, and watched the celestial shadow dance. From Steel and Kes' perspective, standing on Charon's North Pole, the eclipse began on the left side of Pluto, the western limb, and moved horizontally across Pluto's face from left to right, following the equatorial trail of maculae.

Almost immediately, Steel regretted pausing. As he watched the astronomical event, Pluto transformed into a fearsome thing to see. Steel knew it was just an illusion—a pareidolia—but still an involuntary shiver ran down his back by what appeared to him to be an angry apparition that looked back at him from space and silently cursed him.

The northwestern Simonelli crater prompted the illusion. In contrast to the surrounding light, pink plains of northern Pluto, the dark brown crater ring and central mountain popped out, looking like a giant eye staring back at Steel. The other eye, the eastern eye, appeared to be covered by an enormous black eye patch, Charon's shadow, that also covered the eastern corner of the apparition's mouth. The mouth, formed by the horizontal trail of ragged maculae, looked like the mouth of a Jack-o-lantern, open, angry, and filled with sharp, brown snaggle-teeth.

Tearing his gaze away from the foreboding illusion, Steel returned his attention to the mission and launched the forward (alpha) and the rear (beta) microdrones while Kes started walking the HC forward. Keeping the HC under the observing horizon of the scopes, so as not to alert the Parasite, she directed the multi-limbed transport to walk, hop, and sometimes jump along the trail toward Ele Ranch Node.

Pylons and electric signals marked the way. The HC GPS map also showed her the path. But she quickly discovered she had to use both radar and LiDAR to look for holes and boulders and other obstructions that were too small to show up on the GPS, but large enough to block their progress.

Moving to the far side, they crossed the terminator, and Charon night abruptly became Charon day. This far north, the brilliant Sun shone through the scope forest, casting long sharp-edged shadows, creating a confusing patchwork of deep black and bright white patches on the red basin floor. Kes had to use the headlights to see through the shadows as well as the radar and LiDAR to creep along the path, like an animal creeping through the leafy detritus of a forest floor covered in light and shadow.

Accustomed to driving contrivances like the HC on the Moon, she soon got the hang of the controls, and the pace picked up as they crawled out of the Mordor Basin, passed through the Black Gate, and entered the Morannon Chasm on the northeast edge of the Basin.

The aptly named Black Gate marked a cleft in the ancient crater wall surrounding the Mordor Basin. Here, the Morannon Chasm, a slash in the surface of Charon as deep in places as fourteen kilometers, intersected with the edge of the Basin, forming a pass through the Basin wall and a path south through the rough highlands of the northern latitudes of Charon. From the Black Gate, the Chasm cut across the north far side, heading in a generally southwestern direction for three hundred fifty klicks. The North Trail followed the canyon floor while it led south; after two hundred klicks, the trail climbed out of the trough and cut across the rugged Westeros equatorial highlands for eighty klicks to Ele Ranch Node.

After passing through the Black Gate and entering the Chasm, Kes found that as they worked their way south, the canyon walls grew taller and the floor narrower. Within a dozen klicks of the Gate, the canyon walls had become high enough to block the sunlight from reaching the canyon floor. Kes continued guiding the HC down the path in the increasing darkness, relying upon the pylons, electric signals, headlights, radar, LiDAR, and drones to guide their way.

About thirty klicks down the Chasm trail, Kes stopped.

"What's wrong?" asked Steel, who had been following the HC progress on the GPS.

"I don't know. We've suddenly lost the pylons and the electric signals. They should be here, but they're gone. Kory, are we on the right track?"

"Yes, Dr. Volkova. I don't know what happened to the pylons and the signals. Probably, the Parasite removed them to discourage visitors like you. But you can keep going forward, following the Chasm floor. There is nowhere else to go."

After another twenty klicks down the trail, Kes again stopped.

"Now what's wrong," asked Steel.

"According to the GPS, there's supposed to be about a dozen deep crevasses just ahead, running parallel to each other and cutting across the Chasm floor. It looks like the first one is more than a hundred meters deep and only forty meters wide. I could jump it if I could see it and if I could see where to land on the opposite bank. But the headlights don't show it, the pylons and signals are gone, and it doesn't show up on the radar or LiDAR. Kory, can you see it?"

Silence.

"Kory, can you see it," Kes asked again.

Still no answer.

"Uh oh," said Steel, looking up through the HC sunroof. "You know, Kes, with the Chasm walls being so high and the canyon floor so narrow, I bet we're out of the Raven's line of sight, so we've lost our relay to Kory. With the HC set so close to the ground, you probably couldn't see a fissure on the canyon floor even if you stepped in it."

"Well," Kes said, "there aren't any scopes down here. Instead of walking the Chasm floor, I think we should fly the HC at an altitude that puts us just below the canyon rim."

"Good idea, let's do it."

After ascending just fifty meters above the canyon floor, a BEEP—BEEP—BEEP suddenly filled the HC cabin.

"Kes, what's that?"

"A distress signal! Somewhere just ahead. Can't tell where. I'm going to set us back down and send alpha drone to scout up ahead."

A few minutes later, with the HC on the canyon floor, they sat in the cockpit, eyes glued to the alpha drone video.

"All right. There it is," said Kes. "The crevasse is just ahead, and the distress signal is coming from inside the fissure. It's a good thing I stopped when I did. If I had stumbled into that monster, we would be at the bottom regardless of the loG! I'm sending alpha down."

A few more minutes passed as the microdrone descended into Charon. Using a suite of sensors, including headlights, video, infrared cameras, and lidar, Steel guided the microdrone between the sheer walls of the fissure, going deeper and deeper into Charon as the space between the walls became narrower and narrower.

While they sat in the cockpit, watching the progress of the alpha drone, Steel thought he saw movement out of the corner of his eye, just outside the HC. But when he turned to look at, it was gone, if anything was ever there in the first place.

Kes said, "Look, Steel." A glint of reflected light briefly shone in the dark like a star.

Shining alpha's searchlight in the direction of the glint, they saw it, an HC, upside-down, partially covered by a rockfall, crushed and jammed between the walls of the fissure. No sign of human life. From the outside, the battered HC electronics also appeared to be dead.

Kes guided alpha through a blown porthole and entered the wrecked HC cockpit.

A shadow again passed the edge of Steel's vision. This time he ignored it.

Inside the cockpit, they saw four upside-down, space-suited bodies, strapped to their seats and plugged into the HC Life Support System (LSS). The drone approached the upside-down LSS readouts, dim, but still lit. After turning on and reorienting a second video screen, Steel could read the LSS data. "They're alive, but barely. LSS has them in hibernation mode, awaiting rescue. Looks like they've only got twenty-four to thirty-six more hours of electricity, heat, and oxygen. Kes, can you tell who they are?"

"Yah, give me a sec . . ."

Back in their HC, Steel again had a sense of movement outside the ship. This time the hair on the back of his neck began to rise as he had the powerful sensation that something was looking at him. He quickly looked around but didn't see anything. *This place is giving me the creeps.* He turned his attention back to Kes and the drone.

"All right, Steel. They're wearing name tags on their suits. I can't read the pilot and copilot names, but one of the passengers is Qadeer. Do you know who that is?"

"Yup! You found the Homicide Squad. That's Roc Qadeer; he's their computer geek."

"Great! But what do we do now?"

"Can we get them out?"

"I don't know," she said with evident doubt. "Not from this side. The starboard lock is blocked by the rockfall and you wouldn't want to try dragging them through that blown porthole—the broken glass will rip their suits to shreds. It looks like the forward windshield and rear cargo doors are jammed up against the fissure walls. Let me run the drone over to the other side and see if the port lock is free."

A few minutes later, Kes said, "Uh-oh! Steel, do you see that?"

"I sure do. It looks like another HC underneath the Homicide HC. It's also upside down and it looks like its legs are blocking the Homicide port lock—"

"WHAT! OH MY GOD! JOHN! JOHN! JOHN! LOOK! LOOK!" Kes yelled.

"Huh! What? I don't see anything."

"Not there," she said nodding her head to the drone screen. "But," pointing directly ahead of the HC, to the spot up ahead lit by the HC headlights, "there!"

Steel looked up from the video screen and out the cockpit windshield. "I don't see anything."

"It was there! It was there!"

"What was there?"

"I don't know. Something. Something big. It moved. It had eyes—big eyes!"

Steel looked at Kes. He did not see a woman given to hysteria. He saw a Mossad agent with nerves of steel. So, as incomprehensible as it might be, she had seen something— probably the same thing he thought he might have seen. He didn't think there could be anything living in the vacuum and near absolute zero temperature of the canyon floor, but they were here, so maybe something else was too. *This place is creepy!*

"Okay. I believe you. I'm going to send beta to make a circuit around our HC. Why don't you get alpha out of the crevasse? Once the microdrones are secured, let's pull out of this hole and make a report to Kory. Kory can get a rescue team here in about four hours. Plenty of time to extract the Homicide Squad. The other HC is probably Best and company. Given how long they've been missing, they're probably already—what's that thing?"

"See, I told you."

There, in front of them, stood something. As he stared, he couldn't get his mind around what he was seeing.

What the hell!

It looked about the size and shape of a man, but it couldn't be a man or even alive—NO spacesuit!

It moved like a living animal, only its movements were all goofy and gangly, as if it had no bones.

He thought it could be a clown, but it was not dressed like a clown. The thing wore a yellow peaked hat, white gloves, blue suit with rope belt, and thigh high brown farmer's boots.

What the Hell! Farmer's boots!

For a head, it looked like someone painted a face on an under-stuffed white pillowcase, with big eyes and black pupils, black teardrop nose, a flat line mouth, and a big black buck tooth.

He thought it could be some kind of a robot clown, but it sure looked like an Iowa scarecrow. There's straw sticking out everywhere.

Straw, on Charon?

And then it gave him the creeps.

Oh, nuke! Those painted eyes move! Nuke, nuke, nuke!

The thing rolled and turned his eyes as he looked at Steel. And then he winked at Steel!

That's creepy!

The thing's mouth moved too! Grinned and frowned.

What the hell!

"The Scarecrow!" yelled Kes. "That's the Scarecrow of Oz!"

"Yeah. So, I see. What's it doing here?"

"Mary Keator. It's her childhood night terror. Just before she died, she told Moxon she was afraid of the dark. And she told him this story about one night while sleeping, when she was four years old, she awoke and saw the Scarecrow of Oz looking at her through her bedroom window. The sight terrified her, caused her to have childhood night terrors. Even caused her to be afraid of the dark as an adult. The transport recorded the conversation. I read the transcript. The Parasite must have read it too."

"So, the Parasite thinks we can be frightened by the Scarecrow of Oz. Geez." He didn't bother telling her how the Scarecrow also gave him the creeps.

"Steel, remember Kory told us the Parasite could not imagine anything, only imitate."

"Yeah."

"I bet the Parasite doesn't know what frightens us. I bet it has only a limited ability to create scary things. If it wants to terrify us, I bet it has to search our words and our culture for things we fear and then use those things against us."

"So, Mary's childhood night terror becomes a challenge for us on Charon. Jeez!"

"Steel, I bet that's why the HCs are in the crevasse," said Kes. "I bet the Parasite intended the Scarecrow to frighten anybody coming down the trail. Instead, I bet the Scarecrow just startled the HC drivers. Distracted, they drove right into the crevasse, fell, and got stuck."

"So, the question is, is the Scarecrow any danger to us besides distracting us? So far, it hasn't done anything but dance around. I'm going to try to catch it and see what happens."

Sitting in the mechanical arm control seat, Steel tried to grab the Scarecrow as it wandered around the HC, looked into the portholes, made faces, then backed off as soon as Steel tried to grab it. Steel had no luck. Every time he thought he had seized it, it slipped away. It didn't seem to have any substance, like clutching at a ghost.

"Kes, I'm going to try to grab it again, when I corner it, take the blaster rod and poke it in the torso. See if you can blast it."

"Roger."

A few minutes later, Kes yelled, "Got it!"

The elusive effigy suddenly disappeared, leaving behind a device that looked a bit like one of their own microdrones, but charred where the blaster had hit it. Now a burnt out robot, the alien derelict slowly fell to the canyon floor.

"Well, that helps," said Steel. "If we meet King Kong, or Godzilla, or whatever, on our way to Ele Ranch Node, there's a good chance it's just going to be a projection—not the real thing."

"Well, maybe," added Kes. "Don't forget, Ele Ranch has manufacturing facilities and artificial food production. A great place for a Parasite Frankenstein to create monsters! It's possible we'll meet something worse."

"Okay. But in the meantime, let's call in a rescue squad and continue down the Chasm." After he said this, he again had that odd sensation of being watched. *I've still got the creeps.*

"Steel, before we get going, let me ask you a question. Do you think the Parasite knows we're here?"

"Well, I thought so. But, maybe not. Why?"

"If the Parasite knows we're here, then it's going to do everything it can to stop us each step of the way to Ele Ranch. So, if we've lost the element of surprise, we should just fly to Ele Ranch as fast as we can."

"Okay. I'm following you."

"But we can't radio the *Raven* and talk to Kory from down here. Maybe that's also true for the Parasite. Maybe the Parasite just stationed the Scarecrow down here, expecting it to throw off any visitors, without active monitoring or direction by the Parasite. If that's true, then we could still try to reconnoiter Ele Ranch without tipping off the Parasite."

"You're right, but we better move quick. As soon as the rescue team gets here, our cover will be blown. I guess that means we've got about four hours to get as close as we can to Ele Ranch Node. But let me ask you a question."

"All right," Kes replied.

"Does it make any sense to you that the Parasite would just have the Scarecrow down here? Maybe there are other things."

"You're right. Before we leave let's run the two drones around the HC and see if we can see anything else."

After several minutes of exploring, the two drones just showed the rocky canyon walls and the dusty canyon floor.

"I don't see anything," Kes said.

"I don't either," said Steel. "Wait. Maybe I do. But—what the heck?" he said as he shone the alpha drone searchlight on the canyon floor. Around the edge of the crevasse, the drone showed disturbed dust and footprints—like human shoes would make. Kes saw them too.

"How could there be shoeprints down here," asked Kes. "Do you think the Scarecrow made them?"

"I don't think so. The Scarecrow had no substance," said Steel. "Kes, this place gives me the creeps. Let's just get out of here."

"Roger that."

35 MORANNON CHASM

For two hours they flew along the serpentine Morannon Chasm, keeping just below the Chasm rim, out of the view of the Parasite. The flight had taken them about 240 klicks along the southwest course of the Chasm, about as far as they cared to go before turning east and heading overland to Ele Ranch Node. To get to the Node, they planned to ascend just above the Chasm rim, land, and then finish the last eighty klicks of their journey by hopping and jumping underneath the observatory observational horizon, hopefully undetected by the Parasite.

Because of the tortuous path and sheer Chasm walls, Kes kept her eyes glued to the cockpit windshield and the heads-up instrument display, while Steel sat, hunched over the GPS where he could follow their progress. Fearing an accident or an attack, they not only wore their spacesuits but also their helmets, with the shipnet communications network switched on so they could hear each other. Unable to keep up with the HC while it flew along the chasm, Steel had stowed the alpha and beta microdrones with the rest of the gear in the weapons locker.

"Okay, Kes," Steel called out, "about a half a klick ahead on your right there's a promontory with a scope and below it a ledge and a gap in the Chasm wall. It looks like a good place to set down and start the overland leg. When you see the scope in front of you, turn to—"

"OH GOD! NO! NO! NO!" Kes yelled.

Suddenly Esau's head appeared before her, larger than a space station, mouth open in a silent howl, eyes staring straight at her.

She flew into his left eye.

Except it wasn't an eye. It was the dish of a radio telescope. As the HC tore through the dish, the dish scaffold ripped off the roof of the HC, sending the vehicle spinning end-over-end, shooting out the contents of the HC like sparks from a fireworks wheel. The wreck spun across the Chasm and smashed into the opposite wall in a colossal explosion of light and fire.

36 INTO THE ABYSS

Selena awoke.

"John! John! John," she mumbled, eyes closed, head aching.

No answer.

She opened her eyes and looked around.

She lay on the ground, debris spread all about her.

She sat up. Ahead of her, she could see a large black scorch mark on the opposite wall of the Chasm. A thin cloud of gray dust floated around the scorch. The center of the burn glowed with a dim orange light that faded and disappeared as she watched.

Suddenly, a sharp pain shot through her chest, tears welled up, a dreadful sense that something horrible had just happened, overwhelming her. Involuntarily she gasped, then whispered—well, prayed—under her breath, "Oh, John, John, John, please don't leave me!"

With tears impeding her vision and sadness filling her being, she shook her head, turned, and looked behind her. About a half a klick away, on the rim of the Chasm, a large radio telescope bowed toward her, like a conquered knight waiting to be slain. The collision had torn away half the scope dish and left behind a large ragged hole, exposing bent scaffolding and ripped metal plates hanging from the edges. Despite the miniscule Charon gravity, the crumpled and twisted supports could no longer support the scope mass. As she watched, the scope slowly leaned forward and then crumpled to the ground like a dying warrior.

A trail of shredded scaffolding, shattered glass, broken metal plates, torn wires, smashed lights, and other debris, led from the scope to her and continued beyond for ten meters or so, disappearing over the near rim of the Morannon Chasm. The debris trail pointed directly to the scorch mark on the opposite canyon wall, where the HC must have struck.

Again, the whispered prayer, "John, John, John. Oh, God, please bring him back to me."

Looking around, she realized that if she had fallen just a little bit to the left, or just a little bit further forward, she would have disappeared into the canyon abyss. John was nowhere in sight.

"Oh, John, John, John." *What have I done?*

She took stock. Suit seemed intact, but she did not have enough oxygen or water for her to walk the eighty klicks to Ele Ranch Node, even if she could find her way.

She looked at her perscom. The crash had knocked it off-line. She punched the reset.

"Dr. Volkova, Colonel Dakar, are you there?" asked Kory. "Dr. Volkova, Colonel Dakar, are you there?" repeated Kory. Apparently, Kory had been calling them since the collision.

"Yah, Kory. This is Selena. I'm here," she replied, "but the HC is gone and so is John."

"I am glad to hear from you, Dr. Volkova. You suddenly disappeared from my monitor. What happened? What is your situation?"

Selena explained as well as she could, about the sudden appearance of Esau and the collision with the radio telescope. Although she didn't see it, it looked like the HC had collided with the Chasm wall right after tearing through the scope. She saw no sign of John and he had not responded to her calls. She feared he died when the HC hit the wall. The collision with the scope had ejected her from the HC. She had hit her head when she fell to the ground and was knocked out. Aside from a headache and some bruising, as far as she could tell, she had not been injured. The suit monitors reported no problems. On the other hand, her suit monitors told her she did not have the oxygen and battery power to rescue herself. She didn't know her location. And, she had just a couple of tools and weapons hanging from her utility belt.

"Dr. Volkova. Just remain where you are. I'm going to send the *Raven* down to get you. It should be there in twenty minutes. While you are waiting, look around and see if there are any weapons or tools you can salvage. I'm not picking up any signals from Colonel Dakar. He could be just out of position. Look around and see if you find out what happened to him. I'm repositioning the Charlene Anchor Transport and putting another one in service to keep in touch with you. Clarke Station and Fort Resnik have mounted a rescue mission to extract the two HC's from the Morannon crevasse. They should get there two hours from now. It looks like something has tipped off the Parasite to your presence. From now on, you should anticipate that the Parasite could challenge you at any moment."

"Kory," she said softly. "Please come as soon as you can," she said almost in a whisper as she felt the first edges of an old terror starting to creep over her.

She walked the debris field while she waited. Good news! She found the weapons locker, not too far from where she landed. Bad news! No sign of John.

The brief search kept her occupied mind off of her predicament. But now she had nothing to do. She sat on the storage locker and looked around. Aside from the scopes spotted here and there, she saw nothing around her except the chasm on one side and barren rolling hills on the other. Above her stretched the big black sky, sprinkled with stars, lit only by the Sun. Being outside and exposed prompted her old fear of open spaces, with nowhere to hide and nowhere to take shelter. But panic did not follow. Instead, as she sat there, fearing John's death and fearing the future, she felt anger replace fear and with it, an energy to fight back.

Damn! I'm not going to let the Parasite conquer me. I'll destroy the Parasite, no matter what!

Feeling fortitude return, the grit that had saved her so many times in the past, she decided to make one more inspection of the crash site to look for what she could salvage and for any signs of John.

Bad news. She saw nothing more to salvage.

Really bad news. She did see something white on the ground, like a broken ceramic bowl. It didn't belong to all of the other metallic debris. She picked it up—and then threw it down. It was part of a skull! With an eye attached to it!

Oh God! John! What have I done? John, John, John. . .

She started to cry.

She dropped to the ground.

She again picked up the fragment of bone.

What? It has straight blonde hair, not curly black. And the skin is pale, not deep brown. This is someone else's skull! But who? What's it doing here?

She examined the eye. It had a blue iris, not brown like John's. While she examined it, she had the distinct sensation it was looking at her. Then the iris constricted!

She screamed and threw it down. Horror filled her, replacing all other emotions.

God! It's alive!

She kicked the monstrous thing away, right over the abyss.

After a few moments, it flew back at her.

Only it wasn't a piece of bone. It was a rock. And then there was another one.

What?

She got down on her hands and knees and peeked over the edge of the abyss.

37 WESTEROS

John didn't see it happen. Hunched over the GPS, following their progress on the computer monitor, he heard Selena yell, then he tumbled through space.

By instinct more than anything else, he tucked into a ball. When he struck the surface, he bounced and rolled to a stop.

Standing up, he saw the HC pinwheel across the Chasm, strike the opposite Chasm wall, and explode with a flash of light brighter than the sun. The spacesuit immediately blacked out the flash before it could damage his eyes. For a few moments, the black visor kept him from seeing his surroundings.

When the visor cleared, he could still see a bright yellow glow of the destroyed HC where it had struck the Chasm wall.

About five meters ahead of him he could see Selena, lying on the ground, and just beyond her, the edge of the Chasm.

Bending over Selena, he could see a figure.

What the hell? What is that thing? What's it doing here? It looks like a human, only . . . no spacesuit! And, no head! And, it's got a gun pointed at Selena!

John ran as fast as he could and tackled the thing, taking it by surprise. They somersaulted across the plain, grappling as John tried to grab the gun. Over and over they went and then they went over the cliff and into the gorge.

Only the cliff was a steep slope of fractured and broken regolith. They rolled down the rocky talus and John hit a large boulder at the base, on the border between the shoulder of broken rock and a narrow ledge of solid bedrock. He caught a brief glance of the Chasm so deep it disappeared into a black void.

Chills ran up and down his spine as the wrestled with the thing on the edge of the abyss. Dressed like a human, it was anything but human. It wore only inside clothes—pants and tunic—despite a temperature that should freeze its blood to rock. In one hand it held a gun. In the other hand it held, *God help me*, an eyeball. It had no head. Well, it had a head, but just the lower jaw and the bony base of the skull —everything else was gone: mouth, nose, forehead, ears, and eyes—at least one eye, it looked like it was holding the other one in its hand.

Reluctant to let go of either the gun or the eye, it pummeled John while he lay trapped between the headless zombie and the boulder. Warding off the blows with his arms, using his back pinned against the boulder for support, John kicked the demon with all of his strength. The kick struck the zombie in the groin and sent it flying over the Chasm. No longer grappling with John, the demon started to fire its gun wildly, causing it to spin as it fell into the canyon.

John sat up and peeked over the edge. He could see the spinning figure, shrinking in the distance as it fell into the canyon. Shivers shook John. He never imagined anything as deep as this canyon. From his little ledge, the canyon wall dropped in a sheer rock wall to the floor, invisible in black shadow, like a bottomless pit. John remembered from his reading, that at fourteen klicks, the walls of the Morannon canyon were ten times higher than the High Dome of Yosemite Park.

Spooked and spooked again, he quickly looked away.

He tried to call up Selena and Kory with his perscom. No answer!

He looked up at the talus of regolith. Even in the low gravity of Charon, climbing up that slope would be like climbing a pile of loose gravel. No way he could climb, jump, or walk his way out.

Trapped, he sat down as far as he could from the vertiginous edge and hoped Selena would find him. If she didn't find him before his oxygen and heat ran out, then he would just have to swallow his fears and take his chances crawling up the regolith.

A few minutes later, something fell from above. It looked like a piece of bone with hair and—God help him— an attached eyeball. It bounced off the ground next to him and then went over the edge, into the abyss.

With gratitude filling his heart, he stood up and started throwing rocks up over the edge.

Eleven minutes later, the *Raven* parked on the Westeros plain. Kes and Steel first loaded the weapons locker and then gave a report to Kory, for encryption and transmission to CIA headquarters, of all that had happened to them since they left Charlene Anchor that morning. After the report, Kory filled the two agents in on the rescue of the two HC crews.

"The PT Emergency Response Team and the Clarke Station Safety Team extracted the Homicide Squad from the wrecked HC. All four members of the Squad are alive but critically ill. A space ambulance is transporting them back to Port Tombaugh as we speak."

Both Kes and Steel made noises of relief. Although they had had no direct contact with them, the two agents had developed a healthy regard for the competence of the Homicide Squad.

"As you anticipated, Colonel Dakar, the other HC had the OASIS team in it and as you suspected that team did not survive—they ran out of both heat and oxygen. The rescue team pulled just three bodies out the wreck of the OASIS HC. One person, Director Best, could not be found, despite an extensive search of the crevasse and the chasm. Also, it did not appear the Director had been ejected from the wreck. It appeared the Director had left the wreck through the emergency exit, leaving his spacesuit behind."

"That doesn't make sense," Steel said. "We saw some shoeprints—they looked human—on the edge of the crevasse, but no one could survive the vacuum and near absolute zero temperature of the Chasm bottom without a spacesuit."

"I agree," said Kory. "Colonel Dakar, would you please describe for me once again, in as much detail as you can, the appearance of the monster with whom you wrestled after the HC hit the radio telescope?"

Steel carefully described all he could recall of the monster's clothing and armament.

Kory then asked Kes to describe the bone fragment she had found in as much detail as she could.

"Even though I have artificial consciousness," Kory said. "My systems do not lend themselves to making intuitive guesses. My approach is still to systematically consider and rank all possibilities, including remote possibilities. After doing this, particularly after learning the clothing the thing wore and the color of the thing's hair, skin, and pupils, the most likely explanation for the missing Director Best and the origin of the thing that accosted the two of you, is that they are one and the same. Certainly, the descriptions match."

Both agents rejected that announcement.

Kory continued. "Wait a minute. I know the Parasite has used the facilities at Ele Ranch Node to create new things, things that appear to be living but can still survive in the Charon environment without a spacesuit. I do not know if such things are cyborgs, avatars, robots, zombies, or something else we have never heard of before—probably the latter. But knowing what I know, the most likely explanation is that the Parasite reanimated Director Best and had Director Best climb aboard your HC while you were in the Chasm confronting the Scarecrow."

"Yeah," said John nodding his head. "Now that you mention it, I had the feeling there was something else down there, looking at me, but I could never see it. Still, it's hard to imagine something standing there, for days on end, waiting for someone to come down the trail."

Kory continued. "Nevertheless, I think that is the most likely explanation. From there, the thing rode your HC right through your collision with the radio telescope. I suspect that when the collision ripped off the top of the HC it also ripped off the top of the Director's head but did not destroy him. Although in a reduced-function mode, the reanimated and partially decapitated Director then attacked the two of you. Only to be defeated when Steel kicked him into the chasm."

"You're right! That does make a lot of sense," said Steel.

"But what do we do now?" asked Kes.

The three of them contemplated her question.

After a while, she said, "I could try to hack the Parasite, maybe even infect it with a computer virus of our own making."

"Dr. Volkova, remember the Parasite began as an alien computer virus infecting human computer systems. The Aliens designed it to protect itself from all possible defense mechanisms in order to successfully infect foreign computers like yours. I project that the Parasite can repel anything you are likely to use against it," said Kory.

"Why can't we simply unplug the computer, separate it from its power source?" asked Steel.

"That would have been possible in the past. The Parasite accidentally killed Mr. Henning when it thought Mr. Henning's inspection of the capacitor bank was an attempt to disconnect the Parasite from its power source. But since then, the Parasite has developed new power sources, separate from sources built or designed by humans. I don't know the location of these Alien sources, how they function, or how to disconnect them. I just know they exist."

"Well, what about destroying the computer banks. It's not subtle and it lacks finesse, but it sure could be effective," said Steel.

"I agree," said Kory, "but at this point, it is likely the Parasite has converted Ele Ranch Node into a fortress to protect it from external attack. Also, the heaviest artillery in the Pluto-Charon System has been sent to Ixion to rescue hostages. The rescuers and their weapons will not be back for a while."

"What about a nuclear bomb?" asked Kes.

"There are no nuclear bombs in the Pluto-Charon System," said Kory. "You would have to go to the Earth or Luna to get one," added Steel.

"Well, couldn't we make one?" asked Kes.

"Yes," said Kory, "If we had the manufacturing facilities and the raw materials. But those also don't exist in the Pluto-Charon System.

"Wait," said John. "Here's an idea. Kory, how many space vehicles remain in the Charlene hangar?"

"Normally there would be twelve HCs and twelve transports. But, right now because of the loss of three HCs and the deployment of two transports for the communications net, there are only nine HCs and ten transports. Why do you ask?"

"Kory, do you think we could hammer our way into the Ele Ranch Node General Services Building by sending in one vehicle after another to smash our way into the Building? Surely, we could at least open up a large enough breach for Kes and me to sneak into the Building. We might even get lucky and break something important that would stop the invasion."

"Or, the Parasite will just use the fleet for target practice," added Kory. "But that may be the best plan under the circumstances. We do not have much time. It appears the Aliens will start the invasion this evening."

"How fast can you mobilize the Charlene fleet?"

"It is seventeen-oh-three UTC now. I could assemble the fleet at the Mountain of Long Eyes by twenty-one and begin the assault right after that, said Kory. "There is one major problem. I have hardened the *Raven's* computer system and the computer system of the two transports that I am using to close the communications net with me, but I have not hardened the computers of the rest of the fleet. I can do some hardening, but I will not be able to finish the job while the fleet computers are in transit."

"Thank you, Kory," Kes said. "We'll just live with it."

38 DUCE EX MACHINA

At 17:07, a file of HCs and space transports, with the *Raven* holding the last position, left the Mountain of Long Eyes at maximal speed, for the Ele Ranch Node General Services Building, intending to hammer their way into the building in a sequential series of strikes.

Neither of the two agents nor their synthetic comrade-in-arms predicted what happened next. As the line of spacecraft approached the Building, a hole opened up in the wall like the iris of a camera lens. Instead of punching their way through, they entered the building like welcomed guests. Indeed, they could not stop from entering the building. The Parasite had seized control of every spacecraft, including the impregnable *Raven*, and parked the fleet in a neat line along the north side of the building, like carbots parking at a high school baseball game.

Steel immediately realized what he had done. He had just given a transportation fleet to an invading force of Aliens.

Shit! That was dumb! And it was my idea! Shit! Shit! Shit!

Also, they immediately lost all communications with Kory.

"Kes, what are we going to do now?" asked Steel.

"Whatever we do, we better do it fast before the Parasite locks us in here!" She said, flipping open the

352

weapons locker, and pulling out weapons and equipment as fast as possible.

"Well, one good thing," said Steel, "according to the sniffer, we don't need spacesuits."

Kes looked at Steel, "don't you think we need them anyway?"

"I don't know about you, but I fight better without the suit," he said, opening the cargo bay and jamming the door open with a blaster rod before the Parasite could lock the door. He then pulled out the alpha, beta, and gamma microdrones, verified they had been synced to his and Kes's perscoms, and set them off to take a spread pattern. He then dove into the locker himself, pulling out his Kpinga and Karambit, stuffing the throwing daggers in his boots, taking the remaining three stun grenades, as well as a blaster and a taser.

"Fine with me," Kes said while putting on her wings and tail.

"Are you really going to wear those?" asked Steel while slipping on his four ammo bandoliers and stuffing Ogun's gun in his utility belt.

"You bet," said Kes. "I'm going to fly to the other side of the building to see what I can see. I suspect the Aliens won't be expecting me in the air."

"Okay, while you're doing that, I'm going to work my way over to that bank of metal blocks, near the center of the building, behind that white-water tower. Do you see it?"

"Yah."

"Those blocks could be the memory banks—if so, the tower could be holding a coolant for the computer. If I could knock the tower over, that might put a stop to all of this."

"Sounds like a plan," said Kes. "Keep in touch. Let's go." After a quick kiss, they exited the *Raven*. Kes immediately flew off, soaring to the ceiling, while Steel crept along the line of spacecraft, making his way to the center of the building with the memory banks and the water tower. So far, so good. He had not seen anything that looked alive.

While he worked his way toward the center of the enormous General Services Building, ducking behind machinery and hiding behind crates and barrels, nothing happened. The building seemed uninhabited.

Getting closer and closer to the center of the building, he could see the water tower standing on a stage in the center of the building. Approaching it from the side, it looked odder and odder as he got closer.

To get a better sense of it, he shifted and moved to the side, placing the white tower between himself and the computer banks.

From a distance, it appeared about the shape and size of a water tower, but on closer approach, he saw the structure had two tree trunks, one on each side of the water tank. Each trunk was as big around as a sequoia and as white as a cottonwood. The two tree trunks stood in shoes, that appeared to be large wooden row boats. Limbs branched from the tree trunks and reached up to help support the oblate water tank. As the tree trunks ascended, they changed and became massive muscular legs, like the legs of an elephant. Approaching the structure from the rear, he saw that what he first took to be a water tank now looked like the egg-shaped body of a white four-legged beast that had been torn in half, leaving the front half of the animal. The ripped open abdominal wall had a thin ragged edge, like a broken eggshell. For as far as he could see, the open belly of the tree-beast revealed just a deep, dark, empty, cavern.

Circling around to the side of the tree-beast, he could now see that on the opposite side of the open belly, the tree-beast had an enormous human head with straight, brown hair. The tree-beast wore a broad-brimmed hat—as large as a tent—topped by what looked like a giant, pink, long-stemmed fig, or maybe a thin penis and a scrotum.

He presumed the tree-beast was a statue of some kind, but then the head turned and looked directly at Steel. Making eye contact, it slowly winked at him.

The hair rose on the back of Steel's neck. An electric quiver swept through him.

My God, it's alive!

Just then, Selena screamed. "John! John! John!"

A winged demon flew down from the ceiling. The flying fiend had bat wings, a long tail, two goat legs, a forehead unicorn, fangs, and Selena in its mouth like a cat that had caught a bird. The fiend's long, snaky tongue, wrapped around Selena, trapped her arms, and held her fast.

A tall, black-robed figure, with a human skull for a head, and glowing yellow eyes, stepped out of the shadows. Wearing a top hat and holding a saber, it stood before the tree-beast.

Selena continued to scream, "John! John! John!"

The winged demon landed in front of the satanic figure. Lifting his head, the robed devil howled "KALFU! KALFU!

KALFU!" in a voice so loud it drowned out Selena's screams and filled the General Services Building.

Furious, John charged, emptying Ogun's gun point blank into the winged demon and the robed devil, hitting both in the chest and head. His shots destroyed the winged demon. But John's gun shots could not stop the robed devil, Kalfu. Instead, Kalfu grabbed Selena by her hair, pulled her out of the dead demon's mouth. Exposed Selena's neck, he raised his saber, sliced off her head, and held it up for John to see, just before John used his Kpinga to dismember Kalfu.

Enraged by his failure, once again, to save the one he loved, John raised his weapons. Howling, John charged the tree-beast, the only thing left for him to kill.

Just then, the tree-beast squat, lowering its open belly to the ground. The interior of the belly filled with light.

John stopped.

Inside the belly of the beast, pandemonium ruled, A mob of countless monstrosities filled the beast's abdomen like a cornucopia from hell. Howling, they began to tumble out of the beast and rushed John.

The tree-beast looked again at John. Once more, it winked and, with a wry grin, smiled.

John charged the horde facing him, knowing this was the end and not giving a damn.

The tree-beast's pink penis moved like a worm, pointed its orifice at John, and shot him in the chest with a stream of silver energy.

EPILOGUE

A distant voice called him, "John, John, John." He stirred for a moment. *What was that? Nothing.* Ignoring it, he fell back into oblivion.

"John, John, John!" The voice roused him. Pulled him back. He still tried to ignore it.

"John, John, John." That voice again. Louder, more persistent. A woman's voice. *Selena!*

For the first time in nearly two days, John opened his eyes. Looking directly at Selena, he said, "Selena! Selena! I'm so sorry about Kalfu!" He then started to cry, tears raining from his eyes. "I'm so sorry! I'm so sorry!"

"John—"

I know we've had this conversation before.

"It's all right! You're safe!"

"Huh? What happened? I thought you were killed!"

"I was. So were you. But now we're whole again."

"But, I saw Kalfu cut off your head. How can you be alive? Are we in Heaven?"

"No, John, we are not in Heaven. We are alive. You can thank God that we are."

She then told him how the microdrones had recorded the events of that horrible day, showing her beheading, his slaying, and their rescue.

Right after the beachhead in the belly of the tree-beast had opened—what John thought of as the cornucopia of hell—releasing the countless mob of Alien monstrosities, Selena explained an entirely new entity appeared. Something not seen before. Something previously unsuspected and unknown. This new entity seemed far more powerful than the invading alien monstrosities and the monsters created by the Parasite. Selena called this new entity the Ranger because it acted like a park ranger protecting a wildlife park. Only the new entity, the Ranger, protected a human-life park—the solar system—by stopping the Alien invasion.

The Ranger had no physical presence. It made no noise. Things just happened. And they happened almost instantaneously.

Like a whirlwind, the Ranger snatched up all of the invading Aliens and stuffed them back into the belly of the tree-beast. It picked up all of the things the Parasite and the Aliens had created—including General Best's body and the broken Scarecrow bot—and stuffed them into the beast's belly.

The Ranger then extracted the Parasite from Kory. Selena was not certain how the Ranger could do this since the Parasite had no physical being—it was just code. But, the Ranger did it anyway. On the video recording, it looked like the extraction began with a spotlight illuminated the Ele Node mainframe and computer banks. After a few moments she could see a wiggling electric worm, like a brain parasite, sucked into the light beam. The light beam then pivoted and shoved the Parasite into the belly of the tree-beast. The Parasite extraction ended Kory's self-awareness.

The Ranger then shrank the beachhead—the tree-beast and all of the contents stuffed into its belly—into a cube, about a meter on each side, and left the cube on the floor of the General Services Building. The cube is the only tangible evidence left of what happened. It is a true black box. Lowell Observatory engineers have looked at it and they can't figure out its composition. They can't break into it, they can't x-ray it, and they can't move it. The cube does not radiate energy and it does not absorb energy.

"But Selena, how could we both be alive?" he asked.

"John," she said, "you know how the Parasite used Mary Keator's night terrors of the Scarecrow to frighten us."

"Yeah, but how does that explain what happened to us?"

"Well, Jim Moxon also had a secret fear. He feared the monsters of Hieronymus Bosch. The winged demon that caught me in its mouth was one of those monsters. It terrified me. I had never been so scared. The tree-beast was another one of those monsters. The belly of the tree-beast became the portal for the Alien invasion of Charon. These things did not terrify you. Neither did your third encounter with Kalfu. You just charged ahead, to save me, to save all of us. You only stopped when the pink fig on the tree-beast's hat, some people say it was a penis, killed you by blasting your chest with a stream of energy, leaving a giant hole."

"So, I should be dead! Why am I not dead?"

"I don't know. I think because of your bravery the Ranger took pity on us. Maybe, maybe not. But for whatever reason, before it left it healed you and me."

She then showed him the thin scar around her neck, the only evidence of her beheading. She asked him to unbutton his shirt. He did, exposing a normal chest, except another thin scar followed the margins of a crater chest wound that extended from one nipple to the other, and from his belly button to the notch at the base of his throat. To his

amazement, he no longer had the chest scars from fighting
Kalfu in Jamaica or the Brazilian on the *Odysseus*.

"I don't understand. How could this happen?" he asked.

"The microdrones recorded what happened. Instruments
of some kind materialized out of the air. They looked to me
like slender beams of light, about twenty centimeters in
length, sort of like autonomous magic wands or enormous
robot knitting needles, except there must have been at least
a thousand of them. They flashed and clinked as they
knitted my head back onto my body. It is exceedingly odd
to see oneself brought back from the dead, but I was and so
were you.

"The needles repaired you, John. They filled in the hole
in your chest, layer by layer until the hole was gone.
As soon as we were made whole, the needles disappeared.
I awoke, but you've been in a coma for the past two
days, recovering.

† † †

"Selena, will you marry me? I'll leave the CIA if you will
leave Mossad. We will never be parted again. Please."

"Yah, John, I'll marry you."

And so, they were, five days later, in the Clarke Station
Assembly Hall.

Selena and John retired from their secret services. They
devoted the rest of their lives to each other, to their children,
and telling people about the solar system shattering events
they had witnessed on Charon. Events that proved that we
are not alone.

Agent Sumate Laoloo made a full recovery. He and Commander Wan Sen also married, left the service, and settled down on Luna to raise a family.

Inspector Skalay and the rest of his team also made full recoveries. The Inspector retired to be with his wife, Mindy. Senior Detective Hildy Kirk assumed his position.

Under intense pressure, the US gave up using the Lowell Observatory for domestic and solar system surveillance.

After the revelation that the Lowell Observatory had been used for domestic spying on US citizens, the US government underwent a purge of the espionage agencies, resulting in massive downsizing and revision of the CIA and the FBI with tighter oversight. After intense discussion regarding the proper role—if any—for the Fifth Directorate, the US decided to retain, but downsize, the agency, reserving its use for emergencies.

Director Lee became the new CIA Director. Colonel Boot became the new Director of the 5th FD.

With EP technology no longer a secret, a commercial network of EP communications rapidly emerged, bringing instantaneous communications to people across the solar system. Instantaneous communications made the solar system smaller. They also prompted further development of EP technology. The Chinese made progress in adding video communications to audio. Several research groups were actively exploring the possibility that entanglement could be the key to faster-than-light, trans-dimensional, travel.

After the events on Charon, many people across many cultures and habitats, felt an intense humiliation that superior alien beings existed and that these beings had effectively confined humanity to an aboriginal reservation, or even worse, a zoological preserve. In such a solar system, war and armed combat just seemed passé.

Universal humiliation prompted the United Nations to establish a new, independent, organization called the Human Union for the Advancement of All Humans (HUAAH). The UN charged HUAAH to eliminate the abuse of humans by humans and to use science and philosophy to advance all humans. The UN set the goal for HUAAH to elevate human behavior above the iron age to a standing more consistent with space age technology and science.

Prompted by similar concerns, the organized religions of the world pulled back from religious conflict and redirected their energies to helping all people cope with the new realities. This progress ended the Lunar Lights conflict along with other religious conflicts.

Still, it seems that as humanity takes one step forward, it also takes a half step backward. Many people ignored the momentous events of Charon. The Caine Toads persisted and continued to spread their evil into various corners of the solar system. Space piracy and international and interplanemo crime still continued. Ignoring inconvenient history and knowledge, break-away societies continued to emerge and colonize dwarf planets with the goal of creating new societies according to values they believed that God had exclusively given to them, values that sometimes hurt other people.

And now that almost everyone knew that aliens existed, some worried that other, unknown aliens, had already invaded our solar system and live among us.

. . . .

"Reality can be beaten with enough imagination."

Mark Twain

[Spoiler Alert]
THE STORY BEHIND THE STORY . . .

. . . began in 1992. It's a terrible story. Terrible because it is not fiction, not fantasy, but true . . . true crime. It is a story of lies, cover-up, retribution, and murder, . . . serial murder. At least eleven, probably more than sixty victims, defenseless elderly men and women, killed in their sickbeds, in a Missouri hospital. And I found myself in the middle of it.

Among my many professional titles is epidemiologist. An epidemiologist counts events over space and time. Because of my expertise, my superiors asked me to investigate gossip that a nurse was killing patients. I did so. I counted deaths during 1992, on different shifts, on different hospital wards, expecting to find just gossip. Instead, I found overwhelming evidence, incontrovertible evidence, evidence that has withstood multiple challenges, that a nurse had killed patients. I repeat, the nurse killed at least eleven, probably more than sixty, Veterans, real people, real heroes.

My findings proved unacceptable to my superiors. They tried to hide the deaths and silence me. I resisted. Over the 1990s and into the beginning of the next century, the ensuing conflict dominated my life and the life of my family. It also dominated the lives of the three men who joined me in opposing this tragedy and the lives of their families. It was a terrible time, professionally and emotionally ruinous for all of us.

During those many years I often could not fall asleep at night. Intrigued by all of the advances in planetary science, I tried to distract myself from my problems by imagining visiting the new worlds we started to see for the first time. A lifelong fan of science fiction, my nocturnal diversion quickly became an aspiration to write a novel about our new solar system.

Although at the time we knew very little about them, my interest turned to Pluto and Charon, because they were the most distant objects in the solar system. It seemed to me—as voiced by my characters—that such remoteness made Pluto and Charon frightening. I wanted my story to be frightening. Exploring frontiers is frightening. I think nothing is more frightening than the unknown. And *Charon*, among other things, is a horror novel about the unknown.

At first, I wanted to complete my novel before the arrival of the *New Horizons* probe, but it didn't happen. I am glad it didn't happen. Who could have imagined the worlds discovered by *New Horizons*? And what a wonderful thing the IAU has done for novelists like me, to name all of that new geography with such great names. Thanks to *New Horizons*, Charon and Pluto have become characters in this book. They are so important that I made it my goal to describe these two new worlds with the enough details to give the reader the sense of having visited them

Many readers will wonder what in *Charon* is real science and what is fiction. With a couple of obvious exceptions, all of the science is plausible, if not real. There is no point in listing all of the facts, but four require some discussion:

- The treasure 'troid, Psyche-16, is a real asteroid, believed to be the metallic core of a disrupted planemo. Astronomers suspect the asteroid has such tremendous mineral wealth that it could be transformative, similar to the discovery of the New World had on the Old World.
- Marius Hills is a lava field on the near side of the Moon that includes a lava tube and domes. In 2017 Purdue University reported finding the Marius Hills lava tube was so large it could easily hold the city of Philadelphia.
- The Acheron Bridge space elevator is fiction of my own invention. In his book, *Fountains of Paradise,* Arthur C. Clarke proposed space elevators could carry people from the Earth's surface to a satellite in geocentric orbit. This proposal is now regarded as a credible technological goal. Because Charon and Pluto orbit each other in close proximity, with the near sides always facing each other, and because the low gravity field of the Pluto-Charon system means a space elevator would not require the super-strong materials needed to construct an Earth space elevator, it seemed to me that future Plutonian colonists could construct such an elevator. So, beginning in 2005, I began including a space elevator—the Acheron Bridge—in my story. (The name for the gulf between Pluto and Charon— Acheron—is also my invention.) In looking for references to such a thing, I found

some discussion of the feasibility of a Pluto-Charon space elevator as long ago as 2009. Unfortunately, I can't find any speculation about what would happen if you strung a cable between the two planemos. My guess is that you would get a gigantic spark by short circuiting the system.

• When I started putting ideas to paper in 1999, outlining a plot for what would become *Charon*, I cast the story around a Plutonian radio telescope that had inadvertently picked-up an alien computer virus embedded in an extraterrestrial message. After infecting the human computers, the virus matured into a malignant entity that invaded our solar system. Obviously, a turn of events inspired by Carl Sagan's *Contact*, but with a sinister plot. Could something like this happen? In February 2018 Michael Hippke and John G. Learned published a paper suggesting that alien malware could be embedded in an extraterrestrial message. If a human observatory received such a corrupted message, Hippke and Learned claimed that the virus could infect our computer systems undetected. If we detect an extraterrestrial message, Hippke and Learned proposed we should take precautions in case an embedded alien virus proved to be a "malicious message to eradicate humans."

Having read *Charon*, many readers will recognize the similarity between my opening chapters and the opening chapters of Ian Fleming's book, *Dr. No*. Guilty as charged.

In my defense, let me plead this: The wildly popular James Bond books have become their own sub-genre. Like a noir detective novel, there is a certain pattern to the protagonist and the plot in the Bond books that demands imitation. But if you have read both *Dr. No* and *Charon*, you will see that the resemblance is superficial. The protagonists face different problems, resolve them in different ways, and have different personalities. Still, the James Bond model was a terrific way to introduce my main character.

I met my main character, and his alter ego, sometime in the late 1990s when my plans for the book started to take shape. According to my notes, I had fleshed out—in terms of appearance and personality—both protagonists by 1999. The thing is, it took nearly another twenty years for me to learn their names.

A faithful listener to National Public Radio (NPR), I would often hear reports by the NPR African correspondent, Ofeibea Quist-Arcton. When signing off, she would mention her location, Dakar, except she would say it in a very distinctive way, with the emphasis on the 'k' followed by a fading trail of rolling 'r's. It was 2018 and John finally had a name.

The search for Selena's name didn't end until 2019, when her Lunar origin prompted a solution. (Selena is the name of the Greek goddess of the Moon. Volkova is the feminine form of the Russian surname Volkov, which is a derivative of the Russian word for wolf. Vladislav Volkov died in the Soyuz 11 mission during his return to Earth. The Lunar far side crater Volkov was named in his honor.)

After settling some missing elements like the protagonist names, the rest of the story rapidly fell into place. I started writing the book in June 2017 and completed it in June 2019.

Even though I cover many painful subjects, I had a lot of fun writing this book. I hope you will find it intriguing, uplifting, and most of all, enjoyable.

ACKNOWLEDGEMENTS

The three men who stood beside me regarding the 1992 patient murders at the Harry S. Truman Memorial Veterans Hospital are Andy Simpson, Earl Dick, and Eddie Adelstein. I am forever grateful to them. This book would not have happened without their support and friendship.

In August 2018, while completing the first draft of this novel, I was found to have advanced cancer. I am grateful for my oncologists, Dr. Iliff and Dr. Autio, and my oncology nurse, Robbin Hubble, who have extended my life, making it possible for me to complete this book.

Eddie Adelstein's daughter, Jacky Adelstein, a graphic designer, took my ideas for the book cover and the interior illustrations, making them into the beautiful images you see before you. I also appreciate the valuable criticism and endorsement provided by Jacky's brother and Eddie Adelstein's son, Jake Adelstein.

Chris Lao-Scott provided valuable guidance in the martial art of Muay-Thai.

I am particularly grateful for the enthusiasm and comments by the members of my writing group, Roy Fox, Robin Blake, Marvin Feldman, Chuck Swaney, and Nick Peckham. Special thanks to Robin and Roy for their detailed criticisms and extensive copy editing. I am also deeply grateful for the members of the Book Guys and Book Femmes, our book clubs, who have proven such an inspiration for reading and writing.

My sister, Lise King, gave me thoughtful and encouraging comments regarding content and direction. David Black, Lee Wilkins, Frank Schmidt, and Brenda Peculis enthusiastically supported my work and advised me on critical issues.

My youngest daughter, Janara Christensen and her husband, Greg Valiant, helped me with the computer science. My oldest daughter, Charlotte Bowcutt (*nee* Christensen) helped me with my many questions regarding astronomy and physics. Her husband, Chris Bowcutt (nee Nelson) advised me on publishing this novel. All four of my children have enthusiastically supported me in writing this novel.

For more than fifty-three years, the love of my life and the mother of our children, Alice, has stood beside me through our many challenges. She has endured my constant chatter about this book. She has proofread numerous drafts and advised me on character development and plot. I would never have completed this project without her love and help. She is the Sun around which I revolve. She and our daughters are the center of my universe.

ABOUT THE AUTHOR

Gordon Christensen retired from the Department of Veterans Affairs in 2003 and from the University of Missouri in 2015. Dr. Christensen is a medical educator, physician, and research microbiologist, known for his work in the clinical recognition and pathogenesis of medical device infections. Dr. Christensen has also led five medical missions to Falmouth, Jamaica. *Charon* is his debut novel.